A new danger, something very alarming, was hidden within the darkness. Baelfire had felt this evil presence before. Will it never end? she asked herself while fighting feelings of despair and desperation.

THE BLACK SCARLET SAGA

BOOK ONE

BLACK CRYSTAL

BY: R. A. OAKES

Blue Ridge Publishing

Published in the United States by:
Blue Ridge Publishing*PO Box 286*Stuarts Draft*Virginia*24477

Editorial Supervision: Dawn Rogers
Cover Design: Ellen Morris * live4art@comcast.net

ISBN 978-0-615-62088-6 (Tradepaper)

1. Fiction – Epic
2. Fiction – Action and Adventure

ISBN 978-0-615-62088-6

1st Tradepaper printing in the United States of America, June 2012

Acknowledgments

I would like to thank Dawn Rogers, my friend and publicist, whose warrior-woman spirit infuses *Black Crystal* with a real-life woman's attitudes and emotions from beginning to end. I would like to thank Ronna Rothenberger for asking, "Have you ever considered writing warrior-women books?" That one question changed my life forever. I would like to thank the faculty and staff of Blue Ridge Community College, in Weyers Cave, VA, and Dr. Audrey Perselay in particular, for being a never-ending source of encouragement and support. Also, I would like to thank Ellen Morris, a student at Bridgewater College, in Bridgewater, VA, for creating a book cover that's vibrant and captures the spirit of the novel's protagonist.

And most of all, I would like to thank my wife, Ann, who taught me the true meaning of love. My life began the day I met her. She has been my toughest critic and my most steadfast source of support. Without her, life would not be worth living.

Where stories come from is a mystery to me. I never know what my characters are going to do until they do it. I can only thank the creative process for allowing me to be a participant.

Black Crystal

Chapter 1

Charging up the mountain trail, the energy bursting from the leather-clad warrior woman and her stallion tore through the night, as unnerving as a clap of thunder, as piercing as a barrage of arrows yet more silent than a whisper. Rushing towards the imposing edifice of her uncle's castle, Chen, the leader of a band of warrior women, and her guards whipped their warhorses into a frenzied state. There was no reason for pushing themselves and their horses so hard, they had no pressing deadline to meet, but Chen strove for intensity in everything she did, extreme intensity.

As their warhorses reached the castle's drawbridge, the warrior women goaded their animals onward clambering across the thick, wooden boards. Then, reining up hard, Chen pulled her warhorse's head almost back to her chest nearly causing the animal to stumble. But the stallion, having been bred for both speed and endurance, quickly regained its footing.

Before coming to a complete stop, Chen removed her feet from the stirrups, swung her right leg over the animal's powerful neck and leapt from the saddle exuding athletic prowess as she flew through the air and hit the ground running.

The warrior woman's personal guards strained to keep up with her knowing their master's wrath all too well. Chen possessed a ferocious temper and to lag behind would be courting disaster. But the guards were in excellent condition, and they pushed hard trying to shorten the distance between themselves and their master with each stride.

After reaching the main tower, Chen burst into the dungeon brushing past her uncle's warriors who didn't even think of challenging her. Being Lord Daegal's niece was not without its perks, one of which was everyone having to put up with her insufferable rudeness.

Running down the dungeon steps taking two at a time, Chen reached the bottom in short order, then sprinted down a narrow stone hallway stopping in front of one of the cells. With her chest heaving and gasping for breath, Chen smiled at her imprisoned friend who was enormous. His head almost touched the seven-foot ceiling, and his chest was so broad his sheer size made the cell appear even smaller than it actually was. The giant looked like a caged animal possessing such strength he could have ripped the bars apart, thus staying in the cell by his own choice, which wasn't the case. Yet the jail cell couldn't contain his energy, and it poured from him flooding the outside hallway reinvigorating Chen as it washed over her.

The brightness and penetrating nature of his eyes were almost unnerving. As the giant probed deeply into Chen, it seemed like he could feel what she was feeling giving the warrior woman the impression he could sense her motives and intentions, which indeed he could. There was even a certain arrogance about him, as if the giant believed himself to be better off than her, even though he was the one locked in the dungeon cell.

When Chen finally caught her breath and could speak, she said, "Sorry I wasn't able to visit this morning, but I was out."

"Out where?" Pensgraft asked, his eyes darkening.

"I don't have to answer to you," she stormed. Then calming herself, the warrior woman added, "I was out for a ride."

"How many did you kill this time?"

"None."

"How many did you have killed?"

"I don't know, not as many as I would have liked. Right after the battle started, a warrior woman appeared out of nowhere and cut down a lot of my uncle's men. She's the one who did most of the killing and appeared to be enjoying herself immensely."

"And that justifies authorizing the attack?"

"I'm not trying to justify anything. I did what I needed to do," Chen declared in a huff clenching her fists.

"Take it easy, all I did was ask a question."

"Like you never killed anyone."

"I've killed in self-defense or to save the lives of others, but you kill for sport."

"There's nothing else to do around here."

"I don't believe that. There are plenty of other things you could be doing."

"Okay, there's nothing else I want to do. Satisfied?"

"I got an answer, and it's an honest one. But, no, I'm not satisfied."

"Why not?" she demanded.

"Because you deserve better. You're so angry inside that you only experience a sense of relief when someone else dies needlessly," Pensgraft said sincerely worried about her.

"A lot of things happen needlessly. My father didn't need to abandon me years ago, and my uncle, Lord Daegal, doesn't need to climb into my bed every time he gets drunk!"

"Well, it's hard to disagree with you when you're right, at least in those instances," he said in a soothing voice. "I'd heard, though, it was your father who abused you not your uncle."

"It's always been Lord Daegal, my father never did anything like that," Chen said resting her hand on the hilt of her sword. If this man were anyone else, she told herself as she gritted her teeth, I would have rammed my sword through his insolent throat.

Why do I take this from him? she asked herself for the hundredth time. And the answer was always the same. Because I feel I can trust him.

Chen thought back to when she'd first met him. She'd been talking to the jailer when she walked past Pensgraft's cell. There was this giant of a man, and he was holding his head in his hands and looking terribly depressed. Given that she was often depressed herself, Chen's heart unconsciously went out to him. "What's wrong?" she had asked, not realizing how silly the question was given that the man was locked in her uncle's dungeon.

"My daughter needs me, but I'm locked in here," he had groaned.

"Every girl needs her father, god only knows I wish mine were still around."

"I tossed my sword to her," he had said.

"Great, hope she likes it."

"It's not that simple," he'd lamented. "It's a special sword, and there's no one who has any experience wielding it, at least no one alive."

"There are teachers around who'll be able to help her," Chen had said.

"You don't understand, but why should you?"

She'd almost killed him then and there, but had stayed her hand. Worrying about his daughter was what had him so distraught and that was admirable in a way, but nonetheless, it was annoying. Her own father used to be concerned about her, up until he disappeared suddenly when she was 14 years old.

Now, pulling herself back to the present, the young warrior woman considered her current situation.

"What if I talked to my uncle and could get him to release you into my custody? Would you try to escape?"

"Of course."

"You'd still be within the castle walls and most of the time restricted to my chambers. There wouldn't be much opportunity for striking out on your own," she chuckled. "But I do admire your devotion to your daughter."

"Aerylln is very special," Pensgraft said with obvious pride.

"I'm sure she considers you to be rather special yourself."

"It's nice of you to say that, but it's the women in my family who are truly exceptional."

"Do you think I'm exceptional?" Chen asked.

"Yes, exceptionally angry."

"So what? I don't care!" she said defiantly.

"Well, you should."

"Why?"

"I think we'll save that topic for another time."

"Okay, I'll come back later this evening. For now, I'm going to talk to my uncle."

"Do you think he'll listen to you?" Pensgraft asked, his hope rising.

"Oh, he'll listen. The question is, how much will he make me pay for what I want?"

"Pay how?"

"You're so naïve."

"I don't want you doing anything you don't want to do."

"Oh, it's nothing I haven't done before. However, at least this time I'll get something I want out of it."

"What if he doesn't go for your little scheme?"

"Oh, he'll go for it," she laughed. "He'll jump at the chance because I haven't exactly been easy pickings since I got older."

"Older? You're in your early 20s."

"Look at me Pensgraft, look into my eyes. I'm an old woman."

"This is depressing."

"Wait till you try living with me. This is a picnic by comparison."

"You're not so tough," Pensgraft said.

"It's not this half of me you need to be concerned about. But if you ever meet my darker side, you may lose what respect you have for me."

"Things can't be that bad."

"Oh, yes they can be," she laughed. "They can be a whole lot worse."

"I'm sorry to hear that."

Chen shrugged her shoulders, said goodbye and climbed back up the stairs. When she was gone, Pensgraft went over to his bunk and sat down. Suddenly, he realized how safe his jail cell had actually been.

He thought, Chen's so full of inner turmoil that it could be like having a wounded tigress for a jailer. And an animal can be much more dangerous when it's wounded, especially when it feels desperate. Chen's clinging by a thread to what clarity of mind she still has. Sooner or later, that thread is going to snap.

As he closed his eyes to rest, Pensgraft vowed that he wouldn't be around when it happened. He would be with his daughter, and she would have the sword.

Chapter 2

Aerylln rubbed her eyes. How much longer will this take? she wondered.

In the great hall of her castle, Mistress Xan had been chanting for over an hour, Aerylln was certain of that. The young woman's eyelids were getting heavy, and she dared not fall asleep, but it was becoming increasingly difficult to pay attention to the sorceress' incantation.

Suddenly, there was a loud bang as the spell came to a conclusion, and the room filled with a mist that was alive with colors. As Aerylln watched, the colors separated forming six doors, each lavishly decorated with magic runes painted around the edges. Truly her mistress had summoned great magic this night.

"Choose a door, Aerylln," Xan commanded. "It will determine the path that you will walk from this day forward."

Oh, no pressure there, Aerylln thought, feeling nervous and taking a deep breath.

However, Mistress Xan did have a tendency to be rather dramatic, and Aerylln hoped that now was such an instance. But the young woman in her late teens had also learned to take her mistress seriously and do as the sorceress ordered.

So Aerylln rose from her perch, straightened her skirt and brushed aside her long, blond hair absently twirling a lock as she concentrated. The young woman's deep blue eyes darted around the room studying the doors carefully. There were six of them, at least until all but one began fading away.

"Interesting, a scarlet door framed in black seems to have chosen you, and such colors clearly indicate that either you, or the women influencing you in the future, will be outgoing and dominant."

Taking both women by surprise, the scarlet door burst open filling the room with the sounds of clanging steel and hooves prancing on rocky ground, and they saw two powerful warriors locked in battle. Aerylln's eyes were drawn to one of them, instinctively feeling that she knew this man, but how, she didn't know.

Turning his head, the warrior glanced straight at her, his eyes lighting up in recognition, but his opponent instantly exploited the opportunity striking a fierce blow. Falling from his horse, the warrior's head struck a large rock, and he felt himself going unconscious. In desperation, he shouted, "This is yours!" and tossed his sword towards Aerylln, greatly relieved when he saw it sliding to a stop neatly by her feet.

Instantly, as if sensing danger, the scarlet door began closing but not before the second warrior noticed Aerylln and urged his horse towards the opening. Startled by his eyes, which were hypnotic and yellow in color, a chill swept through the teenage girl, and she froze. Acting swiftly, Mistress Xan shouted an incantation, slamming the door shut with a gust of wind and breathing easier only after it disappeared.

Looking down at the sword, Aerylln was awed by its beauty, her eyes, in particular, being drawn to a gemstone set in the top of the hilt. It was purple, then blue, green, yellow, orange, and now it was red. The jewel seemed ever changing with colors swirling around inside of it. Eagerly, yet trembling in anticipation, the young woman leaned down to pick up the sword.

"Wait!" Mistress Xan warned. "We don't know what..."

But it was too late, the sword was already in Aerylln's hand. It was much lighter than she'd thought it would be, and it felt right and natural in her grip. Admiring the exquisite craftsmanship, Aerylln was so lost in thought that she was startled by Mistress Xan's voice when the sorceress said, "Well, it's come down to this has it?"

Pausing briefly, Mistress Xan took a deep breath, and then added, "Aerylln, your path will take you far from my door. I know not the ways of the sword, and thus, by my clan, I'm now forbidden to teach you more of my sorcery. But clearly the sword has chosen you for a reason."

What does Mistress Xan mean, far from her door? Is it possible I'll really have to go? the teenage girl wondered.

"Umm, can't I put it away?" Aerylln pleaded.

"I'm sorry, my child," Xan said. "You must leave in the morning. I can do no more for you." Then, with a sweep of her robes, the sorceress turned away, sat down and began studying her tomes.

Aerylln was stunned. All she'd ever known was in this household. Her mother, before she died, had been a servant to Mistress Xan and planned on Aerylln entering into an apprenticeship when she was of age. Secretly, the young woman had yearned for adventures in the outside world but was terrified now that the opportunity presented itself. How will I defend myself? she wondered. I know little sorcery and have never been trained to use a sword.

Sulking as she entered her room, Aerylln was so angry and disappointed that she flung the sword at the outside wall. Sticking in the wooden frame of the window, it reflected the rays of the morning sun and, acting like a prism, refracted the light into all the colors of a rainbow. However, in no mood to be cheered up, Aerylln flung her cape over the sword and slumped down onto the bed.

Mistress Xan is overreacting! After all, it's just a dumb sword! If I thought Mistress Xan might ask me to leave, I'd have slammed the scarlet door shut before the sword was even tossed to me, the teenage girl grumped to herself. I'll bet that warrior wasn't having any better luck with it than I am, and he just dumped it on me.

Maybe the sword got him into that fight with the yellow-eyed warrior to begin with. Maybe this whole destiny thing of the sword choosing me is hogwash. Yes, he looked straight into my eyes, but I'll bet he hasn't seen a pretty girl in who knows how long? Maybe he was shocked to see me, got caught off guard and tossed this stupid, overgrown knife to me as punishment!

However, Aerylln's depression would have to wait for another time for the sword started "singing" giving off a sound like a high-pitched tuning fork.

Immediately, the outside wall began vibrating and quickly started shaking harder and harder. The whole room was now reverberating from shockwaves pouring out of the sword with dozens of large cracks snaking through all four stonewalls. Next, the sound emanating from the sword turned into a shrill, piercing howl. The entire room began buckling and heaving, and the outside wall collapsed sending tons of stones and debris flying into the surrounding field.

Aerylln fell backward onto her bed watching as the sword disappeared along with the wall. The teenage girl thought, Mistress Xan is not going to be happy about this. She's always telling me to pick up after myself and not leave my room a mess and now this.

After the shockwaves subsided, Aerylln got off her bed and cautiously peeked through the gaping hole. To her surprise, the sword was in the middle of the rubble stuck firmly in the ground standing straight as an arrow with sunlight glistening off its blade and looking very regal.

Once again, the sword began quivering but this time emitted a gentle, warm, comforting sound radiating outward and flowing across the surrounding hillside.

Aerylln gasped as she caught sight of an approaching white horse. It was the most beautiful animal she'd ever seen. As it got closer, the young woman noticed the horse was wearing a jeweled necklace slung around its muscular neck. The gemstones were just like the ones in the sword's handle.

The jewels in both the necklace and the sword began shining brightly as they got closer to each other, and Aerylln wondered, Doesn't this animal look like the horse my warrior was riding, the warrior who tossed this sword to me?

However this horse was fresh, not battle weary, with a glistening coat and eyes that were most intriguing. They looked right into her, just as the warrior had.

The powerful horse trotted up to the young woman nuzzling Aerylln's outstretched palm. The animal's breath was warm causing her hand to tingle and become considerably stronger, yet the teenage girl thought, Maybe it's just my imagination. But it wasn't.

Suddenly an energy surge swept through Aerylln bringing with it a premonition that this horse would take her home, to her true home, one where she would always belong and never be asked to leave. Aerylln was close to tears as she realized all of this might indeed be preplanned, predestined.

Living with Mistress Xan had been just a place for her to grow up, but now she was becoming a woman.

With a bounding stride, she grasped the horse's mane with both hands pulling herself up onto its back. Stretching out her right hand, the sword leapt into it. The sword felt at home in Aerylln's grip, just as she felt at home on the horse's back.

The powerful, white horse began galloping away from the castle as Aerylln looked back over her shoulder at the collapsed wall of her room. The animal's stride was long and graceful, its muscles rippling against her skin, and she felt the horse's warmth on her legs since she was riding bareback. And the horse seemed to glide and gallop at the same time, so graceful were its motions. Aerylln held onto its mane and rode up close to the animal's shoulders, once again feeling the horse's muscles rippling against her own and being impressed with its strength.

As the young woman charged over the hillside with her long, blond hair blowing in the wind, the horse seemed to sense her excitement and galloped even faster while the sword began "singing" again.

Like an epiphany, it hit her that the horse and sword were happy. And with a thrill, Aerylln realized that so was she! After looking over her shoulder again at the crumbled stonewall receding in the distance, the teenage girl swung her sword in circles above her head. Equally enthusiastic, the horse leapt into the air, and the sword glowed, its jewels refracting the sunlight and filling the air around them with all the colors of a prism.

Tilting her head back, Aerylln let out the loudest laugh she'd ever made and thought, Leaving my former life behind isn't so bad.

Throwing one last glance over her shoulder, she saw Mistress Xan on the upper turret of the castle. What's different about her? Aerylln asked herself.

Then it dawned on her.

Mistress Xan had always been so serious, but now she's smiling. Actually smiling! Aerylln thought feeling amazed.

Aerylln could sense the sorceress' emotions reaching out to her even at this distance from the castle, and the teenage girl was hit hard by a second realization and thought, Mistress Xan loves me! She really does!

The young woman burst into tears of gratitude but also realized it was time to venture out on her own. As she rode across the seemingly endless countryside, Aerylln no longer felt alone in the world having found where she belonged. On the back of a valiant horse wielding a sword!

Chapter 3

On her sleek, white horse, Aerylln flew over the vast expanse of landscape as if she were a bird on the wing. She was like an eagle on horseback! A hawk commanding the heavens! A swallow singing its joy!

Feeling a dryness in her throat, she thought, What I am most is thirsty, and I guess my horse needs a drink, too. Oh, and what shall I name her?

"I already have a name. It's Zorya," a voice said in her mind as if by telepathy. And a second voice that had a musical quality filled her mind as well saying, "And my name is Baelfire."

Looking around her, Aerylln was confused. She was galloping along with no other riders in sight. Where did those voices come from? the young woman wondered.

"I know where some water is. There's a very nice stream over to our left by that grove of trees," Zorya said trying to be helpful. Once more, Aerylln heard the voice between her ears, not with her ears.

Stifling a yawn and hoping the voices were the result of fatigue, Aerylln thought, If I have a cool drink and a nap maybe I'll feel better. And having no idea herself where to find water, she allowed the horse to turn and head towards the inviting grove of trees.

Being so tired, Aerylln didn't notice, but she did nothing to make Zorya veer to the left. The young woman didn't nudge the horse or give it any sort of command, the animal just drifted off to the left when Aerylln decided to turn left, as if Zorya had read her mind.

After stopping by a bubbling brook, Aerylln asked herself, What name did I think to call this beautiful animal? For she couldn't imagine that the voices she'd heard were anything other than her own thoughts. However, she couldn't remember hearing her own ideas spoken aloud in her mind before, but she did like the name after recalling what it was.

"Zorya. What a pretty name," she said to the magnificent animal while stroking her mane. Feeling the coolness of the air, Aerylln realized the water would be refreshing and slid off Zorya's back. Running over to the shallow stream, the young woman took her shoes off, waded in up to her knees and bent down splashing water everywhere with her hands. Feeling parched again, she used both hands for a cup drinking her fill of the clear, fresh water.

Zorya gracefully lowered her well-muscled neck, and the little stream bubbled around her snout as she gulped down an amazing amount of water.

Having dropped her sword to the ground when slipping off Zorya's back, Aerylln was surprised to see it stuck in the streambed with its handle moving gently back and forth as if enjoying the cool water flowing around it. Wading over to it and grasping the hilt, Aerylln thought, Yes, I'll call this sword Baelfire, just like I decided earlier. The teenage girl still couldn't believe that Baelfire had actually spoken to her.

Excited over having such a beautiful sword for her very own, she ran splashing out of the water beaming from ear to ear while swinging Baelfire at the tall grasses along the banks of the stream. Aerylln's dress was soaked and its hem dragging in the dirt, but without a care in the world, she ran along the stream bank swinging her sword at the abundant wild flowers.

The young woman cut bunches and bunches of them creating a fragrant bed. Then, she threw herself down onto it gasping for breath and feeling dizzy having been spinning 'round and 'round while swinging Baelfire.

Aerylln lay with her mind drifting and feeling half-asleep when a shadow crept across her body. Slowly, the teenager realized the sun's rays were no longer warming her face and became vaguely aware of a presence close to her. Opening her eyes, she couldn't believe what she saw. A scraggly old man with matted hair, a rough beard, an eyelid closed with a scar running across it and rotting teeth was peering down at her.

"Ahhh!" she shouted rolling away and scrambling to her feet.

"Oh my, young lady, don't be alarmed. I didn't mean to disturb your rest," the old man said in a comforting tone of voice. "I'm just feeling a bit tuckered myself and would like to join you, if you don't mind."

"I don't think so," Aerylln said warily. "There are lots of wildflowers. Maybe you'd be more comfortable with your own bed under that oak tree."

Taking a handkerchief out of her dress pocket, the young woman covered her nose with it. She was disgusted by the vagrant's filthy, sweat-stained shirt, and his body odor was appalling, Aerylln having the misfortune of being downwind.

"Do you dress this nicely every day?" the vagrant asked wearing a wide grin seemingly unaware that his rotten teeth were making the young woman feel even more apprehensive.

"My maidservant set this out for me this morning, and it's nothing special, I assure you," she said. Having lived a sheltered existence, Aerylln took having a personal servant for granted.

"Well, the cloth seems expensive, let me feel it," the vagrant said taking a step towards her.

"I'd rather you didn't, thank you," Aerylln said taking a step backwards while relying on her breeding and good manners to get control of the situation.

"I'll bet you're as comfortable as fresh straw, and as soft. And you're very pretty, why I could look at you all day."

"You'll not have the opportunity, please stand aside," Aerylln said noticing that the vagrant was now between her and Baelfire.

"Just let me touch your sleeve," the vagrant pleaded.

"Don't you put a hand on me!" Aerylln shouted feeling decidedly uncomfortable and taking another step backwards. The young woman thought, I've been taught to be mannerly and polite, but that doesn't seem to be helping. He's too insistent.

Trying to get around the old man, Aerylln moved quickly to her right, but the vagrant stepped into her path blocking her. Noticing that one of the vagrant's knees was giving him trouble, the young woman took advantage of this weakness hiking up her skirts and attempting to run around him. Taken by surprise, the vagrant tried turning quickly but ended up howling in pain when his injured knee gave out. Pitching forward, the grizzled old man tried grabbing at Aerylln to break his fall but missed and made a loud grunt as he hit the ground.

Shocked that the vagrant had fallen towards her almost getting hold of her skirt, Aerylln reached out for Baelfire even though the sword was yards away. But it didn't matter, the magic sword leapt into her outstretched hand exuding an emotion akin to rage. The teenager had never experienced such anger before but was even more surprised when, seemingly of its own accord, her arm shot forward with a wicked thrust causing the vagrant to bury his face in the dirt and lay flat to avoid being skewered.

Regaining her balance, Aerylln took a deep breath to steady her nerves while Baelfire began to glow. The young woman's entire body seemed to be filled with strength beyond her imagination. Had Aerylln been worldlier and not lived such a sheltered life, Baelfire would have reacted with a swiftness that further would have surprised the teenager. But the sword had no desire to frighten her, only to protect her.

With her shoulders squared and sword drawn back, Aerylln was ready to defend herself, pleased by the aura of confidence surrounding her.

After the vagrant had struggled to his feet, the young woman took a step forward, and the grizzled old man stumbled and fell landing on the ground again, this time striking his skull against a rock. Putting a hand behind his head, he touched the stone but, oddly enough, discovered it was attached to a long, hairy post. Turning around, the vagrant realized it wasn't a stone but a horse's hoof he'd fallen against. Glancing up, he was stunned to find himself looking into the eyes of a very angry horse!

Rearing up on her hind legs, Zorya tilted back her head, mane flying wildly in the wind, and let out a battle cry that terrified not only the man but Aerylln as well. Seeing the look of fear on the young woman's face, Zorya, like Baelfire, didn't want to frighten her further. So the powerful horse regained control of her emotions contenting herself with stamping the ground restlessly and snorting in anger at the man who'd dared bother her new master.

Zorya had been grazing over in the next field when she'd heard Aerylln shout. What the horse saw when she looked up made her blood run cold. Her temper was so inflamed, and her desire to trample the vagrant was so overwhelming, that Zorya was frightened she'd accidentally injure Aerylln in her haste to get to the man himself.

Also, the horse knew that Aerylln was unschooled in the arts of war. Thus, Zorya realized that her young master had never seen an enraged warhorse on the attack. In fact, Zorya wondered if Aerylln had ever witnessed a fight of any sort.

Zorya drew on all her strength, not for an attack, but to hold herself in check, lest she further traumatize Aerylln by crushing the vagrant right in front of her. The warhorse felt it might be a long time, if ever, before the teenage girl enjoyed hearing an enemy's bones snapping during battle. Zorya thought, Is Aerylln up to the challenge of being Baelfire's heir and mine? She's the last of her line, so I certainly hope so.

As for the warhorse, the sound of an enemy screaming in pain was like an energizing elixir and one of the spoils of war that Zorya truly loved, even better was the eerie silence that blanketed a battlefield after the last enemy warrior had been vanquished. The profound stillness was a proclamation of victory! Only later, days later, in her heart of hearts, could the warhorse finally admit to herself how afraid she'd actually been and how good it was to be alive.

But for now, life was good, and Zorya took pleasure in standing next to the vagrant while stomping her hooves, snorting and watching the look of fear on the man's face. The warhorse knew she could crush his skull with the flick of a hoof. So easy to dispatch this one, she thought. So easy, and so well-deserved.

Zorya made a quick, vicious move with her head, whipping her snout at the man with her powerful neck causing the vagrant to stumble again and fall flat on his back. Then the warhorse contented herself with the enjoyable sensation of seething in anger. It wasn't much, but Zorya had to think first of the well-being of Aerylln, who at this point was still almost as frightened as the man himself. I hope she doesn't go into shock, the horse thought.

But to Zorya's relief, she heard a sound she'd been comforted by many times after many battles. It was Baelfire "singing" gently to both her and Aerylln, a sound that never failed to calm the warhorse's inner turmoil.

The sword's "singing" also appeared to soothe the old man, who pulled himself together, walked over to Aerylln and said, "You certainly aren't a very good hostess, young lady. Being a good neighbor, I came over to welcome you, and you had the audacity to draw your sword on me."

Aerylln was taken aback. After all, Mistress Xan had always stressed the value of good manners emphasizing over and over how important it was to treat guests well.

"But you tried to grab me," Aerylln protested, though wondering if the vagrant's action had been accidental. Having never seen anyone attacked before, the young woman thought, Certainly, there must be a reasonable explanation.

"I'm sorry. I'm an old man and simply lost my balance. I've an injured knee and only one eye, as you can plainly see. If my infirmities kept me from being agile enough to play the role of a gentleman properly, then you have my sincerest apologies," he said sadly, then sighed forlornly while looking at the ground.

"I don't believe this," Zorya mumbled.

"Patience, patience," the sword counseled. "Aerylln has to learn for herself and develop her own opinions."

"I know, I know," the horse said in resignation.

The vagrant grimaced while hobbling about a little wanting to gain Aerylln's sympathy. Seeing the concerned look on her face, he smiled and said, "Allow me to introduce myself. I'm Smig, and I manage an inn on the village square. As an apology for this unfortunate and regrettable misunderstanding, please let me offer you lodging for the night and a warm meal."

"Well, thank you, but first, who does the laundry around here? My dress is soiled, and I'll need a fresh one for tomorrow," Aerylln said.

"Oh, you can give it to my wife before going to bed. She'll be sure it's washed and mended before breakfast," Smig said lying easily, having neither a wife nor an inn. But his shrewd eyes did notice the coin purse hanging from a cloth belt around Aerylln's waist.

"That's most kind of you, truly," Aerylln said feeling a little guilty and wondering if she'd misjudged the man's intentions.

"Think nothing of it," Smig said bowing gallantly.

"I should have crushed his skull while I had the chance," Zorya said under her breath.

"Patience, patience," Baelfire counseled once more.

"You'll love our peaceful village. It's an oasis of law-abiding citizens, and we've two full-time marshals and severe punishments for troublemakers," Smig said lying effortlessly, though his words were a comfort to Aerylln who tried to see the good in everyone.

After guiding them to the village, Smig made a grand sweeping gesture with his hand saying, "Young lady, I promise you a pleasant evening you'll long remember."

"I think I'm going to be sick," Zorya said.

"Patience," Baelfire said again, but she, too, was getting a little tired of Smig's nonsense.

Sensing their growing irritation with him, Smig found a quick, simple way to neutralize the young woman's chaperones. By the entrance to the village, Aerylln surprised her horse and sword by locating a stable for them, the "innkeeper" having informed her that no one was allowed to carry weapons in town, and that there were no hitching posts for horses in front of any of the village's businesses, including his fictitious inn. Putting them up in a stable was a polite way of helping the horse and sword avoid any personal embarrassment, Smig had assured the young woman, who was touched by the "innkeeper's" concern for her friends.

"Now, this way to the inn," Smig said smiling and motioning for Aerylln to walk in front of him. But as she passed the "innkeeper," the teenager felt a hard tug at her waist and the old man started running down the main road through the village hoping to blend into the crowd.

"He stole my purse! That old man stole my purse!" Aerylln shouted in disbelief, so surprised that she felt rooted to the spot.

Smig's injured knee didn't seem to be bothering him, and he ran ahead shoving his way through a group of village women shouting, "Out of my way! Out of my way!"

But as he ran past a woman traveler with a tall, sturdy walking stick, Aerylln saw her trip the vagrant with her staff and, with blinding speed, bring it down hard on his head. The unconscious purse thief literally had no idea what hit him as he collapsed in a heap on the ground.

Aerylln was amazed that the female traveler's actions seemed so effortless and watched wide-eyed and breathless as her protector retrieved her purse. The woman's neck-length brown hair looked rather unkempt, and Aerylln thought it could use a good brushing. The warrior woman was wearing a black cloth shirt, black leather pants and a tight fitting leather vest laced halfway down the front. Slung over her back was a sword, and Aerylln thought, Smig lied, weapons are allowed in town.

"Lose something?" the warrior woman asked tossing the purse to the teenage girl.

"Thank you."

"Maybe you should choose your friends more carefully."

"I'm new at this, I guess," Aerylln admitted.

"Ah, not long out adventuring, I suppose. Well, my name is Corson. I've been to this village before, and I think I can show you a decent inn. C'mon let's get some dinner. What do you say?"

But at that moment a wagon went speeding past them, the reckless driver holding the reins in one hand, a half-empty bottle of whiskey in the other, and shouting encouragement to the galloping horses.

"That wagon's heading towards the thief lying in the road," Aerylln shouted gasping as the horses trampled the vagrant, the cart bumping twice as both sets of wheels went over him.

"It hit him!" Aerylln exclaimed.

"He shouldn't have stolen your purse," Corson shrugged. "I hope you won't let that spoil your dinner."

Aerylln didn't know what to make of her new friend who appeared kind and thoughtful one moment, yet cold and callous the next. But feeling her tummy rumbling and remembering Mistress Xan's beautiful dining room with its elegant flatware, cut crystal goblets and scrumptious meals, Aerylln didn't think anything could spoil her dinner.

Dreaming of food, Aerylln was lost in thought and trailing along behind Corson when the teenage girl accidentally bumped into her. Startled by how solid Corson's back was,

Aerylln at first thought she'd stumbled into a brick wall. However, while rubbing her forehead, the teenager realized she'd run into Corson instead having bonked her head against the sword slung over the warrior woman's back.

Still feeling unsteady and taking hold of her friend's hips, Aerylln thought, Corson's bottom feels as hard as a blacksmith's anvil. Why would a woman need such powerful muscles?

Aerylln felt her own bottom and thighs, and they were as soft as freshly baked bread. Maybe Corson suffers from some malady? Aerylln worried having always enjoyed curling up and resting her head on Mistress Xan's lap, which was soft and comforting.

I don't understand, Aerylln thought. At Mistress Xan's castle, there had always been plenty of workmen to handle any heavy lifting. Having firm muscles isn't very ladylike, is it?

But Aerylln shook off her confusion as she awakened to the sights and sounds of the village with shops lining both sides of the road and people bustling about.

Suddenly, Aerylln became aware of a disturbance up ahead. A horse and rider were making their way roughly past some pedestrians knocking one down and kicking another aside. Looking annoyed and impatient, the rider was shouting, "Move! Make way!" And that's what Aerylln did stepping quickly aside.

However, in shock and horror, Aerylln noticed Corson was still in the middle of the road directly in the path of the oncoming horse and rider. Yet instead of retreating, the warrior woman calmly uncurled a whip she'd been carrying, hauled back her arm and lashed out catching the horse on the tip of its snout with a loud crack. More startled than injured, the animal reared up on its hind legs promptly dislodging its rider who fell to the ground with a resounding thump!

As Aeryllnrejoined her, the warrior woman stepped on the neck of the fallen man pushing hard with a surge of what Aerylln was learning were rather powerful legs. The teenage girl thought she heard something snap, but wasn't sure giving her friend a confused look not knowing whether to feel horrified or relieved. Was another man dead so soon after the other?

"You can't run from a fight, little one, for if you do, some people will interpret it as weakness, and the world can be harsh to those who cower in fear," Corson instructed.

The warrior woman then abruptly headed towards one of the most tumbledown buildings on the street. As they approached, Aerylln noticed all the windows were dirty and one whole window was missing from the second floor. Or, that is to say, most of it was gone. The frame was shattered looking like something or someone had been thrown through it.

Corson laughed and said, "It doesn't look like much, but the food's good, and they don't mind a person having a good time." She seemed positively jubilant, and Aerylln worried about that given her friend's decidedly different sense of humor.

Striding through the entrance, Corson tossed herself onto a chair like she was throwing herself onto a saddle. The chair had a broken back, but looking around, Aerylln noticed that none of them appeared to be undamaged. Her friend shoved one at her that seemed relatively intact, at least until she sat down and felt it wobble.

Corson grabbed a waiter slamming him down onto a stool and telling him, "We want two steaks and make mine so rare that I can still taste the blood!" She shoved him away with a force that surprised Aerylln, as well as the waiter.

Then she boomed, "Innkeeper, two flagons of your best bitter!" And Aerylln watched in amazement as the little, round man hurried to do Corson's bidding.

Their meal arrived so quickly that the teenage girl thought it must have been prepared with magic until she heard two men on the other side of the room protesting to the innkeeper that their meal had been served to Corson and Aerylln.

The innkeeper smiled nervously as Corson attacked her meat. Red juices flowed down her chin and onto her breasts almost covering them, which was saying something given the size of her friend's chest. Then she downed her ale in one swallow and looked hungrily at Aerylln's, who was more than glad to shove the mug of foul smelling liquid towards her friend. But what bothered the young woman most was that everyone in the tavern was wearing a there-goes-the-neighborhood expression on their faces, and it wasn't much of a neighborhood to begin with.

Corson let out the biggest belch Aerylln had ever heard. She'd heard barnyard animals belch occasionally, but never this loudly. Her friend, the young woman was learning, was clearly in a league of her own. But the real awakening came from what Corson did next.

"Behind you, those men at the table in the far corner have been pointing at us and laughing," Aerylln said. "Maybe we should leave."

"Why?"

"They're making me feel uncomfortable."

"Really? Well, we can't have that," Corson said pounding her fist on the table. Striding over to a half-dozen men, she said, "You're upsetting my friend."

"Really?" one of them chuckled while eyeing Corson up and down.

"Yes, I'm afraid so," the warrior woman said while setting her staff against the bar and unsheathing her sword with one hand and a knife with the other. Instantly, the men were on their feet, but Corson surprised them by turning around, sticking her knife into a wooden post supporting the ceiling and swinging her sword with both hands sinking the blade into it as well.

Now she was virtually an unarmed woman standing alone against six armed men, which in her view evened the odds. Then picking up her wooden staff, she faced the men and said, "I want you to apologize to that young woman."

"Seriously?" the first man asked, who seemed to be the leader.

"Yes."

"And why would we do that?"

With blinding speed, Corson swung her staff bringing it down hard on the tabletop and saying, "Because I'm through asking politely."

"I don't know," the leader said smiling a little less but still amused.

"I won't ask a second time."

The men stared at this woman armed with only a staff, then glanced around at each other, finding the situation totally ludicrous and burst into fits of uproarious laughter.

"So, that's your answer?" Corson asked firmly with an edge to her voice.

"Yes," the leader said, his smile broader than ever but feeling a little confused.

"Then prepare to defend yourselves," Corson purred.

With reflexes and strength that stunned them all, the warrior woman hauled the man closest to her off his feet, using only one hand, and tossed him onto the long, wooden bar dragging him the length of it and driving his head against the wall knocking him unconscious.

All the men were ready to fight, but none went for their swords, Corson being unarmed except for her staff and being a woman as well, although appearing to be anything but helpless.

Striding rapidly back to the table, she held her staff horizontally with both hands and jammed one end into another man's stomach doubling him over as he howled in pain. Two of his friends leapt at Corson, who neatly sidestepped them whacking each on the head with a staff moving so quickly it was a blur.

"Okay, stop! All you want's an apology?" the leader asked, no longer laughing.

"Yep."

"Hey, young lady, we're sorry if we upset you!" he shouted.

Dumbfounded by what was happening, Aerylln didn't know what to say.

"Do you accept his apology, Aerylln?" Corson asked.

"Yes," the teenage girl croaked, barely able to speak.

"Well, that's settled," Corson said smiling and patting the leader on the back. Then pulling her weapons from the wooden post, she sheathed her sword and knife, tossed a few coins on a table to pay for their meal and walked past Aerylln saying, "Come on, kid, let's go."

Both confused and amazed, Aerylln followed her new friend outside leaving a group of rather shaken-up men behind them. But after walking only a short distance, another problem materialized when a horse and rider suddenly appeared out of nowhere galloping right at them. Pulling hard on the reins, the rider brought his horse to an abrupt halt, leapt from his saddle and drew his sword staring all the time at Corson.

Aerylln realized her friend had also drawn her sword, and the two were headed for each other. The swords clashed as the two warriors battled, and it became evident that they were both very skilled. When they had their swords locked above each other, their bodies close, only inches apart, Aerylln saw Corson seductively lick her lips. While the man was distracted, she quickly disarmed him and knocked him to the ground.

As he hit the dirt, she laughed and said, "You always did fall for that one, didn't you?"

The man dusted himself off as he rose, and Corson sheathed her sword.

"You'd think I'd have learned wouldn't you? I guess I still can't resist you, can I?" he said.

Corson shot him a lusty glance. "Why would you want to?" she purred.

Aerylln was confused. What in the world's going on? she wondered. They were fighting, but now they're acting like friends.

The confusion on her face must have been apparent because Corson chuckled and said, "Aerylln, I'd like you to meet Balder. We used to, er, ride together."

Balder laughed as well. "I guess that's one way of putting it."

He approached Aerylln, bowed and said, "I'm pleased to meet you, young lady." Next, Balder turned to Corson and said, "I think I should warn you. Chen's terrorizing again."

"Well that explains a lot," Corson replied. "I dealt with one of Chen's men earlier."

"Ah, that explains the dead man with the horse running around him. For some reason, I thought that was your handiwork."

Walking over to his horse, Balder took it by the reins and said, "I'd best be getting back to my men. I need to drag them out of the tavern and back to camp."

"Oh, were those some of your men?"

"Corson, you didn't?" Balder asked in a stern tone of voice. When the warrior woman shrugged, he laughed and said, "I hope you didn't scare them too much."

"Oh, I think they'll be fine."

"But will I?" Balder asked. "That's the pressing question on my mind. Well, good-bye Corson. Good-bye Aerylln. Perhaps we'll all meet again soon."

Chapter 4

When Balder went into the tavern, his men showed him where Corson's sword had made a gash in the wooden support post. After running his fingers along it pensively, he went over to the front windows and watched her walking gracefully while packed tightly inside her leather pants.

"Those breeches do seem a bit snug," he said smiling at his men.

Balder's right-hand man, Kirtak, the one who'd offered Aerylln a formal apology, came over to him and said, "If she hadn't beaten us so soundly, I might actually have enjoyed the fight."

"If she'd really cut loose, you'd be dead," Balder said. "The last time she got mad at me, she swung her sword at my neck so hard she'd have cut my head off if I hadn't ducked quickly."

All of Balder's men gathered around him as he gazed out the window at the only woman he had ever truly loved.

"What drives a woman to be so mean?" one of the men asked.

"When she was little, she saw her family murdered right in front of her eyes," Balder said sadly. "Sometimes sheer terror can drive a woman so far beyond the breaking point that she can never return to who she was. Corson has an intuitive insight into the human heart that only those who have gone to the brink of insanity can ever imagine."

"So, you're saying Corson's gone mad?" Kirtak asked.

"No, it's worse than that. If she had only gone insane, it wouldn't have been so bad."

"What happened?"

"Corson waited until she felt she was big enough and strong enough, but still barely ten years old, and she walked right into the home of the man who murdered her family . . ."

"What did she do?"

"You just ate dinner and, believe me, you don't want to know," Balder said. "Corson kills just to ease the pain that festers inside of her. For her, killing is medicinal. If she doesn't get into a good scrap at least every few days, the memories get to be too much for her."

"What's it like to make love to her?" one of his men asked, wincing when another warrior elbowed him in the ribs indicating that he shouldn't be asking such a personal question. Balder's men knew their leader's relationship with Corson was, to say the least, complicated.

"It's great," Balder said letting it go at that.

Recalling the early days of his relationship with Corson, Balder knew it had been difficult from the start. He thought, The first time, we were in her kitchen, and she put both arms around my neck and leaned back against the counter. I felt her open up to me inwardly, and it was as if I was looking at the charred remains of a building that had been gutted by fire. The smoke was thick and black. It poured out of her and into my soul flooding and suffocating me, and I pulled back while half-shouting that I was being overwhelmed. She ran to the door opening it for me so I could leave, but once she got away from me, I felt better.

As their leader was silently reminiscing, Balder's men shifted awkwardly wondering what was bothering him. Seeing him tensing up, the warriors figured that whatever he was remembering wasn't very pleasant. And they were right.

Balder was thinking, For the first few months, Corson was almost desperate for friendship and love. But at the same time, she was terrified feeling sure I'd hurt her. Her wounds ran so deeply that they seemed to split the wall between this world and the next, between the physical world and the spiritual world.

All of Balder's warriors, except for Kirtak, drifted over to the far table leaving their leader alone with his thoughts. Turning to his best friend, he said, "Corson doesn't believe she can be killed. She believes she's eternal. Not her body, but her spirit. And she believes the spirit world is more real than the physical world."

"Then, why doesn't she let herself die in battle and be done with it all?" Kirtak asked.

"Corson believes she can't leave this earth until her god allows her to. There has to be a natural exit, and she must give her life to save that of another, or she has to wait till old age takes her."

"So, she's trapped?"

"Yes, trapped between two worlds and a caged animal can be unpredictable and dangerous."

"And we just fought her," Kirtak said shocked over the danger they'd all been in.

"She wouldn't have hurt you seriously," Balder said.

"Why not?"

"She was just defending Aerylln, and that's the first time I've ever known Corson to have a maternal side. But if you see her again, I wouldn't remind her about the fight."

"Why not?"

"For her, the moment's already in the past. Corson lives in the present, and if a person doesn't have relevance to that moment, then it's as if she's forgotten he ever existed. The person's completely out of her thoughts and memory."

"But why not remind her of it?" Kirtak asked.

"Because it takes all of Corson's effort to keep her balance mentally, emotionally and spiritually right now in the present. Even referring to the past can overwhelm her. She can't cope with anything but the present moment."

"Too strange."

"Too deadly," Balder warned.

"Sounds pretty bad," Kirtak said.

"Well, there is one thing worse."

"What's that?"

"If you win Corson's respect and friendship. Because then, if you ever fail her, her disappointment will be compounded and become dramatically out of proportion."

"Does she trust you, Balder?"

"Yes."

"How do you feel about that?" Kirtak asked his old friend.

"When I'm with her, I feel more alive than ever. But it's a slippery slope, and my friendship with Corson puts me on that slope with her. If she goes down, she'll drag me down as well."

"Not if you leave her. Just walk away."

"I can't do that. I have the misfortune of being in love with a woman who already has one foot in the grave and wouldn't mind putting the other one there as well. She takes risks just to feel alive, but those risks could get me killed."

"No matter what happens, I'll always stand by you. You're not alone."

"I don't expect you or any of our warriors to get involved. It's bad enough that I am."

Looking over towards their men, Kirtak said, "Hey, guys, come over here."

Responding quickly, and sensing their leader was in trouble, Balder's warriors surrounded him feeling protective. Gripping Balder's shoulders with both hands, Kirtak said, "No matter the danger, no matter the risks, I will never leave you."

"That might not be wise, old friend," Balder said.

"Well, I never said I was very smart," Kirtak said smiling ruefully. "If you're in trouble, we'll all come to your aid. Many times, you've done as much for each of us. We owe you our lives."

"That's true!" all of his men said almost in unison.

"Anyway, who wants to live forever?" Kirtak added.

"I guess we're all doomed," one man said jokingly, but he took a step back when Balder's other men glared at him.

"Maybe, but maybe not," Balder said. "Corson will be joining us in the coming fight with Chen. And we may welcome a warrior amongst us who, at least spiritually, has been beyond death's door. She'll show no fear, and she won't feel any. It could be the winning edge we need, if we're to survive this coming battle. And come it will. We can't avoid it, and Corson won't try to avoid it, she'll seek it out."

"Straight out of hell she is, is she?" one man asked.

"No, she's not from hell, herself. But when she's in battle, she brings hell with her as her ally."

*

Out on the street, Corson and Aerylln were continuing on their way toward the stable unaware of the men's stares and conversation.

So, Chen is near, is she? Corson asked herself as she reached her arm over her back and felt the handle of her sword. It always brought her comfort. It was one of the few things in life she knew she could trust completely.

Well, if it's a fight she wants, it's a fight she'll get. And death, itself, will be following close on my heels. Where I go, death always follows. I draw negativity to me like a moth to a flame, Corson thought. And there's nothing I can do about it. Something inside my inner self is broken, and I don't even know what it is or how to fix it. She almost cried.

No emotions, she commanded herself. And she shoved her sorrow deep back inside of her. I don't know what's wrong with me, I just don't know! She breathed a sigh that only a person with a truly weary soul can do.

She looked at Aerylln. Maybe she is the hope for the future, Corson wondered.

"I have a magic sword," Aerylln said half to herself as if in a daydream.

"You do?" Corson laughed. "Where is this magic sword?"

"The horse is guarding it."

"What horse?"

"My horse," Aerylln replied.

"You left your sword in the stable?" Corson asked in stunned disbelief. "A warrior never leaves her sword unattended."

"This is not an ordinary horse."

Corson looked in wonder at Aerylln. And then she looked at the stable that was now just up ahead.

A magic sword and a magic horse, she thought skeptically with the cynicism of one who feels lost in a sea of hopelessness.

Corson looked at Aerylln one last time as they approached the stable. What is it that's different about this little one?

As they walked through the doorway of the stable, Corson was about to meet both her future, as well as two weapons so powerful they would bring daylight into the darkest and most remote reaches of her soul. A sword and a horse.

As Aerylln entered the stable, she felt as if she'd entered into an energy that was unlike anything she'd ever experienced before. Corson sensed it, too. It felt like the very walls were so soaked that they radiated a supernatural force.

Corson's hand instinctively went to her sword and raised it an inch out of its scabbard.

"It's okay," Aerylln whispered, as she put a comforting hand on her warrior friend's shoulder. "It isn't a danger to us."

For the first time in her life, Aerylln felt like she was in charge. She moved with the rhythm of the energy like she was born to it, like it was her natural environment, like it was her home, which was perceptive on her part since all of those things were true.

In awe, Aerylln felt the presence flowing in her, through her and around her. She held up her hands, spread her palms wide and felt her flesh pushing up against an invisible living presence.

Corson was totally shaken and unnerved. All color had drained from her face and her skin was flushed.

What is that look in her eyes? Aerylln wondered. In shock, she realized her friend was afraid. Corson looked like a little girl who was lost and unfamiliar with her environment.

Aerylln, by contrast, felt powerful, at peace and was almost drunk on the presence. She wanted nothing more than to just sit down and yield totally to the force itself. To have it flow unobstructed through her, without any particle of her own will blocking the flow. For Aerylln, total surrender was the only response to such a presence.

This was not Corson's first choice of a direction to take in her own life. She felt the presence calling to her, urging her to give herself over to it as Aerylln had. In a state of almost panic, Corson unsheathed her sword and swung it blindly through the air in defiance.

Aerylln watched her friend through an inner peace so profoundly real to her that it was like looking through a haze or an invisible fog. But even being virtually seduced by the energy, she could see her friend's fear of the unknown was beginning to boil over.

With total disregard for Corson's flailing sword, Aerylln walked toward her friend as if she, herself, were in a disembodied state and almost unable to put any tangible value on anything in the physical world, even her own life. She ducked under Corson's arm as the sword took a wicked swipe at nothingness. Aerylln leaned up against her friend's back and, bracing herself, began to shove Corson out of the stable.

The fresh air outside was like a tonic and Corson's head cleared. By contrast, Aerylln felt like a teenage girl again. Everything was once again as it had been.

Aerylln longed to reenter the stable, but Corson wasn't going back in there for any reason, no matter what.

"What was that?" Corson screamed in frustration and rage. Never before had she felt so out of control of her own life, as if who she was, what she did, what she wanted and even what she thought was irrelevant. Which, of course, was the case.

"That was my master," Aerylln said somehow instinctively knowing it to be true.

"What do you mean your master?" Corson shouted.

But Aerylln couldn't explain what she meant or what she'd experienced.

"Well, you can go back inside there with it and bring out my horse along with your own," Corson said firmly feeling assured of herself once more, though still on somewhat shaky ground.

Corson had been accused of being a lot of things in her life, few of them good, but no one had ever referred to her as a philosopher or spiritual artist. Corson would always feel more comfortable with things she could sink her sword into. Something solid.

At that moment, all of life came down to one fact that could be carved in stone. Corson was not going back into that stable.

Let Aerylln's master bring them out if it wants to, Corson thought.

And like so much of life, you need to be careful what you wish for because you just might get it, Corson's massive warhorse, and Aerylln's horse, Zorya, came out of the stable at that very moment.

And the sword came with them, slung over the pommel of a saddle that Zorya was now wearing.

Corson leapt onto her horse, which stood next to Zorya and in doing so almost bumped up against her. Corson felt her body pass through a blinding light and, having had just about all she could stand of that, she spurred her horse and galloped along the street a good block.

Aerylln stood with her face against Zorya's massive head feeling safe and secure in the presence of her protector. She leapt up into the saddle and unconsciously unsheathed Baelfire, her sword, and held it aloft.

Corson was almost knocked from her saddle by the sheer force of the power that struck her. People along the road cleared a path for Aerylln who moved slowly through the crowd with such a blinding radiance that Corson could hardly believe what was happening. Some villagers even felt moved to kneel.

Corson never forgot this moment, for time seemed to stand still and appeared to be at Aerylln's command. And the warrior woman never forgot how relieved she was when she recalled the wizard who lived a few miles outside of town.

I'll take her to see him, Corson thought. This is way too much for me!

And then it hit her that this was the first time she'd ever felt she was in the presence of someone who was greater than herself. And she knew one thing more.

I will give my life in defense of this young woman, if necessary, she said to herself. And somehow intuitively she knew that such a day would come, as sure as nightfall on a rainy day.

And for the first time, Corson experienced an emotion so alien to her that she had no idea what it was. But it caused her chest to ache and her eyes to burn with tears. For the first time in her adult life, Corson experienced what it was like to love another person. And following close on its heels was the fear of loss, another new emotion that was alien to her. For now Corson had someone she never wanted to be without ever again, and at that moment she wedded her own life to Aerylln's. And God have mercy on anyone who tried to hurt Aerylln, for Corson knew that she would not.

Well, we're off to see the wizard, Corson said to herself spurring her warhorse into a gallop as Aerylln, Zorya and Baelfire followed close on her heels. And it was the first time light, rather than darkness, followed her.

*

"The young woman has left Mistress Xan's castle, Lord Daegal," the spy told his master. "And she is already united with Zorya and Baelfire."

"She's not fully united with them yet. She's Lyssa's granddaughter, not Lyssa herself. The young woman is next in Lyssa's line to be drawn into the Trinity, but the three have not become as one yet," the warlord growled.

"They're taking her to see Eldwyn, the wizard," the spy said with some fear in his voice.

"Eldwyn's an old man," Lord Daegal said. "He'll never be able to guide the Trinity into the Light."

"We should kill them all now, my lord. Why risk them being together at all?"

"If we take them down now, we destroy two people, a horse, and a sword. But if we wait until the moment of the transformation when the Light seeks to unify them, then there is a moment of vulnerability when we can invade the Trinity itself and turn it to the Darkness," Lord Daegal informed him.

"But we have the young woman's father," the spy said.

"She's never met her father before. He'll be of no use to us at this point. What's the girl's name?" the warlord asked.

"Aerylln."

Chapter 5

"C'mon, Aerylln, let's have some fun!" Corson shouted nudging her horse, Tempest, and breaking into a full gallop. Aerylln didn't ask where they were going but feeling her shoulders and chest being thrown back, the teenage girl gripped Zorya's mane tightly as her warhorse surged ahead responding to the challenge.

Chasing her friend, Aerylln soon discovered how exhilarating riding a powerful warhorse could be, as the two majestic animals went charging ahead at breakneck speed, the love of racing driving them onward.

Zorya and Tempest thundered across the landscape with their hooves pounding the ground tearing up grass and dirt and sending it flying. The two warhorses didn't just run along at full gallop, they took command of the very earth beneath their feet leaving it shaken and shuddering in their wake.

The warhorses' mighty chests heaved and their powerful hindquarters propelled them forward with such velocity Aerylln felt she was being launched from a catapult. Trying to lessen the wind resistance, the teenage girl bent forward pressing her body against Zorya's neck. Hanging on tightly, and determined to enjoy the experience, Aerylln fought her fear mastering it and shoving it deeply inside of herself. Urging Zorya onward, the young woman thought, I'll trust my horse. She'll take care of me and won't let me get hurt. And sensing Aerylln's confidence in her, Zorya drove herself even harder.

Charging into a forest, the two warhorses and their riders sped along a path through the trees with an intensity Aerylln now found invigorating. Two villagers standing next to the trail stepped back several paces, but it wasn't enough as an invisible field of energy erupting from the raging warhorses knocked them off their feet. Yet even sprawled out on the grass and feeling dazed, the villagers knew Zorya and Tempest were the finest examples of horseflesh they'd ever seen.

Approaching a steep hillside, the warhorses tore up the incline defying the ground beneath their feet and refusing to let it impede their headlong rush. Never having experienced anything like this before, Aerylln gasped as Zorya's energy raced through her like a cleansing wildfire leaving her feeling both exhilarated and exhausted from the sheer excitement. And the energy kept coming, flowing in seemingly endless waves remaking her, rebuilding her.

I could definitely get used to this, Aerylln thought recalling a story Mistress Xan had told her about women in a matriarchal line of succession spanning hundreds of years and producing incredible horsewomen. Aerylln felt she belonged in such a story, as if it was part of her own heritage, and unbeknownst to her, it was. Aerylln's true destiny had been a closely guarded secret, kept even from her, and Zorya and Baelfire's names had never been mentioned.

However, there were a few who knew of her, a very precious few. And nearing the wizard's cottage, the trees began paying homage to Aerylln as the teenage girl rode along unafraid of the energy coursing though her.

"Aerylln, Aerylln," the trees of the forest whispered.

"Aerylln! Aerylln!" the trees began shouting as if welcoming home one of their own. This isn't a dream, the young woman thought. It's not my imagination. But still, she was unafraid.

Reaching the crest of the hill, Zorya and Tempest turned 'round and 'round neighing loudly and stamping the dirt with their hooves.

Up ahead, situated in a grove of oak trees, was a modest stone cottage with smoke drifting out of its chimney radiating a sense of stillness and serenity. After the warhorses cantered up to it, Corson dismounted and said, "I hope this old wizard can help us."

Sliding off her warhorse's back, Aerylln followed Corson to the door as Zorya smiled to herself and thought, This should be interesting.

When Corson knocked on the door, they heard a muffled voice saying, "Who in the world could that be?"

A moment later, the door opened and an old man stood before them. His beard and hair were white with age, and he was wearing what appeared to be wizard robes as far as Aerylln knew. With his eyesight being poor, the old wizard squinted at first, but his eyes grew wide upon seeing Aerylln.

"How's this possible? Lyssa, is that you?" he asked in a whisper. However, looking past Aerylln and seeing Zorya, the old wizard smiled.

Growing impatient with him, Corson pointed at Aerylln and said, "My young friend here has an unusual sword and a rather spooky horse. We're here to ask you about them."

Barely hearing the warrior woman, the wizard made a beeline for Zorya and said, "Oh, my dearest love, how long has it been since I looked into your beautiful eyes?"

"Be careful speaking to a horse like that around witnesses," Zorya said laughing. "There are laws against that sort of behavior."

The wizard wrapped his arms around Zorya's neck running his gnarled fingers through her long, golden mane. She felt the wizard's tears falling upon her shoulder.

"This is embarrassing," Zorya said speaking telepathically, but everyone was able to hear her quite clearly. Then, to the wizard, Zorya whispered, "Eldwyn, not here and not now."

The old wizard squinted again while looking very closely at Zorya and made a rather surprising discovery. "Why, you're a horse! A horse!"

"Does this mean you don't love me anymore?" Zorya laughed. "What happened to how you miss my big, beautiful eyes?"

Feeling confused, Eldwyn backed up a few steps, but Zorya followed and turned sideways bonking him on the head with something solid that was hanging from her saddle. Rubbing his sore forehead, the cobwebs began clearing from his brain. Glancing at what had hit him, the old wizard shouted, "Baelfire, what are you doing here? And where have you been? It's been years!"

Reaching out and touching the sword, the wizard instantly seemed younger. Eldwyn was standing a little straighter, and his skin no longer had such a ghastly pallor to it. A few moments before, he'd seemed more dead than alive, but now the reverse was true.

With quick reflexes that seemed beyond someone his age, the old wizard unsheathed Baelfire swinging the sword in a mighty arc, the blade whistling through the air.

"Stop it, Eldwyn! Put me back in my scabbard!" the sword commanded.

"Put you back? But I haven't seen you since the civil war," the wizard said in frustration though still feeling younger and more animated than he had in years.

"A man can't wield me anymore," the sword explained.

"What do you mean? You never complained before."

"Eldwyn's so fickle, first me, now the sword," Zorya said smiling.

"You just can't hold me anymore," Baelfire said firmly.

"Before, you liked me gripping your handle. You always said I had a gentle touch."

"Oh, please spare me the details," the horse said in disgust.

"I'm sorry, but I can only be touched by a woman now," Baelfire said speaking telepathically like Zorya, but Eldwyn hardly noticed any difference between that and the spoken word.

"I think you're being pretty fussy," the old wizard grumbled.

"If I had a hand, I'd smack him," Zorya said wishing she could kick him but held herself back not wanting to risk breaking his leg.

"I heard that! Why would you want to smack me? Anyway, you're a horse for goodness sake."

"Some say I am, and some say I'm not," Zorya huffed.

"Enough!" Corson said. "Enough of talking horses, fussy swords and crazy old men! I came here seeking answers, not more confusion!"

Taking a look around, Eldwyn said, "Oh, yes, I forgot. We have company."

After Eldwyn slid Baelfire back into her scabbard, Corson overheard him mumble something to Zorya that sounded like, "A horse? What are you doing being a horse?"

Walking briskly over to Corson, the old wizard said, "Answers? You want answers? What do I look like, the town crier?"

"I didn't know who else to ask," the warrior woman said noticing the marked change in the old wizard. A minute ago, Eldwyn had been hobbling about barely able walk, let alone move quickly.

"Okay, so I cured a farmer's sick cattle, ended a prolonged drought and performed countless feats requiring great skill and imagination, but why should I help you?" the old wizard groused though secretly pleased that Corson had heard of him.

"Well, I'm not exactly thrilled by being in the company of a talking horse and sword, and this young woman can ride a warhorse better than most men," Corson said glaring at the wizard. "And you seemed to recognize Aerylln."

"Never saw her before in my life," Eldwyn said in a distracted tone of voice and going back into the cottage.

"What about the horse and sword?" Corson said sputtering in anger. "You did everything but kiss the horse, and you're all upset that the sword won't let you fondle her anymore. Would you care to explain that?"

"Never saw them before."

Corson and Aerylln followed Eldwyn into the cottage, but when Zorya came in behind them, Corson's patience snapped and she exploded shouting, "What are you doing in here? You're a horse!"

"Well, I'm not going to miss out on this. Anyway, you're being picky. How do you think we like being around a prissy warrior?"

"That's going way out of bounds," Corson said instinctively reaching over her shoulder, clutching the handle of her sword and sliding the blade an inch out of its scabbard. "Who are you calling prissy?"

"Well, if you don't want such things being said about you, stop complaining," Zorya huffed.

"At least I wasn't born in a barn," Corson snarled.

"Neither was I," Zorya declared haughtily.

"How would you know where you were born?" Corson shouted in exasperation.

"I was there, and I have a very good memory."

Tilting back her head, Corson screamed, "I'm having a conversation with a horse!"

"Well, I don't want to talk to you either," Zorya said feeling offended and turning around facing away from the warrior woman, which also put the horse's rump right in Corson's face.

The warrior woman looked wild-eyed, like she was ready to pull her hair out.

"Zorya and Baelfire can be quite frustrating," the wizard said in a sympathetic tone. "But they are women, and you know how they are."

"I don't know what you're trying to say, I'm not a man," Corson snapped.

"Not a man?"

"Hey, grandpa, it's okay not to have the best eyesight, but if I were you, I wouldn't insult a woman's personal appearance," Corson purred menacingly.

"You are a woman, aren't you? I was just hoping against hope, I suppose. It would have been nice having some moral support now that those two are back," Eldwyn said nodding at Zorya's backside and Baelfire, who was holding her peace and gently hanging from the saddle's pommel.

"That bottom used to be so small and shapely," the wizard said recalling days long ago.

"When she was a foal?" Corson asked.

"Not exactly," Eldwyn sighed.

"I thought you didn't know Zorya and Baelfire."

"Some people you try to forget," the wizard said still smarting from being rebuffed by them.

"Well, you shouldn't be so grabby," Baelfire said speaking up. "You always were so forward in your affections."

"Well, excuse me, but I haven't touched a woman of your high quality in a long time," Eldwyn said feeling annoyed. "And I haven't heard from any either. I guess some people have forgotten how to write."

"Maybe we'd have more to say, if you were more polite," Zorya said in a snippy tone of voice.

"I'm out of here," Corson said dragging Aerylln with her.

"Why are we going outside?" the teenage girl asked.

Heading over to her warhorse, Corson said, "I don't understand what's going on in there, but it has all the earmarks of a family squabble, and it's better not to get involved in one of those."

"A family squabble?" Aerylln asked following Corson away from the cottage. As the bickering got louder, the young woman thought, Even when Mistress Xan got angry and scolded me, I knew she still loved me. If people truly care, you can feel the love no matter what they say.

"I think they love each other," Aerylln said looking back at the cottage and listening to the angry voices carrying through the still night air.

"That's exactly why we're getting away from them. Stay out of other people's arguments, especially when they're between men and women," Corson said putting her hand squarely in the center of Aerylln's back and pushing her further away from the cottage.

"But it's a horse, a sword and an old man."

"Maybe, but we're playing it safe and sleeping outdoors under the stars."

*

Early the next morning, Aerylln awoke to the feeling of Zorya's sandpapery tongue licking her cheek. As the teenage girl yawned, Zorya tried to keep her from falling back to sleep. The warhorse nuzzled Aerylln's neck and snorted right next to her ear, which sounded as loud as thunder to the young woman. Then, using her snout to nudge Aerylln's chest, Zorya rolled her onto her back. Covering a big yawn, Aerylln sighed realizing that she wasn't going to be allowed to go back to sleep and began rubbing her eyes. Looking up, all that the teenage girl could see was a white horse leaning down filling her vision, but she found Zorya's closeness reassuring.

Turning her head, Aerylln looked over at Corson who was just waking from a troubled sleep. The young woman suspected that, for Corson, a fitful night's sleep was nothing unusual.

Back at the wizard's cabin, Eldwyn awoke from a nightmare worried it was real and not just a dream. Jumping out of bed, he reached into a bucket throwing a handful of water into the air. After transforming into a wall of dense, white fog, Eldwyn's nightmare seemed to come alive within it. First, Lord

Daegal appeared whispering, "Aerylln has surfaced, hasn't she?" But the warlord quickly vanished being replaced by another image that was even more disturbing. Eldwyn gasped as he saw a spy lurking about in the woods outside his cottage.

Hurriedly getting dressed, the wizard thought, Zorya and Baelfire must be warned. Lord Daegal is having us watched, and he knows about Aerylln!

Hearing someone calling her name, Zorya stopped nudging a sleepy Aerylln and looked up. One glance at the wizard's face said it all. Zorya knew the worried look meant bad news, very bad news.

"Zorya, there's a spy in the woods behind my cottage!" Eldwyn shouted.

Watching the old wizard running towards her, Zorya sighed and thought, Now it all begins. Then looking down at Aerylln, the warhorse said, "Well, little one, your destiny approaches."

"What's wrong?" she asked sensing the quiet urgency in her horse's voice.

"Leap up onto my back, Aerylln, quickly."

Without a word, the young woman obeyed.

"Now take Baelfire out of her scabbard and hold her high over your head."

Again, the young woman did as she was told. An enormous shock wave poured out of Baelfire knocking Eldwyn off his feet, then swept past the wizard flowing over his cottage and finding its prey. The spy was incinerated instantly.

"Wow! What was that?" Aerylln asked breathlessly.

"That was hardly anything, my dear, hardly anything at all," Zorya said lowering her head and feeling a profound sadness knowing Aerylln's time of innocence was coming to a close. A tear ran down the warhorse's cheek.

Not completely understanding what had happened, Aerylln watched Corson going over to Eldwyn and helping the old wizard to his feet. The teenage girl could tell he was upset, but wasn't sure why. But the most disconcerting thing was the look on Corson's face. The warrior woman was positively radiant wearing a big, wide smile. And as Eldwyn and Corson got closer, Aerylln noticed one more thing about her friend. Corson appeared to be not only happy but contented as well.

A chill went down Aerylln's spine, and she thought, What could make such a dangerous woman so happy?

Aerylln recalled the reassuring sense of security that had surrounded her during the years she'd spent growing up at Mistress Xan's castle. Taking a deep breath to steady her nerves, the teenage girl felt the weight of the sword in her hand and took comfort from it. Aerylln realized Baelfire belonged with her and could sense the sword's happiness, as if it had found its way home. But, in a way, that also disturbed her and she wondered, What's all this mean?

Aerylln glanced once more at the anxious wizard and the radiant warrior woman. She listened to the quiet sobbing of her horse and felt Baelfire's incredible energy, strength and power still lingering inside of her.

Something's not right, she thought.

After Eldwyn and Corson reached them, Aerylln put Baelfire back in her scabbard and left the sword hanging from the saddle's pommel. Sliding off Zorya's back, the young woman gave Corson a tentative hug wanting to be supportive of the warrior woman's good mood, but still a bit unnerved by it.

"That blast of energy was pretty exciting, what else can Baelfire do?" Corson asked.

"I don't really know," Aerylln confessed. "But Zorya and Eldwyn have more experience with Baelfire, at least I believe so."

"Well?" Corson demanded.

"I'm just a horse," Zorya said.

"Oh, don't start that again. You're a talking horse."

"Not really. Technically speaking, I don't talk at all."

"We all hear you well enough."

"You have good ears."

Suspecting that the wizard, horse and sword wouldn't speak openly in front of the teenage girl, Corson said, "Aerylln, how about if you go for a short walk?"

"Why?"

"We need a few minutes alone."

"It's my sword and horse. I should be allowed to stay."

"True, but humor me, please. And don't go far. Stay in plain sight."

"Oh, all right," Aerylln said sulking a little but going for a walk in the field.

When the young woman was far enough away, Corson turned to Zorya and said, "Okay, let's get down to business. Eldwyn says the dead man's a spy. A spy for whom?"

"Lord Daegal," Zorya said.

"Lord Daegal? He's bad news, I mean really bad news," Corson said. "Why would he want to spy on us?"

Zorya and Eldwyn both looked over at the teenage girl.

"Aerylln?" Corson asked in surprise.

"Yes, she's a catalyst, like her grandmother, Lyssa. At least we hope so, and only she can wield the sword," Eldwyn said.

"I wouldn't mind wielding Baelfire myself."

"It wouldn't work as well for you."

"Why not?"

"It just wouldn't."

"The girl is special is she?" Corson asked.

"Yes!" Zorya and Eldwyn said in unison.

"How special?"

"Special enough to make a talking horse seem like small potatoes," Eldwyn said.

"Watch it," Zorya said. "I like potatoes."

"What can Aerylln do that makes her so unique?" Corson asked.

"What she can't do is a rather short list," Zorya sighed.

Corson's eyes widened considerably, then looking over at Aerylln, the warrior woman said, "She knows nothing about this, does she, Zorya?"

"No."

"What happens now?"

"Lord Daegal won't stop till he has her."

"So, why doesn't he just come and get her?"

"Coming and getting her isn't as easy as it looks," Zorya said with a hint of pride in her voice. "If, like her grandmother, she can be trained to sense rivers of energy flowing through her and blend them into a combustible mix, well, things could get interesting."

"And Baelfire's certainly a deterrent, isn't she?" Corson asked reaching over and unsheathing the sword as Eldwyn gasped!

"Hmm, very well balanced," Corson said, swinging Baelfire back and forth a few times and twirling the sword in her hand.

"If Baelfire didn't like you, you'd be dead by now," Eldwyn said.

"Because I unsheathed the sword?"

"Because you even touched her."

While putting Baelfire back in her scabbard, Corson asked, "So Aerylln's invincible, is she?"

"Not quite, at least not now," Zorya said. "Lord Daegal could take us with a couple hundred warriors at this point."

"I'd feel a lot better about all this, if I was at my friend Balder's military encampment," Corson said.

"You have a friend with more than 200 warriors at his disposal?" Zorya asked.

"Not quite, more like 15."

"Where is this massive military presence?" Zorya asked.

"I'm not sure. They never stay long in the same place."

"Are they on some sort of patrol?"

"Reconnaissance."

"They're spies?"

"No, an enemy sends out spies. Allies go on reconnaissance."

"If we can't find them, they won't do us a whole lot of good," Zorya said.

"There's one place I know where they go for supplies. It's about a half-day's march from here."

"My marching days are behind me, way behind me," Eldwyn said. "But if I walk next to Baelfire, that should help."

"Why?" Corson asked.

"Why not?" Eldwyn countered.

"You could ride the horse," Corson suggested.

"Oh, so I'm back to being a beast of burden, am I? You might want to keep in mind that I'm Aerylln's horse, no one else's."

"Well, I have to say, it wouldn't be the first time I straddled her," Eldwyn said wistfully.

"It'll be your last, if you try it now," Zorya said glaring at him.

"Save your energy for the trek, guys. Let's head out," Corson said.

Aerylln strolled alongside Zorya stroking her mane, as Corson was on point walking a bit ahead of the rest. The warrior woman was always alert and ready, but this time there was an actual threat, and she felt a sense of anticipation. Fighting was the stuff of life for Corson, her reason for living. Everything else was just waiting for the chance to become embroiled in conflict. She was a scrapper, a fighter, and a warrior woman who felt at home in battle.

With Aerylln to defend, Corson had a sense of purpose. She didn't know how much danger they were actually in, but the promise of conflict lurked invitingly around every bend in the road. And what was even better, at least from Corson's point of view, was that things were probably going to get a lot worse.

As the warrior woman walked along, she felt a soft, warm pressure against her back as if a pillow was pushing her. Corson knew it was the sword, and what she felt was Baelfire's aura.

Eldwyn was daydreaming and walking along next to Zorya. The wizard was on the side of the horse opposite Aerylln. Baelfire was hanging from the pommel of the saddle and Eldwyn had his hand on the sword's scabbard. The elderly wizard seemed to be handling the miles without effort.

As for Zorya, she was walking along thoughtfully, wondering what the future held for them all.

Chapter 6

A hundred miles away, Lord Daegal was meeting with Tark, the captain of his personal guards. An imposing, intimidating structure, the warlord's castle was perched high atop a huge outcropping of solid rock. Sheer cliffs protected three sides, and bonfires lit the fourth at night making it impossible to approach unseen. No trees or shrubbery grew upon The Rock, and the access road was so steep many horses became exhausted from the arduous climb.

"I'm expecting Jagatta to report back in a day or two, my lord," Tark said referring to the spy he'd sent to keep an eye on Aerylln and her companions. "Jagatta has always proven to be gifted at his work."

"Don't get too close, I don't want them to become so alarmed that they panic. Just keep a general awareness of their movements and with whom they talk."

"Why not capture the young woman, Lord Daegal? Why give her time to mature? By then, she'll be even more dangerous."

"Aerylln's not much of a threat to us now, and it could be a while before her talents surface."

"But why delay further?"

"We'll have little influence over her feelings, if we put her into prison."

"Her feelings, sire? You're concerned with her feelings?"

"Having lived a sheltered existence, Aerylln might be innocent, naïve and susceptible to outside influence. Maybe her feelings can be molded."

"Molded in what way?" Tark asked while down on one knee, fearful in his master's presence, being well aware of his lord's quick temper.

"We must draw Aerylln close to us, befriend her and get her to trust us."

"Trust us, how?" Tark asked unable to imagine that happening.

"Young women like to experience life, discover who they are and explore the world of young men. After living a sheltered life, Aerylln might be eager to reach out."

"What's that got to do with us?"

"We're going to bring her into contact with people and events that will shape her attitude."

"But Aerylln's already with people who are shaping her attitude."

"We'll introduce her to a few people ourselves. Hopefully, we'll get her to like and trust some people her own age," Lord Daegal said. "Maybe we can have someone save her life."

"I suppose we orchestrate the threat."

"Naturally."

"Zorya will be suspicious of anyone getting close to Aerylln, and she might not allow the young woman to befriend the people you send," Tark pointed out.

"Oh, I hope Zorya tries to keep Aerylln from talking to one person in particular."

"Who?"

"A young man her own age. Someone who's adventurous, intelligent, strong, bold, yet kind, understanding and a good listener. In short, we'll introduce her to a young man who's good at dealing with teenage girls. And if Zorya forbids Aerylln, then she'll take an even greater interest in him."

"And who's this boyish lady killer? Where do you intend to find him?"

"I believe you have a son Aerylln's age, don't you?" Lord Daegal asked.

"Marcheto?" Tark asked in disbelief. "He's a bit of a scamp, don't you think? Are you looking to lead that innocent, young woman into a life of debauchery? I doubt that a sweet girl like her would even look down such a path."

"Marcheto will have to learn finesse," Lord Daegal said.

"Marcheto? My Marcheto? Why, he was seducing household servant girls almost before he could walk. Marcheto's learning finesse with a sword but with women?"

"Would you let a daughter of yours around another man's son, if he was like Marcheto?"

"Never."

"Precisely."

"Well, Zorya will certainly dislike him."

"And more importantly, we want Zorya to forbid Aerylln to see your son," Lord Daegal said.

"Okay, we'll portray Marcheto as a romantic hero," Tark said. "And he'll be sort of a highbred vagabond who rescues Aerylln and her little group from, say, some bandits."

"Now you're getting into the spirit of things," Lord Daegal said smiling.

"The seduction of innocence?"

"Yes."

"It won't take Marcheto long to get his hands up her skirt," Tark said.

"No, that's not what I want. She's important to me, and I don't want her trifled with. In fact, inform Marcheto that if he so much as rubs his manhood against the girl, I'll have him castrated."

Not sure if Lord Daegal was being serious, Tark looked at his master's eyes, but there was no humor in them, and the warlord wasn't smiling.

"Send Marcheto to me," Lord Daegal ordered.

"Sire, putting my son near a young virgin is courting disaster."

"I'll convince him not to harm her in any way."

"How are you going to accomplish that, sire? Marcheto's developing into an excellent warrior, but his weakness is a lack of personal discipline."

"You and Marcheto get along well. And, his being the youngest, haven't you always doted on him?"

"Yes, my lord, Marcheto's a fine son, and we love each other."

"Well, I'll explain to him that if the young woman doesn't remain a virgin, I'll have you killed."

"That should do it," Tark said almost laughing, not taking his master seriously. But as he turned to leave, Tark looked into the warlord's cold eyes and realized Lord Daegal wasn't fooling.

The hairs on the back of Tark's neck stood on end. He would enter eternity, if Marcheto entered the girl. At that moment, Tark gave himself no better than even odds of surviving. If Marcheto and his brothers lost their father, it would be hard on them. It would be hard on everyone in the family. But would Marcheto remember who Tark's death would be most hard on when his rascal son had his own hard on? Tark felt doomed.

Chapter 7

"Ohhhh!" Marcheto groaned falling out of bed and making a resounding thump as he hit the floor. Tangled in the bed sheets, the young man propped himself up on an elbow, struggled to his knees and tried pulling himself back onto the mattress. Feeling spent and exhausted, he nonetheless tried tugging on the covers but fell back onto the floor with another resounding thump! This time he gave up and didn't move.

A feminine hand gripped the edge of the mattress with long, claw-like fingernails. Her skin had a soft luster to it, however Marcheto had discovered this was the only thing soft about the young woman. As sweet and loving as she'd been outside the bedroom, she'd sprung at him like a ravenous wild animal once they crossed the threshold. As it was, the experience had come as a rude awakening to the young man. Up until now, he'd romanced and seduced his share of women, but this time, he was the one being used. And he'd come up short, not meeting the silken tigress' expectations. Not at all.

The young woman slung one of her arms over the edge of the bed and pulled her upper body into view. Long, blond ringlets flowed down obscuring most of the silken tigress' face. Taking a hand and running it through her hair, the young woman held it behind her left ear while gazing at Marcheto with cold, lifeless eyes.

The silken tigress was strikingly beautiful, but her hungry, predatory gaze was her dominant feature. And Marcheto, though approximately the same age, seemed more and more like an old man to her. Feeling annoyed, she wondered if he'd been injured and thought, What did mother say? Oh, yes, older men have weak hearts and can't take much strain.

Noticing that Marcheto's eyes were open but staring vacantly into space, the young woman arched an eyebrow, more out of curiosity than concern, when she couldn't tell if he was still breathing. However, after Marcheto moved his head, blinked a few times and shifted one leg, the silken tigress decided he was showing enough signs of life. Reassured, she slid back into the center of the mattress snuggling in a warm blanket that somehow had remained on the bed.

The young woman heaved a sigh of frustration feeling let down after having heard so much about the young man now lying crumpled on the floor. Marcheto was a legend of sorts around the castle. Yet after just two hours of love making, there he lay almost unconscious by the foot of the bed. Experiencing a sense of emptiness deep inside, she was aching for more but could see that this old man was past his prime. As she slowly drifted off to sleep, she thought, Next time, I'll trust my own instincts instead of listening to rumors.

With a sense of relief, Marcheto heard the young woman's breathing change, then opened his eyes and thought, What an ordeal!

The silken tigress had pushed him past his reserve an hour ago. The only reason he'd continued was after trying to roll off of her, she'd given Marcheto an incredulous look like he'd just grown two heads. "Where are you going!" she had almost shouted.

Marcheto wasn't going anywhere in particular except for getting out from between the legs of this young woman. The silken tigress possessed what seemed to him like hips made of rubber in that they kept flexing, grinding and urging him onward long after he had his fill.

I'm getting too old for this, he thought. When he hadn't been able to pull himself onto the bed and had fallen down a second time, Marcheto felt he was past his prime. As it was, things had turned out badly, and the only way he avoided being openly humiliated was to feign unconsciousness.

I must have peaked as a man almost a year ago, he thought. My days of being able to keep up with a woman like this are over.

The silken tigress was a bundle of energy barely encased in human form, and Marcheto's confidence was shaken. What am I going to do? he asked himself. If I can't keep up with a woman's needs, how can I avoid embarrassment? Fear crept into his heart.

All Marcheto had ever excelled at was being a swordsman in the bedroom and on the battlefield. Now he'd begun doubting himself in one of those areas. Desperately needing to get away, he picked up his clothing and quietly stole out of the bedroom.

Just before reaching the safety of the hallway, as he was almost out the door, the young woman opened one eye and asked, "Are you alright? I hope I didn't hurt you."

"No, I'm fine," Marcheto said cringing, wishing he were invisible.

"You shouldn't be ashamed of being impotent," the silken tigress said. "It's really not your fault. I've heard that it runs in some families."

"Thank you," he croaked, as his face turned bright red.

*

After stumbling into his clothes and walking down the hallway to the foyer, Marcheto glanced into the rooms and thought, I've never been in chambers this nice before. Not that his own rooms weren't impressive, they were, but this residence had something more to it possessing a certain style and elegance.

Marcheto thought, Maybe the young tigress has an older silken tigress for a mother? Anyway, my whole life has revolved around power and political intrigue, but the teenage tigress seems to exist simply to enjoy pleasure.

He recalled how the young tigress had her eyes closed and her delicate jaw set firmly, as she clenched her teeth, tilted back her head and ceased to be anything more than a moving pelvis. The pleasure she'd felt was like a living presence settling upon her. The disturbing thing for Marcheto, however, was that no matter how hard he tried to satisfy her, the young woman's hunger had just increased as she fed off his life energy and funneled it through her inner self.

The silken tigress had a deep, empty well inside of her, and she ached for him to fill it. And even though he'd poured his own soul into the young woman, no matter how much he gave, she always had room inside her for more.

But Marcheto was like a bucket of water being tossed inside a woman who spiritually was like a dry, parched riverbank yearning to be filled. To Marcheto, it had felt like he was being sucked dry. And while he was gradually overwhelmed by fatigue, the silken tigress had become more animated.

Marcheto hadn't understood what was happening to him, but this young woman was a sexually charged bandit of the spiritual world robbing him of his energy. Her stranglehold was the luscious cradle of her open and welcoming thighs, ever so desirable, ever so deadly and impossible to resist. A spiritually dying man would drag himself onto the luxurious plateau of her firm, flat tummy and with the very last shreds of his inner strength would caress the intoxicating nature of the well leading to her inner being.

But having little knowledge of feminine mystical arts, all Marcheto could do was ask over and over, What's wrong with me? What's wrong with me?

Stumbling along dazed and confused, Marcheto bumped into the mother of the silken tigress who was tall, grave and beautiful. Clad in an elegant, white dress, she had golden hair and flawless skin with no signs of age upon her except, perhaps, the depth of her eyes. As he looked into them, they seemed to possess wells of deep memory.

"Marcheto, you have served my daughter well enough but beware of the one to come, for she will prove to be either your savior or your undoing. It will be your choice as far as which way your soul will turn."

Feeling her eyes penetrating his very being, Marcheto wondered if this woman was some sort of prophetess and felt a chill run down his spine. When she released him from her gaze, he felt drained, almost as drained as when he'd tried to please the young tigress. For what seemed like an eternity, he stood there dumbfounded until she turned and walked, or almost glided, down the hallway.

As he felt the chill of her gaze subsiding, Marcheto thought, I'm definitely too old for this, something's got to change.

*

After running up a flight of stairs, Marcheto saw his father at the far end of a hallway. The young man called out to him, and they shared a hug.

"Marcheto, I had a rather interesting talk with Lord Daegal."

"What about father?"

"About you getting me killed more than likely."

"Father, don't say such a thing."

"Lord Daegal's plan might have dangerous repercussions, at least for our family."

"What could be as bad as that? I'm not afraid to die in battle."

"I know you aren't, but this could be more difficult than conventional warfare. It involves a pretty teenage girl. Lord Daegal wants you to get to know her, and he wants you to win her heart."

Marcheto felt sick. Having just escaped the clutches of the silken tigress, he was in no mood for more female entanglements.

"However, Lord Daegal insists that I issue a stern warning to you. Our master says you're not to touch her in any way a virgin may feel is inappropriate. This young woman knows nothing about sex, and you're to keep it that way."

"No sex?"

"No sex, Marcheto," Tark said gravely.

"Lord Daegal specifically said that?" Marcheto asked, his hope rising.

"He said he'd castrate you and kill me, if the girl doesn't remain a virgin."

"That's wonderful news, father, wonderful news!"

Tark looked at his son in disbelief.

"Truly, is she untouched?" Marcheto asked.

"Untouched," his father assured him.

"Unspoiled?"

"Yes, unspoiled, and she's to stay that way. And Lord Daegal has ordered you to stop womanizing and carousing in taverns. You're to focus on this girl alone."

"Oh, this just keeps getting better and better!" Marcheto exclaimed, the joy and relief apparent on his face. The young man hugged his father, kissed him on the cheek and ran off down the hall.

Bewildered by his son's behavior, Tark watched Marcheto bounding along and thought, What's different about him? And then it dawned on him!

Marcheto's happy! The boy's actually happy!

Since the tragic death of his wife and only daughter, Tark hadn't heard his son laugh or seen him smile. And Tark, a battle scarred, old warhorse of a man, turned down a short passageway, put one arm against the wall, lowered his head and wept.

Chapter 8

"Lord Daegal wants to see you," a castle guard had told Marcheto, and so the young man obediently followed the burly soldier to an anteroom outside the warlord's personal chambers. But that was hours ago, and he was still waiting.

I hate waiting, Marcheto thought to himself in frustration as his mind began wandering. Recalling his experience with the silken tigress, he was unhappy with his performance believing himself to have been inadequate.

What's missing? What's wrong with me? Marcheto asked himself sensing an inner emptiness that was leaving him feeling drained and hollow. He suspected there could be something more between men and women but didn't know what since love was a bit of a foreign concept to him. However, the young warrior's disappointment in himself was edging him closer to exploring a new concept. Maturity.

"It's one of the key elements of creativity," his grandmother had once told him. "Nothing of any lasting value is ever attained without it."

"I'm not exactly concerned with lasting value," Marcheto had said politely while smiling at the kindly older woman. "Everything changes. Why pretend otherwise?"

"Unless the ground is solid, you can't use a ladder to scale a wall. Obstacles can't be overcome unless you're on firm ground," the elderly woman had said, her eyes bright and lively.

"There's no firm ground in life, grandmother. None."

"Then create some for yourself," she'd replied patiently.

"How?"

"You'll find a way."

"You and grandfather have been together for a long time."

"Almost 50 years."

"How does one find love, grandmother?"

"Sometimes you just have to stop looking for it."

"But there's nothing worth having, not really, is there?"

"If you know that already, then you've discovered one of life's greatest secrets."

"What?"

"It's only when you possess nothing that you can gain everything."

"That makes no sense, grandmother."

"Maybe not now, but it will."

"How's that relate to girls?"

"Oh, so now I have your attention, have I?"

"So, does it relate to women?" Marcheto had asked smiling broadly.

"Yes."

"How?"

"You can possess a woman's body but still not possess her spirit."

"It's not her spirit I'm after," Marcheto had laughed.

"It will be when the right woman comes along."

"Really? Then how can I possess her spirit?"

"By never trying to possess either her body or her spirit. It's only by your not being possessive that she can freely choose to give you everything."

"I'm lost, grandmother. I don't understand."

"It'll make sense one day."

Staring out a castle window in Lord Daegal's anteroom, Marcheto doubted that anything would ever make sense. Once again, the young man thought about his disastrous encounter with the silken tigress and thought, Maybe the problem is that I finally met a woman who cares even less about love than I do. But do I care about love? Is that what I want? Is that what's missing?

"Marcheto, Lord Daegal will see you now," a castle guard growled.

Whirling around from the window, the young warrior almost stumbled but tried to snap out of his musing saying to himself, Focus! Focus!

What had his father told him when he'd daydream his days away as a child? Oh, yes, Marcheto recalled, his dad would say, "You have to be more effective dealing with reality."

Well, he had. He'd conquered what seemed like half the girls in the castle, if that meant anything, but now he wasn't so sure. He was also good with a sword, and he'd discovered that he was rarely afraid of anything.

But as he watched the hulking guard approaching him, Marcheto lamented the effects that getting older were having on him and wondered if there was anything special about him now.

"Follow me, Marcheto," the guard growled.

Marcheto thought, I need to put my personal problems out of my mind. I have to focus on doors that are opening for me and not on ones that are closing. Dad did say that Lord Daegal has something for me that sounded fun.

And it involved sex that was safe for his wounded ego, which was no sex at all. Which was fine with him. After he was finished with whatever Lord Daegal wanted him to do, maybe he could join a monastery. His life seemed over anyway, or so he thought.

Marcheto and the guard approached a set of massive doors that other guards pulled open to let them pass. They then followed a series of winding passageways leading to a vast great room. There, sitting with his back to them as they entered, was the great Lord Daegal.

Marcheto dropped to one knee in the presence of the warlord and remained silent as the guard left. The young man waited for some sign of recognition or welcome from the master of the castle. He waited for over an hour. His knee got sore, but he dared not shift to his other one. He remained quiet and, gradually, he was silent but also in pain. Maybe the softness of the silken tigress was preferable to . . .

"Marcheto!" Lord Daegal said greeting him as if the young warrior had just arrived.

"Lord Daegal," Marcheto said putting his forehead to the stone floor and holding it there.

The warlord turned back to the table glancing at something he'd overlooked on one of the documents. He picked up the paper, sat back in his chair and proceeded to read several other stacks of papers lost in thought.

The cold from the stone floor started seeping into Marcheto's skull. His teeth began chattering, and he tried to force them to stop afraid that the sound might annoy his master. It wasn't beyond Lord Daegal to have Marcheto's teeth pulled out or his head chopped off if anything about the young man offended the powerful warlord or even served as a distraction.

Marcheto told himself, It's a privilege to kneel here in my master's presence. An honor.

It wasn't unknown for Lord Daegal to kill a person's entire family for the slightest offence. But the problem was that one never quite knew what might offend the warlord.

After having his head against the stone floor for what seemed like hours, Marcheto realized his brain was fogging over from the cold. However, if Lord Daegal wanted a quick answer to something and found Marcheto to be slow witted, then the embarrassment he'd experienced at the hands of the silken tigress would be nothing compared to the warlord's wrath. Marcheto began to shiver, now more from fear than from the cold.

Lord Daegal tossed a paper aside, got up and strode to the window at the far side of the room. "Marcheto come look at this!"

Struggling to get up, he found that both his knees refused to move. They were so stiff they were locked into place like solid bone or rock. Trying to keep from panicking, Marcheto improvised and began rolling over to Lord Daegal. After reaching the window, the young man grasped the ledge and pulled himself up so he could look out and follow his master's gaze.

Only half aware of Marcheto's presence, Lord Daegal said more to himself than to the young warrior, "Look at the vast landscape going on for miles and miles. It looks solid. It looks real. But it isn't, it's just a façade, a temporary façade.

"People plant their crops and harvest them in orderly succession. The rains must come or the crops will fail. Hunger is almost as real as cold and fatigue. They can make things seem real, and they are, but only for a while. Time passes, people get old and they tend to think about what is coming next. Well, what is coming next is eternal boredom. I think I could stand only so much of an afterlife filled with peace and happiness.

"Pain and suffering are realities. They are real in this world and the next. Some people feel pain and some people cause pain. If someone has to be in torment, I would rather it was someone other than me," Lord Daegal said.

"You always have to keep the upper hand, Marcheto. Always! To slip for even a moment is like stepping into quicksand for many people are waiting in the wings for their chance at power, and they will cover you in an instant with their own ambitions.

"There's no time to cultivate the finer things in life. There really are none. Everything dies in the end. Art is but beauty on a gallows.

"You are going to get a chance to help prove that, Marcheto," Lord Daegal said as he looked down at the young warrior. "And we are about to build the grandest gallows of them all, one that will span this world and the next."

After pausing for a moment, Lord Daegal put a hand on the young man's shoulder and said, "Marcheto?"

"Yes, Lord?"

"There's a certain teenage girl who interests me."

"Yes, Lord?"

"I want you to take a sword, a special sword, and kill her with it."

"A girl? You want me to kill a teenage girl?" Marcheto asked looking up at him.

"Well, she's a unique young woman, and she won't be easy to kill. But I want you to meet her, get to know her, gain her trust and lure her away from her traveling companions."

"That should be easy enough," Marcheto said smiling a little. "Who are these traveling companions?"

"A horse, a sword and an old man."

"Is that the sword I'll use to kill her?"

"No, Marcheto, it's not. But whatever you do, don't harm her until after the summer solstice. By then, if all goes well, she won't be so special anymore."

"Won't any sword do in that instance?"

"No, not quite, not even then."

"Why not?"

"Women in her family have a nasty habit of continuing to turn up. Defeat one and 100 years later you'll end up having to fight her great-granddaughter. It's tiresome, but that's the way of it."

"We'll all be dead long before that, Lord Daegal. Why worry about something that far off in the future?"

"Because I still intend on being here. Perform your task well, and you may be as well!"

"When will I get the sword I am to use?"

"It's a dark sword, a sentient being. It will find you."

"How?"

Lord Daegal stood to his full height, glowered at the young warrior at his feet and demanded, "Are you willing to kill the girl for me? Are you?"

"Yes, Lord."

"With all your heart?" Lord Daegal shouted, his anger a terrible thing to see.

"Yes, Lord Daegal, I promise!" Marcheto said backing up against a wall.

"Then the sword will find you, my boy. The sword will find you!"

Chapter 9

The riders came storming out of the east with the sun at their backs, their horses' hooves pounding the dirt filling the air with plumes of dust. Urging their mounts onward, the riders clambered up a slope and around a bend in the road, the same bend Corson was looking at while walking ahead on point. The warrior woman had been waiting and hoping for something dangerous to happen. In an instant, it materialized with a vengeance. Corson smiled.

Unsheathing the sword slung over her back and gripping the hilt with both hands, she planted her feet firmly and raised the weapon above her head. Watching the horses barreling towards her, the warrior woman tried to judge their speed and distance while staring hard at the faces of the riders bearing down upon her. Time ceased to exist. All of life stood on the edge of her sword.

With blinding speed, Corson's blade arced through the air and the lead rider fell from his saddle landing on the ground in a heap. One man tried running down the warrior woman, but at the last moment, Corson sidestepped the horse leaping at the front leg closest to her and gripping it firmly. Never having heard of anyone tackling a horse before, the rider was completely taken by surprise and thrown hard from his saddle. Two horses following close behind tripped over the fallen animal sending their riders flying as well. The horses scrambled to their feet uninjured, but the marauders remained sprawled out motionless on the hard packed earth.

Corson was back up in a flash, striking the next rider so hard that she almost cut him in half. Twirling about, she slashed at another rider cutting through the back half of his thigh severing an artery. Realizing his death was imminent and bursting with rage, the rider spun his horse around and kicked the animal's ribs with the heel of his good leg sending it into a headlong charge. But the rider never made it to Corson, at least not alive. Dying in the saddle, he fell from his horse onto the warrior woman knocking her to the ground. Lying on her back and feeling stunned, she took several deep breaths clearing her head while trying to make a quick assessment of the situation. Standing back up, she again planted her feet firmly, raised her sword and waited for the next assault to begin.

Having made it past Corson unscathed, the few remaining riders stopped, turned around and were utterly amazed at the extent of their losses. Seeing so many crumpled forms lying in the dust, they stared in shock at the carnage. Then as one man, they hurled themselves at the female warrior.

Even with fewer attacking marauders, Corson was still outnumbered which was how she most enjoyed battle. Horses charging, saddle leather creaking, angry riders shouting with swords flailing and all bent on her destruction. Corson felt flattered. Then she calmly cut them down.

Looking at the riders who'd been thrown from their saddles, the warrior woman discovered one had broken his neck when he fell, but two others were alive, though mortally wounded and moaning in pain.

After listening to the cries of her vanquished enemies, savoring the sounds of victory, Corson silenced them with a few quick swipes of her sword. Looking up, the warrior woman watched her traveling companions approaching, especially focusing on Aerylln's face, and asked herself, How will this innocent girl react to what she sees?

Aerylln drifted among the dead like a waif floating through the clouds. She saw what was around her but was still somewhat detached. The teenage girl looked at the dead riders, the blood soaked ground and lastly at Corson's face.

"Life is totally unpredictable, isn't it Corson?"

"Yes, at least it's always been that way for me."

Aerylln continued walking through the human wreckage, the hem of her dress turning crimson so covered was the area with blood. Corson watched her young friend expecting Aerylln to be sickened by what she saw.

Instead, Aerylln seemed to grow stronger, and Corson would later swear that Aerylln had matured at that very moment in time.

"I'm sorry, little one," Zorya said nuzzling the young woman's neck brushing against her golden locks.

"There's nothing to be sorry about. It's just the way things are, I suppose."

And having said that, Aerylln reached for Baelfire who was hanging from the pommel of Zorya's saddle, and the teenage girl unsheathed the sword. Zorya was surprised as the young woman's golden hair fell to the ground, and Aerylln kept cutting until it barely touched her shoulders. Pulling it back and securing her hair with a clip, more of Aerylln's face was exposed making her appear even younger and thinner than before.

Quietly coming over to them, Eldwyn bent down and picked up the locks of golden hair. No one asked him why, knowing the wizard had reasons and ways of his own.

"Who's that?" Aerylln shouted spinning around and pointing at a grove of nearby trees. When a young man's face peeked out from behind a tree limb, Aerylln bolted for it.

Swinging Baelfire and sending the sword whistling through the air, Aerylln slashed at the tree limb cutting through it with effortless ease. Amazed that the tree hadn't even slowed the arcing movement of the sword, Corson wondered, What exactly am I dealing with here?

Aerylln swung Baelfire once more but cut only air.

Never before having seen such a powerful sword, Marcheto tore down a path through the woods with his chest heaving and his eyes wide with shock and surprise. And who was the man who wielded his sword so effectively during the battle? Or was it a woman? he asked himself. It had been hard to tell.

Looking over his shoulder and seeing Aerylln still hot on his heels, Marcheto thought, What a mess! Wait till my father hears about this. That's if anyone's left alive to tell him, including me.

Marcheto focused again on the efficiency of Corson's defense and how she'd fought with an economy of movement. Every motion was lethal. There had been no wasted effort or energy. Marcheto recalled one of his teachers telling him, Simplicity, inner harmony and self-discipline can transform personal combat into a thing of beauty, and in rare instances, into a form of poetry.

Well, whoever that warrior was, he or she'd learned their lessons well, Marcheto thought, totally amazed.

At that moment, a bolt of energy from Baelfire struck Marcheto in the back knocking him off his feet and down an embankment. Being a bit of a romantic, Baelfire had given this little nudge to Marcheto as a way of helping Aerylln along on this, her first foray into the world of young men.

Tumbling through grass, brush and small trees onto the level ground below, Marcheto lay on his back feeling dazed but was still able to reflect on how the day's events had gone so very wrong.

Lord Daegal and his father had arranged this attack, or what had been planned to be a mock assault with no one dying or getting seriously injured. The riders who'd stormed down upon the travelers were to give Marcheto the opportunity to look like a hero. He'd pretend to hack at some of the riders with his sword, make a display of bravery and drive them off. But they hadn't factored in Corson.

I feel like a fool, Marcheto thought. A teenage girl with a very powerful sword is chasing me. What an embarrassment.

Breaking into his reverie, Aerylln came plunging down the embankment and would have tripped and fallen, but Baelfire intervened keeping her upright. Looking on, Marcheto felt sure the young woman had stumbled and was going to come crashing down the hillside as well, but the sword had somehow not fallen with her. Fortunately, Aerylln had been able to maintain her grip on Baelfire, who wasn't in the mood to go bouncing down a dirty hill.

Marcheto watched in horror as Aerylln reached the base of the embankment, raised the sword over her head and took another swipe at him. Regaining his senses and rolling out of the way, he barely escaped the sword as it dug deeply into the earth. Fearing for his life, Marcheto leapt to his feet and was off and running again.

Back at the scene of the battle, Corson turned to Zorya and Eldwyn and asked, "So, what do you suppose Aerylln is up to?"

“Maybe she’s found herself a boyfriend,” Zorya said smiling.

“How do you think it’s going?”

At that moment, Marcheto came running from behind some trees sprinting as hard as he could. Close on his heels was a blond girl who was gritting her teeth as she gave chase.

“I think it’s going pretty well. At least she has him on the run,” Zorya laughed.

“Good, Aerylln’s learned the first rule of dealing with men. Keep them off balance, in the wrong, and never let them feel they have you,” Corson said smiling.

“So what are we going to do with him?” Eldwyn asked.

“I guess we’ll see what the young man has to say for himself,” Corson said. “If Aerylln leaves us anything to question after she catches up with him.”

Marcheto reached the small group of travelers, but Corson, Eldwyn and Zorya showed him no sympathy.

“What are you doing with my sister?” Corson shouted tripping him with her walking stick and sending him sprawling in the dirt.

The powerful warrior woman strode over to the young man, glared down at him and growled, “Did you put a hand on my defenseless little sister?”

Catching up to Marcheto, Aerylln swung Baelfire once more and would have struck him right across the chest, except the sword decided the young warrior had been harried and harassed enough. This time, Baelfire allowed Aerylln to be drawn off balance sending her sprawling into the dirt also and ending up on top of Marcheto.

And Aerylln, who had initiated the chase, pursued Marcheto recklessly, scared Marcheto half to death and almost killed him, hauled back her palm and slapped him full across the face.

How do women get away with hitting men like that? Marcheto thought feeling the welt on his cheek rising.

Aerylln hopped up, looked down at Marcheto and hated him for no other reason than because he was a man, which had been a good enough reason for other young women for hundreds of years and suited her just fine.

Marcheto looked at Eldwyn and Zorya seeking a friendly face. Being a woman herself, Zorya showed him no sympathy and thought, Men deserve to be taken down a notch or two for any reason, at any time, and now's as good a time as any.

Desperate for some show of support, the young warrior looked hopefully at Eldwyn who shook his head and said, "Son, I'm afraid you're on your own. I'm a wizard, but no magic on earth can make a woman's wrath disappear. Maybe you should've let Aerylln kill you, then these women might have felt some regret, or if you'd been severely wounded, they might have come to your aid. But you're a healthy young man, which makes you a prime target."

"But I didn't do anything," Marcheto protested.

"Doesn't matter," Eldwyn said. "A woman can decide you're wrong and come up with a reason why later, if she feels like explaining herself, which she might not."

"So, I back down and let them run all over me?"

"No, they won't respect you if you do that."

"Should I jump up and defy them?"

"No, that wouldn't be wise under the circumstances."

"So what do I do?" Marcheto asked.

"Pretty much just lay there in the dirt, until they decide what they want to do with you."

"How long will that take?"

"Maybe a lifetime. I hope you're not in any rush."

"This is infuriating," Marcheto said.

"Now you're catching on," Eldwyn said smiling ruefully.

Lying on his back looking up at the women, it suddenly dawned on him, and he knew how to respond, the only correct response available to a man no matter when, where or why.

"I'm sorry."

Zorya and Corson looked at each other, and the warrior woman said, "Well, at least he's not as dumb as he looks."

Aerylln stood over Marcheto savoring the victory. It was her first apology from a man, and she liked it.

Marcheto got to his knees, then sat back on his heels and waited, somehow knowing that doing nothing was the best course of action.

His grandmother had once told him that sometimes doing nothing is the best activity. It had made no sense at the time, but now he realized that in this highly charged, estrogen-filled environment around him, quiet was the correct response.

Things were emotionally crowded enough already. There wasn't any room for him. No space was available for his thoughts, opinions, feelings or even his inner spirit. The only acceptable response was nothingness. Marcheto felt a sense of peace and tranquility descending upon him. He was no longer aware of those around him. He was alone. Even he was not there. Only nothingness. He'd never experienced anything like it before.

Realizing what was happening, Eldwyn was impressed and said, "It appears the young man knows how to meditate."

"Do you really think so?" Zorya asked as the women began looking at Marcheto with renewed interest.

"Yes, he may have a gift for it. And I believe it's a new awareness for him. An epiphany of sorts. It seems the young man has stumbled upon himself."

The women forgot their anger, and curiosity replaced it. Watching him carefully, they wondered how Marcheto would handle this new experience.

"How long will he just sit there?" Aerylln asked.

"It's hard to say. He seems to be flowing with the Xao," Eldwyn said.

"The what?" Corson asked.

"The Xao, a universal life force that flows through all things."

"It's an ancient religion," Zorya added.

The small group focused again on the silent young man at their feet.

Marcheto had inadvertently discovered one of the two main rules men should follow when dealing with women. Don't bore them. And, secondly, don't make them mad.

The women accepted his meditative state and moved away to give him room. It was unnecessary. Marcheto had entered a vast inner world greater than any personal space they could have afforded him. For the first time in his life, Marcheto felt at home and at peace.

"How does something like that happen?" Corson asked. "How can he just sit there? It seems like his spirit has left his body."

For Corson to notice it, Marcheto's gift must have been substantial. Ordinarily, the warrior woman focused exclusively on the physical world, and her attention span for spiritual matters was short.

"Let's get moving," Corson said as her interest waned.

When Aerylln, Zorya, Baelfire, Eldwyn and Corson began moving further down the path, Marcheto didn't move. He had no need to move. He had found all he needed.

Corson tossed a stone at Marcheto hitting him gently on the back and causing him to come out of his reverie.

"Let's go!" the warrior woman commanded.

Marcheto got to his feet but was a little disoriented, and his legs felt heavy and lifting them took effort.

Aerylln stood next to him leaning her body up against his for support and putting an arm around him. Marcheto looked at the teenage girl but didn't quite see her.

By accident, the young man discovered one way of getting close to a woman. That is, having his own identity and letting the woman choose to approach him, if and when she got around to it. And always to be grateful that she did. Always.

Without realizing it, at least for now, Marcheto needed Aerylln. And from that moment on, he always would. For though inwardly full and spiritually whole, he would never completely pay attention to his physical environment again. Aerylln sensed that Marcheto was feeling distracted, that the young warrior hadn't totally left his meditative state behind, and that he would need someone to keep an eye on him. Not too much, nothing suffocating or dependent, but he needed her.

In her young heart, Aerylln realized this would give her some control over the young man. It made her feel powerful, and she liked that. Aerylln had fallen in love. Marcheto hadn't noticed, but it wasn't necessary. He would do what she told him, Aerylln decided. All he needed to do was listen to her.

She thought, Life would be so much easier for a man, if he just followed one rule, always do what a woman tells you to do.

"Hey, everyone, let's focus," Corson said bringing them all down to earth. "We need to find Balder and his men. Let's move."

As they headed on, Eldwyn turned to Zorya and said, "Should we ask the young man who he is, and what he was doing here?"

"No, I don't think so. Whoever he was before this moment is already in the past for him," Zorya said. "He'll never be who he was before. All that is changed forever now."

"That's true," the wizard agreed.

"All my life, I've been aware of the Xao, and I doubt this young man has even heard of it. Why should he be given the gift of such total awareness and not me? Why did it just come to him?" Zorya asked feeling a little confused.

"Who can say? Maybe some people are chosen," Eldwyn said.

"Why?" Zorya persisted.

"He probably had nothing meaningful in his life, so the Xao only had to wait for an opening to flow into him," Eldwyn speculated.

"Why now?"

"He was alone, out of his element, a bit scared and the last of what little identity he did have went away. The Xao just flowed in," the wizard said brainstorming out loud.

"I've wanted the Xao to flow into me like that all of my life," Zorya said.

"Your wanting it was a conscious act that might have blocked it."

"And the young man was clueless?" Zorya asked.

"He probably didn't even know any better. He was just an empty vessel ready to be filled."

"That's all it took? His being ready?"

"Pretty much."

"It's not fair," Zorya said.

"Your being a horse is what's not fair. How did that happen?"

"You don't want to know."

"Yes I do."

"I don't know how to get back to being myself," Zorya said in frustration. And for the first time Eldwyn heard a bit of fear in his old friend's voice. "I don't know how to get home, so to speak."

"Be like this young man, possibly."

"Just let it happen?"

"Let's watch him and see how he does it," the wizard advised.

Chapter 10

Only a short distance away, and on the same path, Balder could have used Corson's help. Fighting for his life, the warrior woman's friend and his band of men were engaged in a ferocious battle.

Ducking as a sword swept over his head, Balder pulled a knife from its sheath and stuck it in his opponent's right thigh. Howling in pain, the opposing warrior yanked out the knife with one hand while, to Balder's amazement, continuing to press the attack with another vicious swing of his sword. A second warrior joined the other and both faced Balder, smiling grimly and exuding confidence. The warriors who'd attacked them along the path weren't amateurs but seasoned professionals.

Someone's been watching us and keeping close tabs on our movements. And this ambush was so well-planned, who else but Chen could have orchestrated it? Balder wondered. But where is she? I don't see her anywhere.

As the two opposing warriors prepared to rush Balder, the men hesitated as one pointed towards a woman sprinting down a path and into the small clearing. They smiled and waited for her to reach them as one said to the other, "This should be fun."

From the rise of a nearby hill, Corson had seen Balder's warriors being ambushed and had come running. Balder was her man, and she would help defend him. In a few moments, no one was laughing.

Unsheathing her sword, Corson threw herself at the two warriors threatening Balder without a moment's hesitation. Her opponents had expected a faceoff and counted on the four of them exchanging words and taunting each other prior to combat. Unfortunately for them, Corson never engaged in pleasantries.

Leaping at her two opponents, she thrust her sword into the heart of one and brought her weapon down hard between the neck and shoulder of the other. Both men were dead before they hit the ground. After turning and giving Balder a quick kiss, she rushed forward taking another man down before her boyfriend gathered his wits about him. Corson's prowess in battle always left him speechless, but following her lead, he threw himself into the fray.

Seeing so many of the ambushers dropping to the ground, his men looked on in relief as Corson evened the odds. Feeling much more confidant now, Balder's men seemed to grow in both size and stature. The warrior woman had that effect on men fighting alongside her. But the opposing warriors weren't so happy about Corson's arrival. Two or three of them turned tail and ran. And as more attackers fell to the ground in a heap, others ran for their lives as well. Soon the battle turned into a rout with the enemy scattering in all directions.

"Don't follow them, stay together," Corson shouted as some of Balder's men began to give chase. At the sound of her voice, her boyfriend's men instantly obeyed having fought beside Corson before and knowing her to be an excellent leader. The few who didn't fully respect her judgment obeyed nevertheless, not out of trust but out of fear. However, all obeyed her command.

With the situation under control, both Corson and Balder sheathed their swords and embraced. Balder was special, she believed, in that he had courage, great skill with a sword, wasn't afraid to take initiative and was a born leader. And Balder wasn't insecure, which was good because Corson outclassed him in all the aforementioned areas. Snuggling up against him, she took his earlobe in her teeth and bit down hard tasting blood.

Balder remained still and didn't cry out. Corson had done this before, and he knew it was her idea of displaying affection. Forcing himself not to pull away, he accepted the pain. Balder was eager to show Corson he cared because he did. Very much so.

The warrior woman gave him a long, rough kiss, then swept the battlefield with her eyes and asked, "What started all this?"

"For several weeks, we've been observing Chen's actions. It appears she's killing randomly and for no apparent reason."

"Chen did that a few years ago, but she eventually settled back down," Corson reminded him.

"Being Lord Daegal's niece, Chen feels like she's allowed to do anything, anything at all," Balder said in disgust.

"Chen's full of anger, and I can identify with that," Corson said.

"Yes, but you don't go around killing innocent people for pleasure."

"Well, it doesn't take much to get me upset."

"Chen's a breed apart though," Balder insisted.

"Do you think she was behind this fight here?"

"More than likely, but I'm not sure."

Off in the distance, on a cliff high above them, there was a brief flash as sunlight reflected off armor, a sword, a bottle or something. Looking up, they saw a dark figure dressed in black leather leaping onto her warhorse wrapping her long legs around the animal's sides. The woman had short, dark-brown hair and wore a black cloak that was billowing all around her.

Corson's sharp eyes noticed two female warriors serving as bodyguards for the cloaked figure. One sheathed her sword, which apparently had been the source of the reflection.

"They wanted us to see them," Balder said.

"I suppose so."

"It's Chen," Balder observed.

"Black cloak and women as personal guards. Yea, that was Chen."

"So, what happens now?"

"Anything and everything's possible, if she's willing to be seen openly at this point," Corson said.

"It seems like Lord Daegal allows Chen to kill at will and without provocation. But why would he go along with that?"

"There's more going on here than meets the eye."

"What do you mean?" Balder asked.

"Wait till you see what's tagging along behind me."

At that moment, a little band of travelers arrived including a horse, an old wizard, a young warrior and a teenage girl carrying a sword.

"And these are your companions?"

"Yes."

"And you think they're part of what's going on here?" Balder asked.

"In the grand scheme of things, though I'm not sure exactly how or why."

"What makes you think so?"

"Well, the horse talks and hints that she once was a woman. The old man is Eldwyn the wizard and the boy and girl, well that's when things get really interesting."

"How so?"

"Ask her to take her sword out of its scabbard."

"Okay," Balder said as he headed over to the little group.

"No Balder, I don't really want you to fool with the sword."

"Why not?"

"It's a long story."

"You're smiling!" Balder said in amazement.

Just then, Corson let out a laugh that shook her entire body. She laughed so hard that she leaned forward putting her hands on her knees to support herself.

"What's so funny?" Balder asked in alarm being aware of Corson's perverse sense of humor. "And what's so important about a teenage girl and a sword?"

"Only everything," Corson said, as she held onto her ribs laughing so hard her chest hurt.

"What are we getting into here, Corson?"

"I'd say it's the end of the world as we know it, and maybe the beginning of how we want it to be."

"Say what?"

"That little group gives me hope," Corson said.

"They give you hope? Who in god's name are these people, miracle workers?" Balder asked taking a greater interest in the newcomers.

"Yea, I think so," Corson said laughing.

"Well, with Chen on the loose, we'll need a miracle."

Balder looked up at the cliff where Chen and her personal guards had been standing. He felt a sense of dread. A teenage girl with a sword might be helpful somehow, but what he did know was that a woman with a taste for blood had crawled back out of a nightmarish pit and was on the loose. Heaving a sigh, he watched as off in the distance Chen and her warrior women were galloping along a hilltop while silhouetted against the sky.

"Don't worry, this will be fun," Corson said putting a reassuring hand on his shoulder.

"You're enjoying all this, aren't you? Now, I'm worried for sure."

"It's okay, really, it's good that things are finally coming to a head," Corson said.

"Good? How?"

"Maybe it's time to shake things up."

"I don't know, you'd be playing right into Chen's hands. She thrives on chaos."

"Chen's just the tip of the iceberg. I think Lord Daegal's manipulating her."

"If you're right, we could be walking right into hell."

"Who cares? What's it really matter?"

"Well, there you are, my eternal optimist."

"Chen's hell on a horse," Corson said as she watched the black-cloaked woman riding away. "But if she'd known you were here, Balder, she'd still have run you off, but that's it. Chen wouldn't have ordered an attack."

"Why not?"

Corson remained silent for a few moments, but then she avoided the question saying, "To trigger such retaliation from Chen, you must have been doing some pretty bold reconnaissance. How close did you get to Lord Daegal's castle?"

"Pretty close."

"Well, maybe that's what set her off."

"Are you making excuses for that madwoman?"

"Of course not, I know she's half insane."

"Half insane? Chen's totally insane, but I'll give her one thing, she is beautiful."

"Oh, I'll give her more than that," Corson said. "She's sensuous, elegant, deadly, unpredictable and totally without any sense of boundaries."

"What will you do if you meet her?"

"I suppose I'll fight her if she gets in my way."

"That's my girl," Balder smiled.

As Corson and Balder considered their futures, Chen and her warriors galloped across the countryside. Feeling apprehensive, Chen recalled the warrior woman who'd arrived unexpectedly and thought, Besides me, there's only one woman I know who can fight like that, and I sure hope the wildcat who showed up today wasn't Corson.

Gradually, however, feelings of exhilaration began forcing aside her worries. For some strange reason, seeing people killed or wounded excited Chen. Having been repeatedly abused during her teenage years and now in her early 20s, the woman suffered from horrible, recurring nightmares. But after seeing others suffer, she felt better and the nightmares retreated. Yet they always came back, sometimes reaching out beyond the night and invading her days.

Again wondering if Corson was the mystery woman, Chen thought, If that was Corson, then Balder must have been there. And I hope he wasn't injured, the last thing I need is my best friend angry with me.

The two friends hadn't seen each other in years, not since the night Corson had threatened Chen's abuser at sword point. Things were a little better after that, but Corson had been banned from the castle.

But again, Chen's worries were shoved aside as her inner demons surfaced and took control of her. Thinking about the men who'd just died, her sense of exhilaration returned. The inner darkness receded, her horrendous nightmares evaporated and she was able to breathe.

"Oh, it feels so good!" she shouted feeling cleansed. "It feels so very good!"

Chapter 11

Striding down the castle corridor, Chen's hips swayed as her long legs propelled her forward with crisp, sensuous authority. Armed guards were posted at every hallway intersection as well as every doorway and stairwell, and the warrior woman took pleasure in watching the guards' eyes following her. Not that she had any interest in them, Chen just liked seeing the power she had over men. They looked at her with a mixture of desire, wonder and awe.

Inspired by their stares, her whole body began to sway like a reed bending and yielding in a soft breeze. Her slender, well-muscled arms moved in languid harmony with her willowy figure and strong, supple legs. Adding to Chen's aura was her short, dark-brown hair and tight black-leather outfit. She was a vision of beauty and danger, an intoxicating mix of sensuousness and forbidden fruit.

There were men who, upon doing more than just admiring Chen, found themselves with a slashed hand and missing fingers. Her sword was as quick and deadly as her body was soft and inviting. In short, Chen was more trouble than she was worth, except to Lord Daegal who seemed to revel in her fits of anger. And there were those who suspected the warlord was guilty of encouraging them.

Chen was a dangerous creature with a short fuse that was always set to ignite at the least provocation. She relished any opportunity to vent her spleen on an unsuspecting victim, though how anyone living in the castle for even a few days could be unaware of her hellish temperament would be a mystery.

But today, if she recalled correctly, was the meeting of her uncle and some of his allies from the further reaches of his domain. The word "allies" might be a bit misleading. There was a tense alliance at best with these provinces and The Rock, which was a name often applied not just to Lord Daegal's castle but to his lands as a whole. With a face like flint and a heart to match, Lord Daegal reminded his subjects of a massive boulder whose weight could not be resisted and whose path could not be blocked. No matter what, it just kept coming.

However, in the very furthest reaches of his domain, some still harbored the illusion of autonomy. Being blinded by the distance between their strongholds and the warlord's castle, some felt safe enough to dream of independence, or at least more self-rule, which happened to be the subject of today's meeting.

Chen strode past the warriors guarding the entrance to her uncle's private quarters and entered a great room so long and wide that an accomplished soldier would find it difficult, if not impossible, to throw a spear from one wall to the next.

Thirty nobles were seated around a massive table forty feet in length. Each sat in a high-backed chair that was four inches thick and rose above the occupant's head and shoulders helping to protect him from an attack from behind. Not an unlikely possibility, given the tense atmosphere.

As Chen approached, she noticed an enormous man wrapped in a lion-skin robe, the animal's claws hanging from a gold chain around his neck. The necklace bore witness to the nobleman besting the lion with only a knife for a weapon, something Chen found commendable, but his fierce demeanor bore witness to a defiant attitude, and this Chen found unacceptable. The warrior woman had little use for her uncle personally, but any attack on Lord Daegal's authority was an attack upon herself and her own freedom of movement within the realm.

Sitting on each side of the lion killer were two hulking younger men who were obviously his sons given their bulk and personal appearance. One son wore his own claw necklace and seemed to be the older of the two. All three had beards that gave their lean faces a wolf-like appearance. They were wolves, Chen decided, and they would have to be treated as such.

She noticed that as she approached her uncle, the "wolves" seemed unaware of her presence, although she had captured the attention of everyone else. Chen took personal offense to this.

The warrior woman was so displeased, she leaned up against Lord Daegal partly draping her thin, sensuous body over him and putting a slender arm luxuriously around his thick neck. Lord Daegal was a bull of a man with arms as thick as fence posts, thighs as thick as tree trunks and a back as strong as an oak. Chen allowed her own beauty to compliment and enhance her uncle's regal appearance. They were a pair.

"Lord Daegal," Lion Robe began, "it's nice to see this display of family affection, but what I'd like to see even more is you recognizing a local ruler's right to control his own troops. You draft our finest young men into your own personal army leaving us with insufficient warriors to deal with our neighbors who seek to encroach on our land from areas outside of the boundaries of your domain."

"My domain has no boundaries," Lord Daegal said.

"A domain's boundaries begin where its armies lack sufficient strength, your lordship. You must allow us enough men to defend our own interests."

"There are no other interests, only your lord's interests."

"Then, my lord, make our need for local sovereignty one of your interests!" Lion Robe shouted.

"Local rule is not as important as the overriding concerns of the larger picture!" Lord Daegal shouted back.

"Our crops being stolen, our women being raped and our children being kidnapped by raiders from neighboring lands, are these not part of the bigger picture?" Lion Robe asked.

"Poachers will always be a local problem," Lord Daegal explained. "Still, we can't lose sight of the goals I've determined are in the overall best interest of everyone."

"And those goals are?"

With venom dripping from her voice, Chen said, "Those goals are whatever we feel like having them be."

Lord Daegal's warriors posted around the walls of the great room became fully alert when they heard Chen's voice, which seemed almost like a whisper. If the nobles had no idea what was coming next, the warlord's guards did. They'd seen storm clouds forming over Lord Daegal's niece since she entered the room.

Chen looked at her uncle who gave her a knowing, conspiratorial smile. The warlord took this wild, reckless, angry warrior woman off her leash. Whatever happened next would happen. Lord Daegal relaxed in his chair leaning back against the thick wooden boards. Slouching to the left, he slung an arm over the chair's armrest, putting his right leg over the other armrest and settled back to watch the show. Now his warriors were in a state of total readiness, their hands itching to reach for their swords, but they also knew the opening act of the show belonged to Chen. They'd have to wait for their master's nod before stepping forward to defend his honor.

Chen leapt up onto the huge table like a silken cat prowling for vermin. She was graceful, elegant and not hard to look at, and all of this lulled the nobles into dropping their guards. They took their lead from Lord Daegal who obviously was expecting some form of entertainment. For all they knew, a beautiful dancing girl was strutting down the runway in front of them. Looking up at her, the nobles had quite a view. They could see the young woman's thighs, bottom and the luxurious curve of her back. But none of them watched her eyes.

However, it was the exact opposite for Lord Daegal's warriors, none of whom looked at the warrior woman's body. All were riveted to her eyes, her sword and the knife sheath strapped to her right calf muscle. Chen moved down the table slowly and hypnotically stopping in front of Lion Robe. She lifted her sword's scabbard tilting it behind her, sat down on the table, spread her legs wide dangling them over the edge and almost straddled the man. She leaned back suggestively and let out a sigh.

Unconsciously, the men closest to her on both sides of the table rose part way out of their seats. The lion stood and began climbing onto the table. Stepping on the seat of his chair with his left foot and putting his right knee on the table, Lion Robe placed a hand on one of Chen's thighs and gave it a squeeze. The warrior woman felt soft and warm to the touch.

Wanting both hands on her, he climbed completely onto the table shoving her onto her back. Straddling her, the lion wrapped his right arm under her upper back gripping her right shoulder and placed his other hand on her chest. Chen smiled seductively making him feel younger than he had in a long time. His worries momentarily drifted away, and Lion Robe even thought of a solution to the problems between his province and The Rock. He would ask Lord Daegal to give this woman to him in marriage. The nobleman's wife had died in a raid a year ago and he thought, What better way to cement my relationship with Lord Daegal and further my interests than for this woman to bear me sons? Maybe someday one of our children will ascend the throne.

Snuggling close, Chen kissed the left side of Lion Robe's neck. He smiled feeling reassured that he'd guessed correctly, this young woman had chosen him for her mate. Grimacing as Chen gave him a hard love bite on his neck, the lion began smiling again as she kissed the spot tenderly before biting him even harder. The lion laughed and thought, This one likes it rough.

His excitement over future prospects made Lion Robe feel dizzy. Sweat formed on the left side of the nobleman's neck, and he began feeling lightheaded. Am I getting sick? he asked himself feeling strange. Maybe I'm too old for this young girl. But if that's the case, it doesn't matter. My sons can help me with her.

Glancing at his eldest son, the nobleman was surprised by the alarmed look on his face. Turning to his other son, the lion was shocked upon realizing the boy was close to panicking. Feeling himself beginning to black out, Lion Robe's breathing was labored and sweat began pouring down the left side of his neck and chest soaking his shirt. Wiping his face on a sleeve, he was confused by a red stain the sweat left on his shirt.

As if happening in slow motion, Lion Robe watched as Chen pulled away from him, stood up on the table and did a back flip arcing gracefully through the air and landing solidly with both feet onto the floor.

Next, the nobleman saw his eldest son racing towards Chen with his sword drawn. Why's he fighting her? Lion Robe asked himself. She's such a lovely girl and will make a good wife. But I'm so very tired. Maybe I'd feel better if I rested a little.

Looking down at the tabletop, he noticed it was covered with blood. Now that's odd, he thought glancing around to see who might be injured. Someone must need help.

Lion Robe's younger son wrapped his arms around his dying father holding him against his chest. The lion looked up and saw his son's shirt was covered with blood.

"Who hurt my son?" he gasped trying to reach for his sword, but his arm wouldn't move, nor would it ever again.

The lion didn't realize it, but Chen hadn't only bitten him. She'd nicked his carotid artery, the main source of blood to the brain, with the tip of her knife. He died thinking only of his youngest boy and worrying who had hurt him.

Lowering his father onto the tabletop, the son took his hand off Lion Robe's wound. No amount of pressure had been able to staunch the flow of blood, and his father had died in a matter of minutes. Looking over to where his older brother and Chen were dueling with swords, the warrior woman appeared relaxed and confident. In contrast, his brother was quickly becoming frustrated and furious with himself having been unable to land an effective, decisive blow.

What neither son knew was that as slender as Chen was, her muscles were stronger than the toughest rope. And her skill with a sword was uncanny.

The eldest son, the new head of the family, held his sword with both hands lunging and taking a vicious swipe at Chen who gracefully dodged it. No matter how hard the young lion tried, he couldn't pin the warrior woman down. His skill with a blade was excellent, but his speed and cunning seemed to mean nothing when confronting this adversary. Chen actually smiled at him making him feel foolish and inept. She made him feel like less of a man. And she made him terribly angry.

But most of all, she got him to make a mistake. Out of frustration, he lunged at her once more thrusting his sword directly at her chest and putting so much energy into the move that when Chen sidestepped it, he couldn't stop himself. The warrior woman could have ended it right then by striking the back of his neck but slashed the back of his knee instead, cutting down to the bone.

Hobbling about as best he could, the young lion appeared undeterred in his desire for vengeance. He kept hacking at her with his sword but was cutting only air. Chen humiliated him further by thwacking him with the side of her sword across his face, shoulder and rump. She was knocking him around at will.

Bored with this cat and mouse game, she looked over at the youngest lion and smiled an invitation. This family was not known for their intellectual prowess. Smarter men would have realized they were beaten and would have dropped their swords, declared allegiance to Lord Daegal and thrown themselves on his mercy. Smarter men would have lived to fight another day, but the lions were not smart men.

When the youngest son entered the fray, most of the nobles knew it was already a lost cause. Some called out to the young lions telling the sons they'd satisfied the obligation to avenge their father and that their family honor was intact. No one wanted to witness the coming bloodbath.

However, still not grasping the severity of the situation, the youngest lion swung his sword at a woman so superior to him in battle that she easily parried the blow and with a quick flick of her blade severed the tendons in his left elbow. But she still allowed him to keep his sword arm.

The older brother tried to rush Chen, at least as best as a one-legged man could, and got a thrashing for his efforts. She hit him hard on the forehead with the flat side of her sword almost knocking him out.

The youngest lion stepped in between his older brother and the sensuous killer. It was a mistake. He was no match for this woman. The lions didn't think ahead, but Chen thought through her maneuvers much as if she were playing chess. Each action was to prepare for another action, and then another.

All the nobles waited for the warrior woman to make a kill. Looking at the youngest lion and seeing he was not standing properly, Chen knew she could throw him off balance and cut him down if she wanted to. But she did something even worse.

Turning to the nobles and shrugging her shoulders, the young warrior woman said, "This is too easy." And she walked away from the lions declaring them unworthy of being taken seriously.

Chen cut them down through indifference, mortally wounding their feelings of manhood and depriving them of their self-respect. And worst of all, she allowed them to live.

The warrior woman walked over to the dead lion's body and stripped it of the necklace of lion's claws and in doing so declared him unworthy of the honor. Maybe the lion he killed had been old, sickly or both. It hadn't been, of course, but her disrespect implied it.

Chen walked back to the two brothers who braced for a final assault. But she approached slowly and with the tip of her sword cut the necklace of lion's claws off the older brother as well. The youngest lion made a move to attack the warrior woman, but his brother restrained him.

Further inflicting psychological havoc upon the sons, Chen went over to their father's body removing a massive golden ring from the dead man's hand. It bore the family crest and was a symbol of authority in their home province.

She tossed the ring to the older brother, but it fell short of his outstretched hand and rolled along the floor bumping up against his foot. The family crest had touched the ground, as Chen had intended, and the insult was unbearable. The youngest lion bolted away from his brother dying the instant he came within range of Chen's sword.

The remaining young lion, the last in a line of provincial rulers that had spanned ten generations, put his father's golden ring on the index finger of his left hand and in doing so seemed to grow in size and stature. Looking at his father's corpse and his fallen younger brother, he turned and lifted his sword holding it in front of his face as a tribute to the other nobles.

"She will not have the pleasure of killing the last of my father's line," the young lion declared taking two steps forward and falling on his own sword.

The warrior woman smiled and looked at Lord Daegal to see his approval. It was Chen's only mistake of the evening. Cleverly having feigned his death, the young lion had turned his right side to the warrior woman sliding the sword between his left arm and chest as he fell.

Chen felt the deathblow coming towards her. The warrior woman didn't see it for she was watching her uncle, but she sensed it. What she did notice was how Lord Daegal's face remained a mask giving her no warning of the assault being made upon her. It was a stupid move on her uncle's part because it forced Chen to finally accept how little her life meant to him. And with that realization, the warrior woman turned rogue. Lord Daegal lost what little control he had over her.

As if reading her mind, Lord Daegal wore a smile of satisfaction being totally unconcerned that the last threads of his relationship with his niece were coming undone. In fact, unbeknownst to Chen, the warlord had taken her to the brink of death to insure her feelings of uncontrollable rage were permanently etched into her.

All of the intuitive awareness and emotional upheaval both niece and uncle were experiencing took place simultaneously and instantly. Still one other idea flashed though Chen's mind. There had been a glimmer of joy in Lord Daegal's eyes as the young lion's sword hurtled through the air towards her. But why? Chen asked herself. Then with a shock, the warrior woman realized that her uncle was jealous.

However, forcing herself to focus on the present danger, Chen felt the steel of the young lion's blade arcing towards her unprotected back. Quickly twisting her shoulders sideways, and in doing so throwing herself completely off balance, the sword passed by harmlessly, yet was so close she felt its "breath" upon her neck.

Stumbling and unable to regain her footing, Chen fell to the floor as the sword struck the stones next to her causing a flood of sparks. Instantly, the young lion slashed at her once more, and then again and again, as Chen rolled back and forth desperately trying to avoid death.

Suddenly, the warrior woman saw her opportunity. The young lion's good leg was within reach, and her knife came out of its sheath cutting the tendons in the back of his knee. Down the young lion went with a howl of rage, but he wasn't finished.

Putting one of his wrecked knees over her stomach pinning her onto her back, the young lion lifted his sword to deliver the deathblow. However, a knife maneuvers quicker than a sword and Chen's found its mark in the older brother's throat. Yet Lion Robe's son was so full of adrenaline, nothing short of killing him would stop his momentum. So, obliging him, she twisted the knife and ground it in deeper.

Shoving his leg off of her, Chen leapt to her feet shouting, "Okay, who's next?"

As women from all walks of life and from countless generations will tell you, men often have no common sense, for one nobleman actually raised his hand in a defiant tribute to the fallen lions. Motioning him to come forward, Chen slew him with one blow when he got within range. The noble hadn't even attempted to defend himself knowing his life was forfeit as soon as he challenged this leather-bound, predatory beast. But he'd returned the insult she'd given the two brothers. The nobleman was indifferent to what she did to him. He was uncaring and unafraid.

His action made her look less powerful. It made her appear less dangerous. It made her mad.

Swinging her sword through the air as a further challenge, she glared at the other nobles and screamed, "Anyone else?"

No one moved.

"Good, it's nice to have reached a consensus," Lord Daegal said. "Now, we're all in agreement that my interests are paramount. So, let's move on to the more festive part of the meeting."

The warlord smiled expansively, clapped his hands and servants brought out tray after over-filled tray of mutton, beef, fruits and vegetables and dozens of bottles of wine. A real feast!

Grabbing a leg of mutton, he took a huge bite out of it, red juices from the rare meat running down his chin and he shouted, "Who will join me?"

When no one sat down, Lord Daegal scooped up Lion Robe's body with his massive arms and carefully placed the dead man on a chair. "There, now we can all be friends again," he said ignoring the blood on the table that was enough to take away anyone's appetite.

"Who will join me in the celebration of our united goals?" he shouted once more. When there were still no takers, he sighed and went over to the dead brothers picking them up one at a time and propping them in chairs next to the dead lion. "Okay, all is forgiven, and their spirits can join in the festivities. Come, let's all feast together."

Lord Daegal watched as the nobles approached the table out of respect for the dead lions, but none sat down to join in the feast.

"Let's have a more festive mood," the master of the castle said pouring a jug of wine over several trays of meat and setting them on fire. "Who will join me now?"

Still, there were no takers.

"Maybe I'll give the food to my horses, it seems they're more deserving," Lord Daegal said in disgust turning away from the nobles who began drifting from the great room. Looking at Chen, he gave her a rueful smile and said, "I do believe you've ruined my dinner party."

Moving closer, he patted her hip and said, "It's been so long."

Brushing off his hand and stepping away, Chen said, "Well, it's going to be a while longer. I do want something from you, but that's not it."

"What?" Lord Daegal asked eyeing her appreciatively.

"I want the giant that you have caged in your dungeon."

"I don't know about that. He's sort of a political prisoner. A person of some merit."

"That's nice. I want him sent to the tower in my section of the castle. You can post guards at the bottom of the stairs if you want to, just as long as they don't interfere with the coming and going of my own staff."

"I suppose that can be arranged, but you really don't seem to have any idea of his importance."

"Oh, I know he has a daughter named Aerylln, and he gave her his sword."

Lord Daegal looked at her carefully and said, "If that girl learns about her sword's full power, your own future will be affected. She won't be as easy to get rid of as the men you just killed."

"Maybe I get tired of everything being easy."

"If Aerylln learns about her sword's powers, you'll wish you had more than a conventional steel sword on your hip."

"I'll deal with that when the time comes."

"You might want to deal with it now, while you still can," Lord Daegal advised her.

"What can I do?"

"Your aunt is growing old, and some say she's near death."

"Aunt Glenitant?"

"Yes."

"It's been years since I last saw her."

"Why don't you take a few days and ride over to her castle? You may be interested in knowing that your aunt has a rather unique sword of her own."

"Unique in what way?"

"If Glenitant feels you're worthy, I'm sure she'll tell you all about it."

"Why would she give this sword to me?" Chen asked.

"You have the anger to wield it properly. I've seen to that."

"What does anger have to do with it?"

"Only everything."

Chen pondered the situation. A few minutes ago, her uncle had almost allowed her to be killed. The warrior woman also realized whatever power she currently held rested heavily on the continued patronage of this man who'd almost encouraged her death. At the very least, Lord Daegal had been negligent.

"My own sword," she mused. "A sword with some special power?"

Looking at her uncle again, Chen saw the jealousy on his face. It dawned on her that Lord Daegal wanted the sword for himself, but Aunt Glenitant wouldn't give it to him. And most shocking of all was the realization that Lord Daegal wasn't powerful enough to take it from her.

For the first time, Chen caught a glimpse of her own freedom.

"But Aunt Glenitant's a vicious old crone. She's seething with hatred, and I've never really enjoyed seeing her."

"Glenitant thinks highly of you."

"All she thinks about is hurting people."

"Precisely, and does she remind you of anyone you know?" Lord Daegal asked wearing a mischievous smile.

"She's far worse than me," Chen said glaring at her uncle. Still, the realization that the warlord feared her aunt filled her with excitement. Then, not realizing how appropriate her choice of words was, she asked, "What's that wicked, old witch up to?"

"An old witch?" Lord Daegal asked nervously. "Why, your aunt used to be quite a beauty in her youth."

"My old, hunchbacked aunt, beautiful? What a fall from grace," Chen said smiling and shaking her head.

"She sort of aged before her time," Lord Daegal explained, but what he didn't mention was that Glenitant had begun relinquishing her beauty the day her own mother passed the dark sword on to her.

"I think I'll leave in the morning," Chen decided. "And I'll be taking the giant with me."

"I don't think so. Not outside the castle walls."

"Send along all the men you want to guard him, but he's coming with me!"

"I don't think so," Lord Daegal repeated.

Chen took a step towards her uncle.

Something in her eyes told him that it was time to end this discussion.

"We'll talk about it more tomorrow," he said.

"Have him at the front gate before sunrise," she demanded spinning on her heel and striding from the great room.

Lord Daegal tried hard to keep from laughing. Manipulating Chen was so easy.

Chapter 12

Chen's wolfhounds poured out of the castle gate bounding down the steep terrain of The Rock. Dozens of horses followed with Chen's dark-cloaked figure leading the massive display of raw power as it flowed down the mountainside in an unstoppable torrent.

The mountain was almost totally shrouded in darkness except for the faintest rays of early morning light. On a dare, Chen had once done this blindfolded, so nothing was going to deter the warrior woman's headlong charge that echoed throughout the valley as hoofs pounded against rock shattering the stillness of the night.

No one left Lord Daegal's castle with as much flair as this leather-clad warrior. With a total disregard for her own personal safety, Chen urged her horse down the bleak, imposing cliffs. Following suit, neither her 25 personal guards nor the massive black stallions they rode gave a single thought to the recklessness of their actions. The warrior women made an impressive, if foolhardy, blind assault upon the darkness. It was more like they fell off the mountainside than rode down it, so quickly did the land drop away in front of them.

As Chen neared the bottom, she glanced over her shoulder ready to lash out at any warrior women who'd dared to fall behind, but they'd all kept up. Chen's temper cooled, however, when she realized Lord Daegal's 25 warriors had lost their nerve and were picking their way slowly and carefully down the mountainside.

"Cowards!" the warrior woman shouted further unnerving Lord Daegal's men by appearing to become unhinged and going into a fit of wild laughter.

Embarrassed at having been bested by a group of women, the men wondered why Chen hadn't waited until the sun crested the surrounding mountains and lit their pathway. But it was danger Chen was after, not sunlight. Her warrior women knew this, and so they'd shot down the steep incline with total abandon.

After Chen reined in her horse, the female guards instinctively surrounded their leader as the wolfhounds howled and leapt up to their master eager to feel her reassuring touch. Chen's wolfhounds were powerful, shaggy, black-haired animals possessing the one vital characteristic Chen demanded, a vibrant intensity and an almost uncontrollable restless energy. Unlike her guards, the wolfhounds were male. They were angry, savage beasts whose ferocious nature, however, was forever bonded to their master. And they'd all tasted blood, some having even feasted on the flesh of men.

Chen and her warrior women brazenly mocked Lord Daegal's warriors laughing and shouting insults until they'd finally caught up.

"If archers had been shooting at us, you'd all be dead," Chen said glaring at them.

"But this wasn't a battle or even a training exercise," one man protested.

"Next time, maybe it will be," Chen sneered. "You always need to be prepared for the unexpected."

"What's unexpected is having the misfortune of riding with you," a man said still shaken from the experience.

"Are we feeling a bit cross this morning?" Chen asked placing her hand on the hilt of her sword.

"No, I'm sorry," he said surprised that he'd spoken his thoughts out loud.

"You're one sorry coward, that's what you are."

"Yes, I'm really sorry," he said looking at the ground avoiding her steely gaze that was more penetrating than the sun now peeking over the eastern mountain.

Chen sighed and shook her head. Looking around, the only man who appeared unshaken by the experience was the giant, Pensgraft.

He smiled at Chen, which surprised and pleased her. Chen usually drove people away, except for her warrior women, and it was a long time since she'd had a true male friend.

Lord Daegal's 25 warriors surrounded Pensgraft, but even among the men, horses and banners, the giant was clearly visible being head and shoulders above the rest.

After Chen had Pensgraft brought up to her, they rode along together, and the giant asked, "So where are we going?"

"On a family visit."

"I wasn't aware that you were so domestic," he smirked.

"Watch your mouth, we aren't that far away from the dungeon and can always go back," Chen said laughing.

"So who's the lucky relative?" Pensgraft asked happy to see Chen smile.

"My aunt."

"Does she have your cheerful personality?"

"Pretty much, she's an evil old crone."

"I can't wait to meet her," he laughed. "It must be a fun household."

"You are so bad! She's very ill and near death. I'm paying my last respects."

"And?"

"And what?"

"What's in it for you?"

"Love of family," she joked, and Pensgraft laughed so hard he almost fell off his horse. The warrior woman laughed as well, and said, "So, you can ride down a mountain in almost total darkness, but you can't handle the thought of my enjoying some domestic harmony."

"No, not really. What are you actually after?"

"Anything I can get."

"Well, that sounds more like you," he said smiling, but when he saw the grim look in Chen's eyes, he realized that this woman with a dark heart was up to no good. Again.

*

At that moment, in another mountain fortress ruled by Lord Daegal, the only person who'd ever given Chen a sense of love and belonging was in chains, alone and without hope. After nearly ten years of captivity, Chen's father was huddled in the corner of a damp jail cell dressed in rags.

As wood scraped against wood, a small window slid open at the base of his cell door. Chen's father, Ritalso, perked up and became as animated as a half-dead man could in the morning. In what for him was an enormous display of enthusiasm, he remained motionless but did mange to open one eye. This was the equivalent of Ritalso getting his daily exercise. He didn't move around much.

Some anonymous figure shoved a wooden bowl of gruel inside the cell and slammed the window shut. Ritalso eyed the bowl hungrily but didn't budge. He did, however, mumble something that sounded like, "I wish the servants would hurry and bring my breakfast over to me."

Two rats scurried into the cell, one being heavyset and the other quite thin, and they proceeded to eat from the bowl.

"You two take more than your share every day, and it's been like that for years. I just can't get reliable household help in here," Ritalso said.

"Well, this is one of the few luxuries we still have," the plump rat said. "That is, if you want to call this slop a luxury, but I guess it beats having nothing."

"It's my food," Ritalso protested. "I don't have to share it with anyone."

"Okay, come over and get it."

The old man was too weak to move. He'd been feeling miserable lately and wasn't in the mood for the rat's sarcasm but trying a nicer tone of voice, he asked, "Would you please bring me my breakfast?"

"Of course, your lordship," the thin rat snickered, and both rats put their snouts against the bowl and shoved it over to their master.

"How's that for hospitality?" the thin rat asked smiling.

There's nothing worse than rats with attitudes, Ritalso thought. However, the rats had a right to complain. Prior to Glenitant's casting a spell on them, they'd been Ritalso's personal servants living at The Rock in their master's spacious quarters.

During those years, Ritalso frequently had heated arguments with his brother, Lord Daegal, regarding Chen's upbringing. The warlord wanted Chen's hot temper to be encouraged, but Ritalso resisted the idea and was deeply suspicious of his brother's motives. However, it wasn't until their sister got involved that real problems arose.

Not realizing the extent of Glenitant's corruption by the forces of darkness, Ritalso had ridden over to his sister's castle seeking her counsel and had taken his daughter along with him. While there, Chen had been slighted by one of his sister's groundskeepers. The disrespect had been unintentional, but Glenitant watched in utter amazement as the young woman unleashed a rage upon the groundskeeper that was nothing short of spectacular.

Overjoyed, Glenitant had thought, Chen's the most inconsiderate young woman I've ever known. She's spiteful, hostile, violent, and loses her temper over the least provocation whether it's real or imagined. In short, she's absolutely magnificent!

When it came to encouraging Chen's violent rages, his sister was worse than Lord Daegal taking a perverse pleasure in her niece's descent into madness. Ritalso had tried shielding his daughter from Glenitant's wickedness, but later realized resisting his sister so openly was a mistake. All it did was land him in this dungeon, and being locked up wasn't helping himself or his daughter.

Would Chen even recognize me at this point? he asked himself. But the door to his cell opened for the first time in years interrupting his thoughts and in walked the jailer.

"Pack up your things, you're going for a ride," the man said.

Getting ready to go for a ride hadn't been easy. At first, Ritalso could barely walk but after eating properly for several days and being allowed to walk around the courtyard, he gradually improved.

Looking out over the castle's battlements, Ritalso saw an incredibly barren, mountainous terrain. Later, he had learned the castle was so remote it was nicknamed the Monastery.

I've never seen a land as desolate as this, he thought.

However, Ritalso would later reconsider this idea for he was about to encounter a place even more desolate, his sister Glenitant's heart. Filled with malignant evil, a darker, bleaker, more forbidding place did not exist and few encountering the old crone survived the experience.

Ritalso felt he knew his sister already, but he didn't. During the years he'd been ravaged by imprisonment, Glenitant's life had been even worse. Every moment of every day, Glenitant's evil sword had poisoned her. Ritalso's sister wasn't the depraved woman he'd once known, she was far worse.

Glenitant used to enjoy her wickedness, but those days were far behind her. The malignant evil coursing through the old crone was destroying her. Glenitant's body was wasting away, her mind was clouded, and her heart was darker than the deepest underground cavern.

And now Glenitant had summoned Ritalso back to her sisterly embrace. His only hope would come in the form of an old wizard, a horse, a teenage girl and her sword.

Chapter 13

After reaching Crystal Mountain's summit, the captain of Chen's personal guard was in for quite a shock. Looking at the valley floor, Gwendylln witnessed the grandeur of Glenitant's fortress for the first time. Hardly able to believe her eyes, she found herself gazing upon a castle made completely of black crystal.

Catching up to Gwendylln, Chen joined her friend in gawking at the artistic masterpiece. With the noonday sun blazing in the sky overhead, light was penetrating deeply into the fortress walls making them glow. The entire castle appeared like a luminous, sparkling black jewel that had somehow grown into a breathtaking array of massive crystalline walls and towers.

"When I was here years ago, this castle didn't even exist," Chen said in amazement. "And something else has changed."

"What?" Gwendylln asked.

"A small fortress with a tall watchtower guarded this access path protecting the western entrance to the valley. But it's gone, completely gone. Why would anyone tear down such an important defensive position?"

"At times, appearing vulnerable is a way of displaying power," Pensgraft said who'd ridden up right behind Chen. "Only when invincible can someone afford to appear weak. It's a way of flaunting their strength, almost like daring someone to attack. Your Aunt Glenitant might be more formidable than we realize."

"That or she's just a crazy old lady," Gwendylln pointed out.

"Aunt Glenitant's both, she's powerful and crazy," Chen said aware that this visit could be more dangerous than riding down a mountain cloaked in darkness.

Falling silent and sweeping the ground with their eyes, the warriors noticed a few granite blocks and the remnants of a foundation.

"What do you suppose happened to the granite walls?" Chen asked.

"They could have been used for another building project. If Glenitant's other castle still exists, maybe she used the blocks to reinforce its outer walls," Pensgraft pointed out.

Riding to the edge of a cliff nearby, Gwendylln dismounted, looked over the side and shouted, "What a waste, there must be hundreds of granite blocks at the base of this ravine."

"That's a bold display of power, it has to be," Pensgraft said after Gwendylln had ridden back to the group. "With a black crystal castle, she doesn't need granite blocks anymore."

"But who wouldn't need granite blocks?" Gwendylln asked.

"I suppose we're about to find out," Pensgraft said with a shrug.

"Why would Aunt Glenitant build a marvelous, black crystal castle on the level floor of a valley? She's giving up the high ground, and that doesn't make sense," Chen said as they began riding down the mountain path into the valley.

"That's a serious concern," Pensgraft agreed.

"You haven't seen what's really frightening," she said laughing.

"What?"

"Aunt Glenitant herself."

Laughing along with her, Pensgraft asked, "Will she put the evil eye on me?"

"She might put more on you than that."

"Stop it, you're scaring me and making me homesick for my old cell in your uncle's dungeon," Pensgraft said. "I have to say, you have some pretty strange relatives."

"Tell me about it," Chen sighed.

"Was your dad anything like your aunt and uncle?"

"No. In fact, he seemed like the only one with any common sense, which might be why he ran off."

"What makes you think he ran off?"

"I don't know, but he's not here is he? And he hasn't been around for years."

"Do you miss him?"

"More than you can imagine. He would have killed Uncle Daegal long ago."

"Why?"

"You know, I've told you," Chen said abruptly.

The warriors slowly made their descent along the narrow pathway that wound down the mountain to the valley below. As they entered the fields surrounding the castle, Pensgraft was surprised that no one came out from the fortress to challenge them. He also hadn't seen any soldiers posted on the mountain or anywhere down along the path either.

All he saw in front of him was a huge, dark, monolithic castle that looked like it was made from black marble, except that the sun penetrated its surface similar to how light can filter into the darkest water. It made the black crystal appear translucent giving it an eerie glow.

But most of all, Pensgraft noticed how quiet and still everything was. He also took note of how tightly Chen's warriors surrounded her. Something didn't feel right to them either, and the warrior women were taking no chances.

"I don't see any cause for alarm, do you? All we're doing is approaching an overgrown pile of black crystal that appears to have sprouted right out of the ground," Pensgraft said wearing a mischievous grin. Although meaning it as a joke, the giant wasn't far from the truth regarding the castle's origin.

And why are Chen's women and Lord Daegal's men heading into troubled waters when they're already filled with foreboding? Pensgraft wondered. But as for the giant himself, he wouldn't have missed this for the world. There was uncertainty, danger, intrigue, and the odds were stacked against them. In short, it was Pensgraft's idea of fun.

If curiosity could kill a cat, Pensgraft would have been dead many times over. His biggest character flaw was that he was easily bored. On the other hand, his greatest positive characteristic, the one thing that made his life an adventure, was that he was easily bored. He'd been a trial for his mother while growing up, and he wasn't any better now.

Petulance in a child can be disguised as courage in adulthood. Also, Pensgraft rarely sat still except, that is, when in Lord Daegal's dungeon. But it had taken bars to hold him, and even then he'd paced his cell like a caged animal.

As the band of warriors came closer to the crystal fortress, they noticed something unusual. Looking at Pensgraft, Chen said, "There's no moat."

"And no drawbridge," Pensgraft added.

Lord Daegal's troops and Chen's guards stopped and tried to grasp what they were now witnessing. Even the main gate was wide open with no soldiers around. This black crystal, architectural marvel appeared to be left unattended.

"Now I am worried," Chen said.

"This makes no sense. It's unexplainable, irrational and a bit frightening. And you know what?" Pensgraft asked.

"What?"

"I am going to beat you to the gate!"

Chen's eyes brightened, and the warrior woman thought, Here's someone else who's reckless. Someone who enjoys danger and even needs it.

The truth is, Chen would rather be dead than bored, many times coming close to the first while seeking to avoid the latter.

Spurring their horses into a gallop, they quickly reached the entrance leading to an inner courtyard. Dismounting and walking over to the gate, or to the space where one would normally be, Pensgraft smiled and said, "You go first, and I'll wait here."

"I don't think so."

"But Glenitant's your aunt, and I wouldn't want to intrude."

"You're such a gentleman."

"Glad you noticed."

Standing in front of the huge entrance, they both peered inside and Pensgraft said, "Well, it doesn't look too bad."

"Okay, go ahead, go inside."

Looking back at the others, especially at Lord Daegal's warriors, Pensgraft noticed they were all a bit edgy. Not frightened, mind you, but they weren't in any great rush to come any closer either. The giant thought, I'm free of Lord Daegal, if I go inside.

Squaring his shoulders, he strode boldly into the inner courtyard. And it was incredible! Black crystal was everywhere glistening like polished glass. Standing in front of the main tower and seeing his own reflection, he chuckled and said, "Now there's a handsome fellow."

Glancing at Chen, who had followed him inside, Pensgraft noticed she was looking at her reflection and assessing not just her face but also her figure.

"Your leather outfit looks nice on you," Pensgraft said truly admiring her sense of style. However, just then, a loud, clanking noise began reverberating throughout the courtyard. As the sound continued, the two warriors realized it was coming from inside the main tower, which also had no door or gate protecting it and was wide open.

"Clank, clank, clank!" came the sound. "Clank, clank, clank!"

Chen and Pensgraft looked at each other, and the giant said, "I entered the courtyard first, so maybe you'd like to be first going into the main tower."

"No, let whatever it is come to us," Chen said. And as they waited, neither moving, the noise got louder, "Clank! Clank! Clank!"

Being even more impatient than Chen, which was saying something, Pensgraft remained where he was for a while but finally disregarded the warrior woman's advice and headed over to the tower's entrance.

"Clank! Clank! Clank!" the noise continued reverberating throughout the courtyard as it got closer and louder.

As he walked past Chen, the giant looked at the warrior woman's figure appreciatively and said, "Don't you find it interesting that beauty and danger can coexist in the same moment?"

"Look inside the entrance if you want, but cut the philosophy," she said abruptly trying to hide the fact that she enjoyed his taking an interest.

Stepping through the entrance, the room was pitch dark and the noise was even louder echoing off the walls and seeming to come at him from all directions. Peering into the gloom, Pensgraft said, "I can't see a thing. Come over and sway a little in the doorway. That should get the attention of whoever's inside."

Chen strolled over to her friend smiling invitingly. Taking a deep breath, Pensgraft said, "It's probably not possible to make your leather outfit any tighter, but if you soak it in water and let it dry on you that might do it."

"Already did it," Chen said moving her hips in a languid motion.

"I'm not surprised, you don't miss a trick."

Back outside the castle walls, Gwendylln managed to stay put as long as she could see her leader, but when Chen disappeared from view while walking to the tower entrance, Gwendylln shouted, "Playtime's over!"

The captain of Chen's personal guard spurred her warhorse, and the powerful stallion responded bolting forward. All the warrior women followed in hot pursuit charging through the main entrance without hesitation. Upon reaching Chen, Gwendylln reined in her horse as she and the other warrior women formed a protective circle around their master.

Not being included in the human shield, Pensgraft was feeling a little left out but that didn't last long. A powerful blast of energy shot out of the main tower lifting him off his feet and tossing him, as if launched from a catapult, across the courtyard where he slammed against the outer wall. Black crystal is pretty, but it's also hard as rock, and Pensgraft dropped to the ground unconscious.

Realizing that Chen might be in danger, the warrior women almost went berserk. Gwendylln whirled her stallion around and faced the tower entrance ready to spur her horse once more and charge into the darkness. Had she done so, the 24 other women were ready to follow her in making a blind assault on the unseen enemy. Gwendylln didn't mind a fight, and neither did the other warrior women, especially if it was in defense of their leader.

Years ago, Lord Daegal did one thing right. He'd found 100 athletic young women Chen's age and had them live together with his niece from the age of 15. They were all from poor families, and Lord Daegal had given the parents farmland and enough funds to build barns and buy cattle. The warlord had also relocated the families, so the farms were all within a day's ride of The Rock, which allowed the young women to maintain contact with their loved ones.

It was an older warrior woman who'd actually orchestrated all this on Chen's behalf, but she'd allowed Lord Daegal to take credit for it and chose to remain anonymous. Over the years, all the young women came to despise the warlord, but they'd never forgotten that their families were safe because of Chen's devotion to them. It was she who'd made sure the farms received financial assistance through several hard years of drought, pestilence, crop failure and illness. The women were now, like Chen, in their early 20s and what they may have lacked in size, they made up for in sheer fanatical loyalty to their leader.

So when Gwendylln turned to face the unseen threat, the women under her command couldn't imagine life without Chen and were prepared to die in her defense. Only one thing could stop them from making a headlong charge into the tower, a direct order from their master. And they got one.

"Hold!" Chen shouted, and all the women froze in their tracks. Then Chen led them over to Pensgraft's crumpled body having them form a protective ring around him. Now, at her command, they were prepared to die in his defense.

"Clank! Clank! Clank!"

Chen's guards turned to face the noise wondering what monstrous danger could be approaching them. Gradually, they saw someone emerging from the inner darkness, someone very small who was bent over, hunchbacked and shuffled, barely able to walk.

It looked like an old woman, a very old woman. One so ancient, Chen's guards wondered what was keeping her alive. Feeling enormously relieved, the warrior women began to relax and made a collective sigh of relief.

Then they saw it. They saw the sword.

Aunt Glenitant, the old woman, was struggling along using a sword for a walking stick, which was the source of the noise as it struck the stone floor. The weapon was as black as midnight, as dark as the crystal castle, even as dark as Glenitant's malignant spirit, and Chen smelled danger. Feeling cornered, Chen wanted to lash out at something, anything, as anger welled up inside of her, a deep, violent rage. The warrior woman's mood turned black, which is probably what saved her.

Now cloaked in darkness like Glenitant and her sword, Chen changed tactics dismounting, walking directly up to her aunt and kneeling before her. Glenitant allowed Chen to approach because the old crone could sense the warrior woman's dark mood. Glenitant liked it. So did the sword, which, though made of metal, was a sentient, evil creature.

"Auntie, I'm Chen, your niece."

Auntie sensed that Chen was like a panther ready to strike. Though only weighing 120 pounds, Chen was impressive. Plus she had attitude, and Glenitant loved it.

"Was it you who attacked my friend, Pensgraft?" Chen asked.

"Yes, in a way, but more specifically, it was this sword. But I'm pleased that you haven't lost your edge," Glenitant said.

Auntie looked at her niece, felt Chen's inner anger, and thought, Yes, she has the necessary hatred. The sword might well go to her when I die.

"What do you think, Crystal?" she asked the sentient, evil sword.

The sword liked Chen a lot, even more than Glenitant. And from that moment on, Crystal plotted her master's death.

Glenitant sensed the sword's treachery, and although Auntie had been considering Chen as her heir apparent, the old witch wasn't quite ready to relinquish power just yet. Glenitant was suddenly swamped by jealousy over Chen's youth and vitality and by her sword's sudden switch in allegiance. From that moment on, Auntie plotted her niece's death.

It seems the touching family reunion was short lived.

Gleefully anticipating the coming fight between the two women and the resulting hatred and violence, the sword smiled. Of the three of them, the old witch, the young warrior woman and the sword, Crystal was the worst of all.

Chapter 14

While Chen was at Crystal Castle, in the eastern part of the realm, Aerylln and her small group were encamped a bit to the west of Lord Daegal's castle, The Rock. Aerylln and Marcheto were walking along a woodland path talking about recent events and getting more acquainted.

"When Corson cut down those horsemen, it was a real awakening for me. Walking through a field littered with dead bodies was certainly a new experience," Aerylln said to Marcheto. "So much violence. Do things like that happen a lot in the outside world?"

"Yes," Marcheto said.

The young man didn't know what else to say. Violence was all he had ever known. He, his older brothers and his father trained in the arts of war every day. "A warrior needs to stay sharp."

"What do you mean by sharp?" Aerylln asked. She'd never had a serious conversation before with a young man her own age, Marcheto being only two years older. She felt a closeness to Marcheto and opened her heart and mind up to him.

"During combat, all of one's senses are heightened. Ordinary, day-to-day perceptions of reality simply collapse and are no longer relevant. You can actually feel your opponent's energy," the young warrior explained. "If you lose your edge for even a moment, you'll end up on the ground like one of those lifeless bodies."

"How can you take the life of another person?" Aerylln asked. She hoped she didn't sound too naïve. It was a serious question for the teenage girl, and she hoped he had an answer.

"You kill without killing," Marcheto said simply.

"What do you mean?"

"Well, a swordsman practices for hundreds of hours. He'll go over the same maneuver a thousand times. When he encounters it in battle, he doesn't need to think about what to do. He just does it."

"He's not aware that he's killing?"

"Not really and during training a true warrior will practice doing nothing. Thus in battle, he does nothing and becomes victorious!"

"You're kidding me?" Aerylln laughed.

"No, really, I mean it," Marcheto laughed along with her.

"Try explaining yourself in a way that makes sense," the young woman said as she continued to smile.

"Do you knit? Can you make sweaters and thick socks from yarn?"

"Can you?" Aerylln challenged.

"Yes!" Marcheto said proudly.

"Doesn't your mother do all that for you?" she needled him.

"My mother's dead. My brothers and I make our own clothes."

Aerylln was appalled with herself for being so tactless. "I'm sorry to hear that about your mother. How did she die?"

"Violently. Both she and my only sister," Marcheto said, then he angrily shoved the thought aside in his mind. "But my point is, do you think about moving the needles while you are knitting?"

"No, I just do it."

"Precisely," Marcheto said. "A warrior does the same thing with a sword. At least he does it that way if he wants to stay alive."

"What if you're fighting a warrior who has practiced a move you're unfamiliar with, one that's not ingrained in you?"

"You catch on quickly, don't you?"

"Yes."

"I like that. I've never met a woman like you before. There's a lot going on inside of you isn't there? Thoughts, feelings, hopes and dreams?"

"Yes. You catch on quickly, too, don't you?"

"Yes," he laughed.

"Why are people so violent?" Aerylln asked becoming serious once more.

"Our spirits are too vast for our bodies and for the physical environment we live in. People kill to give themselves more space so they don't feel so cramped," Marcheto said, surprised that he even had a response to such a question.

"Are you saying that the more people kill, the more spiritually whole they become?" Aerylln asked.

"Yes and no," Marcheto said. "Killing can fill a person for a while, but taking life is like a drug. The more you take the more you need to get the same high."

"I'm aware that medicines are called drugs, but I'm not aware of any that cause the response you're talking about," Aerylln said.

"I'm talking about an addiction," the young man tried to explain.

"I have an addiction to daydreaming. At least that's what Mistress Xan always told me," Aerylln said.

"This is a bit worse than that."

Aerylln blushed and felt foolish. She knew she didn't have enough knowledge to really continue the conversation and wondered, "How can I learn about anything without sounding foolish at first?"

"It's better to be a fool than to be dead," Marcheto answered.

Aerylln was surprised. She didn't realize she had spoken her last thought out loud. "Then you don't mind if I keep quizzing you?"

"As long as you allow me to make a fool of myself during our next conversation without thinking less of me as a person. I'll be having plenty of seemingly dumb questions myself."

"Do you think we'll continue to talk openly to each other like this?" Aerylln asked.

"Yes, I do. I'm enjoying myself."

"So am I," the teenage girl said blushing again. She liked this young man and let her shoulder bump up against his. Aerylln recalled how she had tried to kill him when she'd first seen him. But that was all Marcheto's fault, she told herself.

"My trying to kill you was all your fault," Aerylln said out loud speaking her thoughts again, but this time conscious of doing it.

"I realize that. I'm sorry," he said with sincerity.

Aerylln liked him even more now. Two apologies from this young man in one week, it was a heady experience. She stumbled, and her breasts pressed against his arm. Marcheto froze.

"What's wrong?" she asked.

"Nothing," Marcheto said taking a step away from her.

"If nothing's wrong, then why are you so far away?"

"I'm not far away," Marcheto protested.

"You're not walking as close to me as you were."

"You'll think I'm dumb if I tell you about it."

"Oh, good!" she laughed. "It's your turn to feel stupid!"

"I had a bad experience recently," he said, and this time he blushed. Aerylln was watching his face when he turned red. She loved it!

"Tell me about it," the teenage girl said sympathetically. She sensed that things were about to get really interesting.

"I'm not as good in bed as I used to be!" he blurted out. "There, I've said it!"

Aerylln looked at him in astonishment! "You aren't good in bed?"

"No," Marcheto said as he hung his head.

"What do you do? Do you take food to your chambers and eat in bed and get the sheets all messy? Or can't you sleep very well? I'm sorry if you're having a hard time sleeping. That happens to me sometimes," Aerylln said trying to empathize with his situation.

"You're making fun of me!" Marcheto said angrily, and he walked away from her.

"No! No!" she pleaded. "I wasn't making fun of you!"

Aerylln liked this young man, and now he was upset with her. She didn't know what she'd done wrong and began to cry.

Marcheto looked back at her cautiously. He thought that surely her tears must be false. He knew enough about women to know that they used tears to manipulate men. He understood weapons of war. Tears were deadly.

The young man walked back to Aerylln and looked at her carefully. Tears were streaming down her face. "Hey, it's okay if you make fun of me. I'm not angry with you."

"I wasn't trying to make fun of you," the young woman said between sobs.

"Well, you made that joke about sex and bed sheets," Marcheto said in an accusatory tone of voice.

"I never talked about sex," Aerylln said as she continued crying.

"Yes, you did. I opened up to you, telling you how I'm not as good at sex as I used to be, and you started making fun of me!"

"What are you talking about? I told you how I sometimes don't get all the rest I need when I'm worried. What were you talking about?"

Marcheto was astounded. Lord Daegal had said something about Aerylln being a virgin, but the young man had eventually decided that the warlord didn't mean to be taken literally.

Marcheto continued to look at Aerylln with wide-eyed wonder. He'd never really known a virgin before, at least not a girl who'd stayed one for long when he was with her.

"Are you a virgin?" he blurted out.

"How dare you ask me such a question?" she shouted.

He didn't know what to say. He looked at her differently now as if she were some rarity, which, in his world, she would have been. He thought, She actually is a virgin!

Quickly, Marcheto tried to contain the damage.

"My lady, I meant no offense," he said as he bowed to her. "I'm so vulgar and crude. However, I promise never to talk about such a topic again."

Aerylln looked at him to see if this time he was mocking her. But he held his bow and it had been so sweeping and graceful. She began to feel reassured and then began to feel safe again.

"You don't have to go that far," she told him. "Just be careful to clarify what you're talking about."

"Yes, my lady," he said with all sincerity as he continued bowing to her.

Aerylln had never seen anything like this, and she loved it!

All of a sudden, her fears and worries burst forth, and she said, "I'm sorry, as well. I'm such a mess. I was asked to leave the only home I've ever known, and things have been totally chaotic ever since."

Marcheto said nothing. He just listened with an open heart.

"I'm traveling with a magic horse and sword, an old wizard and Corson. And well, Corson, she's the most confusing person I've ever met. However, I like her and trust her. But I've heard them talking about how I'm an heiress to some sort of matriarchal lineage. It's all very frightening."

Marcheto held her in his arms and listened to her sobbing against his chest. He'd never experienced anything more intimate in his entire life. Sex he knew about, but intimacy? He was as unfamiliar with that as Aerylln was about sex.

I like intimacy, he told himself.

The truth was he loved it.

"Hey, we really should be heading back to camp, but we can talk again later," Marcheto said in a soft tone.

"You still want to know me? Won't you be embarrassed to be seen with a weepy girl who's unschooled in the ways of the world?"

"Aerylln, you're the finest woman I've ever known," he said, and he meant it. Every word.

Placing a reassuring hand on each of her shoulders, Marcheto leaned down and kissed her wet cheeks. Feeling tentative and uncertain, he kissed her neck, nose, closed eyelids and brushed his lips gently against hers. Pulling back a little, he stroked her cheek and neck with the tips of his fingers, looked into her eyes and allowed the moment to linger. Marcheto had never given so much of himself to a woman with just a glance, and he felt his soul opening up to hers.

Now, it was Marcheto's turn to be nervous. His mouth was dry, his heart was beating rapidly, and, unconsciously, he was holding his breath.

"It's okay," Aerylln whispered placing one hand behind his neck and running her fingers through his hair.

Feeling Aerylln's touch against his scalp was electrifying. It was a caress from someone warm, sensitive and sincere. Marcheto almost fainted from the sheer excitement of drinking in such a meaningful experience.

Pulling back a little, he gasped and said, "My head's spinning."

"Mine, too."

"I can barely breathe."

Looking up into his eyes, Aerylln realized he was telling the truth, and then she smiled and asked, "Am I too much for you?"

"I've never had anything like this before."

"Neither have I."

Smiling, they kissed again feeling a little less tentative.

After the kiss was over, Aerylln licked her lips and dried her eyes. Putting a protective arm around the young woman's shoulder, Marcheto walked her back to camp. When they returned, several of Balder's men looked up and smirked. Nudging each other, they laughed a bit while looking at Aerylln.

One of the men began walking towards the pretty, blond girl. He smiled at the young warrior standing with her and thought, More than one man can put his arm around her.

Marcheto's hand went to the hilt of his sword, and he took a step away from Aerylln. "Stay here," he said with a sense of urgency. "Please!"

He unsheathed his sword and faced the man who was approaching. At first the older warrior thought Marcheto was joking, but then he looked at the young man's eyes. Death was waiting for him there.

The older warrior put both of his hands up in the air with his open palms facing Marcheto. "Sorry, my mistake," he said sincerely and walked back to the others.

Kirtak, who was Balder's second-in-command, took all of this in and his estimation of Marcheto went way up. He thought, That boy has steel in his spine.

"Okay, everyone, let's break camp," Kirtak said. "I was over on the other side of the stream a few minutes ago, and it looks like Balder and Corson are getting ready to move out." He took one more look at Marcheto and thought, Never underestimate the quiet ones.

Chapter 15

On the other side of the stream, Corson and Balder were sitting together leaning against the trunk of a fallen tree when a group of horsemen rode past them. Corson's hand went for the hilt of her sword, but Balder put his hand gently on hers silently asking her not to unsheathe her weapon.

"We don't even know who they are yet. They may be no danger to us," Balder whispered.

"Better safe than sorry."

"Sometimes a display of trust can deflect hostilities," Balder said.

"The only warrior I trust is a dead one," she said sternly.

"Please, let me handle this," he pleaded.

Corson glared at him.

"Sweetheart, if they kill me, you can slaughter the whole group."

Corson kissed him and smiled.

"Well, you don't have to be that happy about it," he said in an annoyed tone of voice. Looking back over at the warriors, they saw a horse-drawn wagon trailing the riders. It was hauling three coffins.

The driver of the wagon glanced over in Corson and Balder's direction letting out a cry of surprise. Some of the horsemen turned, looked over their shoulders and saw what had alarmed the driver. A beautiful woman, who was almost as big and sturdy as the man next to her, was sitting with her legs spread having one leg laying on the ground and one knee up. No one took notice of Balder's sitting position.

Seeing the hungry looks on their faces, Corson spread her legs a little wider. Most of the men had stopped, but those who hadn't found themselves riding into the horses in front of them. Not realizing what was going on, they saw their friends staring at something and understood immediately when they turned and saw Corson. At that point, everyone forgot where he was or where he'd been heading.

Corson brushed some dust off her thighs, and the men groaned, but Balder doubted that there had been any dust on her leather pants and almost laughed. As he looked at the men gaping at his partner, he thought, Is there anything that cuts as sharply as a woman's beauty? It's quicker and deadlier than any sword.

One of the older warriors was the first to snap out of it and shouted, "We have three bodies in those coffins due to this very same thing. Haven't any of you learned anything from Chen's cutting down three of our own at The Rock a few days ago?

"When you're around a woman, you'd better watch her sword arm at all times and try to determine if she has a knife on her," the older warrior said spelling it out for the younger men. "Her beauty won't kill you, unless you're mesmerized by it while she slits your throat. And we saw that happen recently, didn't we?"

At the mention of Chen's name, Balder slowly stood up raising his hands with palms wide open to show he wasn't holding a weapon and approached the older warrior. After introducing himself and learning that the older man's name was

Dartuke, Balder explained his own run-in with Chen and how he'd lost several good men.

"She's unnatural, that one is," Dartuke declared. "There's something cunningly evil about her."

"Where are you from?" Balder asked.

"About a week's ride to the west, but the way things are going back home, I don't know how much longer we can survive."

"What's wrong?"

"Neighbors further west have been raiding our settlements."

"What's the reason behind it?"

"Lord Daegal has warriors stationed at a garrison about a half-day's ride from us. They're attacking outlying areas ransacking towns and villages and taking plunder back to The Rock. When the western tribes retaliate, we don't have enough warriors to defend ourselves because Lord Daegal keeps drafting our best young men into his army."

"Why not arm your women?" Corson asked him.

"Well, there's a novel idea," Dartuke said scornfully.

"I can make it a lot less novel for you," Corson said inching her sword out of its scabbard. Immediately, two archers in Dartuke's group drew their bows leveling them at Corson who didn't so much as flinch.

Balder stepped between Corson and the archers saying, "My friend won't tolerate men making light of women."

"I meant no offence, but warrior women are extremely rare."

"If men took the time to teach women how to fight, you'd see more of them," Corson hissed.

"True, true," Dartuke said in a calming voice. "But teach them how? Developing an effective training program that helps women overcome their size disadvantage is a mystery to me."

"Not to me," Corson glowered.

"Really?" Dartuke asked perking up. "Maybe this is the solution we've been looking for. Would you consider going home with us and setting up a training program? But, honestly, do you really think women can be taught to fight?"

"Chen killed three of your men, didn't she? I'd say she could fight."

Dartuke and the male warriors around him shifted uneasily in their saddles. Chen's ability with a sword unnerved them. These men were the nobles who'd attended the council meeting in Lord Daegal's great room when Chen performed her ballet of violence.

"But Chen's an exception, don't you think?" Dartuke asked.

"Not really, doesn't she have 100 warrior women at her disposal?" Corson asked.

"How do you know that?" Dartuke demanded.

"I just know."

"How can you possibly know what's going on at The Rock? The security there is incredible. No one gets in or out unnoticed."

"Because, up until a few years ago, I was one of them," Corson said hanging her head sadly. "Things were fine at first, but the senseless violence began and just got worse."

"You knew Chen?" Balder asked staring at his friend in shock.

"Yes, I lived with her for years starting when I was 15."

Balder took a step back and looked at his friend in a new light. He opened his mouth to speak but couldn't think of anything to say. Some of the nobles around him clenched the hilts of their swords, and Dartuke asked, "Why aren't you with her now?"

"I was sort of a black sheep, I guess."

Now Balder found his voice. "You were thrown out? Amazing! Are you telling me that you couldn't even maintain a level of behavior that was acceptable to someone like Chen?"

"Chen wasn't the problem."

"Who was?"

"Lord Daegal."

"You upset the warlord, himself?" Balder asked shaking his head in disbelief.

"Yes, I suppose so."

"How?"

"I took a swipe at him with my sword."

"Lord Daegal is twice my size, and yet you drew your sword on him?" Balder asked while Dartuke and all the male warriors stared at her in surprise.

"He didn't have any clothes on at the time, let alone a sword."

"Why would you attack an unarmed man?" Balder asked. "Although I have to say Lord Daegal's a good person to take a swipe at."

"Let's just say the sword between his legs was going places it didn't belong."

"He was after you?" Balder asked incredulous that anyone would be so foolish as to show Corson unwanted affection.

Corson laughed and said, "No, I would have handled that myself in short order."

"If not you, who?"

"Chen."

Dartuke and Balder looked at each other.

"Chen's father disappeared a year before I went to live with her at the castle. Soon afterwards, Lord Daegal tried taking his place, but gave more of himself than he should, if you know what I mean. Anyway, I haven't seen Chen for a long time, and I miss her," Corson said.

"You miss a woman who's responsible for several of my men being killed?" Balder asked finding it hard to believe.

"No, I don't miss that woman. I miss the girl I once knew."

Looking at Corson with compassion, Dartuke said, "I have a sister who once betrayed me to an enemy. I don't think I've ever gotten over that."

"What none of you seem to realize is that if Chen had some other alternative to living with Lord Daegal, she'd take it. We could even use her against him. Chen needs a place where Lord Daegal isn't always trying to control and manipulate her. He's the real source of her problems. Get her away from him, and I think she could start over again," Corson said.

"Maybe you're letting fond memories of the past cloud your judgment," Dartuke said. "A few days ago, I witnessed Chen doing things that make me believe she's too far gone. That young woman couldn't possibly be of any help to us. Seriously, look at those three coffins in the wagon. Chen killed those men, and the oldest was a close friend of mine."

"If I could somehow talk to her when she's outside the castle, then I could determine how much of my master is still there, how much of the woman I knew is still intact," Corson said.

"Your master?" Balder asked.

"Way down deep, I know that I still love her. We grew up together, and I can't help how I feel about her. Other than you, Balder, she's the only person I've ever loved."

"Do you believe you can help Chen straighten out her life?" Dartuke asked.

"Look, I've seen what she does to people. She kills for pleasure. She kills people who mean her no harm, and who she doesn't even know. But that's the Chen who exists now. What I miss is the girl she used to be."

"And you think meeting her outside the castle would make a difference?" Dartuke asked.

"I don't know, maybe it's hopeless. But she's the only person from my teenage years that I once loved."

Being so distracted by her raw emotions, Corson didn't hear Aerylln walking up behind her. Listening to the warrior woman struggling with her thoughts and feelings about Chen, Aerylln felt badly for her friend. Trying to offer some encouragement, she said, "There's good in everyone, Corson."

The warrior woman jumped. Corson could handle a fight, but a kind teenage girl sneaking up on her was almost more than she could stand. After catching her breath, Corson said, "Aerylln, don't ever do that again. I could have killed you by mistake. And don't try cheering me up. Quite frankly, positive ideas make me sick right now."

Aerylln, Zorya and Tempest, Corson's warhorse, had just returned from the other side of the stream. The teenage girl had waded across it, and her dress was soaked below the knees. The animals had lingered in the bubbling water enjoying a long drink and were feeling refreshed. Even Baelfire was feeling renewed having been dangling in the cool water while hanging from the pommel of Zorya's saddle.

Eldwyn and Marcheto were following close behind, but it was Zorya and Tempest, two massive warhorses, who caught the eye of every one of the nobles. Next, what the nobles noticed was the beautiful necklace Zorya was wearing as well as the magnificent sword hanging from her saddle. Zorya was a horse fit for a king, and Dartuke looked at Balder with new respect assuming the fabulous horse belonged to the male warrior.

"Where did you find such a magnificent animal?" Dartuke asked envying him.

"Zorya's my horse," Aerylln said as she went up to the warhorse and stroked its mane.

Striding over to Aerylln, Corson picked up her young friend and placed her on Zorya's back. The nobles were speechless.

"Aerylln, slide Baelfire out of her scabbard," Corson said.

"No, careful, just ease the blade out a tiny bit," Zorya whispered.

Reaching for her sword, which was hanging from the pommel of Zorya's saddle, Aerylln slid Baelfire from the scabbard, but only slightly, until she saw a hint of the metal blade.

An enormous shockwave surging out of the magic sword nearly knocked the 30 nobles off their saddles, and their warhorses staggered backwards stumbling and almost falling. These warriors were excellent horsemen, but their animals were rearing up in terror, and it was all the men could do to keep control of their mounts. After the chaos passed and things settled down, the stunned nobles looked warily at the teenage girl on the white warhorse.

"Do you still think women can't be warriors?" Corson asked. "If necessary, this girl could whip all of you."

"But don't be alarmed," Zorya said. "We come in peace."

Balder whirled around staring hard at the talking horse, as the nobles' faces wore various expressions running the full spectrum of fear, apprehension, curiosity, amazement and delight. All being leaders in their home districts, the men understood power, or the lack of it, and they knew something remarkable and unbelievable had just happened.

Being women, Zorya and Baelfire weren't against having their beauty appreciated, so the jewels in the warhorse's necklace and the ones in the sword's hilt began glowing brightly. Each of the jewels acted like a prism sending rainbows of light in all directions, and the colors were deep, rich and vibrant.

Thordig, one of the older nobles, nudged his horse riding up beside Aerylln and said, "Years ago, in my youth, I saw a man riding a white warhorse like this one, and he was wearing a sword much like yours. He was a giant, fearsome warrior."

"That's Aerylln's father. I was with him for years," Baelfire said speaking up.

"Well, I recently saw the very same man. I hadn't seen him since that first time, but he was leaving The Rock a few days ago surrounded by dozens of Lord Daegal's men," Thordig said taking a talking sword in stride. "It was just before sunrise in the castle courtyard near the front gate. There were torches along the castle walls, and I could see his face as plain as day."

Zorya and Baelfire looked at each other.

"Not long ago, we were in a skirmish with some of Lord Daegal's warriors," Baelfire said. "Suddenly a door materialized next to us, and Pensgraft tossed me through it. When I discovered I was in Mistress Xan's castle with Aerylln, I knew the time had come for the girl to assume her rightful place as a woman in her family's line of succession."

"After Pensgraft threw Baelfire through the door, he was struck down. Aerylln's father was knocked off my back and in all the confusion, I got separated from him," Zorya explained.

"Well, he's riding with Lord Daegal's warriors now," Thordig said. "And after walking passed him, I looked back and saw Chen and dozens of her warrior women joining him. That hellion and Pensgraft seemed to be on pretty good terms."

"You say Pensgraft was riding with them. Does that mean they left the castle?" Corson asked.

"They were gathering at the main entrance, and when it opened, both Lord Daegal's men and Chen's women stormed through it like there was no tomorrow. I've no idea how many made it down the mountainside uninjured, or if any made it down at all. At the time, it was almost pitch dark."

"My father would never join Lord Daegal," Aerylln said with an air of defiance, although she hadn't seen him in ages and wasn't even sure he was alive until now.

"Pensgraft wasn't tied up, and he held the reins of his own horse."

"I don't believe it," Aerylln said almost in tears.

"You saw Chen leaving the castle. When was that exactly?" Corson asked.

"Three days ago, right before dawn."

"Where were they going?"

"Heading out to see someone named Glenitant, at least that's what I overheard one warrior telling another."

"Chen's Aunt Glenitant has a castle three-day's ride east of The Rock," Corson informed them.

"I've heard of Glenitant, and she's a wicked old crone," Dartuke said. "I wouldn't advise going there by yourselves."

"I've ten warriors at a campsite on the other side of the stream," Balder said.

"A dozen warriors, including you and Corson, won't be enough if you plan on pursuing that bunch. There must have been 50 warriors, or more, leaving The Rock with Chen," Thordig said gravely.

"You'll be coming with us, won't you?" Aerylln asked.

Looking at the teenage girl, the nobles noticed bloodstains on the hem of her white dress, and Dartuke said, "It appears you've had a bit of trouble already, young lady."

"It's not as bad as it looks, and I wasn't hurt. Corson took care of us," Aerylln said smiling at her protector.

"No doubt," Dartuke said glancing at Corson's well-muscled sword arm and the warrior woman's strong legs. "But a three-day ride is quite a distance to travel, and who knows what you'll be heading into."

"I have to find my father," Aerylln insisted.

"And I have to locate Chen," Corson declared.

"We have pressing business at home, and we can't help you," Catara, another of the nobles, said.

"If we can get Chen to unite with us against Lord Daegal, you could break free of the warlord's tyranny," Corson pointed out. "That would accomplish more good than anything you could possibly do in your provinces. As long as Lord Daegal remains in power, you'll always be a repressed people."

"It's in your own best interest. Ride with us," Balder added.

"At least ten of us must go back immediately," Catara said. "If you mount a successful challenge to Lord Daegal, then we must build new alliances with our neighbors, and the warlord's garrison back home must be defeated. Until those things are done, none of our people will venture from their own lands."

"But you believe turning Chen against her uncle will somehow spell the end of Lord Daegal?" Dartuke asked staring directly into Balder's eyes.

"I trust Corson's instincts implicitly," Balder told the nobles. "If she can reach Chen, then Chen might be able to disrupt factions within The Rock. She's crazy, but also devious, cunning and a born strategist. Some factions within the castle might join her. Certainly not all would fight against her. It's worth a try."

"And there's Aerylln's sword," Corson pointed out. "I've seen a little of its power, and Baelfire seems formidable. But I wish we knew if Chen and Pensgraft have reached Glenitant's castle yet."

"I can help you with that," Eldwyn said stepping forward. "Does anyone have a canteen?"

"A canteen, what for?" Thordig asked.

"Just humor him for a minute," Zorya said. The nobles stared at her once more finding it hard to get used to the idea of a talking warhorse.

Catara offered his canteen to Eldwyn who removed the cap, took hold of the canteen with both hands and began waving it about spewing water into the air.

The nobles had been shocked by Zorya and Baelfire's ability to talk, but now they were in for another surprise as the water vaporized transforming into a mist which quickly developed into a dense fog covering the entire area in front of them. An image of Aunt Glenitant's fortress, Crystal Castle, appeared in the white fog, and everyone was in awe of its size and beauty.

They saw Pensgraft being thrown against a wall by an invisible force with Chen and her warrior women racing to form a protective circle around him mounted on their black stallions with swords drawn.

They watched Aunt Glenitant emerging from Crystal Castle's main tower, and Zorya and Baelfire immediately recognized the old crone's dark sword, Crystal. It was obvious to everyone that Glenitant was in poor health, and that the old witch couldn't escape the jaws of death much longer.

Greatly worried, Baelfire said, "Soon, Glenitant's evil sword will be inherited by another. We've got to reach her castle before that happens and break the line of succession."

Zorya and Baelfire watched in horror as Chen knelt before her aunt, and they both felt Crystal's all-consuming desire for Chen to be the heir apparent.

"We can't allow this to happen. It would be disastrous for someone as intelligent, cunning, strong willed and deeply disturbed as Chen to inherit the dark sword. Her potential for evil could be unlimited. We have to leave now!" Baelfire shouted in alarm.

Hearing the fear in Baelfire's voice and realizing the severity of the crisis confronting them, Dartuke and 19 other nobles decided to ride for Crystal Castle. The rest would return and tell those back home to prepare for war, whether against Lord Daegal or his niece, or both, they weren't sure. But conflict was coming.

"Should your women want to join the fight, bring them to me," Corson instructed those returning home. "I'll train them as archers. You bring them to me!"

Although Catara was going back home, he gave horses to Eldwyn and Marcheto, ones formerly belonging to the sons of the dead "lion."

"They're experienced warhorses," Catara said. "Bring honor to them."

A few moments later, Balder's men came across the stream mounted and ready to go. Kirtak, Balder's second-in-command, had seen his captain talking with the nobles and sensed something was up. They approached the group as the nobles returning home were galloping away to the west.

Balder's men were wide-eyed in surprise when they saw the dense fog and the vision of Chen kneeling before Glenitant. The warriors saw the dark sword Glenitant was leaning on for support and shuddered involuntarily.

"We have work to do," Balder shouted to his men and without further explanation, he leapt onto his horse and galloped to the east with his warriors in hot pursuit. Immediately, Dartuke spurred his horse and gave chase as the other nobles followed close on his heels.

Helping Eldwyn get mounted, Corson realized the old wizard actually needed very little assistance. When she'd first met him, Eldwyn could barely walk let alone ride a horse. Yet the longer Baelfire allowed her energy to seep into the old man, the more animated and invigorated he'd become.

Leaping onto Tempest, her warhorse, Corson raced away as she, Eldwyn and Marcheto tried to catch up with the others. Following behind them all was a magic horse with a teenage girl on her back, Zorya having intentionally chosen to pull up the rear.

After galloping for only a few hundred yards, Zorya asked Aerylln to take Baelfire out of her scabbard. The teenage girl expected an explosion of power, but this time the sword gave off a warm, penetrating and energizing radiance. Baelfire filled the air with a light golden haze that spread out in front of them eventually reaching Balder. Giving incredible strength to them all, the golden haze propelled the warhorses and riders forward with supernatural speed. In fact, Aerylln was certain

Zorya's feet were actually leaving the ground as the teenage girl and her magic horse began skimming rapidly along the surface of the earth, as all those in front of them were now doing.

"What's happening?" Aerylln asked looking at Baelfire in surprise.

"Time is of the essence," Baelfire said. "Crystal's my evil twin, and we must get to Chen before the dark sword does."

"If we don't, what will happen?"

"Aunt Glenitant hasn't been particularly good at wielding the dark sword. The old witch and Crystal never really got along and just tolerated each other. But if what I saw and felt is correct, then Crystal has found a kindred spirit in Chen. And that could be a disaster beyond our wildest imagination."

"Maybe it depends on whose imagination you're talking about. Corson's imagination is pretty strange. She's my friend, and I love her, but she sees death and destruction everywhere."

"If we don't stop Chen from inheriting Crystal, even Corson won't be able to fathom the consequences," Baelfire said.

"Corson has nightmares every night, bad ones."

"Not like this!"

Aerylln fell silent, content to ride along and enjoy Zorya's smooth, powerful strides. The teenage girl found the golden haze comforting and thought, Why do I feel good when I'm heading directly towards evil?

At that point, the young woman realized she had no idea what was going on around her. For if she did, Aerylln might have wished she'd never met her horse, her sword and the old wizard.

Chapter 16

Sitting in his great room at The Rock, Lord Daegal was fingering the medallion he wore around his neck. The warlord never took the medallion off, not when he bathed, slept, engaged in battle or celebrated his victories. Never. The medallion was made of polished black crystal, the same type of crystal used to create Aunt Glenitant's fortress. Encircling the black crystal was a thin band of white gold, which provided a striking contrast.

"So, what do you think, Crystal?" Lord Daegal asked the dark sword. The Crystal Medallion enabled the evil sword to communicate with the wearer anywhere and at anytime, precisely what was happening now. Lord Daegal and Crystal were talking even though one was at The Rock and the other at Glenitant's castle.

"About what?" the dark sword asked needling the warlord.

"Don't be impertinent. You know what I mean. What's happening between Chen and my sister, Glenitant?" Lord Daegal asked trying to keep his feelings of irritation in check.

If the dark sword's relationship with Glenitant could be described as tolerable, Crystal's association with Lord Daegal was worse being tedious, filled with mutual suspicion and, at times, hostile. On one hand, having possessed the dark sword for years, Glenitant was tired of it. The old witch was tired of its insatiable evil, tired of its endless demands, and she was even tired of living. Lord Daegal, on the other hand, had envied his sister for years and lusted after Crystal wanting to possess her but unable to do so, as of yet. Lord Daegal craved power and the dark sword exuded it, but the warlord seemed blind to Crystal's malicious mischief. The dark sword had seen this before. Blind desire, and though she liked it, she also felt the warlord was a fool.

But as much as she wanted to, Crystal couldn't totally dismiss Lord Daegal. Possessing the Crystal Medallion, the warlord had the one thing Crystal desperately wanted, something she desired over everything else. Literally within his grasp, Lord Daegal had inherited the Crystal Medallion from his father and the dark sword wanted it badly, very badly, as much as the warlord wanted her.

Crystal had always been a powerful weapon, although not as powerful as Baelfire, but that could change under the right conditions. And the most important condition of all was the dark sword and the medallion being reunited. The Crystal Medallion was actually an extension of Crystal herself, much like how Zorya and Baelfire belonged together and shared a deep, mystical bond. However, Crystal believed Glenitant was weak, far too weak to wield the dark sword and the Crystal Medallion effectively. Chen was another matter.

Crystal thought, Chen, glorious Chen! What a pleasure it will be to have the Crystal Medallion hanging from her neck. And what a joy it will be to feel her rage when she grips me.

In the past, the opportunity to be reunited with the Crystal Medallion had never materialized. Until recently, this hadn't bothered Crystal, at least not overly so, because the dark sword viewed Glenitant as being stupid, coarse and lacking ambition. But with Chen entering the picture, Crystal was increasingly dissatisfied and thought, Glenitant lacks the daring and willingness necessary to take bold risks. Being wielded by an intelligent, determined and fierce warrior woman like Chen would be a welcome relief.

In case the dark sword finally found a way to be reunited with the medallion, Crystal had kept in touch with Lord Daegal. Well, now Crystal wanted it back, and she wanted it for Chen.

To accomplish this, much to her dismay, the dark sword realized she'd need to sweet-talk Lord Daegal. Crystal thought, Just because he wears the Crystal Medallion, Lord Daegal thinks he owns it, when he's just a caretaker. Only a woman can wield us effectively.

But now, as the dark sword listened to Lord Daegal, she realized there was a chance, a good chance, that she and the Crystal Medallion might finally be reunited.

"Crystal, you might enjoy having Chen for a master," Lord Daegal said.

"Oh?"

"Well, temporarily. For a long time, I've wanted to have you here with the Crystal Medallion and me. You know that don't you?" Lord Daegal asked.

"I have always wanted to be with the medallion," Crystal said, and then thought, But not with you.

"Well, Glenitant has never been too smart, but she wields your power well enough to keep me from coming to rescue you," Lord Daegal said.

"Oh, I so wish you would," Crystal said hiding her distain and forcing herself to flatter the warlord. But Crystal was thinking, I'm not going from a lackluster idiot like Glenitant to a crude thug like Lord Daegal.

"Although Chen is a deeply disturbed young woman," Lord Daegal said, "she wouldn't know how to use a sword like yourself to your fullest potential. She's too inexperienced."

She could learn, Crystal thought. But the dark sword held her peace and said, "It would be nice to finally come into my own. I wonder if there's really anyone who can take me there?"

"I might be able to," Lord Daegal said.

"How?"

"If Glenitant should die, Chen would inherit you for herself. However, Chen is inexperienced and her power wouldn't be nearly as great as Glenitant's. So, it's very possible that I could rescue you."

Crystal had no intention of living with Lord Daegal, but she continued to listen as the warlord asked, "Could you provoke Glenitant and Chen into fighting each other?"

"Easily, what would be hard is keeping them from each other's throats."

"If Chen could defeat Glenitant, I'd attack Crystal Castle with as many warriors as necessary to discourage Chen from putting up any resistance. If I showed up with several thousand men, I could defeat my niece even if she tried to use your power."

"I'm looking forward to your arrival," Crystal said honestly but not for Lord Daegal's reasons.

Instead, Crystal was thinking, If I can get Chen to kill her aunt, then we'll have Crystal Castle for ourselves. And if we defeat Lord Daegal's army, then the Crystal Medallion can join Chen and me. With Lord Daegal defeated, there's no one else who could challenge our power. The whole region would be ours.

And that was a very real possibility, but Crystal's plans were about to be disrupted by an old wizard, a horse, a teenage girl and her sword.

Chapter 17

Depressed and discouraged, Chen was sitting in Crystal Castle's great hall in front of an enormous fireplace watching the roaring inferno with her wolfhound, Zenkak, lying at her feet. He was a brutish, vicious beast and leader of the pack. The other wolfhounds brooded as well but kept their distance from Zenkak and their master. The ground nearest Chen was the lead wolfhound's personal domain. None dared challenge him. Zenkak's volcanic, hair-trigger, explosive temper matched Chen's. As it was, pools of flaming, red lava poured into the huge wolfhound's hostile eyes. To him, carrying a grudge was a badge of honor. Anger and survival was one and the same thing.

His master's mood was no better. She glared down at the animal at her feet. Zenkak felt Chen's rage and found the sheer depth of her dark spirit dangerously reassuring. He gave a low, threatening growl of approval. The hairs stood straight up on the other wolfhounds' necks. They knew that for their pack leader being angry was a pleasure. It was something that he savored and enjoyed. Zenkak was a natural born killer. Chen was no better.

Aunt Glenitant had the misfortune of walking into this atmosphere of gloom and doom. At first, the old witch liked it. That is until she became its target.

Chen stood up, walked over to her aunt and said, "Give me the sword."

If the future could be collapsed backwards to a crucial, transforming moment that defined history, this was it.

"Come and take it," Aunt Glenitant said, her voice dripping with venom.

Chen advanced on her aunt with a total disregard for anything other than getting her hands on Crystal. Glenitant was a very frail, thin woman dressed in a drab, gray robe, but when she drew Crystal from her scabbard a malignant evil leapt out of the dark sword. The two women facing each other had embraced hatred for most of their lives, and it was in their blood, but Crystal was worse than both of them put together.

As the dark sword arced out of its scabbard much of the light from the roaring fire was sucked from the air. Its warmth turned to a coldness that pervaded the room. The darkness seemed to be alive. It poured itself onto the ceiling, over the walls and onto the floor. Chen felt evil rising in the room. She felt it covering her feet, then her ankles, and then it crept up her legs.

The evil was so dark, deep and all pervasive that it even seemed to surround itself in its own cloak of darkness. Darkness within darkness. Evil cloaked in evil.

For the first time in a long while, Chen felt fear. Her reaction was instantaneous. She attacked that which she feared.

As she made a headlong rush towards her aunt, Chen drew her own sword. It wasn't magical, however a woman who cared for little else but herself wielded it. Her selfishness gave her strength and focus.

Glenitant had thought Crystal would defend her personally, but she was wrong. There is nothing good in anything truly evil. A dark spirit feeds even on those whom it favors and draws closest to itself. And so, brimming with excitement, Crystal said, "Hey girls, let's have some fun!"

Caught up in the moment, Crystal forgot that she loved Chen. All the dark sword could see was an opportunity to use two people consumed with anger and spite. For Crystal, there was nothing like inflicting a deeply disturbing experience on some deserving victim. In this case, she had two of them, and Crystal couldn't have been happier.

Chen swung her sword at Glenitant with all her might. But the dark sword easily parried the blow and countered by hitting Chen with a powerful energy surge hurling her across the room. The dark sword wasn't taking sides, Crystal simply wanted time to arrange the fight on her terms.

"Put me down, Glenitant," the dark sword commanded.

"What?" Glenitant asked in surprise.

"Put me down."

"No!" Glenitant said alarmed at the prospect of facing Chen by herself.

Realizing the old witch would never let go of her, Crystal began growing heavier and heavier until the dark sword weighed over 100 pounds. At that point, Glenitant had no choice but to let the sword fall to the floor. Glaring down at her traitorous weapon, the old witch asked, "Now what am I supposed to do?"

"Use one of the swords hanging on the wall," Crystal told her.

On the far side of the room, feeling a bit bruised and shaken, Chen scrambled back onto her feet. Glenitant shuddered while watching her executioner slowly and deliberately coming closer as if stalking her prey. Then, to the old witch's surprise, Chen stopped in the middle of the great hall wearing a shocked expression.

Glenitant quickly became equally shocked when a wave of energy emanating from the dark sword swamped the old witch flooding her body and making her feel stronger and younger than she had in years. Examining her arms, legs and waist, Glenitant realized that she didn't just feel young, she was young.

"I thought I'd make this a fair fight," Crystal said.

Twirling her sword in her hand, Chen circled her adversary sizing up her aunt who was now around her own age. Then blood lust filled both of the women, and they leapt at each other swords flailing. Glenitant felt the joy of battle once more. It had been so long. It was as if a long, lost lover had returned.

Glenitant swung her weapon at her niece's head, but Chen ducked, pivoted on one foot and kicked her aunt squarely in the chest knocking her back against a table. Instantly taking the hilt of her sword in both hands, Chen swung her weapon high over her head bringing it down with such force that the warrior woman might have cut her aunt in two if Glenitant hadn't jumped to the right dodging the blow.

Chen's sword cut deeply into the wooden table, so deeply that when the warrior woman tried to free it, the blade wouldn't budge no matter how hard she tugged. Seizing this opportunity, Glenitant struck with blinding speed, forcing Chen to drop to the floor. What saved the warrior woman's life was the wooden bench next to her. The tip of Aunt Glenitant's sword sliced into the wood almost splitting the board, but not quite. As Glenitant yanked her sword free, her niece rolled under a table trying to get away. Auntie, unable to recall the last time she'd fought this well, was thrilled with her newfound youth.

Running to the wall closest to her and sizing up the weapons display, Chen chose a double-bladed axe. The warrior woman swung the axe while spinning around in a circle cutting through the air, and she kept letting the weight of the axe pull her. Chen twirled around faster and faster building momentum. To stop the spinning, Chen held onto the axe tightly while letting it fly high over her head and bringing it down hard onto the black crystal floor biting into it and sending sparks flying.

Glancing at the young woman halfway across the room, Chen smiled, no longer recognizing her. The warrior woman had forgotten it was her aunt. Entering a state of unknowing, a state of being free of conscious thought, Chen even forgot her own identity. She no longer knew her own name. Locked in a fight to the death, her life was stripped down to the fundamental basics of skill and speed. Only if she survived and rejoined the ranks of the living would her name and personal identity matter. Until then, thoughts were an extra step in the fighting process that she could ill afford. But being totally blank like an artist's white canvas, nothing stood in the way of spontaneous action. Flowing with deadly creativity, Chen turned fighting into an art form.

Feeling inspired, the warrior woman spun around, sprinted towards Glenitant swinging her double-bladed axe over her head and bringing it down forcefully at her petrified aunt who, once again, barely sidestepped the attack. Deflecting the axe with her sword, Aunt Glenitant felt a sharp pain in her wrist as the sword was knocked out of her hand and went spinning across the polished floor.

Now it was Glenitant's turn to run to a weapons display, and she selected a lance. It was a long wooden pole with a razor sharp bayonet on the end. She and Chen circled each other once more. Glenitant poked the weapon at her niece seeking a weakness and found it. She could make repeated thrusts while Chen was unable to swing her heavy axe fast enough to constantly fend off the lance. Glenitant's weapon found its mark piercing Chen's thigh.

Glenitant twisted the lance and shoved it deeper into the wound. Chen looked down and saw her own blood. It had a nice, bright color to it, Chen thought always ready to pay herself a compliment deserved or otherwise.

Forgetting about life and death, Chen analyzed the situation in an instant. Glenitant was taking too much satisfaction in her momentary success, focusing only on her lance and the wound in Chen's thigh. It was a deadly mistake. Chen exploited it.

Never underestimating your enemy is an axiom of war Chen always remembered. And what Glenitant underestimated was Chen's ability to accept pain. Great pain.

Chen inherited her tolerance from her mother, who died some years ago, but had gifted her daughter with a capacity to accept a high level of discomfort.

The young warrior woman recalled a story about her birth and how her mother had gone into labor without telling anyone and continued working about her chambers until almost fully dilated. When Chen's mother finally informed her maidservants of her situation, she only had to push six times before her daughter came into the world. Her mother was up and walking around only four hours after giving birth. Chen being born premature with life hanging in the balance had sent adrenaline pumping though her mother's system causing her to pace the halls. But the baby girl fought back from the brink of death and had been fighting ever since.

When only ten years old, one of Chen's teachers had told her mother that she'd never before seen so much anger in a girl this young. To which Chen's mother had responded, "It runs in the family." And it did.

As Chen looked at the lance stuck in her thigh, she figured it couldn't hurt as much as childbirth. So, gritting her teeth, she took a knife out of a boot and threw it at Glenitant catching her in the left shoulder. Her aunt dropped the lance, and Chen yanked it out of her leg. Then with surprising agility for someone having a gash in one leg, Chen jumped at her aunt pushing the knife deeper into her shoulder. Next, hauling back a rock-hard fist, Chen punched Glenitant in the face breaking her nose.

Grimacing a little, Chen stuck her fingers into her own wound to staunch the flow of blood. And she paused for a moment, thinking about a young woman who had once been a member of her personal guard. This warrior woman believed in the superiority of females in battle declaring that after experiencing childbirth, there was little else a woman had to fear.

None of the women in Chen's personal guard had children at that point, but the argument made sense. A sword or a lance cutting into one's body makes a smaller wound than an eight-pound child ripping through a woman's flesh, so men simply weren't as prepared as women to face pain. Chen's friend had never tired of making the point, badgering and baiting the castle guards over the issue.

I miss that girl, Chen thought wistfully. I wonder where Corson is now?

The black leather panther, which is what Chen most resembled when angry, turned her attention back to Glenitant who had succeeded in pulling the knife out of her shoulder without fainting.

Glancing around, Chen noticed the oppressive darkness was leaving the room, and she could feel the heat of the fire once more. Looking over at Crystal, the warrior woman noticed the dark sword was back in her scabbard hanging from the mantle of the fireplace.

Focus and remember what it is you're after, Chen thought. So, ignoring the throbbing in her thigh, she made for the sword. Passing Glenitant, Chen punched her aunt in her wounded shoulder feeling quite gratified when she dropped to her knees howling in agony.

But ignoring her aunt, Chen ran to the fireplace and reached for her prize.

"Not so quick, this isn't over," Crystal said. "Hmmm, is it just my imagination or is the room beginning to rotate?"

Trying to keep her balance, Chen shifted her feet as the floor tilted sharply to the right. The black leather panther watched as the fireplace and dark sword shot up towards the ceiling turning the room onto a corner like a square diamond balancing on its tip. Picking up speed, the floor was now where the left wall had once been, the left wall was on the ceiling, and the right wall became the new floor. Chen quickly began walking to the right keeping pace with the turning room as if walking inside the spinning waterwheel of a gristmill.

I have to get Crystal! the warrior woman thought as the dark sword hung invitingly from the mantle, though way out of reach, and the room continued turning like a windmill.

Seeing Glenitant making a grab for the dark sword, Chen took a crossbow from a weapons display at her feet aiming for her aunt while clutching her wounded thigh. Glenitant, for her part, took hold of a large shield covering herself with it while desperately trying to keep her balance.

Sitting at a table as the actual floor rotated back under her, Chen braced herself, steadied the crossbow and pulled the trigger. Grazing Glenitant's ankle, the arrow opened a flesh wound and chipped a bone causing her to cry out once more.

As pain shot up her leg, Glenitant lost her balance and rolled down onto what now passed for the floor. But continuing to rotate, the floor again tilted at a 45-degree angle jamming Glenitant into the corner at the lowest point of the diamond. Wedged into the corner with her body on one side and her neck bent at a sharp angle, Chen's aunt was more exhausted, shaken up and frightened than anything.

Growing tired of seeing the room moving 'round and 'round, Crystal noticed how exhausted Glenitant was and realized Chen was a much superior warrior. Still, the dark sword wanted more entertainment, especially since all this mayhem was at someone else's expense. The dark sword thought, Using and abusing Chen over the years will be satisfying, but for now I have them both.

Once the floor returned to where it should be, Crystal stopped the room and asked, "So, what's next?" Miffed that neither Chen nor Glenitant were forthcoming with any suggestions, Crystal asked, "Am I the only one enjoying this?"

Met with more silence, the dark sword brooded, feeling underappreciated. With her temper beginning to flare, Crystal thought, No wonder I hate them. They're so ungrateful. If it wasn't for me, their lives would be so dull.

Glaring at the exhausted Glenitant and the ever-alert panther dressed in black leather, Crystal was still not ready to bring all this fun to an end. And so, sighing in frustration, feeling the burden of always being the one having to instigate everything, Crystal asked, "Glenitant, would you like some help?"

"Jewel, I want Jewel," Glenitant wheezed though relieved that Crystal was finally providing some assistance. Eyeing Chen, she grinned wickedly.

And on cue, Jewel made her appearance.

Walking right out of a black crystal wall, she was strikingly beautiful. Jewel was a tall, slender woman with long legs, a trim waist, full breasts and long, slender arms. Her hair was short and brushed back close against her skull. Her face looked as if she'd been sculpted from marble having a firm, chiseled look and appearing very aristocratic. She was attractive. She was desirable. She was awesome. She was not human.

Befitting her name, Jewel was ruby-red from head to toe. A deep, rich, luxurious red, which was enhanced by the light from the roaring fire in the enormous fireplace. She was literally a gem of a woman. Her skin was smooth as glass, and her eyes glittered in the light.

However, Chen was focusing on the weapon Jewel was holding. She was gripping a long, sparkling, ruby-red sword, and Chen asked herself, I wonder if this red devil can fight?

But then, Chen realized she didn't really care. Fighting a woman made of rubies would be a new, exciting experience, and that's what mattered. The warrior woman's dark mood evaporated, and she felt whole, fresh, and ready for anything.

The black leather panther walked over to a wall display and selected a sword. She also picked up a knife and tossed it at Jewel to test her reaction time. The sparkling creature easily deflected the weapon. Chen was pleased and thought, She has excellent reflexes. The black leather panther admired women who could fight.

Chen and Jewel both headed towards the center of the great hall. It was free of furniture and other obstacles that might get in the way of a duel. The women began circling each other. Jewel twirled her sword in her hand. Chen smiled at her ruby-red opponent and found herself liking her.

What is it about this woman that appeals to me? Chen wondered. Oh, I know. She's relaxed, confident and focused. Maybe even dangerous.

Now the dark sword, Crystal, who had instigated this, wasn't the only one having fun. Chen experienced a sense of exhilaration, and her whole body responded. The warrior woman felt sensuous, languid and moved with relaxed elegance. She was ready.

Drifting into sword range, Chen didn't even raise her weapon. The black leather panther held Jewel in contempt, and the ruby-red creature did the same to her. Neither underestimated the other. It was more like issuing a mutual challenge and sending the message, I'm approaching you unafraid. Looking into each other's eyes, the two women sensed their opponent's energy searching for weakness but found none.

They stopped circling one another and stood still. Slowly and silently, each raised her sword and waited for the other to lose her concentration or focus. It didn't happen. Neither woman flinched.

Glenitant stumbled over a wooden bench while backing away from the warriors. There was a loud crash as the bench tipped over, and she went sprawling. Then, having landed on her wounded shoulder, Glenitant gasped from the pain and started screaming.

For just an instant, Jewel shifted her attention to the woman she'd been charged with defending. It was an opening, and Chen took it.

The black leather panther's sword slammed down on Jewel with such lighting speed that the ruby-red woman couldn't deflect the blow. The blade of Chen's sword found its mark slashing Jewel's right thigh. Had the ruby-red woman been human, the fight would have virtually been over. The vicious blow would have made a long, deep gash crippling any other opponent. But gems are made of sterner stuff. As it was, Chen's sword slipped along Jewel's smooth, glass-like surface and struck the crystalline floor without so much as scratching her.

The black leather panther and the ruby-red woman stopped and looked at each other. Before the fight had even started, Jewel knew about her physical advantage, but it came as quite a surprise to Chen. Jewel started laughing, and Chen joined her.

Shrugging her shoulders, the black leather panther sighed and smiled disarmingly. Then, without warning, she struck Jewel's face with the side of her sword, the blow landing with the impact of a sledgehammer. Jewel's face exploded in a shower of rubies that cascaded onto the floor. After keeping its balance for a few moments, her body collapsed into a heap at Chen's feet. Even in death, Jewel was radiant as the solid rubies inside her skull sparkled in the firelight. Jewel was a real gem, a beauty through and through.

As flames from the fireplace reflected on the black crystal great hall, on the rubies scattered across the floor and on Jewel herself, the room was bathed in yellow, orange and red light. Looking out a window at the rest of the castle, the warrior woman saw subdued, white lighting covering the base of the walls and filtering halfway to the top providing a striking contrast to the black crystal.

Chen thought, This is one gorgeous, classy place! I want it!

The black leather panther turned toward the only person standing between her and ownership of the magnificent castle. She looked at a spent, frightened Glenitant and was filled with disdain. The warrior woman almost didn't want to soil her sword with her aunt's blood.

Chen strode towards Glenitant with firelight shimmering on her black leather outfit making her appear even more a part of the castle than her aunt. But Chen stopped in her tracks when Crystal called out a name.

"Flame!" the dark sword shouted.

Chen looked on wide-eyed as a humanoid woman stepped out of the fireplace. She was covered in flames, or more accurately, she was made of fire. The humanoid woman was composed of red-hot coals with flames pouring off of them. Prior to this, Chen had always taken comfort in watching the coals of a fire as the flames began fading at the end of the day. The shimmering black and red embers had seemed alive. How right she was, at least in this instance.

Tonight, however, as the red-hot coals began walking towards her, Chen took no comfort in them. Before reaching the black leather panther, Flame paused near Jewel's crumpled figure, gathered up all the rubies scattered on the floor, turned Jewel on her side and piled the rubies onto the shattered side of her face. Stepping over Jewel, Flame lay down on the floor behind her. This bundle of red-hot fire pressed her body against Jewel's and things really began heating up, literally.

Flame turned herself into an inferno making Jewel's body white-hot and flooding the room with a blinding glare so intense, it was like looking directly into the noonday sun. Gradually, the light subsided, the nighttime darkness returned, and the fireplace gave off the only illumination. It's flickering firelight and dark shadows filled the room once more.

Jewel and Flame were still lying on the floor, the woman of fire having her arm wrapped around the ruby-red body pressed against her own. Chen looked at Jewel's face, and it appeared whole once more.

Suddenly, both humanoid women opened their eyes and sat up. Flame stood and offered Jewel a hand pulling her to her feet. As they turned towards Chen, she saw the anger in their eyes and felt her life expectancy shorten dramatically.

The black leather panther's life flashed before her eyes, and she thought about the failings of her own selfish nature. If she could start over, would she change anything?

"Naw!" Chen said out loud and reached for her sword.

As it was, being self-centered and controlling may have been what saved her. Chen remembered that the dark sword was what she really wanted, and Glenitant stood in the way of her getting it. So the black leather panther ignored the two humanoid women who wanted to kill her and, instead, took the initiative by focusing on the person she wanted to kill.

She ran, or hobbled quickly, towards Glenitant who gave her little resistance. Dragging her aunt off a wooden bench, Chen lifted the woman to her feet, placed a hand against her aunt's back and shoved Glenitant away from her.

Aware of the danger behind her, as much as Chen tried to ignore it, she charged at her aunt who only avoided death by throwing herself to the floor to escape the vicious thrust of Chen's sword. As Glenitant got to her feet, Jewel and Flame were so close Chen could feel heat on the back of her neck.

But the black leather panther smiled upon realizing Glenitant was standing in front of an open window. Chen made her move pivoting on one foot and kicking her aunt in the chest as hard as she could. Glenitant was knocked backwards stumbling and falling over the window ledge. Hanging onto the ledge by her fingertips, Glenitant knew she was doomed. She'd known it ever since Chen first showed up.

"So, you've won. The sword is yours," Glenitant said almost relieved at having the burden taken from her. And a malignant gleam entered her eyes at the thought of Chen having to endure Crystal's insatiable evil. Years ago, seduced by the promise of power, Glenitant had eventually embraced the dark sword only to discover, all too late, its corrosive effects on her. By the time she realized the price of power, her own identity had been worn away. Her own sense of self-worth had been destroyed. All she had left was the dark sword. Without it, she was nothing, or at least that's what Crystal kept telling her.

But now, in the present, upon hearing Glenitant forfeit the dark sword, Jewel and Flame stopped in their tracks. There was about to be a transfer of power, and they didn't want to end up on the wrong side of things. It had been their duty to defend Glenitant, but now their master's life was hanging by a thread, and a very thin one at that.

"Well, Chen, let me give you a hint of what you're in for," Glenitant said wearing a twisted smile. "I killed my own father to satisfy Crystal's lust for evil, but that turned out to be only the beginning. Now, you'll be living with that cruel, deranged weapon, and best of luck, you'll need it. Oh, and one other thing, your father's here at Crystal Castle visiting for a spell."

"He's alive?" Chen asked in amazement. "Where has he been for all these years?"

"Oh, roaming around and visiting far-off countries," Glenitant said lying effortlessly. "You know, diplomatic sort of stuff."

Spinning her own web of evil, she added to the lie and said, "Back then, your father couldn't exactly be carting a young girl around with him, could he? Travel is wearisome enough without having a child tagging along. And who would have looked after you when he was on official business? Having such a hot temper, you'd have always been in trouble. You'd have ended up being a constant source of embarrassment.

"Your father did the right thing leaving you behind. He said so himself many times. And who could blame him?" Glenitant asked making the story up as she went along.

"Go see him, he's right upstairs. But I suspect your father's packing already. He never stays long in the same place. I told him you were here, but your father said he didn't want to see you. Kind of lost interest in you over the years, I suppose," Glenitant said grinding salt into the wound.

"You ought to kill him for what he did. Deserting a young girl like that, it's disgraceful! I don't see how he can even call himself a man! He chose a career as an emissary for Lord Daegal over you. Just like so many other men who choose their work over their loved ones. I wonder what Lord Daegal offered your father for him to sell you out so easily?" Glenitant asked taunting her.

"Stop it!" Chen screamed. "Stop it! My father loved me. He would never have valued anything over me. Never!"

"Well, who can understand men, huh?" Glenitant said with a sympathetic tone. "Give your auntie a hand. Come on, pull me up and we'll confront him together. He never loved you. Not really."

Chen was almost wild with mental and emotional confusion! Her head was pounding and she felt like she wanted to cry, which for Chen was nothing short of astonishing!

"Jewel, Flame," Glenitant called to the humanoid women now standing close to the window. "Give me a hand, pull me back in. We're done for the day. We can talk more about this tomorrow."

Jewel came to the window, stood next to Chen and offered Glenitant, whom she now considered her former master, a hand. Glaring at Jewel, Chen bumped her aside with a hip. Then, the black leather panther took the hilt of her sword in both hands, pointed the blade downward and prepared to ram it through her aunt. But with a mocking laugh, Glenitant let go of the window ledge denying her niece the pleasure of killing her.

Being a long way to the castle courtyard below, Glenitant quickly disappeared into the darkness, once more taking the form of a cold, vicious old hag. With her last breath, Glenitant cursed Crystal for ruining her life. Her body struck the courtyard floor with a barely discernable thud, and a lifetime of evil was over.

Turning around, Chen found Jewel and Flame on their knees bowing their heads to the floor. Fuming, the black leather panther said, "I'll deal with you two later."

Chen strode towards Crystal who hung invitingly from the fireplace mantle. Tingling with anticipation, the dark sword thought, Yes, I'll admit, I almost killed Chen. But that was in a moment of excess. I want Chen to hold me, to feel her touch.

But as the dark sword dreamed of yielding herself body and soul to the approaching warrior woman, total chaos suddenly broke loose all around her.

Having immobilized Chen's wolfhounds during the fight, Crystal had released them as the black leather panther came closer. With Zenkak in the lead, the wolfhounds bounded toward the stairwell, the source of all the commotion.

Zenkak leapt towards the first person reaching the top of the stairs opening his jaws to crush the neck of a blond-haired girl carrying a magnificent sword.

"Get back!" Baelfire shouted as two-dozen stunned wolfhounds were thrown forcefully to the other side of the room.

Baelfire leapt out of her scabbard throwing herself at Crystal who had unsheathed herself as well. The titans of good and evil crashed against each other in a shower of sparks, smoke, and flame. Chen, Aerylln, and those who were running up the castle steps were knocked onto their backs from the force of the collision. The energy flowing from the conflict was so intense that Aerylln felt like a ton of rocks was piled on her chest.

Baelfire realized the fight had to be taken outside, or the humans would be destroyed by the energy crashing against them like a churning whitewater river pounding the sides of a narrow canyon. The good sword flew out the nearest window shooting straight up into the sky. Crystal was hot on her heels seething with sibling rivalry.

In a way, the magic swords were sisters. Centuries ago, they had been created by a master craftsman who was a wizard of great renown. Baelfire had been forged first and was created from megentum, a metal so rare it took 100 years to collect enough to craft a single sword. At the same time, Baelfire had been infused with a woman's spirit to help the good sword anticipate the motives and actions of a dangerous, demonic evil spirit who was also a woman.

Almost as an afterthought, the unused portion of megentum went into Crytsal. It wasn't much, but there was enough for her to claim a common heritage with Baelfire.

The quality of megentum was so refined that it was like being created from golden silk. It was luxurious, it was seductive, it was bold, and it existed in an extremely limited quantity. Crystal had enough of it to wish she had more, just enough to make her realize what she was missing.

Torn between the megentum and the lesser metals used to create her, Crystal had developed a dual personality. A noble one sprung from the megentum, which had been used in great quantity in Baelfire, her sister sword. The second sprung from another rare metal of enormous value, but more common than megentum, and it had been used to craft the majority of Crystal's blade. It was an exquisite metal, but due to its increased availability, more prone to the ways of this world and more easily influenced.

It was after the craftsman's hammer had ceased its work, and the wizard plunged Crystal into a barrel of cold, brisk water, that a consciousness of her own existence had awakened within her.

At first, Crystal had been proud of herself, justifiably proud of her beauty, strength and incredible rarity. She had felt fresh, whole and full of life.

But then, she had looked at her hilt and saw it was made of plain, ordinary iron. The craftsman had run out of the megentum used for Baelfire, and he'd also run out of the exquisite metal used for the majority of Crystal's blade. Thus, the handle of her sword, which was an important part of her own body, had been made of tempered iron. It was of the best quality craftsmanship, but it was not a rare metal.

Crystal was shocked by the commonness of her hilt. She had tried to will it away from her, but it was firmly attached for all eternity.

Still, she consoled herself with the knowledge that she was the finest sword ever made. She must have been. Looking at her creator's face, she had seen how proud and excited he was.

He had achieved his dream. Two beautiful, powerful swords.

Two swords? Crystal had asked herself in shock. What did he mean by dreaming about two swords? Maybe he meant a knife? That's it! Maybe he created a matching knife. Whew! Why was I worried?

Anyway, given her own rarity, she could be forgiven if she was a bit concerned about her station in life and a tad vain. Just look at her beauty. Even the well-crafted iron hilt looked good actually, if one took into account her overall appearance. And so, she smiled with smug self-satisfaction.

Then she saw Baelfire, and her heart went cold with fear.

Baelfire was a sword of unparalleled grace and charm. She was elegant. Her blade shimmered as if the sun's rays were bouncing off of it, but the two swords were not even outside.

Baelfire lay on the craftsman's workbench in languid splendor. She was so supreme in her self-confidence that she didn't mind Crystal being created partly in her own image. Baelfire had even smiled a warm welcome to her new half-sister. It made Crystal furious!

She didn't want to be loved by some superior being!

And hatred began seeping into her heart.

So, since they were forged, bad blood had been brewing between them.

Crystal was in an almost constant rage over being second best. And although nothing else in the world could be compared to her beauty, she hadn't known that when she was born. Her sister was an eminently more beautiful sword and, for all Crystal knew, she herself could be common as stone.

In those early days, things had been said between Baelfire and Crystal that neither of them would ever forget. And not long after their creation, Baelfire had grown tired of her half-sister's way of venting her personal anger and disappointment on others.

Crystal's anger and bitterness had eventually evolved into evil and malice. And Crystal liked it that way, at least that's what she had told herself. But now, to make matters worse, Baelfire had come into the hands of a young, innocent teenage girl and all of life seemed to be opening up before her.

So, as Baelfire and Crystal now found themselves flying up into the sky together, this fight had been brewing for a long time. A very long time.

Baelfire was short and to the point.

"Crystal, you are not going to have Chen as your master! I'll never allow that! You have enough problems without joining up with a troubled young woman!"

"I've found a friend, someone like me," Crystal countered. "You have Aerylln, and now you're trying to prevent me from having my own true love! I notice you never complained much about Glenitant."

"Well, Glenitant wasn't what I'd call a spectacular catch," Baelfire laughed before she could stop herself.

Crystal glared at her half-sister. "All right, if you want to fight, come on!"

Baelfire and Crystal collided with a force so powerful it would have leveled the trees on the mountains surrounding Crystal Castle, if the swords hadn't been so high above the ground. Crystal heard her half-sister grunt from the impact, took heart, and charged again. This time, she aimed at the middle of Baelfire's blade hoping to split it in two. What Crystal got instead was another humiliating revelation. A hairline crack formed along her blade, a very tiny one, but Crystal became hysterical. The dark sword had always known she wasn't as attractive as her half-sister, but in her wildest imagination had never considered the possibility that she wasn't as strong as Baelfire.

Always having felt competent, vital, powerful and dangerous, the dark sword took one look at her half-sister floating unscathed in front of her, having received not so much as a scratch, and panicked.

Crystal fled back to the castle with all the speed she could muster. She had to get back to Chen. The young, black leather panther would make her powerful once more, far more powerful than her goody-two-shoes sister and the little piece of fluff Baelfire had taken as her new master.

Chen would make things right. Before this, Chen's rage had always been a source of amusement to her, now it was a matter of the dark sword's survival. At least that's how Crystal interpreted things. Her dark heart had long ago blinded her judgment.

Diving through a castle window and into the great hall once more, Crystal saw Chen by the fireplace mantle, and the evil sword's heart swelled in anticipation of the young hellion's hand gripping her.

What Crystal saw next stopped her heart.

Eldwyn, the wizard, was standing between Crystal and Chen. If the dark sword had hair, she would have torn it out in frustration.

Crystal made a quick swing to the wizard's right side hoping to slip past him, but then she heard it, those terrible words.

Wizard's robes flowing all around him, Eldwyn spread his arms wide lifting them above his shoulders, the long, draping sleeves hanging down below his waist. Eldwyn's robes seemed dull, worn and frayed, but looking into his eyes, Crystal realized they were as sharp and penetrating as ever. The dark sword's blood went cold.

Bentar ulray candas temantus! Bentar ulray candas temantus!" Eldwyn shouted.

The old wizard repeated the incantation over and over, the force of his voice and the sensation of power increasing with each repetition.

Crystal, feeling the air beginning to swirl around inside the room, was further surprised upon seeing a horse appear at the top of the stairwell. And it wasn't just any horse. It was Zorya.

"Life is so unfair!" Crystal screamed, but her words were lost in the roar of the wind hurling about the room.

As Eldwyn drove himself into a mystical frenzy, the jewels on Zorya's necklace began glowing. Turning around, Crystal saw her half-sister behind her, and the jewels on Baelfire's hilt were glowing as well. Beams of purple, blue, green, yellow, orange and red light shot out in all directions, rainbows filling the air with deep, vibrant colors. The jewels on Zorya's necklace and Baelfire's hilt were acting like prisms refracting light and splashing it all over the walls. It was like an artist gone wild!

The dark sword watched in horror as Eldwyn reached into a pouch lifting out a few strands of long, blond hair. Crystal's eyes darted to the girl standing next to Zorya and instantly saw how short Aerylln's blond hair was.

"It's that little tramp's hair!" Crystal wailed.

The dark sword tried to run, but Baelfire blocked her way. In desperation, Crystal flew towards the teenage girl figuring that killing her might help, but Zorya reared up and gave a deafening battle cry.

Crystal glanced around anxiously trying to come up with another alternative, but then something in front of her sparkled catching her attention. Eldwyn was holding up the strands of blond hair, ones he'd saved after Aerylln used Baelfire to cut her hair. And they were glowing.

Eldwyn tossed them into the air, and they headed towards Crystal. Approaching her, the thin strands became longer and thicker transforming into golden ropes. As the ropes surrounded the dark sword and began wrapping themselves around her, Crystal felt her strength and willpower being drained away. Now greatly weakened, exhausted and ready to faint, Crystal collapsed onto the floor. The cool, black crystal floor.

Suddenly, remembering the Crystal Medallion in Lord Daegal's possession, the dark sword called out to it. With her last shreds of strength, she cried out in anger and frustration. And although The Rock was several days hard ride from Crystal Castle, the Crystal Medallion heard the dark sword's cry.

"Lord Daegal, we must go to Glenitant's castle and rescue Crystal!" the medallion pleaded, her voice filled with urgency.

"Yes, of course. That will come soon enough, but first I have plans to make and troops to call back from furthest reaches of the realm," he explained. "We'll be launching an attack on Crystal Castle in due time."

"No, we must go now!" the Crystal Medallion insisted.

"We're not leaving yet. Preparation's half of any battle. I'll go when I'm ready."

Gradually, Crystal's voice faded, and the medallion could no longer hear her cries. The Crystal Medallion thought, What's going on? Is Glenitant doing something to her?

Neither Lord Daegal nor the medallion knew of Glenitant's death. It was the golden ropes, not Glenitant, who were contributing to Crystal's demise. Trussed up like a turkey, the dark sword was lying at the feet of Aerylln, who was holding Baelfire once more. Things were looking pretty bleak for the dark sword.

"Easy come, easy go," Chen said shrugging her shoulders.

"Oh, that's just great. Love me and leave me, why don't you?" Crystal said, her voice dripping with scorn.

"Not a bad idea, given the current state of affairs," Chen groused who, if anything, was a realist.

Chapter 18

With Crystal bound with golden ropes, Chen was again feeling depressed and discouraged, but when the black leather panther glanced over towards the stairwell, what she saw brought true joy to her heart.

"Corson! You old battle-axe, what are you doing here?" she asked while hobbling over to her friend.

After standing quietly and looking at each other for several moments, they smiled and fell into each other's arms. Any apprehension Corson felt about seeing her former master again evaporated.

"How do you like my castle?" Chen asked.

"Black Crystal and black leather are a good fit," Corson said smiling.

Balder, who had come up the stairs after Corson, was watching the two women with some apprehension. Looking over Corson's shoulder, Chen saw Balder and glared at him, hating the man from the moment she saw him. Chen thought, He's a typical man, all muscles and no brains! For Balder, that was far from the truth, but when Chen decided to hate someone, she never went about it halfway.

However Chen was distracted from Balder, for the moment at least, by a young man who reached the top of the stairs, walked quickly over to Aerylln and held her hand. It was Marcheto.

"They deserve each other," Chen said to Corson mocking them.

"He's Aerylln's first boyfriend," Corson said smiling.

"First boy? I had my first man before I was her age."

"Well, that's you."

"It didn't happen again until later, at least not voluntarily," Chen said, anger rising within her at the thought of Lord Daegal's drunken visits to her bedchamber.

Corson already knew that, but something else surprised her. She'd enjoyed Chen's arm being around her, finding it very reassuring, but now she noticed her friend's hand sliding down onto her hip. And she felt Chen's hand giving her a little squeeze.

"So who's your man now?" Corson asked looking closely at her friend.

"I don't have a man, I don't need one, and I'm not looking for one!"

Corson smiled and shook her head, finding Chen as defiant and opinionated as ever.

When a man of towering proportions climbed to the top of the stairs, the subject changed abruptly. It was Pensgraft.

"Of course, there's always an exception to the rule," Chen said making her way over to her only real male friend.

"Did you come up to see what the commotion was all about?" Chen asked smiling at the giant. Leaning up against him, it felt like she was pressed against solid rock. He was massive. Pensgraft made her feel safe, feminine, and he even made her feel happy.

Suddenly, Chen stepped back in alarm! Looking up at him, she felt a bit frightened. For a long time, the black leather panther hadn't depended on anyone but herself, and the thought of actually having someone special in her life unnerved her.

"What's the matter?" Pensgraft asked.

"Nothing," Chen said, but she still had a worried expression on her face. Shaking off her feelings of apprehension, she smiled and said, "Come here and meet this bunch of characters. And I thought I was different!"

Brightening at that thought, she laughed and Pensgraft smiled. The giant liked it when Chen was happy.

Heading over towards the others, Chen was still feeling unsettled. From experience, Chen knew that after being in a relationship for a while, men often got possessive and tried to control the woman. They'd attempt to tell the woman where she could go, what she could do and with whom. Such futile attempts to limit Chen's freedom got on her nerves, as if she'd give up being herself and being in control of her own life for a man. Not likely.

Because guys tried to set rules, every relationship she'd ever been in had ended with Chen walking out. They tried to control her, but all men ever succeeded in doing was making her mad.

On top of that, sooner or later, she would get bored. She'd never yet met a man who could sustain her interest. And Chen didn't like being bored. No one did, not really, and Chen least of all. Once boredom set in, the man was shoved out, regardless of the cost to herself or to him. The uncertainty of change was preferable to being ground down by a relationship that was more like a millstone than anything else.

Fortunately for Chen, she had stumbled upon the joy of confrontation, and it became her one, true passion. Defying and fighting, twin pleasures serving as outlets for her frustration and anger.

Yet walking next to Pensgraft, she was discovering that friendship, itself, could be a good thing. Less pressure, no boundaries, intellectual conversation and not having to be around him all the time.

But a nagging little voice at the back of her consciousness was reminding her that friendship involves trust! Gads!

Sex she might give a man, but trust? No way!

But as she reached Aerylln, Zorya, Baelfire, Eldwyn, Corson and Balder, a band of creative malcontents, as she saw them, Chen began to relax. She also quickly realized that this giant already knew some of them.

"Nice to see you again, Pensgraft," Baelfire said.

"I'm happy to see you're all right," Zorya added with a sigh of relief.

"Thank you both, but can someone explain why I wasn't able to get up the stairway until now?" Pensgraft asked.

"Oh, was the stairway blocked?" Baelfire asked innocently.

"So, it was you? I should have known," Pensgraft laughed.

"When I came up those stairs with Aerylln, I didn't know what I was getting into. So, I figured it was best to keep most people downstairs," Baelfire said.

"Oh, I see. Your protective maternal instincts kicked in again, did they?"

"Yes, something like that," Baelfire admitted. "After some hundreds of years, one starts to feel one knows best."

"Well, sister, after some hundreds of years, I feel I know what's best, too. And what's best is for you to untie me and let me be with Chen," Crystal said in a huff.

"Some of us learn slower than others," Baelfire said looking sternly at her half-sister.

"If I had a wizard of my own, I wouldn't be in this mess," Crystal grumped. "And if I had my own magic horse, I would be long gone!"

"Since it was you who turned me into a horse, why don't you go out and get yourself another one?" Zorya asked, her hooves tramping close to Crystal's hilt.

"Well, you were one of a kind. It's not exactly easy to find women like you."

"How about changing me back now?"

"Untie me, and I will."

"I'd rather be a horse than see you on the loose again."

"Fine, then enjoy being a horse because you're going to stay one for a long time," Crystal said taunting her.

Aerylln walked over to Zorya, stroked her mane and said, "I like my horse."

Crystal wanted to say something caustic, but she held her peace for fear of Baelfire. After all, by Baelfire's own choice, the teenage girl was now her half-sister's master.

Although Crystal couldn't speak freely, she thought, Let me catch you away from Baelfire, and I'll change you into a horse, too. And we'll see how much you like that.

Suddenly, Aerylln felt something cold and slimy creeping up next to her. Turning around, she didn't see anyone, and the feeling went away. For now.

Very gently, Baelfire began to broach a sensitive topic with Aerylln. The young woman's father was just a few feet from her, and she didn't even know it. Baelfire thought, After so many years apart, how do I introduce them? Baelfire decided to try approaching the subject from an historical perspective.

"Aerylln, I didn't mention it before, but I knew your grandmother," Baelfire said.

"Really? What was she like?"

"She was a noble, courageous woman, and her name was Lyssa."

"That's a pretty name."

"Yes, it is. Well, your grandmother only had one child, a boy. He grew up to be a man, and that man and your mother had you."

"I remember my mother a little, but I can't remember my father at all. I try hard to see his face, but I can't."

Pensgraft almost died inside when he heard that, and the giant felt like he needed to sit down. Chen put a hand against his back to steady him.

It's amazing how a man this big can be cut down by a girl this small, Chen thought. That's why I don't trust love. All it ever does is cause pain.

As Aerylln was speaking, Baelfire kept a cautious eye on Pensgraft.

"I always wanted a father, but now I guess it doesn't matter. I have you, Zorya, Corson and Eldwyn. And Marcheto," Aerylln said looking at him and squeezing his hand.

Pensgraft took a real hard look at Marcheto. The young man wasn't that much older than Aerylln, but he was still older, and old enough to know more than she did, a lot more. And like fathers down through the ages, Pensgraft wanted to ask him a few questions. Have you touched my daughter? was at the top of the list.

Clenching his fist, Pensgraft almost took a step towards the young warrior. Quickly using her energy, Baelfire gave Pensgraft a restraining push. Taking the hint, Pensgraft remained still.

"Aerylln, you are your father's only child. I'm sure he misses you very much and would love to hold you in his arms again," Baelfire said.

"If he misses me so much, why didn't he ever visit me?"

"Because you are the sole heir, the only woman left in an unbroken matriarchal chain going back 500 years. And from the day you were born, you were always vulnerable to anyone who might want to kidnap or hurt you."

"Who would want to do that?"

"Many people," Baelfire said, and she thought, With Lord Daegal at the top of the list. "Aerylln, for your own protection, you had to stay at Mistress Xan's castle. And your father couldn't visit because I was in his care, and we dared not risk putting you and me together before you came of age. We'd have made too tempting a target."

"But with you, my father could have defended me."

"No, Aerylln, he couldn't. What have I told you about men, women and me?"

"You said men are caretakers, and women are masters."

"Yes, and as a caretaker, your father didn't even have the power you have now. In a man's hands, I'm not much better than an ordinary sword. He couldn't have protected you."

"So, I never really needed him at all," Aerylln said pouting.

Sighing in frustration, Baelfire looked upward for guidance.

Pensgraft looked at Baelfire, and he shook his head. The sword read her former custodian's mind as Pensgraft thought, For now, don't pursue it further. It's not the right time.

Feeling greatly saddened, Baelfire thought, Once again, the price of power is that, often times, a person's all alone. In this case, it's a teenage girl who's trying to be very brave.

"If anyone's interested, which I doubt, Glenitant said my father's here. He abandoned me, the great Ambassador Ritalso, and I want to find him," Chen said angrily.

Chen knew Aerylln was Pensgraft's daughter, but the warrior woman wasn't hoping for a tearful reunion with her own father. She just wanted to tell him off, and thought, He'd better be holding a sword when I meet him. If he's not, someone should give him one real quick. If I don't like what he has to say, he might need it.

At that moment, Gwendylln appeared at the top of the stairs, and Chen asked, "So what are you doing, Baelfire? Letting people up here one at a time?"

"Pretty much. I just thought you might need her for moral support."

"Are you serious? Gwendylln doesn't have any scruples, let alone morals," Chen said laughing. "But what she can do is fight."

"It's just a phrase. I meant..."

"I know what you meant. You're saying I can't handle my own father."

"No, that's not it. However, Gwendylln might keep you from murdering him. You wouldn't kill Gwendylln, would you?"

"No, I owe her too much, my life several times over, for example. But how did you know what I was thinking about my father? Are you a mind reader, on top of everything else?"

"Something like that, I suppose."

"I can read minds, too," Crystal said piping up.

"Keep quiet, no one asked for your opinion," Baelfire told her half-sister.

"I am so under appreciated," the dark sword laughed.

"When I go see my father, can I take Crystal with me?" Chen asked Baelfire.

"Oh, how I love family reunions!" Crystal said laughing already knowing that Baelfire would never let her go along.

"Listen here, young lady, don't ever touch that sword. Not ever!" Eldwyn said, all too aware of Crystal's potential for treachery.

"Is that right, grandpa?" Chen sneered.

"Hey, I like the old guy," Corson said.

"Oh, please, tell me there's nothing going on between you and this old geezer," Chen said looking at Corson in amazement.

"No, not yet," Corson laughed. "But if he's near Baelfire much longer, he might be a target. When I first met Eldwyn, he could barely walk and was blind as a bat. Now he's an excellent horseman, and he took those steps coming up here two at a time."

"Well, I'm glad you both get along so well," Chen said cynically. And then, with a mischievous grin on her face, she added, "You know what I'd like to see you do with him?"

"Not in front of Aerylln," Corson cautioned.

"Who is this girl?" Chen asked in frustration. "Why doesn't someone send her out to play, or off to bed, or something?"

"Let's go find your father," Corson said changing the subject.

Catching Chen's eye, Gwendylln smiled, and the three warrior women headed upstairs.

"If I were her father and knew she was coming, I would run," Pensgraft said. And he meant it.

Chapter 19

Stopping for a moment and counting on the good sword's telepathic ability to read minds, Chen wondered, Baelfire, does Crystal know exactly where my father is?

"Hold on there! Why are you asking my sister anything?" Crystal telepathically asked in a huff. "I know where your father is, but I should warn you, what Glenitant told you about him isn't quite correct."

"What do you mean?"

"You'll see. Your father's room is two flights up, the first door on the left."

Wearing a sword, the scabbard hanging from a belt around her waist, Chen headed upstairs with the tip bumping against each step. The warrior woman walked the whole way up with her sword going, "Clank, clank, clank!"

Chen's father, Ritalso, locked in a room at the top of the stairs, heard the noise echoing throughout the stairwell. To him, it sounded like Glenitant was approaching. Whenever the old witch moved about, she had used Crystal like a walking stick and always made that same clanking sound.

Going over to the window and looking down on the courtyard below, Ritalso noticed that nothing was stirring in this incredible fortress, other than his sister it seemed. Feeling a sense of wonder once more, the elderly gentleman knew he'd never seen a castle as beautiful as this.

When Ritalso had first arrived, he was amazed. The white-haired gentleman, prison having aged him prematurely, had marveled at the awesome beauty of Crystal Castle. He was so impressed by its sheer artistic elegance that he'd felt sure his sister must have changed while he was away.

But Ritalso had overestimated his sister's capacity for self-healing. In fact, Glenitant seemed meaner and older than before, constant exposure to Crystal having aged her prematurely as well.

What Ritalso didn't know was that Glenitant and Crystal had been having serious problems with their relationship. It was endlessly stressful and a serious emotional strain affecting Glenitant mentally and physically. The grating tension between herself and the evil sword wasn't exactly good for her health.

Being at odds with a magic sword, and a dark one at that, had worn her out. Crystal, well aware of this, was intentionally driving Glenitant into an early grave. As it was, the dark sword had succeeded.

However, alone in his chambers, Ritalso knew nothing of Glenitant's death and had no idea Chen was even at Crystal Castle.

When the clanking stopped outside his door, Ritalso listened for the sound of a key being inserted into the lock. What came instead was a knock.

"Come in," the elderly gentleman said having no idea why his sister would be knocking on the door of his jail cell. Well, it wasn't actually a jail cell, but he was being confined behind a locked door.

When Ritalso had arrived at Crystal Castle, Glenitant openly admitted she intended on using him to influence Chen. He figured his sister had some wild scheme, but Ritalso wasn't sure what to do. After being imprisoned, he was a broken man both emotionally and physically. Swamped with despair, Ritalso knew he no longer had the strength to resist Glenitant.

In his weakened condition, Ritalso was frightened that he would sell out his daughter rather than go back to jail. He loved Chen and would gladly die for her, but he could no longer stand imprisonment.

As he waited for Glenitant to enter the room, Ritalso dreaded what was coming next. But instead of the door swinging wide open, he heard an angry, unfamiliar voice making threats.

"Open this door, or we'll kick it in!" the woman shouted.

"It's locked," Ritalso said in a weak, raspy voice.

"We know it's locked, you fool. Unlock it now!" the woman shouted.

"I can't."

"You can't or you won't?" Chen asked. Impatient to get her hands around her father's throat, she didn't wait for an answer. Turning to Gwendylln, she told the captain of her personal guard to kick in the door.

The sound of splintering wood echoed down the hallway while Chen, Gwendylln and Corson unsheathed their swords and rushed into the room. Feelings of anger, confusion and sadness over having been abandoned for years welled up inside of Chen, and she gripped her sword tightly. She was about to meet a man she once loved, but who was now, to her, nothing more than a stranger. Yes, her father helped bring her into this world, but now she was tempted to give him death in return.

Stepping from behind Gwendylln, who'd entered the room first, Chen saw a sickly, half-starved man in front of her. Ignoring him, she strode over to a door and ripped it open ready to confront the man who'd ruined her life, but she didn't find anyone. It was just a closet.

Undaunted, Chen returned to the frail, old man and shouted, "Where's Ambassador Ritalso?"

"I've never heard of an Ambassador Ritalso," the sickly man said.

Chen was in no mood to argue. The black leather panther wanted to find the ambassador, and she wanted to find him now! Shoving the old man up against a wall, Chen put a hand on his throat.

"I was told Ambassador Ritalso was in this room! Are you one of his personal retainers? Where is he?"

The warrior woman put her face up against his. Ritalso felt like his head was in the mouth of a hungry lion, except Chen was far more dangerous. A lion killed for food and to protect its turf, but Chen sometimes killed for no reason at all. And the frail old man was getting mighty close to finding that out.

"I'm Ritalso," the frightened man squeaked as Chen tightened her grip on his throat.

"Ambassador Ritalso?" Chen asked in surprise.

"No, just Ritalso."

"Are you the man who traveled about representing Lord Daegal throughout the furthest reaches of his realm?" she asked glaring at him.

Ritalso felt like he was ready to black out.

"No, I've been in one of Lord Daegal's dungeons, at least until recently," he said before collapsing. That is, he would have fallen down if Chen weren't holding him firmly against the wall by his throat. As it was, his legs just went limp.

"Let him go," Corson whispered in Chen's ear.

Gwendylln looked at Corson as if she'd lost her mind.

"Wow, you really have been away for a long time, haven't you?" Gwendylln said unable to think of another reason to explain Corson's suicidal behavior. When Chen was in a foul mood, to interfere was virtually a death wish.

Whirling around, Chen punched Corson in the chest with a rock hard fist knocking her completely off balance. Without hesitation, Chen unsheathed her sword and spun around whipping the blade at the surprised warrior woman.

In a flash, Corson's own sword was out, and she parried the blow. Gaining momentum, Chen swung her sword over her head, but the blade struck the black crystal ceiling above her. The warrior woman realized they shouldn't be fighting with swords in a confined space, so she threw it aside and drew her knife. Problem solved.

Blinded by rage, Chen had no idea who she was fighting. To her, Corson was a faceless, nameless opponent, a stranger to attack and kill.

Most warriors, men or women, would have been terrified by the sheer savagery of Chen's assault, but this was Corson she was fighting.

However, Corson wasn't smiling or amused, and the warrior woman knew she was fighting for her life. But there was something Chen didn't know. Corson had made peace with death a long time ago and didn't care if she lived or died. Thus, Corson could take greater risks and counterattack more fiercely.

But Corson was unaware of an important part of Chen's psychological makeup. The black leather panther didn't care whether she lived or died either. This allowed Chen to take enormous risks and to continue the ferocity of her attack.

In short, they were evenly matched.

And so, the ever-resourceful Corson, seeking the quickest and simplest solution to the problem, kicked her former boss in her wounded thigh, the wound Chen had earlier received from Glenitant's lance.

When Chen didn't seem to notice the pain, Corson was impressed. And, almost as a compliment, she kicked Chen's wounded thigh again. This time, Corson saw Chen blink, but the pain didn't slow the black leather panther's arm when she swung a knife at Corson's throat.

Swelling with pride over Chen's prowess as a warrior, Corson decided that she owed the black leather panther the best she could throw at her.

However, Chen had felt both blows to her thigh, the kicks causing enough pain to clear her mind. And so now, the black leather panther was fully aware of whom she was fighting, and she was impressed with Corson's willingness to exploit her wounded thigh. Chen was proud of Corson and felt she owed this tough warrior woman the best she could throw at her. Squaring off, they went at each other like wild animals.

Knives flew through the air with blinding speed, and they were both starting to enjoy themselves. After one particularly wicked thrust, Chen looked into Corson's eyes, and the women smiled at each other.

Wanting to end the fight, but not willing to yield, Chen kicked Corson in the chest sending the warrior woman flying. Bouncing off the opposite wall and making a good, solid thud, it sounded like Corson was in excellent condition. That made Chen want to kick her again, but the black leather panther fell down laughing instead. Having ended up sitting on the floor, Corson leaned back and joined in the laughter.

"Was it good for you?" Chen asked laughing so hard she was almost in tears.

"I'd have brought you some flowers, or something, if I knew you were going to be that good," Corson said smiling.

"But will you respect me in the morning?" Chen asked continuing to laugh.

"I don't see why. I never respected you before, why should I start now?" Corson chuckled.

After they caught their breath, Chen pointed at the crumpled figure on the other side of the room. "Who do you think that is?"

"Well, I hate to say it, but I think that's what's left of your father."

After getting to her feet, Chen glared down scornfully at the elderly-looking man on the floor. "No doubt he wasted himself away on women, booze, and whatever while traveling for years."

Corson looked at her friend compassionately, but this time remained silent.

Smiling grimly at Corson, Gwendylln thought, Good, you've learned the most important rule. When Chen's upset, keep quiet.

"All through my teenage years, my father wasn't there for me, and now he's still no use to me. I hate him," the black leather panther said scowling.

That's the end of Chen and her father, Gwendylln thought. He could be dying of starvation or freezing to death, and Chen wouldn't toss him a crust of bread or a blanket. So much for family.

Corson and Gwendylln followed Chen back downstairs leaving Ritalso to his own devices, which mainly included lying on the floor unconscious and moaning occasionally.

A few doors down the hallway, Baelfire, Aerylln and Marcheto observed the warrior women leaving. Baelfire had wanted to be in the vicinity in case things got out of hand, but she decided not to intervene when Chen and Corson were fighting. At the time, Baelfire had thought, After all, that's what warriors do, isn't it?

Creeping along the hallway, Baelfire, Aerylln and Marcheto looked down the stairwell wanting to make sure the warrior women were gone. After watching them entering the great hall, the rescue team rushed into Ritalso's room.

Taking one look at the emaciated man on the floor, Aerylln's heart went out to him. The teenage girl's helpful, innocent nature surfaced and fortunately being openly vulnerable was safe, up to a point. In the guise of Baelfire, Aerylln had a guardian angel watching over her. Hurting this teenager would not go unpunished.

Kneeling down beside Ritalso, Aerylln placed Baelfire on his chest. Suddenly, Chen's father took a deep breath, his chest arching upward and eyes opening wide. The gray pallor left his skin, and he seemed to be putting on weight. Within half an hour, Ritalso was able to sit up.

"The leader of the women who came crashing in here, who was she?" Ritalso asked.

Baelfire didn't have the heart to tell him it was Chen, the daughter for whom he'd sacrificed so much. So, being vague and evasive, the good sword said, "Oh, she sort of owns Crystal Castle."

"She owns it? What about Glenitant?"

"Well, Glenitant's no longer with us," Baelfire informed him.

"Where did she go?"

"Out a great hall window, I'm afraid."

"Good riddance."

"That's exactly how we feel," Baelfire agreed. "So, are you well enough to come downstairs?"

"Yes, I believe so. But tell me, who does Glenitant's sword, Crystal, belong to now?"

"No one at the moment, she's sort of indisposed. Tied up, that is," Baelfire said.

"I was afraid my daughter, Chen, would inherit that miserable sword."

"No, Chen almost got hold of Crystal, but Baelfire stopped her. Chen owns the castle, but not Crystal," Aerylln said in a rush.

"I thought the leader of those warrior women owns the castle?" Ritalso said.

"Well, yes, she does," Baelfire admitted, and the good sword waited as Ritalso put two and two together.

"You mean, that woman was Chen?" he asked feeling shocked and surprised. "My daughter is the owner of Crystal Castle?"

"Yes," Aerylln said trying to be helpful.

"But she doesn't own Crystal, the dark sword?"

"No," Aerylln assured him.

"But what do I do now? How can I possibly communicate with a daughter who's that hostile?"

"I'd give her some time," Baelfire counseled.

"I didn't recognize my own daughter. I've missed out on everything. I'm so empty and alone, how do I even begin to rebuild?"

"I'm not sure, but it's an interesting question," Marcheto said. "Maybe we can begin by simply looking around this room. Using your powers of observation, what do you see?"

"Nothing but a window, a small closet and the four of us."

"What else?"

"Nothing."

"Okay, I agree, the rest of the room is empty," Marcheto said. "But we're sitting within that emptiness, aren't we?"

"I don't understand."

"We can sit here on the floor only because the room is empty. Look outside the door. See the hallway wall?"

"Yes?" Ritalso said wondering where Marcheto was heading with all this.

"Go over to the wall and walk into it."

"I can't."

"And why not?"

"Because the wall is solid. I can't walk into a solid wall."

"So, can we agree that emptiness is needed?"

"Yes," Ritalso said. "But I'm not a room, I'm a person."

"Then, I wonder if emptiness works the same way with people? All I'm saying is that where there's nothing, there's great potential."

"Marcheto, I don't have the strength to rebuild," Ritalso said.

"What if you allowed the emptiness to rebuild your life for you?"

"What do you mean?"

"Your inner emptiness might be of great value to someone who needs a close friend. Eager to be filled, you're receptive to the thoughts and feelings of others. You would make a great listener. It's a rare person, indeed, who's genuinely interested in the lives of others."

"I hope you're right," Ritalso said. "Otherwise, it's going to be a long, lonely life."

Chapter 20

While Chen, Gwendylln and Corson were upstairs in Ritalso's room, Pensgraft and over 50 warriors were gathering in Crystal Castle's courtyard discussing the ramifications of Glenitant's death. Dartuke and the noblemen, Balder and his men, and Chen's warrior women were present, which was virtually everyone living in Crystal Castle. Everyone human.

All agreed that Lord Daegal's warriors, who'd escorted Pensgraft and were camped outside the castle walls, should be stopped from returning to The Rock. It was imperative that they be kept from reporting Glenitant's death and about the dark sword being taken prisoner.

"Crystal Castle's extremely vulnerable, and if word reaches Lord Daegal, we'll be in serious trouble," Pensgraft said gravely.

After quickly consulting with the other nobles, Dartuke said, "Yes, if Lord Daegal realizes our predicament, he'll most certainly attack."

"We need time to build up our forces," Thordig, another of the nobles, said. "But if Lord Daegal discovers that we intend on using Crystal Castle as a base for a rebellion, he'll move against us even faster."

Malavika, third in command of Chen's warrior women, said, "So let me get this straight. You're talking about the 25 warriors Lord Daegal sent along to guard Pensgraft? Is that correct?"

"Yes, to prevent me from escaping," Pensgraft said.

"And we can't allow any of them to get away. We must decide on a plan of attack," Dartuke said, a sense of urgency filling his voice.

"Isn't the course of action obvious?" Malavika asked winking at the warrior women under her command. Mounted on their black stallions, the women were shaking their heads and smiling.

"Listen guys, how about letting the girls handle this one?" Malavika said chuckling. "We'll approach them under the covers. I mean under the cover of darkness."

The warrior women shifted in their saddles.

"But first, I need to find Chen and tell her about this," Malavika added, but she didn't have to look far.

Chen, Gwendylln, and Corson walked out of the tower entrance into the courtyard. The black leather panther didn't recognize the nobles, but they knew her, and their mood turned hostile. Reacting instantly, Chen's warrior women dismounted and formed a protective circle around her.

"What's the matter? Haven't my women been nice to you?" Chen sneered seeing the angry expressions on the nobles' faces.

Feeling annoyed, Dartuke took a step in Chen's direction. Gwendylln quickly unsheathed her sword holding it to his throat. Immediately, all the nobles reached for their swords, Chen's warrior women following suit, and dozens of weapons leapt from their scabbards.

"Oh, this is a great beginning," Balder said. "Why don't we save Lord Daegal the trouble by killing each other? That way, he can walk into Crystal Castle unopposed."

Chen gave Balder a withering look. It made her feel a little better.

"Don't you remember us, Chen?" Dartuke asked.

"No, why?"

"Not long ago, you murdered my friend and his two sons," Dartuke said. "Have you forgotten so soon?"

The black leather panther probably had forgotten about it.

Due to her highly independent nature, Chen rarely connected with other people's wants and needs. Most people, upon interacting with her, found this to be a great source of irritation. Also, at least to others, Chen's view of life could be frustratingly narrow. If something wasn't on the black leather panther's personal agenda, it didn't exist.

And for Chen, life wasn't so much divided by hours, days and weeks but by seconds and minutes. The warrior woman was intensely aware of every waking moment of every hour. Therefore, asking Chen to recall what happened last week was like asking her to dig up an ancient artifact. To her, it had been buried long ago.

Adding to the complexity, Chen saw everything around her in fractions. For every one thing most people noticed, Chen saw not only that but all its component parts. The black leather panther saw life in enormous detail, and this went on all day, every day. Therefore, if something took place last week, it had already been relegated to life's dusty archives.

Chen wasn't imagining these problems. They were real for her. Chen was brilliant, but the strain of being herself took its toll on the black leather panther and on everyone around her.

However, the nobles considered Chen nothing more than a gifted killer, a murderer. Balder, for that matter, had recently lost several men to her madness. Yet, for Chen, this was all in the past.

"Just let go of it," the black leather panther said providing Dartuke with her brief and direct advice.

"Letting go isn't easy. He was a good friend."

"Then come join him in death!" Chen shouted pushing past Gwendylln.

Corson wanted to help, but she knew better than to get between Chen and Dartuke. When the black leather panther was on stage, which is what a fight was to her, it was wise not to disrupt the flow of the play. Chen had an extremely tight mental focus. She intimidated telepathically, locking onto an opponent's psyche and letting him feel the force of her willpower. Being around Chen was an education and could be very instructive, if it didn't make you a nervous wreck.

Keeping well away from Chen, Corson spoke up. "We have serious differences, but keep in mind that it was Chen who secured Crystal Castle, thus providing us with a base of operations. And whom do you want more, Chen or Lord Daegal?"

"Both," Thordig growled.

"Chen has allies at The Rock who may prove useful," Corson said. "Also, the dark sword views Chen as her master. Even tied up, Crystal could still be dangerous, and we may need to rely on Chen to control her."

"Plus, she's our leader, and we'll need her approval, if we're going to dispatch Lord Daegal's warriors for you," Malavika reminded the nobles.

Chen gave her a questioning look.

"We can't allow Lord Daegal's warriors to return home, can we? Well, Dartuke favors a conventional attack, but I pointed out that a blanket can be more powerful than a sword."

"Sounds like a party," Gwendylln said wearing a grim smile, having participated in a similar operation that was dangerous, devious and seductive.

"Can't I be away for an hour without you thinking about men and sex?" Chen laughed.

"Oh, we'll kill them all, eventually," Malavika assured her.

"Gwendylln, would you like to be in charge of this rather unorthodox military maneuver?" Chen asked, very aware of what Malavika was suggesting.

"My pleasure."

"Okay girls, put on your makeup," Chen said, a code phrase ordering her warrior women to prepare for battle.

Chapter 21

At dusk, Gwendylln mounted her black stallion and rode out of Crystal Castle heading for the encampment where Lord Daegal's men were staying. Mentally she readied herself to implement the course of action she and the other warrior women had decided upon. They would use as little sex as necessary to lure the men into dropping their guards, then kill them as quickly and efficiently as possible.

War is unpredictable and something can always go wrong, but as Gwendylln got closer to the encampment, she put all concerns and doubts out of her mind. Riding past a sentry, he recognized her and waved the warrior woman onward.

Gwendylln saw Lord Daegal's men gathered around their cooking fires finishing their evening meal. Taking a deep breath, she steadied herself and rode boldly into their midst.

"How about a little dessert?" she shouted heartily, overcoming her fears with brash behavior.

"I'll have some!" one man called out.

Gwendylln dismounted and literally took matters into her own hands. Striding up to a warrior, she gripped his face with both hands proceeding to kiss him roughly, so roughly it appeared to onlookers like she was chewing off his lips.

After nearly devouring the man, Gwendylln pulled back and smiled. Covered with teeth marks, the warrior's mouth was bleeding from several puncture wounds where she'd cut deeply into his skin.

"Who's next?" Gwendylln shouted shoving him aside.

As the warriors formed a circle around her, she saw the lust in their eyes. This was the moment Gwendylln had been dreading, the development of a mob mentality. Making a quick decision, she threw them off balance by striking first. Slamming a forearm against one warrior's chest, she knocked him down and began unlacing his pants. Mesmerized by this unexpected development, Lord Daegal's men froze and looked on in amazement.

However, sneaking up from behind, one warrior grabbed her shoulder. Having been taken by surprise, Gwendylln's years of relentless training took over, and her knife was out in a flash. Whirling around and lashing out at him, the blade cut along the upper palm of the man's hand severing two fingers.

Looking at his mangled hand, he began screaming but unsheathed a knife with his good hand and lunged at Gwendylln. Another male warrior intervened punching the attacker square in the jaw, and the wounded man dropped to the ground in a crumpled heap. Gwendylln's defender, and most of the men, didn't want such a pretty woman cut up, at least not yet.

On Chen's command, Malavika and three other warrior women performed a flanking maneuver entering the encampment from the east. After making their way towards a roaring campfire, they allowed their figures to be in silhouette so their curves and flowing hair were clearly outlined. They appeared to be dark warriors engulfed in flames.

"You've finished eating, but how about rustling up something for us?" Malavika shouted trying to draw attention to herself and women with her.

This tactic caused about half the men to turn from Gwendylln and head over towards the flaming angels of death. With the encampment in disarray, Chen now led a frontal attack with 22 seasoned warrior women calmly riding in and dismounting by a different fire. Each woman picked out a target and walked towards him dropping articles of clothing along the way. By the time a woman reached her man, he was already defeated whether he realized it or not.

After allowing the men to kiss them, each of the women led her man into the darkness away from the others for privacy. At least that's what they told them.

Dividing and conquering can be an effective strategy, and Chen's warriors used it to their full advantage.

Gradually, here and there, sharp grunts punctuated the air sounding like a release, but it was too early for that. Instead, they were death cries. The women were killing the men quietly and efficiently.

The cries continued disturbing the stillness of the night, and each woman took whatever time was necessary to tempt her man into dropping his guard. When he did, the man died quickly and silently.

Some of Lord Daegal's men were more difficult to fool, so some got more than others, but it ended up the same way, a knife shoved into a critical and lethal area. To Chen's warriors, the shock and surprise on the men's faces was almost comical, but none of the women laughed outright. A few of their sisters were still engaged in the task at hand, and stealth was vital.

But suddenly horses began neighing wildly, men started shouting and the clash of metal against metal filled the air. Chen had anticipated this, so before arriving at the encampment, she'd told Corson to dispatch her man as quickly as possible.

Chen wanted Corson ready to help troubleshoot any problems that might arise.

As sounds of combat filled the air, some of Lord Daegal's other warriors shoved their women aside. Then, jumping up to see what the commotion was all about, and finally being distracted, they died at the hands of a female assassin.

From experience, Chen had learned there were a few men, very few, who were ruled by their minds, not their genitalia. Such men were rare enough to be considered an endangered species. And tonight, Chen intended on endangering them even more.

When the fighting broke out, the black leather panther and Corson were already mounted and ready. Both women knew conflicts might arise, and Chen was excellent at planning for various contingencies.

In addition to Corson, the black leather panther had ordered four more of her best warriors to dispatch their men almost instantly. These women were fully dressed as well and mounted on their black stallions. One was stationed north of the encampment, one stationed south, another to the east, and a fourth to the west of the battlefield.

Being highly disciplined, experienced warrior women, when pockets of resistance did break out, they remained where they were in case trouble arose in their own sector, their primary task being to prevent escape.

Chen and Corson were rovers, and their role was to head for any trouble and quell resistance before an escape was attempted. However, there was one thing Chen hadn't anticipated. Several men were willing to die helping another get away to inform Lord Daegal.

Even before seeing them, Chen realized several of her warrior women could already be dead. That knowledge made the black leather panther angry enough to remain calm. She forced herself to think clearly and to observe what was happening.

With swords drawn, three men were fighting back-to-back against six warrior women who were in a frenzy to prevent them from escaping. The three men died, but the one they were protecting was riding off into the darkness.

Spurring their horses into action, Chen and Corson rode after the male warrior who was heading west towards The Rock. The warrior woman stationed in that sector darted towards him, but the man turned in the saddle, raised his bow and launched an arrow at her. When Chen heard her warrior crying out and saw the woman clutching her right shoulder, the black leather panther decided enough was enough.

Earlier, a few of Lord Daegal's men had been snooping around inside the castle, Chen remembered. So, does this man know about Glenitant's death? Or about the dark sword being taken prisoner?

Chen wasn't sure of the answer, but she knew he could still report that 24 of Lord Daegal's warriors were dead. And the black leather panther certainly didn't want that information reaching her uncle's ears.

Chapter 22

Chen instinctively took the lead but remembering Corson's remarkable eyesight, her old friend having incredible night vision, the black leather panther yielded her place out in front. Being an excellent commander, Chen put the mission first and herself second.

Additionally, Corson's mare, Tempest, was exceptional in her own right possessing an incredible level of endurance. When other horses had run themselves into the ground, Tempest would still have a mile or two left in her. And so Corson's strategy was simple, she would push the male warrior's horse to the point of exhaustion, and then kill the rider.

Corson rarely gave any thought to taking someone prisoner. And as far as Chen, she didn't know what a prisoner was. Oh, the black leather panther had seen people in jail but never put anyone in a cell personally. And she'd never buried any of her enemies, leaving them on the ground where they died. After having suffered repeated abuse as a teen, she often appeared remorseless. But for whatever reason, both Corson and Chen were out for the kill.

The path of the male warrior was obvious for there was only one western entrance into the valley and one way out. So, what it came down to was an uphill horserace. And the switchback trail leading up the mountain was a four-mile stretch of well-packed earth. The endurance race from hell.

What the male warrior had going for him were his feelings of desperation since such people are often unpredictable and dangerous. However, the two warrior women chasing him were always unpredictable and dangerous, whether desperate or not, and the man's predicament had simply lifted him to their level of readiness.

With his horse charging up the mountain, the male warrior was riding with relentless determination. And the warhorse was smart, tough and ready to die before letting another horse overtake him. The man riding him was a good master, and the horse had known none other, the male warrior having raised the warhorse from a foal.

As adrenaline poured into the animal's bloodstream, the warhorse knew today was the reason he'd been born. All of life converged on this moment. Now was the day to give back to a master who'd given so much to him. The warhorse would go to his death proudly and without hesitation. And so, gritting his teeth, the animal stretched out his neck and lengthened his stride.

Chasing this noble animal up the mountain path, Chen and Corson had made a serious error. They didn't respect the man, but they should have respected the horse. Instead, the two warrior women had underestimated the enemy.

Their true enemy was the horse. His name was Zenithstar.

Listening to the horses behind him, Zenithstar noticed that the sound of their hooves was getting louder, which meant they were gaining on him. Fear entered his heart. Not fear of death, but fear of failure.

As the grueling race wore on, Zenithstar's mind was fogging over from pain and becoming dull, but he raced upward determined to get as much as possible from every stride. Even as the pain worsened, seeping into his shoulders, Zenithstar raced ahead detaching himself from his own flesh, unconsciously stepping outside of his own body. He wasn't going to allow the enormous strain on his body to ruin his chances for reaching the top of the mountain first. And this became his goal. He begged his flesh to last that long. And he refused to panic.

A lesser horse would have surrendered, but Zenithstar thought, I just can't lose. I can't. Please, anything but that. Give me strength!

Drawing on energy from a higher power, Zenithstar found himself getting his second wind. It was more like sneaking past death, the warhorse nearing total exhaustion and close to collapsing.

Yet as noise from the horses behind him receded, Zenithstar realized he was going to win and felt so relieved that he almost wept. Taking a deep breath, the warhorse thought, Now I'll show those other horses who they're dealing with!

However, Zenithstar had no need to prove himself to anyone, especially not to Corson's warhorse, Tempest, who already knew she was dealing with a contender. Tempest respected her opponent, paid homage to him and honored him. Tempest even gave Zenithstar the ultimate compliment considering the warhorse to be worth killing.

This awareness of Zenithstar's quality made the chase important to Tempest, who decided to test her own ability against the raging horseflesh in front of her.

If necessary, Tempest was willing to chase Zenithstar through hell. In fact, she kind of savored the thought. Tempest was as strong as Corson, and as tough as Chen. Still, Tempest had her hands full with the beast in front of her.

Before Zenithstar had gotten his second wind, and when he'd been at the very height of his pain, the noble warhorse was driving his body mercilessly and was worried that his aching limbs would cause him to stumble. Unable to shake the torment in his body, Zenithstar had lost track of where his legs were. The warhorse knew he was moving forward at a quick pace, he just could no longer tell why.

But that was all behind him now, and he raced at top speed feeling a sense of exhilaration.

Charging ahead, Zenithstar began distancing himself from the horses behind him. He wasn't exactly leaving them in his wake, but they weren't gaining on him either. The warhorse was so happy that he almost laughed. Immediately taking this as a warning sign, Zenithstar thought, If I'm becoming giddy, I must be near my breaking point.

But then, to his total amazement, he reached the mountaintop. Hardly able to believe his good fortune, Zenithstar thought, I've achieved my goal, and my struggle is over. I've made it!

The warhorse couldn't handle the idea of going any further, and so now it was the rider's turn to take control. Pulling on Zenithstar's reins, he did what a warrior had to do in battle. He expected even more from his horse. The rider realized that they should never have made it as far as they did, but somehow they had. And demanding more wasn't easy.

Having raised this horse, the male warrior had fed Zenithstar carrots and apples and, on several occasions when the animal was ill, had slept with him in the barn at night. Now, with a heavy heart, he needed to ask more of his friend, though Zenithstar wasn't just a horse, he was a part of the rider's own soul. And yet, near tears, the rider did something he'd thought he'd never do. He took his whip and beat his horse.

When Zenithstar felt the whip on his flesh, he was stunned. The warhorse had never tasted the bite of a whip before. It hurt, and it just kept coming! The whip landed again and again searing his backside. In the past, Zenithstar had felt a sword's steel blade ripping his flesh, and he knew what it was like to endure battle wounds.

But whipped? he thought in surprise. Whipped!

He found the experience humiliating. It told Zenithstar that his master no longer trusted him to give everything. Gritting his teeth, the warhorse was determined to prove his master wrong.

Chen looked ahead at Tempest trying to will Corson's horse to go faster. Chen's stallion had performed admirably, but now the black leather panther was up against something greater than combat, greater than exhaustion, and even greater than the power of death.

Corson, Tempest, Chen and her black stallion were fighting the love of a horse for its master. And when the male rider dug his heels into Zenithstar's sides, the horse leapt forward.

Be careful, and don't stumble, Zenithstar thought heading down the path. The warhorse knew most accidents happened going down a mountain. Most travelers are alert while going up, but they become lax going down figuring the difficult part of the trip is behind them.

However, feeling overwhelmed by a sense of bone-crushing fatigue, Zenithstar knew that going down this mountain was going to be a nightmare. He could barely stand, let alone gallop down a winding path cloaked in darkness with two warriors on horseback trying to kill his rider and himself.

The clatter of hooves pounding on the hard-packed trail continued echoing throughout the mountains disrupting the serenity of the night. And as Zenithstar faltered, Corson and Chen began gaining ground.

Zenithstar had done all he could do. His body was shutting down. The valiant horse was dying.

Getting closer, Corson unsheathed her knife and tossed it at the male warrior nicking his cheek. Glancing behind him, while tasting his own blood, the man was almost thrown from the saddle when Zenithstar stumbled, and stumbled hard. Knowing his horse was done for, the rider drew his sword and prepared to dismount, determined to fight till the end.

But that was not to be, for Zenithstar took a sharp turn to the right, doing so when considerably shy of the approaching right-hand, hairpin turn of the switchback.

Stepping off the trail into thin air, Zenithstar fell like a stone.

When his front hooves touched down on the mountainside, they buckled causing the warhorse to pitch forward launching his rider into the night air. Zenithstar tucked his head, rolling forward and letting the saddle take most of the blow as his back crashed against the steep embankment. Somehow, the shock cleared his mind reinvigorating Zenithstar, at least a little, and he jammed his hooves into the hillside sending stones and dirt flying.

Zenithstar felt his master's hands grasping his mane and the pommel of his saddle. The male warrior was up and mounted in an instant, which might not have been such a good idea. Zenithstar was still fighting gravity and a very steep incline.

But the two put their trust in each other, which gave them some company since no one else would have given them the slightest chance of surviving. Except, it turned out, for Chen who didn't hesitate to follow her prey.

The black leather panther launched herself over the side of the trail and into the air with such flair that Zenithstar's death-defying act paled by comparison. As her stallion was falling, Chen slid onto the horse's rump. Then, placing her feet on the back of the saddle, she pushed off throwing herself closer to the hillside where she broke her fall by grasping onto roots and tree limbs. However, she still ended up glancing off trees and boulders on the way down.

By the time she reached the path below, Chen was bruised and shaken, but she quickly realized she'd fallen in front of the male warrior and his horse.

Looking up the trail, the black leather panther saw Zenithstar and his rider approaching. And with great satisfaction, the warrior woman noticed that her black stallion had regained his footing and was standing on the trail further down blocking it.

Stepping back into the trees to avoid being seen, Chen grabbed onto the back of Zenithstar's saddle when the male warrior rode past and pulled herself up onto the horse's rump right behind the rider. Quickly reaching down to her boot, the warrior woman pulled out a knife.

The male rider had felt something landing behind him and thought a falling tree limb or rock from above had struck Zenithstar, but it was something far worse.

With Zenithstar about to crash into Chen's stallion, the black leather panther wrapped an arm around the startled man in front of her and held on tight.

Suddenly, Chen decided on a different strategy. Standing up on the horse's rump, she held her knife directly behind where the male warrior's heart would be. Jumping against his back and using him for a springboard, she propelled herself off the horse.

And though this worked out for Chen, it didn't for the male warrior, the black leather panther having kicked the handle of the knife driving it into the man's back and through his heart.

As pain was exploding inside his chest, the male warrior watched in horror as Zenithstar was about to crash into a dusty black stallion. Hoping to avoid the collision, not fully realizing he was dying, the man tried sliding off his saddle only to see the stallion stepping aside and allowing them to pass. The black warhorse's eyes glinted in the moonlight looking smooth as glass.

Then, after falling from his horse, the male warrior saw Zenithstar rearing up and letting out a blistering cry of frustration and rage.

Feeling the horse's love, the warrior died a happy man. He'd done his best, had run a good race and, most of all, his horse was still alive. Neither should have survived this grueling test but one of them did, and the man was glad it was his horse.

Collecting himself, Zenithstar ignored the stallion and swept the path with his eyes coming upon Chen. Somehow, the warhorse instantly knew she was the person who'd killed his master, and Zenithstar hated the black leather panther with all his heart.

"Stand in line," Chen said reading his mind.

Through a haze of exhaustion, Zenithstar realized he had the black leather panther all to himself and exploded in a headlong rush for the warrior woman.

But given the warhorse's level of fatigue, the grieving animal pretty much ended up trotting towards Chen. And even that was agonizing for Zenithstar, so broken was he in mind, body and spirit.

Corson was now beside Chen, and they both watched Zenithstar as the half-dead warhorse attempted to seek revenge.

The loyal horse's valiant effort would have tugged at the heartstrings of most other warriors, but it was wasted on Chen and Corson. Chen didn't have any heartstrings, and Corson's had worn out long ago from seeing too many senseless tragedies in battle.

However, Chen and Corson looked at each other and smiled. They both knew that this horse was worth keeping.

Walking up to Zenithstar, Corson said, "Time to go home big guy."

Zenithstar didn't mind this warrior, but when Chen came over and petted him, the horse glared at her.

Zenithstar realized they wanted him. But his owner was dead, and the warhorse felt like he had nothing to live for, that is, until he studied Chen carefully, deciding that one day he would kill this woman.

Chen smiled, intuitively knowing what the horse was thinking. She'd seen that look on the faces of men, women and even animals before. However, from experience, the black leather panther had learned that self-interest frequently neutralizes hate.

Chen decided that she'd observe Zenithstar and wait until the horse wanted or cared about something. Then, the black leather panther would make the warhorse understand that he'd either behave, or she'd keep him from getting whatever it was he wanted. And Chen would teach Zenithstar that her continued safety was the key to keeping it.

"I'll give this warhorse to Pensgraft," Chen told Corson. After all, the giant had penetrated her own dark heart and won her trust, and Chen was interested in seeing if Pensgraft could work his magic again, this time on a war-ravaged animal.

The black leather panther's interest in the warhorse was purely pragmatic. Zenithstar was simply one amazing piece of horseflesh, and she wanted him functional.

Well, enough of that, she thought.

Next!

Nothing held Chen's interest for long, not beyond its practical value, except for Pensgraft who was virtually her only friend, her only male friend.

Chen turned to Corson. "I have to get my warrior women out of Lord Daegal's castle. We can't hide what's going on at Crystal Castle forever. I'll need the other 75 with me for when things really get bad."

There were 100 young women who'd been raised with Chen since she was 15-years-old. Some were at Crystal Castle, but the majority were still at The Rock.

Chen made a decision.

"I'm riding to The Rock. Tell Gwendylln she's in charge of Crystal Castle till I get back."

Chapter 23

Spinning her black stallion around, Chen spurred him into a headlong gallop through the woods intent on reaching her warrior women at The Rock as quickly as possible. However, now that Lord Daegal's warriors had been dispatched, such a dramatic sense of urgency seemed unnecessary. Who was left to inform the warlord of recent events at Crystal Castle?

But when she wasn't upset or desperate about something, Chen felt a nagging emptiness deep inside of her. Therefore, having decided to go somewhere, she was going to get there as fast as she could. Emotional intensity was Chen's opiate of choice, her favorites being anger, aggression and recklessness. Such feelings helped fill the empty well inside of her, a depth that went down to eternity. And it could be all consuming.

She tried plugging the hole with constant activity, but as soon as one situation was under control, the nagging emptiness would drive her relentlessly into some other crisis. Anything to keep herself occupied, anything to keep the feelings of emptiness and boredom at bay. It was like living with a vacuum inside of her that could trigger an implosion.

The black leather panther had tried building a fence, an emotional barrier, around the well inside of her, for the deep hole was dangerous. She could fall in, or even worse, others might see into her. Deeply into her.

How to keep others out of the well? she often wondered.

Blocking it out and blinding people to its existence was a start, and no one could see through Chen's intensity. A goal itself wasn't as important as being in motion, and Chen felt safe as long as she was moving, while stopping gave her time to reflect on her vulnerability. But regardless of how much Chen feared the deep well, at other times, she welcomed it. The vast emptiness called to her. It was both a black hole and a gateway to freedom. She felt tempted to rest and to yield to the endlessness.

She yielded now.

Why now? Needing a fresh mount, she had to stop.

Chen's stallion slogged his way to the front door of a farmhouse. The horse could go no further, but now he could rest. Maybe he could investigate the mystery of limitless inner space.

The black leather panther dismounted and looked around. Walking over to the barn, she stepped through the open double doors. It was pitch dark, no moonlight penetrating the interior. But she smelled horses and smiled.

However, hearing her own horse whinny, Chen's hand went to her sword.

The black leather panther's musings were instantly forgotten. The emotional barrier surrounding her inner well seemingly turned into one of solid steel. And when Chen walked out of the barn, she was back in control of her feelings. Whatever philosophical side she possessed was now buried in a landslide of practicality.

"Who's there?" an older woman asked.

Chen said nothing.

"Don't be frightened, young lady, we won't hurt you," the woman said reassuringly.

Chen's hand tightened on her sword.

"I have a nice stew simmering, come inside and have a bowl," she coaxed.

Chen turned grim inside. Sincerity was an unpredictable emotion, and she hated it. Therefore, she froze out the older woman. A mild depression coated by a layer of silent anger shielded Chen. Confident now in her armor, she spoke up. "How did you know I was a woman?"

"Why honey, the lightness of your boots upon the grass was like a calling card."

"How did you know I was young?"

"Who else but a young person would be out alone at night?"

"Are you saying that older people have more common sense?"

"No, nothing like that. The young are more restless, that's all," the woman said in her soothing tone of voice. "You sound quite tired. Have you traveled a long way today?"

"Not too far, but I sort of had a race over the mountain."

"Then let's tend to your horse," the older woman said. Turning to the farmhouse front door, she shouted, "Pa! Pa! There's a young woman's horse that needs tending out here in the yard."

When a huge silhouette appeared in the doorway, Chen's sword inched out of its scabbard. Light from the fireplace inside the farmhouse glinted off the polished metal.

"Now, now, none of that, my dear," the farmwife gently chided her. "Pa, keep a polite distance from this young woman and give her some elbow room, but tend to her horse, please."

The man quietly did as he was told. Chen liked that.

Striding over to the farmhouse, the black leather panther leapt up two steps onto the porch. Placing a firm hand against the open front door, she held it in place until she could check behind it. Then, she performed a quick inspection walking throughout the house. Lastly, she opened the backdoor and looked outside. Satisfied, Chen returned to the main room.

The older woman acted as if having her home searched by a total stranger was an everyday occurrence. She patted a chair indicating for Chen to sit there, so naturally Chen sat in one of the other chairs. One with her back against the wall.

"A little cramped there behind the table, honey, don't you think?"

"It'll do," Chen said crisply.

After setting a bowl in front of Chen, the farmwife brought a pot of stew over to the table. The older woman was about to ladle some stew into it when Chen stopped her.

"I'll do that, thank you," Chen said wondering where the "thank you" had come from. The black leather panther couldn't recall the last time she'd thanked anyone for anything. This farmwife was starting to frighten Chen, and she thought, I could run an enemy through with my sword and that will stop him, but how do I keep this woman's kindness from touching me?

Unconsciously, Chen reached for the knife in her boot.

"Oh, sweetheart, maybe you'd like one of ours, we don't really use them," the older woman said going into the next room and coming back with an apron full of sheathed knives.

Chen was up out of her chair in an instant, her sword in one hand and knife in the other. Her chest was heaving, and she was breathing deeply, hyperventilating, gulping air, almost gasping.

The farmwife had known the young warrior woman would respond in this manner. She'd gone for the knives as a way of bringing her visitor's fears to the surface where they could be dealt with openly.

Well, the one thing Chen was very open about was violence. The black leather panther was very sharing and giving in that capacity, and she'd almost leapt at the older woman.

Totally confused, Chen's brain shrieked!

"What's going on here?" Chen screamed, genuinely frightened for the first time she could remember in years. "Stew and knives! Where did you get the recipe for that?"

The black leather panther thought, What's wrong with me? Just kill this woman and get out of here! But instead, Chen remained standing with her back against the wall and a weapon in each hand gaping at the farmwife.

The older woman almost laughed, but chastised herself thinking, Stop your foolish pranks. Yet, she couldn't hold back from teasing Chen further. "What's the matter? Don't you like the knives? I assure you, they're all well crafted."

Finally, Chen ripped herself back to reality and said, "You're really pushing it, you know?"

"I'm aware of that, honey. I was wielding a sword decades before you were even born. You'd be Chen, right? Daegal's little niece, right?" she asked. "Honey, you'd better sit down and eat before your stew gets cold."

Chen obeyed. Her obedience stunned her.

The older woman wisely stayed clear of the table. Chen was near snapping. Anyone else, anyone Chen had ever known in her entire life, would be dead by now if they did this to her. As it was, the young guest was quietly eating her dinner. The farmwife struggled not to enjoy all of this too much.

"How is your stew, Chen?"

Chen felt refreshed, and it was great having a warm meal in her stomach. But she said nothing. The young warrior had accidentally thanked the farmwife once already, and she wasn't going to give this woman a compliment on the food no matter how tasty it was.

"It's really good!" Chen found herself saying in spite of what she'd been thinking.

The farmwife ladled more stew into Chen's bowl and gave the young woman a reassuring pat on the back. Chen liked it. She felt like she was losing her mind.

In a shower of red-hot embers, a log fell from the fireplace and rolled onto the floor. The older woman quickly took a step back, then lifted her skirt and brushed it with her hand.

The black leather panther noticed a scar running the length of the woman's right calf muscle and another on the back of her left leg as the farmwife turned while continuing to brush her skirt. Chen also saw several scars on the older woman's left forearm and a small one below her right ear.

"I see you've had several farm accidents. Don't you have adult children to help with difficult tasks?"

Before the farmwife could answer, the front door opened and the woman's husband entered the room. "That poor stallion's pretty beaten up, and it's going to take me about a week to get him rested and fit. If you think you'll be heading back this way anytime soon, maybe you'd like to borrow one of ours?"

Looking at the man's kind eyes, Chen saw they were filled with concern for a horse the farmer had never even seen before. Speaking with a gentle, polite tone of voice, the farmer added, "Why not come out to the barn and see if you like any of our ponies?"

Getting up from the table, Chen shook her head imagining the sad-looking bunch of animals these old folks must have. Smiling good naturedly, the farmer lit a torch and headed outside with Chen reluctantly tagging along feeling skeptical.

Ponies? Who raises ponies anymore? And I'm not going to be seen riding on a tiny horse, Chen thought adamantly, the mere idea making her feel embarrassed.

But after they entered the barn, Chen was shocked to be looking at some of the best horseflesh she'd ever seen. After patting each of the "ponies" on their rumps, the farmer said, "Go ahead, pick yourself out a horse."

Running her hands over one of the animals, and with her voice filled with awe, Chen said, "These are incredible warhorses, but why do you raise them?"

"Oh, it's sort of one of my wife's hobbies."

"Raising warhorses for a hobby?"

"Well, some old habits die hard. And my wife says having a good horse can be more important than a sword."

Then, in the flickering torchlight, Chen got a further surprise. Across from the horse stalls, an entire wall was covered with weapons. There were broad axes, swords, bows, quivers of arrows and a collection of knives.

Chen thought, I don't believe it, more knives, as if they don't have enough of them already.

Reading Chen's mind, the farmer said, "Andrina is partial to knives, never having used a shield. She'd block with her sword and deliver the deathblow with a knife."

"Your wife can fight, and she's been in battles?"

"Andrina has seen plenty of action. Years ago, when civil war broke out after his father's death, my wife and I both fought on Lord Daegal's side."

"I've no great respect for my uncle," Chen said firmly and coldly.

"Well, in those days, we believed in him. Back then, Lord Daegal was a fearless leader and treated his warriors well. As a reward for our service, he bestowed this farm upon us."

"What did you do to deserve that?"

"Me? Not a whole lot. I mostly guarded my wife's back. But Andrina was one of the best natural-born fighters anyone had ever seen. And make no mistake about it, young lady, that's one dangerous woman in there. Even at her age, she has a quick temper, muscles as hard as rock and excellent reflexes. Oh, she can't strike with lightning speed like she used to, but if you ever get Andrina upset, even you would have your hands full."

Thrilled by the farmer's description of his wife, the black leather panther's eyes were sparkling. And she was wearing a big, wide grin while radiating a sense of excitement and enthusiasm.

Looking at Chen, the farmer smiled realizing she and his wife were a lot alike. Even while walking back to the house, Chen felt deeply moved by what she'd learned about Andrina. Somehow, knowing the older woman was an accomplished warrior made Chen feel more secure. The black leather panther no longer felt so alone.

When Chen entered the house, she took one look at Andrina and started tearing up. The older warrior woman spread her arms wide, and Chen ran to her burying her head in the farmwife's bosom and sobbing.

"My father left me when I was 14, and I've been alone since then. I've been so frightened for so long," Chen said weeping.

And then it all spilled out. The dam came tumbling down. She cried for the loss of her father and for all the years she'd lived feeling vulnerable and abandoned. She cried over the loss of the safety and security she'd known as a child. And most of all, she cried for the warrior women who'd died earlier this evening fighting Lord Daegal's men.

Chen cried for the loss of her innocence and for what she'd turned into. She knew she was mean and spiteful. The young warrior woman knew she hurt other people but didn't know how to stop herself. Everything always seemed so out of control. Chen had started killing as a way of keeping her fears from overwhelming her, and she just didn't know what else to do!

"I've killed a lot of people," Chen sobbed. "You'd hate me if you knew how many people I've killed. It's all I know how to do. It's all I am good at."

"I know, sweetheart, I know all about it," the older warrior woman said as she rocked Chen in her arms like a baby. "I know all too well about it."

"How would you know about me?"

"I'm the one who suggested to Lord Daegal about surrounding you with 100 women your own age. I even helped select some of them," she told a surprised Chen. "Have they been good to you?"

"Oh, yes, very good!"

"There was one girl I was particularly impressed with, a big girl who could be really vicious, if provoked."

"Corson!" Chen said smiling.

"Yes," the woman laughed as Chen's tears began to dry. "Corson! What ever happened to that tough little girl?"

"Well, she grew into a tough big girl. She can almost outfight me!"

"And that's saying something."

"Yes, it is," Chen agreed feeling proud of Corson. "She's over at Crystal Castle, or at least she's heading back there now."

The older woman froze. "Corson's living with Glenitant?"

"No, Glenitant's dead."

The farmer rose and looked at his wife with all seriousness.

"What happened to her sword? Who has Crystal now?" Andrina asked cautiously.

"No one really," Chen said as she wiped her face and rubbed her eyes. "Well, I do, sort of. But Crystal is all tied up. Some other sword arrived with a blond girl and took Crystal prisoner."

"So what's the status of Crystal Castle?" Andrina asked.

"It's mine now, I guess. At least that's what everyone seems to think, including Crystal."

"What's happening over there?" the farmwife asked.

"Well, I have around 25 of my warrior women at Crystal Castle, but the rest are back at The Rock. I plan on getting them and taking them to my castle."

Chen liked the sound of the words "my castle."

"About 20 nobles from the western lands are at Crystal Castle, and Corson said more will be arriving at some point. But for now, there aren't many of us at all," Chen said. "However, I don't understand about the blond girl's sword everyone's so impressed with. Why aren't they counting on that sword to help out more? I've heard Baelfire's powerful."

"Along with the sword and girl, is there a horse? A white horse wearing a large necklace inset with rare jewels?"

"Yes, a white warhorse named Zorya, and she looks powerful, too."

"My understanding of it is that the three of them must go through some sort of ritual or initiation before the girl can come into her own. And Baelfire will be restricted by the girl's own limitations until that time."

"I'm not allowed to use my sword," Chen frowned. "Even Corson says I shouldn't lay a hand on Crystal, not even to pick her up. Corson also says I should listen to some wizard named Eldwyn."

"Eldwyn's there?"

"I guess. That's what they call him anyway."

"What does Lord Daegal know about all of this?" Andrina asked.

"Nothing yet, but my girls and I killed a bunch of my uncle's men earlier this evening after dark. I'm here now because we chased down one who had tried to get away. Now I'm on my way to The Rock to get the rest of my warrior women out."

"How about if you head back to Crystal Castle and I go visit your girls?" the farmwife asked.

"I don't know. I want to be sure I get all of them out."

"Yes, of course, I understand you want them all. And Lord Daegal will probably allow me to see them, but we have got to remove your warrior women from the castle in such a way as to avoid suspicion. We can't just go in there and take them all out in one group. That would be like waving a red flag right in front of your uncle's eyes."

"How would you go about it?"

"I would prefer to have them leave a few at a time," the farmwife counseled Chen. "And to buy us more time, the rest of the young women can stay confined to your chambers."

"Why?"

"I want people living at The Rock to get used to not seeing them around the castle for a while. That way we can gradually slip your warrior women out without being so obvious, and people will be less likely to know how many are gone. Also, even after they are all out, their absence may not be noticed for a while."

Chen looked at the farmer. "So Andrina's the brains of the family, is she?"

"You won't find a better battle tactician anywhere in the realm," the farmer said proudly.

"Well, how about if we get a good night's sleep and start out fresh tomorrow morning?" the farmwife asked.

Andrina's farmhouse was spacious, with three extra bedrooms. Chen was snuggled deeply into the covers on a large, soft mattress that smelled of fresh sheets. Chen smiled as she fell into a deep, restful slumber.

"That girl needs a mother," Andrina said.

The farmer smiled and thought, It looks to me like she's found one.

The husky woman with the many battle scars went into her bedroom. She put on sturdy breeches and a loose-fitting, heavy cotton shirt and headed out to the barn with her husband in tow.

Andrina put on a wide belt with a scabbard hanging from it. She hefted her favorite sword, admired its balance once more and stuck it into the scabbard. In addition to that, she put a knife in her belt, a knife in each of her boots and one in a sheath hanging down her back.

Feeling sufficiently armed, Andrina mounted a massive warhorse that had been bred for both strength and speed. She kissed her husband, rode out of the barn and headed down a trail leading west to The Rock.

As the farmer watched his wife riding off into the darkness, he felt an old, familiar fear. He wondered if he'd ever see his wife alive again. Then he forced the idea from his mind. She'd been in countless battles and always survived. But the farmer had always been with her guarding her back, and he thought, Who will protect her back now?

The farmer had pleaded with his wife to let him go with her, but she wanted him to watch over the young woman sleeping in their home. Chen was now very important to the farmer and his wife for the older warrior woman and her husband were a childless couple.

Andrina hadn't seen Chen in years, and they'd never actually been formally introduced. The black leather panther had changed in appearance growing into an incredibly beautiful and strong woman. Yet when Chen entered her home, the older warrior woman recognized her immediately. Andrina took one look at Chen and realized that standing before her was the daughter she'd always wanted.

The farmer and his wife had tried to have children for years but had experienced disappointment and frustration. Finally, they'd gotten pregnant, but the baby had been a casualty of war.

Those were tumultuous times. Lord Daegal's father had died, and civil war had broken out. Andrina and her husband fought on the side loyal to Lord Daegal. One day, there was a surprise attack on their encampment, and they'd been surrounded with no chance for escape. The farmer had tried to get his pregnant wife to safety, but it was hopeless. The battle was raging around them on all sides.

He remembered how, during the battle, Andrina had gone into labor. She'd been fighting desperately, killing any enemy who came near her and the baby. However, his wife's labor pains had gotten so great that she could no longer withstand the agony and finally lay down. Andrina had struggled to stay on her feet, but the baby was insistent and was coming, war or no war.

Andrina had been fighting so well that her heroic efforts greatly inspired those around her. When her fellow warriors, all men in those days, saw what was happening, they encircled Andrina and fought for her life. Many a brave man died that day in the defense of this incredibly courageous woman.

But it had all been to no avail. The baby was stillborn. And so, when the farmer had seen Chen by their hearth a few hours ago, the look in his wife's eyes was undeniable. He'd seen the child hunger on her face before. For after that one baby, she'd never become pregnant again.

Yet after all of that, Chen had come into their lives, and his wife finally had what she wanted, a daughter to nurture, protect, defend and care for. If Andrina was dangerous before, she was doubly so now.

The farmer didn't know what the changes at Crystal Castle meant for Lord Daegal, but he knew one thing. If that architectural masterpiece was indeed Chen's, then his wife would fight anyone who attempted to take it from her. And he knew that Lord Daegal wasn't going to allow a fortress like that to slip through his fingers, if he could do anything about it.

Once Lord Daegal learned of Glenitant's death, he would respond in force.

Chapter 24

Crystal was seething in anger and frustration. Eldwyn had captured the dark sword days ago, and she'd been languishing on the great room floor bound with golden ropes made from strands of Aerylln's hair.

Even life with Glenitant was better than this, and she never amounted to much, Crystal thought bitterly, the old witch having been easy to dominate but incredibly difficult to motivate. Sighing in exasperation, Crystal recalled how Glenitant had never wanted to leave the valley.

By contrast, the dark sword wanted to travel far and wide. She wanted evil adventures, warped excitement and cruel initiatives. In short, she wanted to spread her mischief-making as far a field as possible. But that was not to be, for Crystal and Glenitant were as different as night and day.

No matter what enticements I offered, they were all to no avail, Crystal thought. When I had Crystal Castle rise up from nothing, right out of the bare ground, I'd hoped it would inspire Glenitant and make her want more out of life.

But to the dark sword's disappointment, it hadn't.

And yet, such a magnificent fortress would have inspired the imagination of many others, for the beauty and elegance of Crystal Castle was undeniable. However, in the end, Crystal had discovered that giving Glenitant such a luxurious home was a mistake. Rather than inspiring her former mistress to greatness, it just made Glenitant even more contented. And then, without a doubt, she wanted to spend all of her days in Crystal Valley.

The valley was a beautiful place with lush, green fields, wondrous mountains and fine weather. But Crystal longed for the widespread suffering, devastation and death of a battlefield.

Glenitant was driving me insane, and if Chen hadn't arrived, I would have gone mad, Crystal thought. But what Crystal ignored about herself was that she'd gone insane long ago.

But Crystal loved Chen. The dark sword thought, That woman's a fighter! She'd never be satisfied to stay in one place, not her. But what am I going to do now?

Looking around the great room, the dark sword thought, The black crystal floor I'm lying on is stunningly beautiful but languishing here isn't doing me any good. I've got to escape.

While Crystal was pondering her fate, Aerylln was also in the great room wondering about her own future. Unfortunately, while in a particularly morose mood, the dark sword's eyes settled on the teenage girl.

Aerylln jumped when she felt Crystal's penetrating gaze and quickly turned around seeing the dark sword lying bound and gagged on the floor. Being a very sensitive soul, Aerylln became acutely aware of the sword's discomfort. The young woman hated to see anything or anyone in such torment and so, feeling sympathy for the weapon, she walked over to it.

Looking down at Crystal, Aerylln felt a darkness she'd never encountered before. There was also something else, something even worse.

What is it? Aerylln asked herself. But then, she started wondering why others feared this sword being that it was so beautiful, even an artistic masterpiece.

Aerylln noticed that Crystal wasn't as incredibly beautiful as Baelfire, but she could see the high quality workmanship that had gone into making this very attractive sword.

As she marveled at the sword, Aerylln thought, Crystal really is an example of exquisite craftsmanship.

Delicate patterns had been etched into Crystal's scabbard, and Aerylln found herself beginning to drift along and daydream as she followed the designs. Without even thinking about it, the teenage girl found being near Crystal to be restful.

Aerylln thought, Baelfire is always so intense and driven.

However, once again, Aerylln felt something disturbing about Crystal but couldn't exactly put her finger on what it was.

Suddenly, Aerylln felt Crystal reaching out to her, comforting her and inviting her to get closer. The young woman leaned down to look more carefully at the intricate designs and felt herself being swept up by a strange power. It was as if someone or something had gripped her by both shoulders and was pulling her towards the dark sword.

Eldwyn, Zorya, Marcheto and Ritalso were in the great room with Aerylln, but they had wandered over to a window and were calling out to someone below in the courtyard. Even Baelfire was off a ways lying quietly on a table near the massive fireplace.

Frightened and confused, Aerylln tried calling out to her friends but found she couldn't speak, almost as if she were mute.

The grip on the teenage girl's shoulders tightened. Aerylln tried pulling away but found herself being drawn ever closer to the dark sword. Suddenly a deep, dark pit opened up in front of her, and she found herself balancing precariously on the very edge. Waving her arms around wildly, Aerylln struggled to keep her balance but felt her body tilting forward. Terrified, she screamed, but it was a soundless cry of desperation, nothing came out.

Wide-eyed with fear, Aerylln saw Crystal hovering near the surface. Glancing down and seeing only fathomless darkness, the young woman somehow knew she was looking into insanity itself. Crystal came closer, now directly in front of her, and Aerylln sensed the perverse joy the dark sword was taking in her predicament, a gloating gleefulness.

Whatever this is, it's a horrible place, Aerylln thought while trying not to panic. The teenage girl could almost hear Mistress Xan saying, When in danger, be disciplined. Discipline is more important than brilliance, more important than any gift or talent. Without it, there's nothing, only chaos.

Desperately attempting to control and discipline her fears, Aerylln tried tearing her eyes away from the pit but could not. Peering into the darkness, she looked into the very origin of chaos, into the heart of madness!

Feeling herself beginning to faint, Aerylln gripped the sides of her head with the palms of her hands and screamed within her inner being using every ounce of strength she had!

Sitting straight up, instantly springing from the tabletop and balancing on the point of her scabbard, Baelfire quickly surveyed the room. In shock, she saw what her half-sister, Crystal, was up to!

Baelfire began shaking violently along the entire length of her blade and handle. Outraged, the magic sword was convulsing as though having a seizure. Baelfire fell from the table, where Aerylln had placed her, and landed on the black crystal floor with a clatter.

Immediately, cracks began forming in the highly-polished surface accompanied by a sound like shattering glass. The floor splintered erupting into broken shards of very hard, durable black crystal. It would have taken an enormous weight pounding down upon it to even scratch the floor, let alone shatter the entire surface, but it didn't stop there.

Hairline fissures began threading their way up the walls and creeping across the ceiling. All four sides of the great room shuddered violently while the sound of shattering crystal intensified as the surface of the walls began exploding and filling the floor with piles of black shards.

Staring in awe at Baelfire, the dark sword quickly closed her deep pit of insanity and lay trembling on a floor still erupting all around her.

Materializing out of nowhere, a bright light shot down from the ceiling and slammed onto Baelfire with the intensity of a hurricane. The pulverizing, high-speed, thundershower of light particles radiated enormous energy like gale-force winds of incredible velocity and fury. With this unimaginable display of power, the Creative Light shot straight down on Baelfire.

Then, as quickly as it began, it was over.

But Eldwyn, already lost in meditation, had opened himself to the very depths of eternity. When the Creative Light appeared, the old wizard had instantly closed his eyes dropping down a well within his very being. Detaching from the world around him so rapidly and so deeply, Eldwyn no longer knew which was more real, the inner well or Crystal Castle's great room. The surface world could easily have been a dream, as far as he knew. But the forces of creation were not a dream. At this level, they were real, very real.

"Cathrak dantay sechum tasterak! Cathrak dantay sechum tasterak!" Eldwyn shouted while throwing his arms

wide projecting more Light energy into all those near him, including a very surprised Aerylln.

The young woman was sitting on a chair with Baelfire at her feet, the good sword recovering from the intensity of the Creative Light's infusion of power into her. But Crystal was nowhere to be seen having been banished to the furthest corner of the great room.

Looking down at the good sword, Aerylln saw Baelfire was glowing red-hot with a little whiff of smoke curling up from her. The young woman, herself, had been so infused with Light energy that she appeared to be made of translucent porcelain.

But Aerylln stayed calm. For even though overwhelming, the encounter was strangely familiar, as if she'd experienced it before. The Light energy shining through her began fading, and she was once again herself, yet not quite. Something was different about her. When the Creative Light shot through her, it had altered her physical appearance.

Aerylln's long, white dress had been replaced by a new outfit. Now, she was wearing white leather pants, a matching jacket, a white long-sleeved blouse and knee-high riding boots made of white leather. Further enhancing her appearance was ultra-white hair flowing luxuriously down her back to her waist.

Aerylln still had the face of an innocent young woman, but for the first time there was a hint of power, or of power yet to come. It was subtle, but it was there and everyone recognized it, except for Aerylln who wondered why they were looking at her.

Eldwyn turned to Baelfire, who was exhausted after her encounter with the Creative Light, and said, "It's been a long time since I saw or felt anything like that."

"I'd forgotten what it was like," Baelfire admitted. "I think it's going to take some getting used to."

"There's no getting used to that," Eldwyn said.

"Only total submission to nothingness can be the response to a power like that," Aerylln said absentmindedly. "Going blank inside, your mind and emotions blank, being as fresh as an artist's white canvas. Being open to nothing and everything."

"You're right, so completely right," Marcheto said proudly slipping behind her on the chair and wrapping his arms around her. Resting his head upon Aerylln's shoulder, they both seemed lost in another world.

"Who does she sound like?" Zorya asked, still a bit shocked from the suddenness of the Creative Light's reappearance after so many years.

"Lyssa," Eldwyn said with joy and relief. "Aerylln's grandmother had that same mystical look about her."

Looking up at her master, Baelfire smiled and said, "People once referred to me as the Sword of Light."

"They'll do so again," Zorya said encouragingly. "I'm sure the process of our transformation into the Trinity of Light has begun."

"Yes, it's begun," Eldwyn agreed, "the formation of the Trinity has begun."

The old wizard, almost breathless with excitement, added, "Did you see how Aerylln handled it all?"

"Yes, she did really well. When infused with the Creative Light for my first time, I didn't stay nearly as calm," Baelfire said.

"You're not as calm as Aerylln, even now," Zorya laughed. "And as I recall, on your first encounter, you flew around the room in a panic."

"You weren't any better, not your first time," Baelfire laughed remembering Zorya screaming hysterically as a torrential surge of Creative Light careened through her body.

But their reminiscing was cut short. Barely having recovered from the Light's first appearance, a second energy surge was unleashed upon them. This time, it was Zorya, not Aerylln, who began glowing brighter and brighter.

Knowing what was coming next, Zorya headed for the nearest window leaping over the ledge and falling like a stone towards the courtyard below. Feeling a rapid buildup of the Creative Light's energy within her, the warhorse braced herself as it came hurtling out with a vengeance. Exploding with prism light, Zorya's body transformed into clear crystal as she shot upward through the sky leaving a stream of purple, blue, green, yellow, orange and red in her wake.

I feel strong and whole for the first time in, how long has it been? Zorya wondered. But then, as she began weakening, the warhorse sighed in frustration and flew back to the castle gliding to a soft landing in the great room.

"That was quite a ride!" Eldwyn said, his eyes wide with excitement.

"It didn't last very long," Zorya lamented.

"Every time the Creative Light appears, we'll be able to sustain the energy longer and longer," Baelfire reminded her.

"Honestly, I've been apprehensive over Aerylln's readiness to serve as a catalyst," Eldwyn admitted. "Only Baelfire's heir can trigger the transformation, but I wasn't sure if Aerylln was up to it."

"Yes, Lyssa was much more outgoing," Baelfire agreed. "But this encounter was encouraging, and Aerylln shows great promise."

"For now, we should go down to the courtyard and find Pensgraft and Dartuke," Eldwyn said. "They'll be interested in learning about the mess we just made of the entire great room."

"And they might want an explanation for why a warhorse went shooting through the sky like an arrow," Marcheto said smiling.

"Yes, true, but I'm not responsible for turning the great room into a shambles," Zorya said looking over at Baelfire.

"Don't blame me, Crystal was the one starting trouble," the good sword said.

"Oh, that's it, we'll blame everything on your half-sister," Zorya chuckled.

As they headed downstairs, Crystal was over in the far corner of the great room plotting her revenge. And it would be no laughing matter. The dark sword was now desperately seeking a way out, any way out.

Chapter 25

In the great hall of The Rock, Lord Daegal was in a foul mood.

The warlord was angry and frustrated that, as of yet, he lacked sufficient troop strength to wage a decisive assault on Crystal Castle. Lord Daegal wanted to possess the dark sword, Crystal, with all his heart but was unable to act.

Over the years, he'd tried taking Crystal from Glenitant, but each effort had ended in failure. Glenitant wasn't all that smart, but she was far from being stupid. On several occasions, Lord Daegal had found out the hard way that his sister possessed an innate cunning, a knack for survival.

Also working to his disadvantage, Lord Daegal had always been way too impulsive. Repeatedly, the warlord had made the mistake of behaving impatiently and even rashly when dealing with Glenitant. Being that she was his younger sister, Lord Daegal had frequently underestimated her.

"I wish I knew what was happening at Crystal Castle between Glenitant and Chen," the warlord growled at Tark, the captain of his personal guard. "It would be helpful if I knew whether Glenitant was dead or alive."

Having thrown Chen at his sister like a winged predator, Lord Daegal was reluctant to send spies into Crystal Valley. The warlord didn't want it to appear obvious that he was behind the black leather panther's arrival at Glenitant's castle. He wanted to hedge his bets in case things didn't work out.

"What bothers me most, Tark, is that we haven't heard back from the warriors I sent along to guard Pensgraft when he and Chen rode off together," Lord Daegal said, the lack of information grating on his nerves.

"Yes, sire, they should have sent word by now."

"What about Marcheto? Have you heard anything from your son?" Lord Daegal asked glaring at the captain of his personal guard.

"No, sire. All we have is a report from our scouts telling us about the 'bandits' being massacred."

"I had those warriors attack Aerylln, Baelfire, Zorya and Eldwyn so Marcheto could play the hero. How did things go that badly?" Lord Daegal demanded.

"I should have sent additional spies, but I figured all the 'bandits' would still be alive to report back," Tark confessed.

"At least Marcheto's body wasn't found among the dead."

"Yes, sire, and I've sent scouts everywhere searching for some sign of him. That is, everywhere but into Crystal Valley. It's possible he may have headed over that way."

"What news of Aerylln and her companions?"

"Nothing, sire, it's as if they vanished."

"Well, if you don't want to vanish along with them, I'd suggest you find them."

Just then, the Crystal Medallion that Lord Daegal always wore around his neck began trembling against his chest and glowing. Although anxious for news from Crystal Castle, the warlord was powerless to initiate contact with the dark sword. She had to contact him. Lord Daegal knew Crystal and the medallion were linked together somehow, which is why he constantly kept it with him.

However, the warlord was completely unprepared for the level of hysteria in Crystal's voice. He was truly shocked. In all the years Lord Daegal had known the dark sword, she'd never been less than totally confident. Devious, untrustworthy, spoiled, ruthless and hate filled, yes. But lacking in confidence? Never.

Lord Daegal actually held his breath waiting for Crystal to impart her news. And now it was Tark's turn to stare in amazement at his master. Lord Daegal had never been hesitant about anything. Reckless, yes, but uncertain? Never.

For Lord Daegal, life was about to take a major deviation from comfortable familiarity, a dramatic, irreversible change of direction.

"Lord Daegal, it's Crystal!" the dark sword shouted stating the obvious. No one else had ever contacted the warlord via the medallion.

"Yes, Crystal?" Lord Daegal said in a calm voice as he forced himself to regain his composure.

"The great room here is in shambles! There are black crystal shards everywhere! The whole place is falling apart! I'm lying in a heap of black crystal rubble!" the dark sword screamed.

Lord Daegal was convinced that his once reliable, if treacherous, ally was babbling incoherently. The warlord thought, Maybe Glenitant found out we're plotting against her and is punishing the sword somehow. This could be a disaster!

"What was I thinking when I sent Chen over there?" Lord Daegal said under his breath to the captain of his personal guard.

Once again, Tark was dumbfounded and thought, Is that fear I'm hearing in my master's voice?

"What's Glenitant doing?" the warlord asked the dark sword.

"Nothing, she's dead!" Crystal shrieked.

Feeling confused, Lord Daegal thought, That's great news, isn't it? Why would Glenitant's demise bother Crystal?

"What about Chen?" Lord Daegal asked.

"That hellion's the person who killed Glenitant!"

"Well, that's fantastic, right? That's what we hoped for," Lord Daegal said, the confusion in his voice readily apparent to Tark.

"It would be if the traitor hadn't changed sides leaving me to rot while tied up!" Crystal yelled at the top of her lungs.

"What are you talking about? What other side? Crystal, please take your time and tell me what happened. Try to be objective and stick to the facts," Lord Daegal said hoping to calm the dark sword by listening carefully and allowing her to vent.

"Facts, you want facts? Okay, Chen kicked Glenitant out of an open window here in the great room, and the old witch fell to her death on the courtyard below. That's fact number one," Crystal said.

"Okay, but that's good. What else?"

"Your men are dead!" Crystal said as she began laughing hysterically.

"Dead? How many are dead?" Lord Daegal asked genuinely shocked.

Gloating over the opportunity to convey bad news to Lord Daegal, Crystal broke into a fit of psychotic laughter and said, "All the men you sent over with Pensgraft, Chen and her warrior women. Every last one of them!"

"How's that possible? Glenitant couldn't have killed them all, not all of them, unless it was a clever trap. My sister never kept an army, not even a personal guard. She always believed you were all the protection she'd ever need."

"Well, she was wrong."

"Glenitant couldn't have managed this without your help. How did they die?" Lord Daegal demanded.

"It wasn't me, and it wasn't Glenitant, it was Chen."

"Why?"

"Chen's taken over Crystal Castle and wants it for herself," Crystal said as she finally started getting control of her emotions and calming down.

Now it was Lord Daegal's turn to be sarcastic, and he said, "What a surprise! Come on, Crystal, get a grip on yourself. I know what Chen wants, which is why I'm raising an army over here. You and I've talked about it, don't you remember? I said I'd raise an army of several thousand warriors to insure victory even with Chen being your new master.

"And since Chen has no experience wielding a magic sword, I mentioned that maybe I could back her down with a sufficient show of force," Lord Daegal said, a hint of suspicion creeping into his voice. Wondering if Crystal was up to something, he gave her a stern warning. "If you betray me, you'll never see this Crystal Medallion again. I'll destroy it."

"Don't worry about me. I won't help Chen at all," Crystal assured him frightened at the prospect of losing the medallion forever. If it was destroyed, Crystal's hope of creating a dark trinity would die along with the medallion.

"Listen to me very carefully, if you help her, you're going to regret it."

"I won't," the dark sword said genuinely terrified.

"Okay, that's good. So tell me, what does Chen gain by killing my men?"

"She wants to keep you from finding out a few things."

"Such as?"

"Such as my being taken captive and being tied up with some sort of golden ropes that sap almost all of my strength. I've been tied up for days," Crystal said almost crying in frustration.

"Taken captive by whom?"

"By Eldwyn, the wizard!"

"Who's with him?"

"Who do you think? Baelfire, Zorya and Lyssa's granddaughter, Aerylln! And that little tramp even looks like her grandmother!"

"What's Baelfire up to?"

"The transformation into the Trinity, what else?" Crystal asked, her voice mocking him.

"What about the Trinity? Have Baelfire, Zorya and Aerylln joined together creating the Trinity of Light?" Lord Daegal asked genuinely alarmed.

"No, not yet, but Baelfire caught me tormenting Aerylln and went berserk trashing the entire great room. Both Baelfire and Zorya have experienced the Creative Light, and Zorya was outside flying around like a meteor."

"What about Aerylln?"

"That teenage girl's going to grow up real quick if you don't put a stop to all this. And I mean now."

"There's no Trinity yet, so Baelfire and Zorya's powers will still be limited," Lord Daegal said thinking out loud.

"I'm telling you, if you don't want things getting a whole lot worse, you'd better get over here right away."

"And no one's tried using you as a defensive weapon?" Lord Daegal asked starting to feel more hopeful.

"No, Chen's turned into a goody-goody," Crystal said in disgust.

"I don't believe that for a second."

"Her friend, Corson, showed up and convinced Chen not to even touch me. Anyway, I'm indisposed at the moment. I'm tied up with magic rope of some type."

"That can change," Lord Daegal said trying to encourage her. "If the Trinity hasn't formed yet, then keeping you imprisoned is taking a lot of effort on someone's part, either Baelfire's or Eldwyn's. What we have to do is give them something really big to worry about, something that might serve as a major distraction and a heavy drain on their energy. I believe we can wear them down."

"If you can take Baelfire, Zorya and Eldwyn out of commission, there won't be much more to deal with," Crystal said. "The whole castle's being defended by maybe 50 warriors."

"I'm coming over," Lord Daegal assured the dark sword. "I was waiting till more of my warriors returned from other regions where they're currently stationed. But I think I can take Crystal Castle with a thousand warriors that I have within a day's ride of The Rock. I should be able to move soon."

"Until then, I'm all alone," Crystal sighed, feeling depressed.

"Maybe not totally alone," Lord Daegal said.

"What do you mean?"

"Is there a young man hanging around Aerylln?"

"Yes, his name's Marcheto."

"Wait till I tell his father," Lord Daegal said having waved Tark out of earshot, the captain now being over by a window.

"What are you talking about?"

"Marcheto's the son of the captain of my personal guard. He's a spy. He's ours."

"I don't believe it."

"Well, he is, I personally arranged for him to meet Aerylln," Lord Daegal said.

"But those two are head-over-heels in love."

"How sweet, just let that young warrior know I want to speak with him."

"I'm telling you, Aerylln has him all wrapped up at this point. She's done everything but put a bow on him."

"It doesn't matter, I have something that will bring him back down to reality very quickly," Lord Daegal said.

"What?"

"His father, and I'll kill him if Marcheto doesn't listen to me. And those two are very close."

"That should get Marcheto's attention."

"Will you get a chance to see him?"

"This great room's a mess. I don't know if they'll be coming back here, but I'll try to get to see him somehow," Crystal said. "And I appreciate your help. In fact, there may be something I can do for you in return."

"Such as?"

"Well, I'm not totally powerless," Crystal said.

"But you've been taken captive."

"Yes, I'm very weak, but once you get into Crystal Valley, I might be able to help."

"How?"

"I could enhance the fighting skill of some of your warriors."

"How many?"

"In my weakened state, I'm not sure. But I could make them into incredibly fearsome warriors, at least temporarily."

"What do you mean by temporarily?"

"I'm not sure how long I could sustain the change at this point. The golden ropes Eldwyn used to bind me with are continually eating away at my strength. In fact, if you don't get over here soon, I might not be able to help at all."

"This all sounds highly unreliable."

"Maybe you're right," Crystal conceded. "But I would be turning your warriors into shock troops that are savage, high impact and extremely intimidating. Their very presence on the battlefield will create terror in the hearts of all those defending Crystal Castle. And regardless of how many I can change into such berserk fighters, or for how long I can sustain the change, the psychological effect on those in Crystal Castle will be devastating."

"How devastating?"

"Take the Crystal Medallion from around your neck and hold it in the palm of your hand."

"Why?"

"I'm going to give you an example of what I can do."

The warlord took off the medallion holding it on an open palm. "Now what?"

The dark sword didn't answer. Instead, Crystal was concentrating with all her might trying to use the medallion to project her energy into Lord Daegal. But nothing happened.

"I'm waiting."

"Try forming a fist around the medallion and raise it above your head."

"Oh, this is working out just great," the warlord said feeling skeptical.

However, when he did as Crystal requested, the dark sword sensed an explosive surge of energy building up deep within her. Erupting from her scabbard with enormous velocity, an invisible bolt of black lightning shot out of a window and blasted through the sky towards The Rock and the Crystal Medallion.

Hurtling down upon the warlord, the dark light struck with such force that Lord Daegal was knocked to the ground. Immediately, the warlord's hand turned dark gray, then black.

Lord Daegal watched in horror as the hand holding the medallion began making cracking, popping sounds that echoed off the walls. In disbelief, the warlord watched as his fist turned into highly-polished black crystal.

Then, it began traveling up the length of his forearm.

The warlord leapt to his feet and stumbled into the sunlight streaming through a nearby window. As the sun's rays reflected off of him, light sparkled and danced along the various planes of black crystalline surfaces causing his entire forearm to take on the appearance of a long, polished gemstone. It looked like the wondrous work of a master jeweler.

Staring at his arm in amazement, Lord Daegal watched as his biceps and shoulder grew and expanded tearing his shirt and revealing massive, black crystalline muscles exuding strength and power.

Looking down at his feet, the warlord was stunned to discover they'd also turned to black crystal. As the process of crystallization continued, it traveled up the length of his legs and thighs until Lord Daegal finally bent over in agony, and his whole chest began shuddering and heaving. Tripping over his huge feet and stumbling once more, he looked with apprehension at his shadow on the floor watching it growing larger, taller, and broader, rapidly expanding into monstrous proportions.

Tilting back his head, Lord Daegal let out a terrifying, ferocious growl! Then, looking around wildly, he saw Tark who immediately turned and ran for the entrance to the great hall.

Sprinting through the opening, the captain of Lord Daegal's personal guard shouted for his warriors to close the thick, wooden double doors and to be quick about it. Grabbing a double-bladed axe from one of his warriors, Tark thrust its shaft through the door handles and did the same with a second axe.

Now, the captain of the guard squared his shoulders and faced the steel-reinforced doors as an enormous weight fell upon them. When the wood began splintering, Tark saw his men step back as what sounded like an enraged animal was pounding upon the double doors with all its might.

Turning to their leader, Tark's men gave him a questioning look. These were hard, seasoned warriors, but they weren't exactly encouraged by their captain's quick exit from the great hall.

"Captain, shouldn't we do something? What about Lord Daegal?" Rory, his second-in-command, asked.

"No, we'll stay here. And as for Lord Daegal, that's a little difficult to explain at the moment."

Drawing their swords, two warriors placed themselves directly in front of the entrance ready to attack anything strong enough to break through such thick, wooden, steel-reinforced doors. The men were almost eager to confront such an adversary.

"Guys, I'd stand back if I were you," Tark said. "This is one of the times when it's okay to run. We can't attack whatever that is, even if it comes crashing out of there."

Surprised, his warriors stared at him. But suddenly there was total silence, like an eerie peace and quiet after a terrible, horrific storm.

"What was that, Captain?" one of his men whispered.

"Trouble," Tark said, deeply relieved the doors had held.

Glancing around and seeing the apprehension and confusion on their faces, Tark realized his men were looking to him for leadership.

"It's just all in a day's work, guys. All in a day's work," Tark said smiling grimly.

Turning back to the double doors, he realized his master was inside and in some form of danger. However, as he weighed the pros and cons of unbarring them, Tark heard several low, rumbling, threatening growls and decided to wait a while longer. After a few moments, he heard Lord Daegal's voice filtering through the doors.

"Tark?"

"Yes, Lord?"

"Begin assembling the warriors we have within a day's ride of the castle. I want to move out as soon as possible."

"Yes, Lord."

"And Tark, place our best, most experienced warriors in a separate unit. I have a little surprise waiting for them once we reach Crystal Valley."

"Anything else, sire?"

"Yes, tell the men to get ready, we're going to storm Crystal Castle. It's ours for the taking."

Chapter 26

Chen's warrior women at The Rock were seething in anger and frustration as Andrina told them what their leader had been going through at Crystal Castle.

When Andrina, the retired warrior woman Chen had met at the farmhouse, first arrived at Lord Daegal's castle, she'd been welcomed with the full status of a visiting dignitary. The warlord had openly embraced her and given her the complete run of the castle.

Not having seen Andrina in years, Lord Daegal was unaware of her change of heart towards him. And he was unaware of her interest in Chen. Had he been, the warlord would have tossed her deep into his dungeon.

However, as it was, she was still in her former master's good graces. But that would all change before nightfall.

Andrina had wanted to take Chen's warrior women out of The Rock in stages, having their exit be more clandestine. But the older woman knew plans could change quickly, sometimes in the blink of an eye.

Now was such an instance.

When Kato, one of Lord Daegal's personal guards, entered Chen's chambers, swords leapt from their scabbards. Being in a vicious mood, the women almost advanced on him, and the situation could have rapidly gone against Kato except one of the warrior women quickly claimed him as her man.

After seeing that, the others settled for eyeing him up and down evaluating his potential usefulness.

Kato wasted no time getting to the point.

"Lord Daegal knows Chen and some of your sister warriors killed 25 of his men at Crystal Castle."

Without missing a beat, Andrina said, "It's time to go!"

As she rose, 75 warrior women stood as one and went to gather their battle gear.

"No heavy armor," Andrina cautioned them.

When they looked at her in surprise, she added, "We're going to try to walk out of here as if nothing has happened."

Turning back to Kato, Andrina asked, "Has Lord Daegal ordered our arrest?"

"No, he hasn't, at least not yet. It was Tark who told us about it. Lord Daegal, himself, was pretty shaken up by something that happened in the great hall a little while ago."

"What happened?"

"I don't really know. But Tark came running out of the great hall, had us slam those big doors shut and jammed some axes into the door handles. It sounded like a mule was kicking the doors from the inside, a big mule! And there was this wild, hideous growling!"

When the women just stood there looking at him, he said, "It doesn't make any sense to me either, but Tark says Lord Daegal knows what Chen did."

"I want everyone to bring her bow and plenty of arrows just in case we do have to shoot our way out of here," Andrina said wearing a grim expression.

Within a few minutes, the warrior women were assembled, and the whole group stepped out into the hallway. This was one grim, hostile bunch of women itching for a fight.

Fortunately, they made their way down to the stables and saddled their horses without incident.

When all 75 warrior women, mounted on black stallions, approached the main castle gate, the slightest spark of trouble would have ignited the entire group into action. Hundreds of arrows would have flown in all directions within a matter of seconds. Lord Daegal's warriors would have died by the dozens almost instantly. Chen's own warrior women could have also sustained casualties. One never knows for certain what will happen when the dogs of war are unleashed, which is both the intoxicating elixir of battle and the tragedy of it all.

A lesser woman than Andrina might have been tempted to fight her way out of the castle. Often times, inexperienced or reckless warriors can't resist the desire for violence. For them, confrontation can become more important than strategy. But Andrina had seen enough death to last her a lifetime and took no pleasure in killing.

She was focused, instead, on one rational goal, leaving the castle. If it could be accomplished without violence, and by doing so preserve Chen's warrior women for the coming battle with Lord Daegal over Crystal Castle, then that's what she would do. Andrina knew the fight would eventually come to them. It was unavoidable. But she was determined to avoid fighting that was either unnecessary or premature.

As it was, Lord Daegal's guards at the main entrance had witnessed the warlord welcoming Andrina into the castle earlier this very day. To the guards at the gate, these warrior women mounted on their magnificent black stallions appeared to be a natural entourage for such a famous warrior as Andrina.

With pride, the men saluted and raised the castle gate honoring Andrina and Chen's warrior women, then watched transfixed as the women rode by with their strong, well-muscled thighs straddling powerful, massive warhorses. The men were enthralled by all the creaking saddle leather, black knee-high riding boots, black cloth blouses, black leather pants, leather wrist protectors, and tons and tons of long, luxurious hair blowing in the wind.

It was a sight many would long remember, except for the sergeant on duty. He'd be dead by nightfall. Lord Daegal would be furious with the sergeant for not even questioning the necessity of such a large honor guard.

Andrina's prestige alone had gotten Chen's warrior women out of the castle. Andrina was an amazing woman, and Chen's warriors would be finding that out even more so very shortly.

Chapter 27

Hundreds of Lord Daegal's warriors were pouring into Crystal Valley.

Andrina, who at the moment was alone and pacing along a walkway above Crystal Castle's front wall, was surprised when she saw the warlord's army making its way through the mountain's western pass and winding its way down the switchback trail leading to the valley floor.

Marcheto had volunteered to keep watch at an overlook located a few miles west of Crystal Castle on the other side of the mountain. It afforded him an almost unobstructed view of land that Lord Daegal's troops would have to traverse in order to reach the black crystalline fortress. Repeatedly over the last few days, Marcheto had reported that there was no sign at all of Lord Daegal's warriors.

Suspecting some form of treachery, Andrina thought, And now this! How could that young man possibly have missed an army of this size?

Marcheto had been reporting to several nobles who established a reconnaissance post at Crystal Mountain's western pass and who, in turn, reported back to Crystal Castle. Just this morning, Marcheto informed the nobles that he hadn't seen so much as a single warrior on horseback.

This had been welcome news given their state of readiness, or their lack of it.

Even now, with Chen having all her warrior women at the castle, there were still less than 150 warriors defending the black crystalline fortress. And that included the nobles, as well as Balder and his men, and Aerylln, Zorya, Baelfire, Pensgraft, Corson, Ritalso and Marcheto.

Andrina thought, This small number is tantamount to no defense at all. The most we can hope for is to put up a brief resistance. And is that really worth dying for? It was a question she'd been asking herself for the last few days.

It wasn't that Andrina was afraid of dying in battle. In fact, she had no great desire to drift quietly into old age. Her fighting ability was still intact, and she had no desire to live beyond her days of being an able warrior.

Andrina was also well aware of her violent temper. And she knew that, sooner or later, she'd speak her mind to the wrong person and not be able to back it up properly with her sword. It was only a matter of time.

Andrina's sense of pride was such that, rather than a mocking smile, she wanted to see fear in the eyes of the warrior who took her life. The warrior woman felt strongly that when she could no longer prove to be a credible threat, well, life just wouldn't be worth living.

It wasn't death she feared but public humiliation. She lived in dread of others seeing her fight badly.

I'll be dead before that happens, Andrina reassured herself.

In fact, her death might well be in the very near future, the warrior woman realized, given the way things were shaping up at Crystal Castle.

Everything had happened so quickly. First, there was Glenitant's death at Chen's hands, or feet, since she'd kicked the old witch out of an upper-storey window. Second, Crystal was now a prisoner. Third, Crystal Castle was up for grabs. Fourth, there was her own surprise at seeing Chen again after so many years.

Also, there were Aerylln, Baelfire and Zorya.

Andrina thought, What exactly is this transformation they talk about, and when is it going to happen? Whatever they're going to do, they'd better do it quickly. We need their help now, not later. The sun may come up tomorrow, but that won't do us any good if it shines on us when we're dead.

Standing on one of the front wall's battlements, Andrina looked out over the valley floor and was surprised to see Marcheto riding towards the castle.

Andrina thought, What can he possibly say to justify his behavior? But then, she realized Marcheto wasn't interested in explaining his motives to her or the other warrior women. He was going after Aerylln!

And Andrina thought, Does that young man think he can betray his friends and still have the woman he loves?

Marcheto's answer to that question would have been, no! However, he wasn't willing to give up trying. And so, seemingly oblivious to the risks involved in returning to Crystal Castle, the prodigal son barreled through the entrance, which had no drawbridge, door or gate blocking him, such barriers never having been needed before.

As Marcheto dismounted, Corson, Chen and her warrior women swarmed around him seeking news of Lord Daegal's army. They were also wondering why he'd left his job as scout and returned to the castle.

However, looking up at the battlements and making eye contact with Andrina, Marcheto was unnerved by the way she was glaring at him. Shuddering, he realized that from her vantage point atop the castle walls, Andrina was watching Lord Daegal's army entering Crystal Valley.

"They have my father!" Marcheto blurted out to Chen.

"What are you talking about, and why should I care?" Chen asked, almost laughing at him, such talk seeming irrelevant.

"My father's name is Tark," Marcheto confessed, a look of anguish on his face. "He's the captain of Lord Daegal's personal guard."

"I know who Captain Tark is, and he has a bunch of sons, doesn't he?"

"Yes, I'm one of them. The youngest."

"Why haven't I seen you around the castle?" Chen asked eyeing him suspiciously.

"Being the youngest, I was at work taking care of my older brothers' horses and gear, as well as having my own training. All that goes on from dawn to dusk, day after day, so I don't exactly get out much."

"Tark's youngest son? Maybe I have heard about you," Chen said smiling. "Are you that oversexed young man who's seduced half the women in the castle?"

"I guess that's me, but I'm not like that now. I've never even touched Aerylln inappropriately."

"Why are you telling me this?" Chen asked.

"Lord Daegal ordered me to become a spy by ingratiating myself with Aerylln."

"You tricked that innocent, teenage girl? And you're a spy?" Chen asked feeling genuine surprise. "Well, you had me fooled, I thought you loved her."

"I do love her!"

"And yet, Marcheto, you used her to become a spy? I'll tell you what you are, you're a traitor," Chen said reaching for her knife.

"If you kill me, Aerylln will never believe my crime. You'd best let me live long enough to tell her myself."

"You're going to admit to Aerylln that you betrayed us all? She's never even known a man before, and you're going to tell her that the only man she ever loved is a traitor?"

"Yes."

Chen almost killed him for that alone.

Then, nearly 100 warrior women parted as a teenage girl with a very powerful sword approached them.

Having run downstairs to greet her boyfriend, Aerylln was breathless and smiling. From an upper-storey window in the tower, she'd seen Marcheto entering the courtyard. But after taking one look at the warrior women surrounding him, Aerylln knew Marcheto was in trouble, serious trouble.

Walking up to him, she took his right hand in both of hers, looked up into his eyes and said, "Tell me what happened."

"I'm a traitor! My father's the captain of Lord Daegal's personal guard. I lied about the location of Lord Daegal's army, and now it's pouring into Crystal Valley! But Aerylln, Lord Daegal said he'd kill my father if I didn't help him!"

Aerylln took in the news calmly.

"You've made a serious mistake, and the consequences will be severe. You realize that, don't you?" she asked quietly.

"Yes," Marcheto whispered.

Looking at the faces of the women surrounding them, Aerylln realized Marcheto might soon be dead. If she let go of his hand and turned her back on him, Marcheto would be executed before she took two steps away from him.

Desperate to explain himself, the young man looked at the only woman he'd ever loved, the only woman who'd ever loved him in return, and implored her to understand.

"Lord Daegal would have killed my father!" Marcheto said again, the torment and anguish in his voice readily apparent. Though not fearing death, he didn't want to meet his demise before receiving Aerylln's forgiveness.

"Does your father love you?" Aerylln asked, her voice quietly chastising him.

"Yes."

"Then, you should have trusted his love. He'd rather be dead, himself, than witness what you're doing now, betraying those who trusted you."

"Maybe you're right, but after Lord Daegal threatened to kill him, my father was really upset," Marcheto said. "I heard the fear in his voice."

"Yes, I'm sure he was distraught, but a father would rather bear any burden than see his son turn traitor. You should have known that, Marcheto, you should have trusted your father to rise to the occasion. No one respects a traitor, no matter what side he's on. As it is, you denied your father a proud death, and, if he survives this coming battle, you'll have caused him to live in shame," Aerylln said squeezing Marcheto's hand while sighing over his shortsightedness.

"More than likely, Lord Daegal will kill your father anyway. He won't trust him anymore, not when Lord Daegal's virtually responsible for your death. So, your father will end up dying for nothing," Aerylln said sadly.

All the warrior women, including Andrina, who'd come down from the battlements, marveled at the young woman's wisdom.

Aerylln let go of Marcheto's hand. "I want him left alive," was all she said as she turned and walked away.

No one disputed Aerylln's quiet authority, so the warrior women began dispersing while looking at the young man in disgust. That is, until Gwendylln walked over to Marcheto and punched him with a rock-hard fist. Stumbling backwards, his breastbone fractured, Marcheto's chest exploded shooting excruciating pain throughout his entire body.

Next, Malavika walked up to Marcheto throwing a devastating left hook, and everyone in the courtyard heard his skull crack. Then the punishment began in earnest as each warrior woman took her turn, all except for Chen, Corson and Andrina. Chen knew if she so much as touched him, she wouldn't be able to stop from killing him. Corson held back because Aerylln was her friend. And Andrina knew that no amount of physical pain would cleanse the young man of his crime.

However, their self-restraint didn't stop the others, and the beating went on for what seemed like an eternity.

When the last woman walked away, Marcheto lay on the floor of the courtyard only a step or two from dying. But he was alive. So they had honored Aerylln's request but only by the slimmest of margins.

Chapter 28

Chen's savage wolfhounds bounded out of Crystal Castle like black meteors of death.

They were long-haired, shaggy beasts with massive jaws, enormous chests and hind legs possessing the strength of catapults. Almost two-dozen of these fearsome creatures were ripping through an expanse of thick grassland stretching out in front of Crystal Castle as far as the eye could see.

Unaware of the approaching danger and taking comfort in its vastly superior numbers, Lord Daegal's army continued winding its way down the mountain trail. Several hundred warriors had already reached the base of Crystal Valley and were milling about waiting for orders to form into battle groups.

The first warriors to see the four-legged behemoths hurtling at them stared in stunned disbelief at the sheer size and speed of these incredible animals.

Some of Lord Daegal's personal guards were formulating attack plans when the wolfhounds were sighted. Tark, Rory and Kato were present and, looking up, saw the wolfhounds descending upon them.

Zenkak's back and shoulder muscles rippled with each stride as the pack leader charged towards his prey with eager anticipation.

When the wolfhounds reached Lord Daegal's men, some launched themselves into the air with powerful hind legs flying over the first row of warriors and falling upon those behind them like black rain. It was a thundershower of madness, and the wolfhounds unleashed hell all around them.

Other wolfhounds ran right through the front line penetrating deeply into the ranks and stopping only after clamping onto a human who acted like an anchor slowing the animal's momentum. The strongest wolfhounds charged even deeper into the fray, the shaggy beasts' powerful muscles straining as they dragged screaming men by their arms and legs while horrified humans fled the torrential downpour of pain and agony.

With an enormous mouth filled with gleaming incisors, one gigantic wolfhound clamped his jaws around a man's midriff lifting the warrior off the ground with feet and legs dangling out one side of beast's mouth, his head and shoulders the other.

Running back through the ranks of Lord Daegal's warriors who were scattering in all directions, the massive wolfhound bounded into the open grassland while carrying his trophy. The shaggy beast charged along the entire length of the hundreds of warriors gathered on the valley floor. Anytime his human cargo stopped screaming, the giant wolfhound clamped down harder digging long, sharp teeth deeper into the man's ravaged middle.

As the wolfhounds continued their relentless attack, the howls of pain were deafening. Those warriors fortunate enough to escape shut their ears to the agony and ran away as far and as fast as they could.

For some, it just wasn't far or fast enough.

Filling the pastoral setting with an air of unreality, the high-pitched wailing and shrieking seemed incongruous with the natural beauty of the valley. But as almost two-dozen hungry wolfhounds continued pursuing their enemy, the cries became prevalent enough.

"Mortally wound your enemy but don't kill him. Instead, let him scream," Zenkak had instructed his hounds before making their charge. "One man screaming in agony will unnerve a dozen. And the more warriors you intimidate, the fewer you'll have to fight."

And now, putting his teachings into effect, the pack leader clamped his jaws down on an unfortunate warrior's leg whipping the hysterical man back and forth in the air. Then with one powerful sweep of his neck, Zenkak tossed the warrior aside.

With a sense of exhilaration, the pack leader tilted back his head and cut loose with a ferocious battle cry. It had the desired effect, and the warriors closest to him put as much distance between themselves and this monstrous king of beasts as possible.

Looking around for his next victim, Zenkak settled on Tark, the captain of Lord Daegal's personal guard, and lunged at him. But Tark didn't flinch and didn't try to escape. He stood his ground.

Zenkak, lowering himself as if getting ready to spring, prowled slowly in a circle around his adversary while making deep, rumbling growls.

Unafraid, Tark twirled his sword in his hand and watched carefully.

But the attack came from an unexpected direction. With blinding speed, Lothar, Zenkak's second-in-command, hurled himself at Tark landing on the captain's back and sinking his fangs into the warrior's shoulder. Warm liquid flowed into the wolfhound's mouth spilling over his tongue. Lothar liked the taste of blood, but this time it proved a nearly fatal distraction.

Exploiting this opportunity, Tark sank his sword into the animal's thick, muscular neck finding red meat beneath the surface. And though his shirt was becoming soaked with the wolfhound's blood, Tark stayed focused. Next, the captain's knife found Lothar's soft underbelly, and he shoved it in deeply.

Hearing Lothar howling in pain, two wolfhounds rushed to help him. One knocked Tark to the ground, but as he fell, the captain shoved his thick shield into the wolfhound's huge, slavering mouth. Next, Tark plunged his sword into the frenzied beast's heart, and the animal died instantly.

Running interference, the second wolfhound placed himself between Tark and Lothar, then after cautiously backing away, helped the wounded animal reach the open field.

However, Zenkak remained in the thick of things and, glancing around, settled on Kato as his next victim. Earlier, back at The Rock, he was the one who'd warned Andrina and Chen's warrior women that Lord Daegal knew about their sister warriors killing 25 of his men.

Letting out a tremendous growl, Zenkak leapt at Kato clamping onto the warrior's left thigh and thrashing him around in the air. But there was something different about this young man. He wasn't yelling as loudly, and he hadn't panicked.

Zenkak sensed trouble.

In the next instant, the pack leader felt a knife digging into his flesh and raking across his shoulder blades. Reacting quickly, the giant wolfhound began spinning around causing the young warrior to lay flat, stretching him out and keeping the hand with the knife as far away as possible. Zenkak continued whipping around in a circle building momentum, then let go of Kato and watched him sailing over the heads of the other warriors.

Next, looking to his right, the pack leader was greatly impressed by what another of his wolfhounds was doing. The animal was missing his right ear and had a deep wound running down one side of his face but was giving his all, even fighting to the death. Just a few moments ago, a dozen warriors had formed a defensive circle facing outward at the wolfhounds menacing them on all sides, yet this daring animal had broken through and was now in the center. The beast was clawing the backs of the warriors and sinking his teeth into as many as possible. But when the uninjured warriors turned and faced him, the wolfhound was doomed, caught within a circle of swords.

Lying on the ground mortally wounded, the noble animal summoned up his last ounce of strength, turned his massive head, gripped a warrior's sword arm and bit down hard. Even though life was rapidly draining out of him, the wolfhound heard the man screaming and died contented.

Looking around and assessing the situation, Zenkak realized his wolfhounds had done well. Many of Lord Daegal's warriors were running away in disarray. It was a rewarding sight, but the price had been high, and the pack leader could see that he'd lost at least half of his wolfhounds. However, having accomplished their mission, which was to create confusion, fear and panic, Zenkak gave a high-pitched howl signaling his hounds to fall back.

Tragically, as one wolfhound was turning away, a warrior took a swipe at him cutting off the lower half of a hind leg. Unaware of his injury, though limping badly, the animal raced to where Zenkak and the others were gathering at a safe distance from the enemy atop a small hill. However, upon reaching the other animals, he noticed the concern on their faces, looked at his hind leg and realized he was ruined as a warrior.

And though huddling around him reassuringly, all the animals knew that a wolfhound without four good legs was useless in battle.

"Say goodbye to Chen for me," the wounded hound growled. Then, turning towards Lord Daegal's men, he ran as best he could and plunged into their ranks taking off a warrior's sword arm before the others cut him down.

As he lay on his side dying, the wolfhound made eye contact with Zenkak who held his gaze until the last flicker of life drifted from the fallen animal's eyes.

Leaping into the air in a savage rage, Zenkak nonetheless fought to get his temper under control. If it weren't for the coming battle at Crystal Castle, where the wolfhounds would be sorely needed, they would have all charged into death without hesitation.

"We'll be joining him soon enough, possibly by nightfall," the pack leader said trying to console them.

And with that, Zenkak and his wolfhounds sped back to Crystal Castle.

Chapter 29

Even before Zenkak and his wolfhounds made it back to Crystal Castle, almost 100 warrior women riding black stallions came thundering out of the entrance. It was a raging torrent of dominant, assertive, determined women on horses with long, outstretched legs, glistening coats, flowing manes and pounding hooves and all racing towards Lord Daegal's men.

At the same time, at the base of the mountain, male warriors were tending to their wounded and beginning to regroup, and many were ashamed of the way they'd fled from Zenkak's surprise attack.

"I ran like a girl," one young man lamented.

"Don't beat yourself up over it," a seasoned warrior said. "I saw plenty of good, experienced men behaving just like you did."

"I've never faced wild animals before, at least not giant ones," the young warrior said trying to justify to himself, more than anyone else, why he ran away.

"There's nothing to be embarrassed about. I was almost sick, myself, when I saw those wolfhounds clamping their jaws onto some of my friends and thrashing them about."

"You didn't run," the young man pointed out. "You stood your ground."

"Yes, but I didn't advance on them either."

"If I could do it over again, maybe I wouldn't run."

"Possibly, but I've never seen or heard of anything like that before. It was enough to unnerve anyone."

"I just wish I had another chance to prove myself."

"Be careful what you wish for, you might get it." And at that moment, the veteran warrior heard something and glanced up. What he saw wasn't encouraging.

Chen and her warrior women were shouting battle cries and firing a barrage of arrows that flew across the sky in waves and rained down upon the unsuspecting warriors with devastating effect.

Redefining the phrase "running like a girl," a thundering horde of female barbarians stormed through the ranks of men firing their bows at will. And now, not only were Lord Daegal's warriors screaming from wounds caused by wolfhounds, but also from broken arms and legs, or worse, caused by being trampled by powerful warhorses being ridden by women who were more free spirited and filled with more restless energy than the stallions themselves.

"Women are unpredictable!" Gwendylln shouted upon realizing that no one had expected a second attack so soon after the first. Charging deeply into the army of stunned, disbelieving men, she launched arrow after arrow. But Gwendylln also knew it was important to make the most of the men's confusion while it lasted and then to retreat.

"Snap out of it!" Tark bellowed trying to rouse the men to action while protecting himself from the arrows with his shield.

Malavika, having ridden almost as deeply into the ranks of the surprised warriors as Gwendylln, was firing over and over at the men nearest to her. Keeping them at bay wasn't hard, at least for the moment, since few held their ground against the warrior women, just as most everyone had been caught off guard by the wolfhounds.

Men are so predictable, Malavika thought as her arrows repeatedly struck home. But like Gwendylln, she knew the men wouldn't stay shocked forever.

Fortunately, on other parts of the battlefield, Chen and her warrior women were meeting with similar success. Six women had formed a circle facing outward and were firing rapidly, clearing the area around them of any opposition.

Another group of warrior women and their stallions had formed two rows of ten. Each row was lined up side-by-side, the women's legs almost touching. The rows were facing in opposite directions, their horses' rumps almost touching, and the women in one row had their backs to the women in the other.

Added to that, the archers in both rows began firing in alternate sequence. That is, every other woman fired her bow, and as she paused to reload, the women on either side of her were firing. This alternating system provided a continuous stream of arrows that mowed down the men around them with ruthless efficiency. It allowed for no pause in the firing that the men could exploit to make a run at the women.

Almost 100 warrior women firing continually can do a lot of damage, and Lord Daegal's men were being cut down left and right. Chen was in her glory.

But for as passionately intense as Chen was about everything she did, one survival skill she'd perfected more than any other was having the self-discipline not to overplay her hand. And so, sensing they'd done as much as they could, Chen ordered her women to retreat.

To the men's despair, Chen's retreat was as aggressive as her opening assault. While carefully making their way back to the open field, her warrior women continued putting pressure on their male adversaries. Glancing around and doing a quick count, Chen was relieved to discover that her warrior women hadn't suffered a single casualty.

And then, the unexpected happened.

Glenda, the last warrior woman exiting the battlefield, was dragged from her horse by a man who jumped up behind her, pinned the woman's arms to her sides by wrapping his arms around hers, and then rolled off of the warhorse with both of them crashing to the ground a short distance from the main body of men.

Having hit the ground hard, Glenda was sprawled out on the grass with the wind knocked out of her and her head spinning, but she could sense the men gathering around her. However, the first man to touch Glenda discovered she wasn't as helpless as she appeared, and the warrior woman slashed the back of his wrist with her knife. Then, struggling to her knees, Glenda made several wicked thrusts with her knife before being struck from behind. As her skull seemed to explode, the warrior woman blacked out completely and fell to the ground unconscious.

Unaware of Glenda's plight, the other warrior women were racing through the field when Chen suddenly heard Malavika shout in alarm. Wheeling her horse around, the black leather panther saw Malavika standing in her stirrups and pointing at something.

Taking the scene in at a glance, all thoughts of caution and self-preservation left Chen, and she spurred her warhorse and went back to get her sister warrior. Having been raised with these women since she was 15-years-old, Chen wasn't about to leave anyone behind, not as long as she was alive.

As Chen charged to the rescue, all the warrior women galloped after her creating a wedge formation with their leader on point. As soon as they got within range, the women began shooting arrows at any man within 100 yards of their fallen sister.

Pulling her warhorse to an abrupt halt, Chen leapt from the saddle, hauled out her sword and threw herself at the men who were pinning Glenda down. Three were dead before they even knew what hit them. Two more saw the black leather panther leaping at them, but the warrior woman's sword was a blur, and they were powerless against her.

Chen was an avenging angel of death.

The last of the men surrounding Glenda put up a brief resistance, which ended when Chen's sword rammed right through his chest. Afterwards, when she pulled out her weapon, the man was still standing, so she punched him in the jaw knocking him to the ground.

Looking about, Chen was wild with rage. Few could work themselves into a battle frenzy like the black leather panther.

After Gwendylln helped an unsteady Glenda back onto her feet, all three women mounted their warhorses, and the entire deadly sisterhood galloped off into the open field leaving devastation in their wake.

"There's more where that came from," Chen yelled over her shoulder at Lord Daegal's men. She was stating the obvious, and no one doubted her.

*

Less than an hour earlier, Lord Daegal was on the mountain trail several hundred feet above the valley floor watching helplessly as Chen's wolfhounds plowed into his troops.

The warlord realized he'd made a serious mistake allowing his infantry units to make their way down the mountain ahead of his archery and cavalry units. He'd underestimated his niece and was furious with himself for doing so.

With the dark sword, Crystal, almost within his grasp, Lord Daegal knew this wasn't the time to be making such errors in judgment.

"I want that sword!" the warlord shouted more to himself than anyone else. "I'd hoped Chen would take Crystal from Glenitant, and then kill the old witch. And I'm not surprised Chen wants to keep Crystal, but I didn't actually expect her to try to keep the castle!"

Lord Daegal failed to understand how desperately Chen wanted a place of her own, a place where she'd feel safe and secure.

To Chen, the loss of her father had been a devastating blow to her sense of security. But Lord Daegal had felt differently about his brother, Chen's father, viewing him as useless.

Thinking back to when Ritalso had lived at The Rock, Lord Daegal smiled as he recalled his brother's greatest weakness. The warlord thought, Ritalso cares about those around him, and because of that, it was easy to take advantage of him. Plus, it wasn't like Chen and her father got along. My niece was always lording herself over Ritalso, bossing him around and making him do things. She was more a parent to him than he was to her.

Still surprised at her reaction, the warlord recalled the shock on Chen's face when he'd told her about her father's supposed disappearance. He thought, I didn't realize she'd take it so hard. Why would Chen care that such a weakling had come up missing? She never listened to him anyway.

Without Chen's knowledge, Lord Daegal had imprisoned Ritalso in the Monastery Castle hoping to keep his brother out of the way. Ritalso had been resisting Lord Daegal who'd wanted to turn Chen into a disturbed young woman with a violent temper.

After having Ritalso quietly and secretly kidnapped, Lord Daegal had repeatedly preyed upon the teenage girl. And so, feeling abandoned by her father and being assaulted by her uncle, Chen was pushed beyond the breaking point, and she'd become consumed by anger and hatred, which was exactly what Lord Daegal had wanted to happen. The warlord knew that such dark emotions were required if Chen was to win Crystal's acceptance for the evil sword thrived on women who were deeply disturbed and extremely negative.

Lord Daegal had counted on Crystal being unable to resist the opportunity to be inherited by Chen who was in the direct line of succession. Glenitant had no children, and Chen was her only niece making the black leather panther the sole heir. Crystal could have decided to skip a generation waiting for another girl child to be born, but with Chen being so filled with dark thoughts and feelings, Crystal was only too eager to accept her.

However, Lord Daegal was upset that he needed Chen at all, though there was good reason why the warlord needed her help. On several occasions, he'd tried unsuccessfully to take Crystal from Glenitant, but the old witch had always proven to be a more difficult opponent than he'd expected.

But now that Chen had inherited Crystal, Lord Daegal was hoping his niece's lack of experience wielding the dark sword would enable him to ride over the mountain with his army and take the sword from her. Blinded by his desire for power, Lord Daegal had refused to believe the truth, that only a woman could wield the dark sword effectively, even though the same was true of Baelfire, her half-sister.

And so, after years of planning and plotting, the warlord was riding down the mountain trail into Crystal Valley, but he still couldn't understand why his niece was resisting.

"I'll never allow Chen to keep Crystal Castle, but she could live here," he said thinking out loud while marveling at the castle's incredible beauty. More than just a fortress, it truly was an architectural masterpiece.

He smiled and thought, Of course, I'd want to visit her at night to confer. Then, laughing out loud, he shouted, "And confer and confer and confer!"

Somehow, it had never occurred to Lord Daegal that assaulting his niece repeatedly over the years, along with kidnapping her father, would make Chen want Crystal Castle as her own for a safe haven. Being so focused on turning Chen into a woman Crystal would want, Lord Daegal had forgotten to take into account what so much emotional damage would cause Chen to want.

However, once again, Lord Daegal thought about how good it would feel to have Chen back in a more subservient role. The warlord still didn't understand, and he never would, which is why Chen was determined to keep Crystal Castle for herself or die trying.

But Lord Daegal's ambitions went beyond his desire to possess Crystal, the dark sword, and Crystal Castle.

He thought, If I can get Crystal and also be present during the transformation of Aerylln, Baelfire and Zorya into the Trinity, I might be able to inject some of Crystal's malignant evil into those three, and then Crystal's hold on them would be substantial.

"And I'll be holding Crystal!" Lord Daegal shouted. "I'll finally have the undisputed power I've always wanted!"

Still, it angered him that his lack of preparation had allowed Chen to send those wolfhounds at his men. But he was about to get even angrier.

Watching in disbelief, Lord Daegal saw Chen and her warrior women pouring out of Crystal Castle and storming into the ranks of his army, an army already made jittery from the wolfhound attack.

The warlord watched in dismay as his infantry began scattering in all directions, ending up in total disarray.

As the warriors closest to him shifted nervously in their saddles, Lord Daegal realized he had failed them. Thus far in this campaign, he'd proven to be a poor leader and was being bested, and sorely embarrassed, by his niece. Scores of his warriors were dying down below on the valley floor, and it was his fault.

"You'll pay for this, Chen! You'll pay!" Lord Daegal screamed in frustration.

Chapter 30

Chen's warrior women charged through the castle's entrance their jaws set, their eyes hard and their stallions' hooves thundering on the stone pavement. It was a display of power that would intimidate anyone, including Marcheto who was sitting on the courtyard floor, leaning against a wall and nursing his wounds. Aerylln, hovering protectively, was standing nearby.

As the warrior women dismounted, many looked over at Marcheto. Fresh from battle, they were filled with restless energy and adrenaline was flooding through their veins. When Gwendylln saw the young man, she spat on the ground in anger. Just the sight of him enraged her. Some warrior women headed over towards Marcheto and Aerylln, anger filling their eyes and their fists clenched.

Marcheto felt a sense of hopelessness as the ferocious-looking women strode towards him. The young man knew he couldn't survive another beating. His body was already so wracked with pain that he could hardly bear it. Having fainted only a few minutes ago, Marcheto was still dizzy, and his stomach felt sick.

As the women continued making their way across the courtyard, Aerylln quietly stepped between them and her boyfriend while placing a hand on Baelfire's hilt. That was enough to stop two of the warrior women, but five others ignored her warning and kept on coming.

Squaring her shoulders, Aerylln drew Baelfire ever so slightly out of her scabbard exposing the metal blade a fraction of an inch. A thin sheet of blinding light instantly burst from the sword, and the approaching warrior women stopped and covered their eyes. Sliding the blade back into its scabbard, Aerylln faced the women and didn't blink. Her gaze was steady, firm and determined.

The message was clear, This is my man, keep your distance!

The warrior women backed away and rejoined their sisters, but now all of them were glaring at Marcheto.

Glancing over at the castle's main tower, Aerylln saw Chen's father coming out of the entrance. Ritalso and Chen hadn't reconciled their differences, but she permitted him free and safe passage throughout the castle. And, at the moment, Ritalso was performing an important errand for Aerylln.

While watching Chen's father heading towards them, Marcheto noticed he was carrying a wooden shield, a sword and a knife. Upon reaching the younger man, Ritalso laid the armaments next to Marcheto who stared at them in silence.

"You know what you have to do," Aerylln said. "You have to ask Lord Daegal to honor the ancient ritual of trial by combat."

"Yes, I've thought about that myself," Marcheto said looking over at Chen's warrior women who were still glowering at him. "I'd have to fight someone from Lord Daegal's army who's an excellent warrior, someone good enough to kill me. Then, should I survive, I'd be welcomed back into the good graces of those who now want me dead. But I don't know, it sounds like a long shot to me."

“Well, you can’t stay here, not after what you did,” Aerylln said. “If you want me, you’re going to have to fight for me.”

That was exactly what Marcheto needed to hear. He wanted Aerylln more than anything, even more than his own life, and he’d do whatever it took to win her back. Being in love made Marcheto feel more alive than he’d ever felt before.

“I’ve been such a fool,” the young man said deeply regretting how he’d betrayed everyone at Crystal Castle. “But I felt trapped, and I didn’t know what else to do.”

“Like I told you before, if you’d trusted me more, we could have talked about it,” Aerylln said looking at him with a level gaze. “Now get up!”

Forcing himself off the courtyard floor and onto his hands and knees, Marcheto tried getting onto his feet, but his head was spinning, and he collapsed. After struggling repeatedly, trying again and again to make it to his feet, Marcheto was close to passing out from exhaustion.

Realizing she’d have to intervene, Baelfire began by expressing her own displeasure saying, “Aerylln’s very important to me, Marcheto, not only as my master but as a friend. And you hurt my friend, young man. You broke her heart.”

Remaining silent, Marcheto looked at the powerful sword Aerylln was holding with both hands.

“You’re alive only because Aerylln wants it that way. Were it up to me, I’d reduce you to a pile of cinders.”

Marcheto held his breath and didn’t move.

“As it is, Aerylln and I had a talk, and I agree that trial by combat is the only honorable way out for you, and it would lessen Aerylln’s embarrassment. Remember, we’re the ones who brought you to this castle. So, we share in your shame, and I don't like that one bit!"

Marcheto remained silent even after the sword finished speaking, which probably saved his life, at least for the moment, for Baelfire was on the edge of losing her temper. But Aerylln shook Baelfire gently, and the sword calmed down a little.

"Well, are you willing to ask Lord Daegal for trial by combat?" Baelfire asked.

"Yes, but I can hardly move. How can I endure trial by combat if I can't even walk out the castle entrance?"

"We might be able to help in that area," Baelfire said, her tone softening.

Aerylln gave the sword an affectionate squeeze, pleased that Baelfire was giving her boyfriend a second chance.

"Okay, take hold of my scabbard," Baelfire said.

Marcheto hesitated and looked at Aerylln who nodded. Summoning what strength was left in his body, the young man gripped Baelfire as tightly as possible.

The relief from pain was instantaneous. Marcheto could feel life pouring back into his body. His wounds began to heal. His throbbing headache left him. He no longer felt like he had been trampled by a mob of wild horses. He felt energized and whole again.

The young man got to his feet and took up the sword, shield and knife. He bent down to give Aerylln a kiss, but she turned away.

"Not until you've earned it," she said while secretly wanting the kiss as much as he did.

Marcheto ached inside for he'd wanted that kiss very badly. He wanted not just one kiss but a hundred of them. Yet most of all, he wanted Aerylln back.

Looking at the wide-open castle entrance, the young warrior realized it was his one chance for redemption. Striding over to it, Marcheto stepped outside with a sense of grim determination. Walking through the field towards Lord Daegal's army, the young warrior's greatest fear was that the warlord wouldn't take him seriously and might even laugh at him.

Looking over his shoulder, Marcheto saw Aerylln, Baelfire, Zorya, Eldwyn, and Ritalso standing on the walkway behind the castle's front wall and watching through the battlements. He also saw Chen and her warrior women along the top of the front wall on the parapets and watching as well. Dartuke, Thordig and the other 20 nobles from the western lands were also there. And lastly, he noticed that Balder and his 10 men had joined the nobles.

Marcheto thought, Regardless of what Lord Daegal might say, this is no laughing matter. It's a matter of honor. Everyone in the castle shares in my shame. They feel they've been duped, which is why they want me dead, out of the castle, or both.

Both, Chen would have told him.

Rather than killing Marcheto themselves, as they'd wanted to, the warrior women were now all watching him.

"I hope he doesn't embarrass us again," Gwendylln said to Chen who was standing next to her. "He needs to at least put forth a good effort, or there's no reason for us to have allowed him to go out there."

"Why did you listen to Aerylln when she asked you to permit this?" Malavika asked Chen.

"Because, as a sign of respect, Aerylln sought out my counsel on this matter, even though that really wasn't necessary. However, it shows that Aerylln recognizes my ownership of

Crystal Castle. She sees it as my home and is willing to live by my rules. So, it was hard for me to say no."

"Then why did you allow us to keep threatening Marcheto? Why didn't you tell us to stop?" Gwendylln asked.

"I want to be sure Marcheto understands how we feel, and that he realizes the severity of what he did. But Aerylln believes he deserves a second chance and maybe she's right. I know I needed one badly.

"Having Crystal Castle is my second chance at life. Trial by combat is Marcheto's second chance," Chen said. "But I agree with Gwendylln, let's hope he at least puts up a decent fight."

As Marcheto continued making his way down the field towards Lord Daegal and his men, the young warrior passed several sentries who'd been posted as a precaution just in case there were more surprise attacks.

As he passed the third sentry, Marcheto glanced back over his shoulder and saw Pensgraft riding out alone towards him. The giant warrior looked so regal astride his massive warhorse that the younger man actually gasped.

After reaching Marcheto, Pensgraft pulled up on his reins and said, "No one should have to die alone. I'll serve as a witness to what happens here today. And I'll bring your body back for proper burial if that's necessary, although I hope it's not. Remember, Marcheto, you have nothing to lose now. Don't play it safe at all. Attack from the very moment the fight starts and keep attacking. Never go on the defensive. Never!"

Pensgraft then leaned down and extended his hand to the younger warrior. Marcheto was greatly in need of acceptance and shook the giant's hand with gratitude. Sighing with relief, he no longer felt so alone and turned to face his destiny.

However, in addition to that, he found himself facing his father and three older brothers who were riding towards him.

"Marcheto, what's going on?" Tark asked as he pulled his warhorse up next to his son.

"I want trial by combat."

"Why?" Tark asked in surprise. "If you're in trouble, we'll all stand together. You don't ever have to go it alone in this family. You know that."

"I know father, but this is something I have to do myself."

"You're not here because of that young woman, are you? Oh, please, tell me you're not risking your life to impress Aerylln."

"I don't believe it," Kirnochak, the oldest brother, said in disgust as he dismounted and walked over to the young warrior.

"But father's right, this is about that teenage girl, isn't it?" Kirnochak said smacking Marcheto on the back of the head.

"Don't do that again!"

"What are you going to do about it?" Kirnochak taunted him.

Marcheto raised his shield.

"Oh, you want to fight?" Kirnochak asked taking his own shield down from where it was hanging on the pommel of his saddle. Being older and stronger, Kirnochak managed the heavy shield easily and walked back over towards his youngest brother.

"I'd be a little careful, if I were you. Remember, Marcheto may be small, but he's quick, tough and smart," Xandaric, the second oldest, cautioned Kirnochak.

"I'm well aware he can fight! I didn't say he couldn't," Kirnochak protested.

As he got closer, Kirnochak and Marcheto made eye contact. They looked into each other, deeply into each other.

Equally aware of Marcheto's sensitive nature, Kirnochak knew his youngest brother could sense things, things that no one else could.

You have a better feel for the politics of the castle than anyone else, Kirnochak had once told Marcheto. His youngest brother had simply replied that it was all very obvious to him. And it was.

After maintaining eye contact for what seemed like a long, long time, Kirnochak sighed and asked, "So what's really wrong?"

But before his brother responded, Kirnochak felt a powerful force touching him and, glancing up, saw Pensgraft watching him closely. Looking into the giant's eyes, he realized that this mountain of a man had the same intuitive gift as Marcheto.

"What are you doing here?" Kirnochak asked.

"I didn't want your brother to have to stand alone."

"I appreciate that, but we're here now, so you can leave if you want," Kirnochak said.

"I think I'll stay."

"Well then, how do you feel about all this?" Tark asked.

"Your son is about to become a man."

"He may die in the process."

"Sometimes they go hand in hand."

"That's easy for you to say, he's not your son."

Pensgraft remained silent and held his peace.

"Marcheto, what's on your mind?" Tark asked his youngest son, who was also his favorite.

"I'm a traitor."

"You can't be a traitor," Xandaric said in exasperation. "You were following Lord Daegal's orders, and you owe him your allegiance."

"I've changed since you last saw me."

"No you haven't, not really," Kirnochak said. "You've always had insights into situations that none of us were able to pick up on at first. And you've always been right, at least in the long haul."

"Then listen to me now, Lord Daegal is finished."

"How's that possible? You have what, maybe 200 warriors at Crystal Castle?" Kirnochak asked. "Look over there, Lord Daegal has over 1,000 warriors even after the debacle with Chen's wolfhounds and archers."

"He's finished. Aerylln's the future."

Kirnochak tried to fathom Marcheto's prediction suspecting that his youngest brother possessed a sixth sense enabling him to pick up on things quicker and make correct assessments faster.

"Okay, maybe, but let's stick to what's happening right now," Kirnochak suggested. "Who do you plan on fighting in this trial by combat?"

"Tredax, son of Gornic!"

Tark and Kirnochak looked at each other.

Amazed, Xandaric whistled, turned to Pensgraft and said, "You have to look out for this one. Marcheto can come out of nowhere with one of those ideas of his."

Leaning back his head, Xandaric let out a battle cry, then said, "What a wild man you are, Marcheto. How did you come up with that one?"

"It just came to me while I was walking out here."

"They couldn't refuse us!" Xandaric exclaimed. "They would be humiliated in front of everyone!"

Feeling a sense of fatherly pride, Tark lowered his head and smiled. Marcheto had just outmaneuvered a rival family that had been a thorn in his side for years.

"Brilliant!" was all Adexsus, the next youngest son, could think of to say. "Absolutely brilliant!"

"I'll ask Lord Daegal about this, but I think he'll go for it," Tark said.

"Why are you so sure?" Pensgraft asked.

"Because it's going to be one hell of a fight!"

Chapter 31

Meanwhile, on the walkway atop Crystal Castle's front wall, Aerylln, Corson and the others were watching as Tark rode back to Lord Daegal's army.

"Should Marcheto lose, I'll kill his opponent for you," Corson told her friend.

"No, I'll do it myself," Aerylln said. "After all, I'm the one who sent him out there."

"Yes, but if you hadn't, Chen's women would have killed him eventually. And it would have been sooner rather than later."

"I know."

Falling silent, Corson and Aerylln watched Tark disappearing into the ranks of Lord Daegal's warriors, all of whom had reached the valley floor. The infantry, cavalry and archers were beginning to form into battle groups, and Corson could feel the tension building in the air.

After searching for Lord Daegal, Tark located the warlord, explained what Marcheto wanted and, as he'd suspected, found his master to be quite receptive.

"I hope you're right, I hope Aerylln put him up to this, or at least suggested it," Lord Daegal said. "If they're in a genuine relationship, then that could work to our advantage."

"Sire, Marcheto may not be much use to us," Tark said. "By now, he may have gone over to the other side completely."

"If everyone in Crystal Castle's dead, there won't be another side for him to join," Lord Daegal said smiling grimly.

"Well, that would solve the problem."

"And remember, Marcheto believes you're a dead man if he disobeys me. Plus, if I need to, I'll use your other three sons as hostages. When Marcheto has to choose between obedience and the loss of his entire family, he'll do what he's told."

"I hope so," Tark said, but he doubted that anyone could control a young man in love. And Tark didn't like having his family threatened. He knew a threat could easily become reality, if Lord Daegal lost his temper. And the warlord's temper was a horrible thing to see.

Having been the captain of Lord Daegal's personal guard for over 20 years, Tark knew his life and his very reason for living were tied to this violent and unpredictable man. But as he rode away from his master, Tark admitted to himself that Lord Daegal had changed, and changed for the worse, over the years.

Sighing deeply, Marcheto's father realized he'd spent much of his life defending a man who turned out to be a disappointment. However, forcing this out of his mind, Tark headed for General Gornic's encampment.

Lord Daegal had been pleased that Marcheto wanted Gornic's son, Tredax, to be his opponent. Just a few minutes earlier, the warlord had smiled at Tark and said, "This fight's been brewing for a long time."

"Yes, my lord, it has," Tark had readily agreed.

"And we should give Tredax something extra to fight for. Let him know that if he wins, I'll let him have Chen. He's a few years younger than her, but I don't think he'll mind having an experienced woman in his bed," Lord Daegal had said.

At first Tark had been shocked by this offer, but then he admitted to himself that nothing Lord Daegal did should come as a surprise anymore. To the warlord, selling out his niece and Tark's entire family in an effort to get his hands on Crystal and Crystal Castle seemed perfectly reasonable.

But approaching General Gornic's command post, Tark put these thoughts out of his mind as well. The general's four sons quickly surrounded the captain of Lord Daegal's personal guard, almost laughing at him for falling into their hands so easily. Having ridden in, they were in no mood to let Tark ride out, at least not alive.

Although feeling somewhat shaken over being in the hands of his personal enemy, Tark got a grip on himself, focused on business and said, "Marcheto wants trial by combat, and Lord Daegal says he's to fight Tredax."

"When?" Gornic asked.

"Now, and Lord Daegal says that if Tredax wins, he'll get Chen as a prize."

General Gornic's eyes opened wide over that comment. The general realized that any sons Tredax and Lord Daegal's niece had together would be in line to inherit The Rock, as well as all the lands in the warlord's domain.

"But first, let's see how Tredax stacks up against Marcheto now that my son will be allowed to fight back," Tark said glaring at his adversary.

"Your son's a coward, that's always been Marcheto's main problem. If he had any guts, he'd have put an end to Tredax bullying him a long time ago," Gornic sneered.

"Your son's bullied Marcheto since they were children, and Tredax always had a size advantage over my boy," Tark said.

"Yes, a big size advantage," Gornic laughed. "Tredax can shove Marcheto around pretty much at will."

"Maybe, but Marcheto's a better swordsman. Yet he couldn't take advantage of his skill because the bullying never quite went far enough to threaten Marcheto's life, though it came mighty close on several occasions."

"That's rubbish, Marcheto could have challenged Tredax to a swordfight anytime he wanted," Gornic insisted.

"Marcheto challenged Tredax more than once, but your son refused to fight, and you know it."

"Well, this time, you'll be sorry when Tredax accepts the challenge. You haven't seen him lately. He's even bigger, and he's a better swordsman than Marcheto is or ever will be."

"Stop bragging and let him prove it. Get Tredax onto the field of honor. But I think Marcheto's going to take him down, and he'll do it in front of everyone."

Wheeling his warhorse around, Tark began charging his way through Gornic's sons who still had him surrounded. When they went for their swords, Tark pulled his as well.

"No!" Gornic shouted. "Let the coward's father go free. He'll regret showing his face here soon enough."

Tark glared at Gornic as if the general's sons weren't even there. He looked past them at the man he'd hated for years, the man responsible for the death of Tark's wife and only daughter. The desire to kill the general was almost overwhelming, and Tark fought hard to keep himself from going out of control. But then, he thought of Marcheto humiliating Tredax in front of the entire army, and he wanted to live to see that, so he sheathed his sword.

"Marcheto will be waiting," Tark said digging his heels into his warhorse's sides and galloping away. But the young warrior wasn't kept waiting for long. Right after Tark returned to his family, Gornic and his sons were already riding out into the field towards them.

"Marcheto?" Tark said.

"Yes, father?"

"I want you to do something for me."

"What?"

"Kill that rotten son-of-a-bitch," Tark said pointing at Tredax.

"Yes, father," Marcheto said filled with grim determination.

"Take my horse, Ramhorn," Kirnochak said handing his brother the reins.

"Thanks," the young warrior said leaping onto Ramhorn's saddle.

The warhorse pranced around restlessly as he felt the mood of the men changing. Ramhorn sensed he was about to be taken into action, and his heart began racing, his nostrils flared, and his muscles tensed. It was all the warhorse could do to contain himself. The tension kept building, and he became almost wild with the desire to spring forward.

Finally, Ramhorn could stand the wait no longer, and he began edging closer to defying his rider who was keeping him in check. Reaching his breaking point, with his patience ready to snap, the warhorse got the command he was so desperate for.

Marcheto nudged Ramhorn's ribs with his heels, and that was all the permission the animal wanted or needed.

Screaming out his rage over having been held back, the warhorse burst forward with such energy that his bulging, straining muscles seemed ready to rip right through his hide. Feeling a ferocious anger that was beyond any rational reason, his hooves pounded against the grass and dirt punishing them for being in his way. Having worked himself into a blind frenzy, all Ramhorn wanted was to find someone or something to throw himself against.

At that very moment, Tredax galloped past his father and brothers who had halted their advance and rode out into the field alone. But he wasn't going to be alone for long. Having seen the other horse and rider, Ramhorn made them his target and went in for the kill.

As the warhorse began increasing his speed with each stride, Marcheto was impressed by the animal's focus and devotion to duty. The young warrior hoped he could perform as well as this magnificent beast.

And Marcheto hoped for one other thing. The young man hoped he could leap off Ramhorn before the two horses collided and do so without Tredax suspecting his intentions. For this strategy to work, Marcheto knew he'd have to wait until the last possible moment to make his move and jump clear.

Realizing that Tredax was more brawn than brains, and that the bully was extremely proud of his size, Marcheto was eager to exploit his opponent's overconfidence.

To start with, as Tredax got closer, Marcheto made a point of making and maintaining eye contact with his opponent.

Marcheto wanted Tredax to think that this coming collision was a personal challenge, a test of their manhood.

Marcheto also wanted Tredax to think that flinching from this challenge would be tantamount to declaring oneself a coward.

And so, with the warhorses thundering towards each other, Tredax, being dull minded and brutish, glared at Marcheto and braced for impact. In return, Marcheto glared back at his opponent appearing to be equally committed. But at the last second, with only a few yards between them, Marcheto, being far too intelligent to take this kind of male posturing seriously, leapt from his horse.

In doing so, Marcheto was obeying a basic axiom of war, which is to take the momentum of one's enemy and use it against him. For example, if an opponent wants to force open a door, and if he's running hard and ready to throw himself against it, then the best alternative is to just open the door. That way, the enemy can run in, quickly reach a surprisingly nearby wall, fall over a window ledge and land several flights below.

And so, knowing that Tredax always relied on blunt force, Marcheto encouraged his opponent to do so once more and then sidestepped the whole situation.

The impact of the two warhorses lifted both animals off the ground sending Tredax flying through the air where his skull cracked against his horse's head as the animal's neck snapped back in response to the force of the collision.

After sailing through the air half-conscious, Tredax landed with a loud grunt followed by a snapping sound as something broke somewhere in the crumpled heap. Marcheto fared much better having rolled neatly to a stop, and he got back up uninjured.

"What a dope," Marcheto said looking down at his mangled opponent. For a while, he stood pondering the crumpled figure of a man who'd bullied him for most of his life. Then Marcheto leaned down, took Tredax's sword and stuck it into the ground next to the fallen warrior's chest.

Marcheto glanced over towards Gornic and his sons, and the message was clear, I could have killed Tredax, but I didn't.

Looking back at the crumpled bully, Marcheto thought, Maybe sparing his life will help bridge the rift between our two families.

But after further pondering his act of mercy, Marcheto wondered, What about Tredax, himself? Will things change, or will he interpret my kindness as a sign of weakness?

However, after glancing over at their warhorses, he quickly shifted his attention. The powerful animals were standing on their hind legs and flailing away with their front hooves like wild stallions.

Surging forward, Ramhorn stretched out his neck biting his opponent, then followed through by landing a vicious right hook, or right hoof, against the other warhorse's jaw knocking the animal to the ground unconscious.

And so, a few minutes after the collision, it was all over.

Marcheto made no attempt to approach Ramhorn who was taking a lot longer to calm down. The warhorse belonged to Kirnochak, not Marcheto, and so the young warrior waited until the animal's breathing returned to normal. After all, Marcheto hadn't raised this warhorse from a foal, his oldest brother had.

When Ramhorn was sufficiently calm, Marcheto slowly walked up to him, and the horse nuzzled the young warrior's face rubbing his snout against Marcheto's cheek making it all wet.

But suddenly, Marcheto felt the animal tremble. Looking on Ramhorn's left side, the young warrior could see nothing amiss, but when he examined the warhorse's right, Marcheto couldn't believe his eyes. The handle of a sword and a few inches of its blade were sticking out of the warhorse's neck, the majority of the blade being imbedded in the animal. And standing next to Ramhorn, a very scratched and bruised Tredax had his hand on the weapon and a big smile on his face.

"Sorry about your horse, punk," Tredax laughed while Marcheto stood there stunned by the senseless attack.

As Tredax hobbled back over to his horse, Ramhorn fell to his knees, rolled onto his side and died. In shock, Marcheto looked down at the animal having never seen anyone intentionally kill a horse before. It left him shaken.

"You never deserved a warhorse like that anyway," Tredax chided him. "I don't know how the animal put up with you."

Marcheto stared blankly at his enemy.

"Well, look on the bright side. You won't have to clean his stall anymore," Tredax said laughing derisively.

When Marcheto's brain began to clear, it dawned on him that Tredax thought Ramhorn was his horse, not Kirnochak's.

How would he know otherwise? the young warrior mused. Then, as if on cue, Marcheto fell to his knees and tears began flowing down his cheeks. Upon seeing this, Tredax laughed even harder. This is just what the bully had expected.

Seemingly overwhelmed with grief, Marcheto jumped up and stumbled towards Tredax swinging his sword wildly.

Unsheathing a spare sword attached to the saddle of his still unconscious warhorse, Tredax watched Marcheto and smiled broadly as the smaller warrior tripped and fell appearing to be half blinded by tears.

"You always were worthless," Tredax laughed. "You never could fight worth a damn."

When Marcheto got within range, Tredax swung his sword at his opponent's neck and, much to his surprise, missed.

With amazing reflexes for someone appearing so distraught, Marcheto ducked to avoid the blow and reached for a knife strapped to his lower leg with his left hand. Then, looking up at the burly warrior, Marcheto rammed the blade deep into Tredax's right armpit, so deep it went all the way through. Staring at the knife in disbelief, Tredax tried lashing out once more at Marcheto making the blade slice even further into his shoulder. Howling in pain and wild with rage, Tredax dropped his sword but refused to yield, instead leaning down and grasping it with his left hand. However, standing back up, he found himself facing a very dry-eyed and angry Marcheto.

Unable to accept what was happening, unable to imagine that someone he'd been bullying for years could ever get the better of him, Tredax rushed at Marcheto screaming like a madman slashing and hacking repeatedly at the smaller warrior. But he ended up crying out in frustration as he cut only air, Marcheto skillfully dodging each blow.

"Stand still!" Tredax shouted, so Marcheto obliged going down on one knee to avoid another vicious swipe of the taller warrior's sword, and then rammed his own weapon into the bully's stomach. Staring at the protruding blade, Tredax gasped, stumbled and fell to his knees.

Yet having been taught never to underestimate his enemy, Marcheto walked back to Ramhorn's inert form and took a spare sword out of its sheath. Tredax was mortally wounded, but he wasn't dead yet, and Marcheto stayed alert and cautious.

Going back over to his opponent, Marcheto said, "If you drop your sword, I'll allow you to live long enough to say goodbye to your father and brothers."

When Tredax let go of his weapon, Marcheto began turning away but stopped for a moment and said, "You shouldn't have killed my brother's horse."

The burly warrior looked at Marcheto with uncomprehending eyes, and Marcheto shook his head in disgust realizing Tredax was an example of what happens when aggression and a lack of intelligence reside in the same person.

Suddenly, hearing raised voices, Marcheto glanced over in the direction of Lord Daegal's army and saw two of General Gornic's sons riding at him with their swords drawn. The general was desperately trying to restrain his other two sons, but soon they were charging towards him as well.

Watching Tredax's brothers behaving shamefully, Marcheto knew there was no excuse for their lack of discipline, and so he held his ground. If he was going to die, he would do so with dignity and refused to run.

Marcheto now faced a battle with the odds of four to one. And those men coming at him were mounted, whereas he was still on foot. Even so, the young warrior made no attempt to revive Tredax's horse, which still lay unconscious.

Marcheto just took comfort in the fact that around 1,000 men were watching Gornic's family make fools of themselves. The young man knew he'd be defeated, but even Lord Daegal wouldn't put up with this type of treachery. Gornic's sons were as good as dead no matter how things played out here today.

But then, Marcheto thought of Aerylln and turned to her hoping Baelfire might be able to help him. But Baelfire, Zorya and Aerylln hadn't been fully forged into the Trinity of Light, and Marcheto lay beyond the good sword's range.

As soon as Tark and his sons saw what Gornic's sons were doing, they wanted to race to get to Marcheto first.

"Stop!" Pensgraft commanded while instantly taking on the appearance of being every inch a magnificent warlord. The giant looked the same physically, yet everything about him was different.

Glancing at Pensgraft, Tark realized that some men are just born to rule and that this giant warrior was one of them.

"You'll never get to Marcheto in time. If you race out there, all you'll do is make what Gornic's sons are doing seem acceptable," Pensgraft shouted.

"What else can we do?" Kirnochak asked.

Pensgraft looked back over his shoulder at Zorya and Baelfire.

When both the sword and the horse saw Pensgraft looking to them for help, it almost broke their hearts for they viewed him as their son.

Lyssa had been Pensgraft's mother and Aerylln's grandmother. She had wielded Baelfire for a decade and was the sword's heir even before Zorya had become a horse. But Lyssa was killed 25 years ago during the civil war. When she died, Pensgraft was left an orphan, and so Baelfire and Zorya took him in as their own.

Aerylln, Baelfire and Zorya wanted to become a Trinity, but Aerylln's grandmother had accomplished it. Lyssa had successfully united three as one. However, in those days, Zorya had been known as the Lady of the Well. She'd been tall and willowy with an aristocratic bearing, and her movements were languid, graceful and hypnotic. Too hypnotic, some said. But all of that changed when the dark sword, Crystal, put a spell on her.

But whether as a magnificent horse or a beautiful spirit-woman who had taken human form, Zorya was a permanent member of the Trinity and had been so for centuries. However, the unification was not indestructible. Its weakest link was the human element, and with Lyssa's death, the Trinity had been broken.

That Lyssa had no other children besides Pensgraft, especially female children, made matters even worse.

She had no sisters and no nieces either.

Thus, Lyssa had no heir!

Being a woman, Baelfire's power was based on a matriarchal line of succession, and the sword could only be passed down to a female member of the clan. The problem was that there weren't any, neither in Lyssa's generation nor in Pensgraft's.

And so, the sword fell into a sort of limbo, and Pensgraft became its custodian.

In turn, Baelfire and Zorya became his guardians, and they watched him grow into manhood. The sword and the horse had waited patiently for their son to become a man, fall in love and have a child. To their relief, it was a girl.

Still, they had to endure another prolonged wait until the baby grew into a fine young woman and came of age.

And Aerylln, the young woman, was now at Crystal Castle watching Pensgraft as he looked at Baelfire and Zorya, his eyes pleading for help. Yet she was confused by the intensity of her friends' reaction to this giant of a man. To her, Pensgraft was a battle-scarred warrior, but to the sword and horse, he was still a young boy, and he needed them. Turning to each other, Baelfire and Zorya swore they wouldn't fail their only child, who was also the father of their only grandchild, Aerylln.

Suddenly, a solution presented itself. The Creative Light, an enormously powerful, life-giving force, appeared for the second time shooting down on Baelfire like a thunderbolt, just as it had in the great room of Crystal Castle when the surface of the floor and walls shattered into thousands of black crystal shards.

Simultaneously, Zorya began shining brightly, and the explosive buildup of energy that she'd experienced in the great room returned to her. Zorya stepped to Aerylln's left side, while

Baelfire floated in the air on her right, and Eldwyn, the wizard, positioned himself directly behind her.

"Cathrak, dantay, sechum, tasterak!" Eldwyn shouted as he threw his arms wide open. *"Cathrak, dantay, sechum, tasterak!"* This was the same incantation he'd used when the Creative Light appeared to them before.

Suddenly, Aerylln looked to be 30 years old, then 65 years old, then 20, 55 and 40. But after a while, Aerylln returned to looking like a young woman.

Eldwyn moved closer to Aerylln, as did the horse and sword. The teenage girl once more began shape shifting and moving rapidly up and down her body's timeline altering her appearance from that of a young woman to that of a 45 year old. Aerylln next took a dramatic leap to how she would look when she was 70. Following that, she dropped down to being 20. But that lasted only for an instant, and suddenly she appeared to be an elderly woman of 85. Her appearance continued shifting wildly as her age seesawed faster and faster.

"Do it now, Aerylln! Now!" Baelfire shouted, fearful that the transformation might not be permanent and that the Light might fade away once more. Somehow, Aerylln knew what Baelfire wanted her to do, so she stretched out her arm and pointed a finger at Pensgraft.

Instantly, a bolt of energy made of pure, white plasma shot from the tip of her finger across the vast expanse of field in front of Crystal Castle and struck Pensgraft.

The giant absorbed the energy and began to shine. It wasn't an overcast day, but Pensgraft looked as if a beam of sunlight had broken through clouds on a stormy day and was streaming down upon him.

But as everyone at Crystal Castle held their breath and watched in eager anticipation, nothing happened. Nothing at all.

"Well, that was a waste," Corson grumbled.

"Patience, Corson, patience," Eldwyn smiled.

"What is patience anyway?" she chided him. "I've never had any. Why don't you tell me about it?"

"Watch and learn," the wizard said, quietly pointing back towards Pensgraft and the others.

Corson did as she was told and found herself learning quite a bit!

The bright light surrounding Pensgraft had faded from view, but twinkling little sparks of prism light, like tiny purple, blue, green, yellow, orange and red stars, began flowing all around him. The giant nudged the sides of his warhorse with his heels, and, in the next instant, he was standing next to Marcheto. The young warrior was concentrating on Gornic's four sons as they raced across the field and hadn't noticed Pensgraft riding up behind him. But neither had anyone else. The giant had just materialized.

However, Marcheto did notice what happened next.

Pensgraft unsheathed his sword and pointed it at one of Gornic's sons who was almost upon them. A stream of multicolored light shot out towards the enemy warrior, and he just …disappeared!

Next, Pensgraft pointed his sword at another of Gornic's sons, and another, and another, until they all simply vanished.

"That man there," Marcheto said pointing at General Gornic. "Do that to him as well."

"No," Pensgraft said softly.

"Why not?"

"Because he's not attacking us," Pensgraft explained.

"When Lord Daegal gives the order, he'll be coming at us!"

"We'll deal with that when the time comes."

"That man's my father's sworn enemy, kill him!" Marcheto shouted.

"Not now, maybe later."

"I want him dead!" Marcheto almost screamed in frustration.

"Listen to me very carefully. Any man can kill, it's in our blood, and it's very easy to take that route," Pensgraft said. "What's hard, what really takes experience and discipline, is holding oneself in check when the desire to take a life becomes almost overpowering. Conquering others is one thing, Marcheto, but a real man first learns to conquer himself. And that's the hardest battle of all."

"We'll have to fight him eventually, and kill him. So, what's the difference between doing it now or later? I don't understand."

"Later means it's a while longer before we have to take another life," Pensgraft tried to explain. "It's a small reprieve, but it's still a reprieve."

"General Gornic doesn't deserve a reprieve."

"Not a reprieve for him, it's a reprieve for me. My soul grows weary of battle," Pensgraft sighed.

"How can you be a leader, if you're tired of killing?"

"It's only after you tire of it that you can truly lead," the giant said.

"Why?"

"Because there has to be something that enables us to fight and fight hard. When we kill, our goal should be to save lives not to take them. With every life we take, we should be looking to save two others. It's the only way a real warrior can keep on fighting when the going gets tough."

"I'm still not sure I understand," Marcheto said.

"You'd better learn to understand these things, if you're going to be in a relationship with my daughter," Pensgraft said.

"With your daughter?"

"Aerylln."

"Aerylln's your daughter?" Marcheto asked, a bit alarmed.

"Yes, and while I have you here, I want to ask you one question."

"Yes, sir?"

"Have you ever touched my daughter? And you know what I mean, touched her inappropriately?" Pensgraft growled.

"No, sir! Aaaask Baelfire!" Marcheto said as he began to sweat.

"If you ever hurt my daughter, you'll think facing General Gornic's sons was a picnic," Pensgraft said almost in a whisper.

"I'll tttttreat her prrrrroperly," the young man stammered.

"Good decision!" Pensgraft said hoisting Marcheto up behind him on the saddle and heading back over to the young warrior's family.

Chapter 32

Before Marcheto could be reunited with his father and brothers, the field he and Pensgraft were riding through began to change. It started first around Crystal Castle and spread outward in concentric circles much like a pebble creating circular ripples when dropped in a pool of water.

The young warrior and the giant watched in amazement as an oil-like, black liquid came pouring out of Crystal Castle flooding the entire valley floor. At the same time, hundreds of Lord Daegal's warriors and their horses began stepping up and down in the ooze as it rose above their ankles and hooves.

Pensgraft and Marcheto clung to their horse as it pranced around trying to keep from being trapped in the mire, which was quickly beginning to solidify. In a matter of minutes, the grassy fields around the castle had changed into vast, unbroken sheets of black crystal.

But they didn't remain unbroken for long.

The valley floor quickly began to buckle and heave shattering the smooth, polished surface into seemingly endless piles of black crystal shards.

Crystal, the dark sword, being the one who'd initiated this chaos, was enjoying herself immensely as she sensed the confusion and fear people were experiencing all over the valley. Her valley. Not Glenitant's and not Chen's. Hers!

The dark sword, with moves worthy of an escape artist, had been thrashing about twisting and wiggling until nearly half her handle was free of the golden ropes that were ensnaring her. It wasn't much, but it was enough.

"The bitch is back!" Crystal had laughed.

Then she'd gone to work, flooding the valley with black ooze.

The dark sword wanted to be united with Chen, but when Baelfire put a stop to that, Crystal had turned to Lord Daegal begging him to rescue her. She'd promised the warlord her help, but the dark sword was growing weaker and weaker with each passing day as the ropes drained both her power and her will to resist.

Yet Crystal's willpower was strong, stronger than anyone had realized.

And now, to a small degree, the dark sword had been able to free herself, and she reached out to her savior, a man she hated, and sought to bring him victory.

"Lord Daegal!" Crystal shouted using the Crystal Medallion to contact him.

"Where have you been?" the warlord demanded.

"I've been half dead, thanks for your concern."

"I have plenty of men who are more than half dead," Lord Daegal fumed.

With an effort, Crystal held her tongue but thought, If I have my way, you'll be joining them soon enough! However, getting her temper under control, she said, "I realize that I haven't lived up to my end of the bargain. You wanted to wait and gather thousands of warriors, but, at my request, you rushed over here with only 1,000. I'm sorry."

"That doesn't do me any good, especially with Baelfire becoming more powerful. Your half-sister and Pensgraft killed four of my men. She could prove to be a real problem."

"Quit worrying. If Baelfire, Zorya and Aerylln had any real power, they'd have stopped you the moment you reached Crystal Valley."

"Maybe, but the way Baelfire helped Pensgraft was pretty spectacular."

"Spectacular? I'll show you spectacular!" the dark sword shouted cutting loose with a bolt of energy that leapt from her scabbard, shot out of the castle and landed directly on the warlord.

The change was immediate and dramatic.

First, Lord Daegal's warhorse went wild as its hooves and legs began turning to black crystal. Its nostrils flared, and its eyes bulged, and the animal reared up on its hind legs. But nothing, not even blind panic, could reverse the process, and soon the warhorse was more crystalline than flesh and blood. Even its head and neck, the last parts to change, appeared to be made of highly-polished black marble, and the warhorse's facial features were chiseled and angular.

After the change was complete, the warhorse really came alive, racing over the black crystal shards as if storming across a field of shattered glass was its natural and preferred habitat, which it was.

With every stride, the warhorse seemed to be growing bigger, taller, more muscular and far more powerful. The black crystal charger became so large that Lord Daegal looked small by comparison, and the warlord was anything but that. Yet no matter how hard he struggled to master the giant warhorse, it proved too much for him, and Lord Daegal had to cling to the saddle just to keep from being thrown.

But then, the warlord felt a tingling sensation in his legs, and he realized they were growing longer, much longer. Wrapping them around the animal's rib cage, Lord Daegal, with a strength that surprised him, squeezed the warhorse's sides so hard that the black crystal charger turned its head and looked at its rider with newfound respect.

However, respect quickly turned to fear, and justifiably so. What the animal saw was enough to terrify anyone!

Lord Daegal was the perfect size to be riding such a warhorse, which meant he was now enormous! And Lord Daegal gave the horse such a murderous look that the animal surrendered to its master once more.

Like his warhorse, Lord Daegal had become a black crystalline, raging inferno of raw power. Flames leapt from his eyes and mouth, and his body smoldered with an intensity that caused his hands and forearms to glow red as if they were made of hot coals.

Lord Daegal was now at least 15 feet tall, and his warhorse was twice that size when it reared up on its hind legs. The horse spit fire and smoke, and its hooves gave off a reddish glow and were covered in flames.

Lord Daegal's intellect and personality remained unchanged, and he loved it as he rode through his army calling his officers by name. The most astute recognized his voice and knew it was their ruler, but many leaders and their warriors were terrified as what looked like a bonfire illuminating midnight darkness went thundering by on four legs. It was dusk, and light was fading from the sky, adding to the dramatic nature of Lord Daegal's appearance.

I could really get used to Crystal's help, he thought, while leaning back and letting out a monstrous roar that reverberated throughout the valley. It never dawned on Lord

Daegal that Crystal might be playing him and had her own agenda.

Thus, blissfully unaware and brimming with excitement, Lord Daegal rode over to General Gornic's camp and was pleased to see him smiling.

"Nice touch," General Gornic said, impressed by the forbidding spectacle. "And you just dug that costume out of a closet?"

"Nothing much surprises you, does it, general?" Lord Daegal laughed.

"Oh, I don't know, maybe I just like being surprised."

Years of training and discipline enabled General Gornic to put the tragic loss of his sons into a separate compartment of his mind to be dealt with later. He'd kill Pensgraft, he knew that much. But for now, he had his master and a coming battle to think about.

"Get 200 elite warriors, the best of the best, mounted and ready," Lord Daegal commanded.

"With pleasure, my lord," General Gornic said as he leapt onto his warhorse and began barking out orders to his staff.

Within a few minutes, 200 battle-hardened warriors were sitting astride their warhorses feeling rather unnerved by Lord Daegal's personal appearance. They were about to become even more unnerved.

"Gather 'round, boys, gather 'round!" Lord Daegal shouted glaring at his men and testing their resolve.

To his surprise, a few warriors appeared relatively calm, as if reporting to a black crystalline giant spouting flames was a normal part of their daily routine.

Lord Daegal respected such men, that is, ones possessing the strength and courage to act unafraid even in the face of totally unexpected situations. Further testing their nerves, however, he had his warhorse rear up on its hind legs, and he took out his sword as both horse and rider burst into flames. The horse let out the most unnatural, horrifying battle cry anyone had ever heard, and Lord Daegal shouted with such horrendous, barbarous intensity that men and warhorses backed up a step.

Lord Daegal and his warhorse continued bellowing while bolts of lightning erupted out of the warlord's chest striking each of the warriors in front of him. Suddenly, the crushing intensity of Lord Daegal's battle cries seemed more manageable to his men and not so overwhelming. Many of Lord Daegal's warriors began feeling the need to join in and lifted their voices with guttural growls, frenzied howls and wild snarling.

"Don't you think this is a bit bizarre?" one warrior asked the man next to him and was shocked to find that his neighbor looked like a smaller version of Lord Daegal. The man wasn't 15 feet tall. In fact, his height hadn't changed. But a six-foot tall, fire-breathing warrior made of gleaming black crystal wasn't exactly what he'd expected to see.

Then, looking at his own body, he discovered his legs and lower torso were turning into black crystal. Soon, all the howling and snarling going on around him seemed natural, and he joined in as well.

Now, hungering to make a kill and eager to release the violence churning inside of him, what he wanted most was something to attack. Feeling exactly the same way, Lord Daegal reared up on his charger once more, pointed his sword at the architectural masterpiece and shouted, "Take Crystal Castle!"

All 200 black crystal warriors turned as one man and galloped towards their objective, howling, growling and snarling along the way. Once there, they halted and rallied 'round Lord Daegal.

"Have no mercy on them! Kill them all! And bring me the swords Baelfire and Crystal!" the warlord shouted.

"How will we know the swords you want, my lord?" one warrior asked.

"You'll know Baelfire. She'll be the one trying to kill most of you. As for Crystal, she's tied up in the main tower."

But turning back towards Crystal Castle, they found the entrance blocked by a young woman, a sword, a horse and an old wizard.

"Take me out of my scabbard," Baelfire told Aerylln.

The teenage girl did as she was told, and the battle was joined.

Pointing Baelfire at the black crystal warriors directly in front of her, Aerylln watched in amazement as a powerful beam of multicolored prism light shot out from the sword with tremendous velocity catapulting dozens of fire-breathing monsters through the nighttime sky like meteors.

In a flanking maneuver, General Gornic brought his army into play marching his warriors towards the western and southern walls of the castle. But looking into the sky, the general was dismayed to see many of Lord Daegal's elite warriors sailing overhead and falling to earth far behind his advancing troops.

Baelfire kept throwing Lord Daegal's warriors off into the distance. But soon the good sword realized her strength was waning. In her first attempt, Baelfire had catapulted nearly 25 warriors away from the castle but now could barely manage four or five.

With at least 100 black crystal warriors still closing in on the castle entrance, Eldwyn reached into a pocket of his robe searching for a tiny stick about the size of his index finger.

Finding it, the wizard placed it in the palm of his hand and, for a few moments, became lost in thought recalling the adventures they'd had together. He and this small, seemingly inconsequential stick had relied on each other many times in the past.

The wizard also recalled the first time he'd seen Zorya, the Lady of the Well, many, many years ago when he was a young man. Zorya had been in danger and desperately needed to cross a turbulent stream to make her getaway. But before she could even attempt a crossing, the water had burst into flames, and a hideous face materialized within the inferno making its way closer and closer to her.

Eldwyn had been breathless, and not just from running, but because of Zorya's incredible beauty. She was the most enticing woman he'd ever seen. And Eldwyn had wanted to come to her rescue but was tall, gangly and unsure of himself. However, he was so captivated and so determined that his self-doubt had evaporated. Even so, the young man had been confused about what to do.

All the young Eldwyn had in his possession was a small stick, about the size of a twig, which his grandfather had given him upon his death. The tiny stick was supposed to be wise and powerful, or so his grandfather had said, but Eldwyn thought the old man delusional at the time. Yet as the hideous face moved closer to Zorya, the young man had reached for the stick, just as he was doing now.

"Snap out of it!" Zorya shouted stamping her hooves impatiently and glaring at him. When he saw the look of disapproval on the majestic warhorse's face, Eldwyn yanked his mind back to the present and found himself looking down the throats of dozens of fire-breathing, black crystal warriors who were now almost upon them.

Shaking himself out of his reverie, Eldwyn took a deep breath, grasped the tiny stick tightly and squeezed. Instantly, beams of multicolored light shot out of his clenched fist, followed by a blinding flash of white light, and the wizard found himself in possession of a full-length walking stick.

Taking a long step with his right foot, Eldwyn bent his knee and leaned forward as if preparing to withstand a terrible windstorm. Grasping the staff with both hands and thrusting it outward in a horizontal position, Eldwyn braced himself, looked at Baelfire and said, "I'm ready."

Shooting her remaining energy at Eldwyn's staff, Baelfire changed it from wood into a long, cylindrical, clear-crystal prism. Almost immediately, Eldwyn recoiled from the kick as a long, thin beam of purple, blue, green, yellow, orange and red light exploded outward from the staff slamming into the fire-breathing, black crystal warriors with the force of a hurricane.

The gale-force winds stopped them in their tracks sending Lord Daegal and his warriors flying. It was an incredible lightshow with refracted light from the prism staff shooting into the darkness and launching enemy warriors who now seemed like dozens of bits of flames and smoldering coals tumbling end over end until disappearing from view. A ball of flame larger than the others appeared as a comet in the nighttime sky but in reality was the warlord himself getting an unexpected aerial view of Crystal Castle after dark.

That castle is breathtaking, and I want it! Lord Daegal thought as he sailed through the air while trying to calm his terrified horse, which had also taken flight. But feeling angry and frustrated over the turn of events, the warlord gripped the Crystal Medallion and shouted into it.

"Crystal, I'm flying like an eagle across a vast expanse of darkness with the castle quickly receding from view. And, though I have to admit, it's a rather unique experience, I'd prefer to save it for another day when I have time for it."

The warlord was being cynical, but Crystal, for whom sarcasm was an art form, wasn't impressed by his attempt at nonchalance or his effort at being witty.

"My half-sister's giving you a rough time, is she? But you and 200 of your men are black crystal warriors, what else could you possibly need?" Crystal asked, her voice dripping with scorn.

"A lot more of us would be nice," Lord Daegal grumbled.

"I'll work on it," Crystal said derisively. "However, I don't think my sister can keep up this pace. You're wearing her down."

"From where I'm at, she's looking pretty powerful," Lord Daegal said while falling from the sky, crashing onto the ground and rolling to a stop. Feeling battered, shaken and surprised to still be alive, the warlord listened to the black crystal warriors all around him groaning in pain and asked, "What makes you think Baelfire's losing steam?"

"When the Creative Light appeared earlier today, Baelfire was infused with energy but without a continuous supply of energy running through her, she can wear out just like anyone else."

"She doesn't seem worn out, at least not to me," Lord Daegal said grimacing while massaging a crack in his black crystal right leg, as well as a sore spot on his left shoulder that had been chipped during his rough landing.

"But she is wearing out," Crystal insisted. "I know her limitations, and Baelfire can't possibly have enough energy to perform another counterattack. Not without a direct infusion of energy from the Creative Light."

"So, what's your advice?"

"Regroup and make a second attack. If you do it before the Creative Light shows up again, Baelfire will break under the strain."

"Why doesn't the Creative Light stay with her? Why does it come and go?" the warlord asked.

"When the Light appears, Aerylln has to coordinate rivers of energy flowing through herself, Baelfire and Zorya. It's not easy. As I recall, it took Aerylln's grandmother, Lyssa, six attempts before everything clicked."

"Well, I need more of my men brought from other parts of the realm like I'd originally intended, and I need a lot more black crystal warriors if we're to succeed."

"I'll work on it."

"Do that," the warlord growled.

"Quit complaining and get back into the fight. We aren't done yet! Not by a long shot!"

Chapter 33

Back at the castle entrance, Crystal's prediction had come true.

Exhausted and struggling to catch her breath, Zorya had collapsed onto the courtyard floor. Aerylln, feeling faint and gasping for air, was draped across her friend's massive neck resting her cheek against the warhorse's soft mane. And Baelfire, feeling like she was made of lead, was lying on the courtyard floor savoring its coolness against her blade.

Only Eldwyn was exerting any effort, and he was leaning against a wall to keep from falling down, but it wasn't just any wall. Standing inside the castle's unprotected entrance, the wizard was sealing it off with a force field emanating from his staff. However, with his head throbbing, his heart pounding and his legs ready to give out, Eldwyn didn't know how much longer he could hold on.

Exploiting the situation, General Gornic had posted runners outside the entrance with orders to notify him the moment Eldwyn collapsed. Additionally, keeping constant pressure on the force field, and on the old wizard, mounted warriors were taking turns trying to break through it, charging at the invisible energy shield over and over. Other warriors were on foot beating against it with axes and swords.

Though desperate to remain on his feet, Eldwyn could feel his life energy ebbing away. The wizard now looked far older than when his companions had first arrived at his cottage. Glancing over his shoulder, Eldwyn saw Andrina striding along a walkway on the western wall and was encouraged by her obvious strength and confidence. Filled with admiration, he thought, That woman certainly doesn't mind a fight.

And Eldwyn was right on the mark. Andrina watched with growing anticipation as hundreds of General Gornic's warriors approached the western and southern walls of the castle. These were more vulnerable than the eastern wall, which was protected by a steep, downward slope. While Lord Daegal was attacking the castle's entrance, General Gornic, as part of a two-pronged attack, had been gathering his troops for an assault on the walls.

Andrina observed the way the enemy was positioning its warriors and also took note of their swords, armor, helmets and siege ladders. Making a quick count, the warrior woman calculated the odds against them at maybe ten to one.

"What do you think? Good odds, huh?" Andrina asked Balder who was next to her.

Shrugging his shoulders, Balder thought, Corson was bad enough, and now we have Andrina. For without a doubt, he knew that either woman would provoke a fight just to have one.

However, not beyond some grim humor, he said, "I don't know, Andrina. Unless Lord Daegal gets reinforcements, the battle won't last over a day or two. It's hardly worth fighting."

"Well, it's better than nothing," Andrina said taking his comment seriously. She didn't want her first battle in years to be viewed as easy, although it was far from that.

"Oh, I'm sure there's a good chance we'll all be dead by morning," he reassured her.

"That could be," Andrina said feeling a little better, an optimistic tone creeping into her voice. Balder shook his head and walked away from the warrior woman.

Going over to his men, he told Kirtak, his second-in-command, "If I'm going to die tonight, I'd rather be around people who are at least sane."

"I'd rather have her with us than against us," Kirtak said.

"Oh, hell yes! I just don't enjoy fighting as much as Andrina does."

"You like a good fight."

"True, but it's a little spooky being around someone who loves it more than I do. The only other person I know like that is Corson."

"Speak of the devil," Kirtak said pointing at the warrior woman walking towards them.

Aroused by the threat of violence, Corson began purring as she approached Balder, and then shoved him against a battlement pressing her body against his. When the warrior woman began biting his throat and clawing at his shoulders, Balder knew what was coming next. That people were milling about meant nothing to Corson.

"I was just talking with Andrina," Balder said trying to change the topic, "and she seems like a woman after your own heart."

"I don't know, she's so self-involved," Corson complained.

Balder looked over at Kirtak and rolled his eyes.

At that moment, a siege ladder fell against the wall next to them, a warrior already near the top and getting ready to climb over it. However, when Corson glared at him, the warrior knew he was a dead man. He didn't know how, but he knew.

Even so, the man was stunned when Corson's reflexes proved so quick that he didn't see her knife until it entered his throat.

Had he lived long enough, what would have further surprised him was how angry Corson got over her foreplay with Balder being interrupted. Clenching her fists, Corson's eyes hardened, her face became flushed, her body tensed, and she completely lost her temper.

When most people lose control, they make mistakes that could get them killed. However, Balder knew it was different with Corson. Fascinated, he watched as the warrior woman leapt onto a battlement proceeding to kill warrior after warrior as she climbed down the ladder.

"They shouldn't have made her mad," Kirtak observed.

Seeing Corson besting so many of the enemy, Andrina was envious. But soon another opportunity presented itself when two siege ladders fell against the wall only a few paces away.

Leaping up on the battlement and standing between the ladders, Andrina was excited as she took out her sword and waited for the men to reach the top. However, always willing to improvise, Andrina got an idea when 20 of Chen's warrior women walked past carrying spears.

"Gwendylln!" Andrina called out as she saw Chen's second-in-command. "I could use two of the spears your women are carrying."

Intrigued by the request and wondering what devilment this famous warrior was up to, Gwendylln quickly got Andrina what she needed.

The older warrior woman continued watching both ladders until it was obvious the first warrior on the left was going to beat the first warrior on the right by a wide margin. At that point, Andrina gave him her undivided attention.

When the faster warrior got a few rungs from the top, Andrina took one of the spears and, without hesitation, jammed the weapon into the man's neck right above his metal breastplate. Leaning forward, she used her weight to drive the spear down through the warrior's body and out the other side. The man was still alive when the tip of the spear exited his lower back right below his armor.

Stepping onto the top rung of the ladder and changing her stance to get more leverage, Andrina leaned even harder on her end of the spear. When she finally stopped pushing, four feet of the spear protruded out of the warrior's lower back and four feet was still sticking out of his neck.

After a few moments, the light went out of the warrior's eyes, and his legs dropped into the space between two rungs of the ladder. But he didn't fall far, the spear catching on the rungs above and below the hole.

Bent at the waist, the man was face down against the ladder with his legs dangling in midair making it almost impossible for those behind him to reach the top. Any warrior trying to climb over the dead man would be turning himself into an easy target.

Thus having finished securing the ladder to her left, she took her second spear and repeated the process with the warrior nearing the top of the ladder to her right. By killing just two warriors, Andrina had blocked dozens of others and effectively put two siege ladders out of commission.

Gwendylln waved for Chen to join them and both stood there marveling at Andrina's handiwork.

"A little trick I learned some years back," Andrina explained.

Chen quickly focused on the male warriors trapped on the ladder closest to her. Instinctively, the black leather panther put an arrow into a bow she was carrying and began pulling back on the bowstring. But then, she caught herself and, turning to Andrina, asked permission to launch the arrow.

"Do you mind?" Chen asked.

"No, of course not," the older warrior woman said feeling like a mother contributing to the advancement of her daughter's career. This is very satisfying, she said to herself.

Feeling a little apprehensive, Gwendylln put an arrow in her bow but worried that Andrina wouldn't give her permission to address the other ladder.

"It's okay, go ahead," Andrina said knowing that Chen and Gwendylln were close friends.

In her heart, Andrina had secretly adopted Chen, but the young warrior woman hadn't caught on, at least not yet, which was a good thing. Had Chen known, she probably would have felt uncomfortable. The black leather panther didn't mind being near people. She just didn't want to be close to them.

As Chen and Gwendylln let their arrows fly, some of the men near the bottom tried to climb back down. Such was not to be for Corson, having already cleared her ladder, had come over to help with Andrina's. Corson was now working her way up, killing those who were trying to retreat. In short order, the warrior woman made her way to the top and climbed over the castle wall.

Once Corson had rejoined Chen, Gwendylln and Andrina on the walkway, they looked around and assessed their situation.

There were over a dozen siege ladders up against the southern wall, and General Gornic's men were pouring over it. The general had attacked that side of the castle with overwhelming numbers and speed.

However, Andrina wasn't surprised. After observing General Gornic's initial maneuver where he attacked the western wall using fewer warriors and siege ladders, the warrior woman had suspected he was up to something.

"I've seen this done before," Andrina had told Chen. "As a diversion, one wall is attacked first to bring as many defending warriors as possible to that side of the castle. Then, a second wall is attacked using twice as many men and siege ladders."

"Well, if General Gornic gains control of one outside wall, it's all over," Chen had said, clearly stating their predicament.

However, having anticipated the general's strategy, Andrina had arranged a welcoming committee. First, she'd allowed the general to think his plan was working by packing the western wall with Dartuke, Thordig, the other 18 nobles, Pensgraft, Balder, his ten men and 75 of Chen's warrior women.

On the southern wall, General Gornic's real target, were just 20 of Chen's women along with Marcheto, his father, Tark, and his brothers Kirnochak, Xandaric and Adexsus.

"Okay, listen carefully," Andrina had said. "When General Gornic puts his siege ladders against the southern wall, I want those defending it to fall back to the courtyard floor. And I want 50 of Chen's warriors from the western wall to join them."

"Andrina, once my women are in the courtyard, do you want them shooting arrows at General Gornic's men as they come over the southern wall?" Chen had asked.

"Yes," Andrina had said, pleased that Chen's mind worked so quickly.

And now, Corson, Chen, Gwendylln and Andrina were watching as hundreds of General Gornic's men made their way over the castle's southern wall and headed downstairs to the courtyard below.

At first, Chen's archers devastated the enemy but became less effective when General Gornic's men began taking shields from those who'd been killed. Carrying two shields each, the enemy warriors were forming a protective wall down the full length of the stairs. After only a few minutes, a warrior was standing on each step holding two shields, one above the other, protecting his entire body while providing cover for dozens of other warriors heading to the courtyard below.

Soon hundreds of General Gornic's men were making their way downstairs behind a nearly impenetrable barrier of shields, but the protective wall didn't stop there. Upon reaching the bottom, the general's men began forming another wall of double shields at least 40 warriors wide. Then, the wall began advancing towards Chen's archers while more of the general's men formed up behind it holding shields over their heads.

General Gornic's forces now controlled the castle's southern wall and a portion of the courtyard floor, but his men didn't stop there and continued pressing forward sensing victory and exuding confidence.

Deeply concerned, though ever unflappable, Corson nudged Chen and pointed at Crystal Castle's entrance. Bordering on total exhaustion, Eldwyn was sitting on the ground gasping for breath and leaning against Zorya's massive back. The wizard was still blocking the entrance with the energy remaining in his staff, but it was obvious he couldn't hold up much longer.

Peering into the darkness, Gwendylln pointed at hundreds of tiny flames off in the distance that appeared to be closing in on Crystal Castle. Filled with uncontrollable rage,

Lord Daegal and his fire-breathing, black crystal warriors were headed this way.

"We have a few minutes until they arrive," Andrina said.

"What good's that going to do us?" Corson asked.

After pausing for a moment and taking a deep breath, Andrina said, "Chen, this isn't the path I would've chosen for you. You deserve better."

"I'm not afraid of death," Chen declared looking around and seeing the tide of the battle turning against them.

"We may not have to turn our backs on life, at least not yet. There's still one alternative, but it leads down a path that's dark and fraught with danger."

"What do you mean?"

"I want you to know that should you choose this route, you'll not travel it alone. I'll walk it with you."

"What path?"

"When Eldwyn's unable to protect the entrance, he could also be too weak to keep Crystal a prisoner."

Chen's eyes widened.

"And if that happens, you'll be able to untie Eldwyn's golden ropes and set the dark sword free," Andrina said.

"How much longer do you think Eldwyn can last?" Chen asked.

"I don't know, but we need to be ready. We have to reach Crystal, and quickly. Let's head for the great room."

With that, Chen, Andrina, Corson and Gwendylln ran downstairs to the courtyard and sprinted to the castle's main tower. After making their way upstairs to the great room and over to Crystal, the warrior women surrounded the dark sword who was lying on the floor covered with black crystal shards from earlier when the surface had shattered.

As Chen was trying to catch her breath, she looked at Andrina in amazement. While running over to the great hall, the older warrior woman had been in the lead almost the entire way. For a few moments, Chen had kept a pace or two ahead of Andrina, but it had taken an enormous effort to do so.

If she's this good now, what was Andrina like when she was my age? Chen wondered, but then the black leather panther focused on the present situation as she and the others looked down upon the dark sword.

"What's the matter? Having a busy day?" Crystal asked.

"There's a bit of a ruckus out in the courtyard," Chen replied.

"Do tell?"

"Maybe you'd like to help," Chen suggested.

"Maybe another time, I'm rather indisposed at the moment."

"Eldwyn has collapsed from exhaustion and may soon be drifting into unconsciousness," Chen informed her.

That got Crystal's attention.

"Untie me!"

Kneeling down, Chen tried to remove the golden ropes, but they held fast. "They're too tight, I can't even loosen them."

"Then kill him!" the dark sword screamed.

"Kill whom?"

"Kill Eldwyn!"

They all looked at each other.

"I don't think so," Chen said.

"If you want Crystal Castle, then you'll have to kill that meddling wizard. I should have done it years ago when I had the chance."

Chen glanced over at Andrina who was by a window overlooking the courtyard. The older warrior woman could see

Eldwyn down below protecting the entrance. After observing the wizard for a few moments, Andrina walked back to the dark sword and said, "There are going to be some new rules."

"You aren't in a position to make rules. I can feel General Gornic's troops getting closer. Have they penetrated the castle yet? They have, haven't they?" Crystal asked mocking the older warrior woman.

"We could just choose to keep you tied up," Andrina said.

"I can't see through the prism-light shield emanating from Eldwyn's staff. Prism light blinds me, so I can't tell exactly how weak he is. But I can see in darkness, and I know who's riding at you right now. Lord Daegal is on his way back."

Kneeling down next to Crystal, Chen gently stroked her scabbard, and the dark sword felt chills rippling along the length of her blade.

"You don't want to be owned by a man, do you? And if I had to go through life without you, I just don't know what I'd do," Chen said, and she began to sob. The black leather panther was quite an actress.

Crystal felt her heart opening up for the first time in a long, long while. Glenitant had never touched the dark sword on a deep emotional level. And before her, Crystal had no great affection for Glenitant's mother, but Chen made the sword feel like a girl again.

Crystal's inner spirit was so dark that, to her, Chen's damaged soul seemed as bright as the noonday sun, and Chen's spirit was so dark that even a night owl couldn't penetrate its gloom. The black leather panther had physically survived her upbringing, but her inner self had not.

Yet it was to this damaged, shattered young woman that Crystal was turning for help.

"Chen, I'm responsible for Lord Daegal and his men being changed into fire-breathing, black crystal warriors," Crystal confessed.

"Tell us something we don't already know," Andrina said scornfully.

"So change them back now," Chen said soothingly. "You have me. You've got what you want."

"It's not that simple."

"It had better be," Andrina growled.

"You don't understand. Lord Daegal has the Crystal Medallion and wears her around his neck," the dark sword said fearfully. "If it becomes obvious that I've double-crossed him, the warlord might hurt her."

"What's the medallion to you?" Gwendylln asked.

"She's part of my own trinity. With Chen, myself and the Crystal Medallion, I could become as powerful as when Baelfire, Zorya, and Lyssa, Aerylln's grandmother, were together."

"Why didn't you do that with Glenitant?" Corson asked.

"That old crone was weak and stupid. She couldn't have handled it. Plus, the Crystal Medallion was taken from me years ago and given to Lord Daegal's father, Lord Glenhaven."

"Before that, had you ever achieved a trinity?" Gwendylln pressed her.

"No, the women who inherited me were always too weak."

"You mean none of them could handle the toxic nature of your own inner evil," Andrina said. "You destroy all those who come close to you, don't you?"

"Say what you will, but with the right woman, I could be the most powerful force in the land. I could shove Baelfire into a dungeon so dark and deep that even she couldn't see her way out of it."

"Wait a second. I thought we were coming to this sword for help. I don't see a whole lot of benefit from this arrangement," Corson said.

"Neither do I," Andrina agreed. "Let's try to get out of the castle and just leave Crystal to Lord Daegal."

They all began leaving, except for Chen who played her part convincingly.

"Is there nothing we can do?" the black leather panther said to Crystal as she kissed the dark sword's hilt and rested her cheek against it. Crystal almost fainted.

"Well, maybe I could go along with a few rules, if they're small ones," Crystal said lying languidly on the floor waiting for Chen to go further.

Instead Chen, who treated men like dirt and could do the same thing to women, jumped up and said, "No, I can't give up my friends. They're all I have."

Quickly catching up with the others, Chen, Andrina, Corson and Gwendylln headed for the stairwell.

"This was a waste of time," Andrina said loudly enough for Crystal to hear. "Let's get our warrior women and head out before Lord Daegal arrives. Eldwyn should be able to put a shield around us until we can make our way up the eastern mountain on the other side of Crystal Valley."

"Yes, let's leave this sword for Lord Daegal," Gwendylln said speaking loudly as well. "Once he finds out she's of no use to him personally, since he's a man, I'm sure he'll let his warriors have their fun with her. Maybe they'll pass her around so everyone can wear her."

Laughing boisterously, the four women began walking downstairs pretending to ignore the dark sword as she shouted, "Wait! Let's not be too hasty about this. Let's talk."

But Crystal's words appeared to fall on deaf ears as the warrior women made their way further down the stairwell.

"Wait! I'm willing to negotiate!"

Silence.

"Help!" Crystal screamed. "Don't let me fall into the hands of Lord Daegal! I can't stand him! Help me! I'll do anything!"

More silence.

Fear started seeping into Crystal's heart, a fear of being abandoned. The dark sword knew she'd begun the alliance with Lord Daegal, but, Crystal reasoned, that was only after Baelfire refused to allow Chen to be her new master. It's all my half-sister's fault! Crystal fumed.

But I'm losing the woman I've been grooming for years, Crystal thought frantically. I had Chen's father taken from her. I suggested to Lord Daegal that he make nighttime visits to Chen's bedchamber. And now my foolish pride is pushing her away.

"Chen! Chen!" Crystal began shouting. "Come back! I'll do whatever you want! Anything!"

Reappearing at the top of the stairwell, the black leather panther began walking toward the dark sword with an air of cool detachment. Chen wasn't playing a role now. This time she'd shown up as herself, a tough, decisive, no nonsense warrior woman, and a natural born leader used being in command.

"I want this battle with Lord Daegal ended now," Chen demanded.

"I can't do that," Crystal said.

Chen glared at the sword hating her, then spun on her heel and stormed off. But before the black leather panther had gotten even a few steps away, Crystal became hysterical shouting, "I'll end it! I'll end it! I'll end it!"

The warrior woman turned around and stared hard at the dark sword despising Crystal and feeling no pity for her. The black leather panther wanted only one thing, the sword's submission to her will.

"Could we please save the Crystal Medallion first?" Crystal begged.

"Why?"

"She could be a help to us."

"How?"

"In a variety of ways," Crystal said vaguely.

Chen began turning away once more.

"Wait! The medallion can extend your power over a greater distance. She can give you a greater range!"

"That could be useful," Chen agreed.

"So, what are these rules Andrina was talking about?" Crystal asked.

"There's really only one rule."

"And it is?"

"Whatever I want, whenever I want it."

"Why am I not surprised?" Crystal asked.

Chen smiled.

"So, how do we go about rescuing the medallion?" Crystal asked.

"I want to meet with Jewel and flame."

Immediately, Jewel stepped out of a wall to Chen's left, and Flame walked out of the roaring fire in the great room's hearth. Looking sheepishly at their new master, both were painfully aware that they hadn't met on the best of terms,

Crystal having made them join with Glenitant to fight the black leather panther. When Chen had killed Glenitant anyway, it made things awkward for Jewel and Flame. Chen was their new master, at least until Baelfire and Eldwyn had blocked the warrior woman from inheriting the dark sword.

But that was all in the past, provided Jewel and Flame could deliver on what Chen wanted now. And what the black leather panther needed most was an army of her own.

"How many others like you are there?" Chen asked.

"Just us," Jewel replied.

"Come look out here," Chen said.

Jewel, Flame and their new master went to a window looking out over the castle's western wall.

"The warriors defending that wall are having a pretty difficult time," Jewel commented.

"Lean over the edge, crane your necks out a bit and look at the southern wall," Chen told them.

Hesitantly they obeyed. Jewel and Flame recalled how Chen had kicked their former master, Glenitant, out this very window. Gingerly, the ruby-red woman and the woman of fire leaned out and looked south. Hundreds and hundreds of General Gornic's warriors were now massed on the southern wall and in the courtyard directly below it.

"This isn't good," Flame said.

"What if I were to send you down there to fight your way through that horde of men?" Chen asked.

"That wouldn't be my first choice of how to spend my day," Jewel said.

"Nor mine," Flame added.

"Take a look out this other window," Chen said.

Walking to a window overlooking the front courtyard and the fields beyond the castle's entrance, Chen pointed at the bits of flame moving towards them in the darkness.

"More bad news," Jewel sighed. The ruby-red woman and the woman of fire both knew what they were looking at, they'd seen it before.

Feeling jittery, Flame looked at the roaring fireplace, and Jewel looked at the black crystal walls. Both women wanted to make an exit.

"Don't even think about it," Chen warned them. "You two know Crystal Castle, and I want to know my options. What are they?"

"There's a trapdoor leading to the roof of this tower. We can lock ourselves in up there," Jewel suggested.

"It has a nice view in the daytime," Flame added.

"Listen to me," Chen said angrily. "You're either going to come up with an alternative, or I'll use the two of you for a welcoming committee when Lord Daegal and his men come riding through the castle entrance."

"Why? There's that nice, elderly man who's already blocking the entrance with a very sturdy looking walking stick," Jewel said as she smiled at Chen awkwardly. "But I do have something to confess. We aren't exactly warriors. We're mostly for ornamentation."

"What do you mean?" Chen asked nervously.

In response, Jewel and Flame both began walking around swaying in a very seductive, inviting way.

"Oh, spare me! I can do that much myself. What can you do that will actually be useful at a time like this?"

"We can multiply," Jewel and Flame said at the same time.

Instantly, an exact replica of Jewel stepped out of, well, right out of Jewel herself! The same thing happened with Flame as a duplicate walked directly out of her own body. Next, the number of ruby-red women doubled from two to four, and they kept on doubling until there were eight, 16, 32 and finally 64 of them. Once again, the same thing happened with Flame. The humanoid woman made of shimmering coals duplicated herself over and over until 64 bodies of fire were standing before Chen.

Some of the women, now numbering 128 in total, began swaying and moving languidly as they walked around. Others just stood in one place, put their long, slender arms over their heads and proceeded to slowly rock back and forth.

"I need an army not a harem!" Chen yelled. Then, sighing in frustration, she looked over at Crystal who was still tied up and lying on the floor. "I could use a little help over here! Last time I saw those two they were carrying swords and were real fighters! What happened to them?"

"You've got to get these golden ropes off of me," Crystal said. "They're robbing me of my strength."

Chen looked down on the courtyard below and saw Eldwyn still holding his staff and blocking the entrance with its energy. Feeling desperate, the black leather panther began glancing around for something to toss at the old wizard to knock him unconscious.

Fortunately for her, Eldwyn took that moment to collapse. An energy field of prism light was still covering the wizard, Aerylln, Baelfire and Zorya providing them with protection, but the entrance was now wide open.

Chen ran over to Crystal and tore the golden ropes off of her.

"Take me out of my scabbard!" the dark sword shouted.

"Not yet," Chen said wanting to get the feel of her sword's powers before unleashing her even more so. "Just get those women ready for battle."

"With pleasure, but first send them downstairs to the courtyard. Once I give them horses and swords we're going to need more room."

"All right ladies, let's head downstairs," Chen said.

They stopped and looked at her moodily.

"Please!"

Appeased momentarily, they began walking towards the stairwell.

In exasperation, Chen glanced at Gwendylln who said, "Don't look at me. I wouldn't take any of them even as raw recruits."

"I'll get them whipped into shape in a minute," Crystal promised.

"You had better do something," Chen said.

Once all the women were in the courtyard, the first thing Crystal did was reseal the entrance. Chen looked at the dark sword and said, "Not bad, at least for starters."

"Well, I may be sluggish, but I'm not stupid," Crystal said.

However, Chen and Crystal watched in amazement as the women began waving to General Gornic's men who were staring back at them dumbfounded.

"You'd better put a stop to this nonsense, and I mean now!" Chen said glaring at Crystal.

"Take me out of my scabbard, even just a little. Let me get some air!"

Chen slid the dark sword ever so slightly out of her sheath.

In an instant, the women were mounted on magnificent warhorses some of which were ruby-red while others looked like bonfires, and all the women were holding shields and wielding swords.

But far more important, from Chen's perspective, was the change in their attitudes. The women in front of her now appeared to be battle-hardened veterans. Their bodies were leaner, firmer and tougher, and they radiated a sense of grim determination.

"Nice job," Chen said. "I could use 200 more just like them."

"Not without the Crystal Medallion," Crystal informed the black leather panther. "Without her, I'm not up to my full potential."

"Not you, too? I thought Baelfire was the one with limitations. You gave me the impression of being more self-reliant."

"With only Glenitant around, I had to be self-reliant. But Baelfire and I are half-sisters. We both have our strengths and weaknesses."

"Well, you picked a great time to tell me," Chen said.

"Forget the battle inside the castle, that won't make or break us. To win, we must focus on getting the Crystal Medallion. Once we get her, I can give up any pretence of supporting Lord Daegal, and I'll change his black crystal warriors back to normal."

"But in the meantime, my warrior women will be getting slaughtered by General Gornic's men."

"It's the price of war," Crystal countered.

"No, that's unacceptable. I grew up with those women."

Striding over to a ruby-red warrior, the black leather panther asked, "Are you Jewel? And if not, which one is she?"

"We are all Jewel," the woman informed her. "We share the same mind."

"You mean a communal consciousness?"

"No, there's no one else here but me. We're not made up of a collective of minds. There's only my mind. Go ahead, talk to one of the other women. Ask her name."

Walking past three or four of the ruby-red women, Chen turned to one and asked, "Are you Jewel?"

"Yes," Jewel said. "In battle, if you tell one ruby woman what you want, then all the others will automatically know. No matter which one you talk to, you'll be talking directly to me. There's no one else here, just me."

"It works the same for both of us," Flame added.

"So what are we going to do?" Crystal asked Chen.

"Would anyone care to hear my thoughts on the matter?" Andrina asked.

"Only everyone," Chen said as she, Gwendylln and Corson turned to the older warrior woman giving her their undivided attention.

Crystal looked at Andrina in a very guarded manner. Even though Chen remained outwardly calm, Crystal could sense how relieved she was that Andrina had a suggestion.

Chen has a child-like faith in Andrina, and I don't like that one bit, the dark sword thought becoming filled with suspicion and jealousy.

However, Crystal's personal concerns would have to wait. Battle plans had to be made and quickly!

"You have ten wolfhounds that you've been holding in reserve, right?" Andrina asked the black leather panther.

"Yes, but only five are healthy. The rest are wounded. Over a dozen died earlier when they attacked Lord Daegal's army."

"Can the wounded ones fight?"

"Yes."

"Well, here's what I propose. We have 64 flame warriors and 64 ruby ones. I think we should have 100 of them reinforce your archers in the center of the courtyard."

"No!" Crystal shouted. "Lord Daegal and his 200 black crystal warriors will rip right through the 28 that are left!"

Andrina gave Crystal a stern look of disapproval. The older warrior woman didn't like being interrupted when explaining battle strategy. And she didn't suffer fools gladly.

Horrified that Crystal had interrupted her mentor, Chen shook the dark sword as a warning and said, "Show some respect."

Crystal was shocked. In 500 years, no one had spoken to her like that. No one had dared, fearing the consequences. The dark sword glared at Andrina with a look of pure hatred filled with malignant evil. Conjuring up hideous mental images with her imagination, she attempted to project them into Andrina's consciousness hoping to cripple the warrior woman with terror.

Feeling confident, Crystal waited for Andrina to crumble in the face of such intimidation tactics, but the older warrior woman didn't even blink.

"Nice try," Andrina said dismissing the dark sword's temper tantrum.

This made Crystal so angry that she began shaking, but Chen thought the dark sword was trembling in fear over the coming fight with Lord Daegal.

"Don't be frightened. Just stay calm, keep your wits about you and obey Andrina," the black leather panther said reassuringly.

Upon hearing that, Crystal's temper went from red hot to white hot. Having to endure Chen's patronizing attitude on top of everything else was just too much. The dark sword's blade got so hot that smoke began seeping out of her scabbard. However, Chen took this as an encouraging sign and thought Crystal was trying to summon up her courage.

"That's right, get mad. Anger can drive away fear," Chen said trying to be encouraging.

Andrina didn't smile or take pleasure in Crystal's discomfort even though the older warrior woman knew how much the dark sword disliked her. Instead, Andrina stayed focused, stuck to the task at hand, kept a balanced attitude and was, well, very professional. Crystal, by comparison, appeared to be emotionally immature.

The dark sword was learning what it's like to be around intelligent, powerful women who are experienced, competent and fearless. These warrior women were a far cry from her former master, Glenitant, and Crystal didn't like it.

"As I mentioned before, I want 100 warriors to reinforce Chen's archers," Andrina said. Then, looking at Jewel and Flame, she added, "At first, all I want you to do is fight a holding action. I'll be sending you 75 more ruby warriors and 75 more flame warriors as reinforcements. At that point, you take back the courtyard and the castle walls."

"How long until reinforcements arrive?" Jewel asked.

"Soon after the rest of us ride out to confront Lord Daegal."

Crystal was dumbfounded!

"Could I have permission to speak?" she asked.

Chen smiled at the dark sword pleased that Crystal was showing Andrina the proper deference.

"Yes, you can speak," the older warrior woman said.

"I haven't the energy to create more Jewels and Flames as reinforcements."

"I realize that," Andrina said without further explanation.

Looking back at Jewel and Flame, the older warrior woman added, "You'll get your reinforcements within the hour. But I want you to engage the enemy now and hit them hard."

With that, a total of 100 Jewels and Flames turned, raised their swords and charged at General Gornic's men.

"I need to talk to Aerylln and Eldwyn," Andrina said as she watched the warrior women charging into battle. "While I do that, Corson and Gwendylln could you get our horses, please? Also, Chen, it would be a big help if you'd get Zenkak and the other wolfhounds."

When Corson, Gwendylln and Chen ran to do Andrina's bidding, the older warrior woman went over to Aerylln, Zorya, Baelfire and Eldwyn.

"Please lower your energy shield, I need to speak with you and Aerylln," Andrina told the elderly wizard who was greatly relieved at not having to keep up the effort.

After kneeling next to Aerylln who was exhausted but awake, Andrina asked, "Could you and Eldwyn erect an invisible wall 300 yards long, five feet high and place it between us and Lord Daegal's black crystal warriors?"

"How long will you need it to be there?" the young woman asked.

"Once we leave the castle, wait until they're almost upon us, and then raise the invisible wall. You can drop it right after they slam into it."

"We have the energy we were using for our protective shield, but it's all we have left, and I can't promise it will withstand the weight of 200 mounted, black crystal warriors. They might crash through it."

"Could it withstand the force of 100 mounted warriors?"

"Possibly, but the effort could kill Eldwyn. He's near death now," Aerylln said wondering what trick Andrina had up her sleeve.

They both looked at the wizard who appeared to be very frail.

"Eldwyn," Andrina said softly.

Turning his head and looking up at the warrior woman, Eldwyn said, "I've been listening to you. I don't know if I can help."

"If you can't, we're all dead," Andrina said in a tense whisper. She didn't want anyone overhearing her gloomy assessment of the situation.

"Well, not exactly," the wizard said. "Life never really ends. All that changes is the form it takes."

"I'm sure you're right," Andrina said humoring the old man. "But I'd like to spend a bit more time in this world, so what I need to know is will the wall hold?"

After struggling to his knees, Andrina helped Eldwyn to his feet. Assessing the situation, he saw the battle raging in the courtyard. Next, glancing out the entrance into the darkness, he watched the bits of flame getting closer. Then, he leaned on his staff seemingly lost in thought.

"Eldwyn, I need to know. Will the wall hold?"

The wizard took a deep breath, squared his shoulders, looked Andrina in the eye and said, "Yes, the wall will hold. I'll make it a foot thick out of clear crystal."

At that moment, Corson and Gwendylln approached with their horses. Corson mounted her own warhorse, Tempest, while Gwendylln, Andrina and Chen mounted the black stallions her warrior women were famous for.

Zenkak and the other wolfhounds were surrounding Chen growling and looking ferocious, which was the way they appeared most of the time. However, suffering from their wounds, some of the shaggy beasts were especially irritable and eager for a fight.

Taking a last, tentative look at the old wizard, Andrina sighed knowing her survival and the lives of all those with her depended upon him. Mustering her strength, she forced the feelings of apprehension from her mind.

"Let's ride!" Andrina shouted.

Chapter 34

Andrina charged out of Crystal Castle with Chen, Gwendylln, Corson, 14 ruby-red warriors, 14 flame warriors and 10 wolfhounds trailing behind her. They ran at breakneck speed across a terrain made up of black crystal shards.

Chen had to ride hard to keep up with Andrina. Is there anything this woman can't do better than everyone else? the black leather panther asked herself.

Had Andrina known what Chen was thinking, she would have laughed. The older warrior woman found exceptional ability to be a double-edged sword. It cut both ways.

As a result of Andrina's conceptual and strategic planning skills, she was right so often that it got on people's nerves. Insecure people began doubting themselves, ambitious people saw her as a rival, talented people felt overshadowed by her, and powerful people feared losing their influence. She made enemies easily.

Andrina had made an enemy of Crystal. The dark sword knew that she would never gain Chen's confidence as long as the older warrior woman was alive.

Andrina was a complicated woman, except during battle.

The older warrior woman was riding out to confront fire-breathing, black crystal warriors and was out numbered six to one. Her own warriors consisted of Chen, Gwendylln and Corson, who were three extremely confrontational women. She also had humanoid women riding on horseback who looked like they'd been soaked in flammable liquid and set on fire. Those fires shed light on glistening ruby warriors turning them a deep blood red. For Andrina, this was simplicity.

Riding out of Crystal Castle's entrance, she'd felt more relief than fear. With a sense of eager anticipation pumping adrenaline through her system, the older warrior woman watched as the gap between herself and Lord Daegal and his men shrank dramatically. Raising a hand into the air, she signaled for her warriors to stop, and they came to rest on a small rise in the field of black crystal shards.

The small group of 32 female combatants and 10 wolfhounds waited as the black crystal warlord and his 200 fire-breathing warriors bore down upon them.

When Lord Daegal saw all the Jewels and Flames, he wondered what was going on. But the warlord also noticed their small numbers and was determined not to allow them to impede his progress. Lord Daegal decided to run down his opponents and pound them into the ground. Digging his heels into his black crystal warhorse's sides, the animal leapt forward.

As he got closer, Lord Daegal realized Chen was among the small band of warrior women and with a broad smile, he headed straight for her.

"Crystal, change the black crystal warriors behind Lord Daegal, and to his far left and right, back to human form," Andrina said.

"But he'll notice and hurt the Crystal Medallion!"

"No, he won't. He's not watching anyone other than Chen. If you look carefully, you'll see he's headed directly for her. Start now!"

Almost immediately, there were fewer bits of flame making their way towards them in the darkness. However, a large, central core surrounding Lord Daegal was still filled with fire-breathing warriors hungry for battle. And they were riding black crystal horses snorting smoke and flames, with red-hot hoofs covered in yellow and orange fire.

Black crystal shards flew in all directions as the warhorses kicked up sharp glass-like pieces of the shattered valley floor. Crystal had earlier paved the vast fields surrounding the castle with smooth, polished sheets of black crystal. That beauty had only lasted a short while before the dark sword had exploded the glossy surface into tens of thousands of sharp fragments. Andrina suspected that the dark sword never grew tired of making trouble, and she was right.

The older warrior woman realized Crystal was unreliable but calmly proceeded with the strategy she'd formulated. Getting the Crystal Medallion from Lord Daegal would either buy the dark sword's cooperation or it wouldn't. Being a realist, Andrina was hoping a sadistic magic sword was better than no magic sword at all, at least for now. And so the master strategist focused on the problem at hand, which was to defeat Lord Daegal.

"Crystal, concentrate on the Jewels and Flames back in the castle courtyard. Project your energy onto them. You've returned about half of Lord Daegal's men to human form, so you should have enough energy to create 100 more warrior women as reinforcements," Andrina said. "Do it now!"

Projecting her energy at the castle, a bolt of black lightning shot out of the dark sword flying through the nighttime sky, then slammed into the courtyard exploding right in the middle of the Jewels and Flames. Instantly, they began multiplying, and the courtyard became filled with ruby-red warriors, as well as women made of flaming red and black coals. General Gornic wasn't easily unnerved, but he was deeply concerned about the number of reinforcements that arrived and by the way they'd materialized.

Back in a field outside Crystal Castle, Lord Daegal was in for a rude awakening of his own.

Andrina, Chen, Gwendylln, Corson, the Jewels and the Flames watched in apprehension as the fire-breathing, black crystal warriors got closer. But when almost upon them, Lord Daegal and his men just stopped.

Well, "stopped" may be too mild of a word. They crashed, slammed, careened and plowed, and they hit hard.

Dozens of fire-breathing warhorses lay crumpled behind a solid wall of…nothing! Scores of black crystal warriors were thrown from their saddles and flew over …nothing!

Eldwyn's invisible wall had held, and vanished!

The black crystal, fire-breathing horses ran into a chest-high wall stopping them cold and sending their riders flying. The men sailed headfirst over the wall and went sprawling onto the ground.

As quickly as the clear-crystal barrier appeared, it disappeared. Most of the fire-breathing warhorses fell forward collapsing onto a valley floor already covered with shards. In the darkness, the animals looked like piles of burning logs strewn along a row 200 yards long.

"Crystal, turn all these black crystal horses back to normal and conserve your energy," Andrina commanded.

In a moment, it was as if the row of fire had been extinguished.

The only horse making it over the wall was Lord Daegal's massive charger. It was so gigantic that the wall had caught the animal well below the chest. The massive, black crystal horse had been sent sprawling over the barrier flipping onto its back. And the massive warhorse smashed down on

Lord Daegal, who made a loud grunt before slipping into unconsciousness.

"Now!" Andrina shouted, and her human, ruby and flaming warriors leapt forward into battle.

Sadly, from Lord Daegal's black crystal warriors' point of view, Chen had a major trick up her sleeve. When the black leather panther had fought Glenitant, and then Jewel and Flame, the warrior woman learned an important lesson. She'd discovered that a sword isn't the best weapon to use against a ruby or crystal warrior. Jewel's body was so hard that it had deflected a blow from Chen's sword with the metal edge sliding along the ruby warrior's leg rather than cutting into it. Ever highly adaptable, Chen had solved the problem by smashing Jewel in the face with the flat side of her sword shattering one whole side of the ruby-red woman's head and sending gems flying all over the castle floor.

Chen had learned her lesson well, and as the warrior women now rode towards the black crystal warriors, they all reached for maces hanging from the pommels of their saddles. They were metal, sledgehammer-like weapons that could be slammed against the enemy.

Before leaving the castle, Chen had explained to the warrior women that you don't cut crystal, you shatter it!

Chen's mace had a wooden handle with one end of a chain attached to the top. The other end was connected to a large, iron ball with spikes sticking out of it. Holding the handle in her right hand, the black leather panther whirled the metal ball around and around over her head. Picking a target, Chen rode towards a black crystal warrior struggling to get back on his feet. When he saw the warrior woman coming at him, he drew his sword, but it did him no good.

The black leather panther swung the iron ball bringing it down upon his chest, and the warrior exploded in a shower of black crystal shards that flew in all directions.

Seeing that, Andrina smiled. She liked Chen's inventiveness. As for herself, the older warrior woman was wielding two maces, one in each hand. She fought as well with her left arm as she did with her right.

Andrina's maces had no chains attached, simply having a wooden handle with a heavy iron ball at the end. The wooden shaft was inserted into the iron ball and secured making the wood and metal as one.

The older warrior woman was in her element and rode along the line of black crystal warriors sprawled on the ground smashing heads like pumpkins. War is brutal, and Andrina was a gifted warrior, but that didn't mean she enjoyed it. Battle required a cold-hearted practicality that she'd mastered long ago, much to her regret. She knew that every life she took made her more callous, that her own sensitivity was damaged by it. How could it not? Only by emotionally distancing herself from her own actions could Andrina do what was required of her. After a prolonged battle, it was days before she could feel anything, a numbness settling on her like a protective shield keeping her from having to endure the brunt of life's necessary cruelty.

But for Chen, it was another matter. Her tortured upbringing had already made her numb to her own feelings. And so, pushing firmly ahead, Chen grabbed Crystal by her scabbard and gave the dark sword a direct order to return more black crystal warriors to human form. But as the black leather panther continued whirling her mace over her head and bringing it down hard on her opponents, she failed to notice Crystal was disobeying her.

Instead of doing what she was told, Crystal took the energy she'd saved by returning the black crystal warhorses to normal and used it to put a force field around Lord Daegal. He'd been lying on the ground pinned under his massive warhorse, but now he was even worse off than before, the force field immobilizing him pinning his hands and arms to his sides.

But the dark sword now had what she wanted! The Crystal Medallion was safe!

It's time for some fun, Crystal thought smiling to herself. She eagerly watched the sights and sounds of battle and had no intention of ending this conflict.

Zenkak and his wolfhounds were bounding around terrorizing Lord Daegal's men, and the wolfhounds were having more success attacking the 100 warriors that Crystal had turned back to normal. These men had slammed into Eldwyn's clear-crystal wall but hadn't put as much strain on it since they weren't as heavy as their black crystal counterparts. Being more fragile, however, they'd fared poorly when their human bodies flew over the wall and crashed against the sharp black shards covering the valley floor.

Upon hitting the ground, many of the humans had been cut to pieces. And the smell of so much blood was driving the wolfhounds wild. They sank their teeth into human flesh flailing the bodies back and forth through the air. A few of the beasts were so consumed by the taste of blood that they couldn't distinguish between those who were alive and those who weren't. Some of the men being thrashed about were already dead. Normally, Zenkak wouldn't have allowed such undisciplined behavior, but he felt that his wolfhounds had earned their pleasure.

"Enjoy yourselves!" the leader of the pack shouted. But he, himself, stuck to business. All the humans had been stunned upon slamming into the wall, but many were still alive. However, Zenkak began lessening their numbers. Grabbing one after another by the throat, he snapped their necks with a flick of his own powerful neck.

The leader of the pack was gratified to see that further down the line, Lothar, his second-in-command, was following his example. Zenkak stopped and indulged himself for a moment listening to the sound of men screaming before Lothar bit down hard on their throats and silenced them.

As Chen's wolfhounds were putting an end to human resistance, Jewel and Flame had been focusing on men made of black crystal. There had been 100 men still in the form of fire-breathing warriors when they crashed into Eldwyn's invisible wall. By contrast, there were only 30 fighters on Chen's side, and they were outnumbered three to one. Hoping to even the odds, Flame became inventive.

Flame, mounted on a fiery warhorse, had a duplicate of herself leap up behind her. The duplicate wrapped her arms around the other woman of fire and put her head against the other's back. This created quite a bonfire, but it did something more. It turned them into a humanoid flame-thrower.

Flame reached out and fire shot out of her hand. Focusing on one black crystal warrior at a time, she waited until the crystal became so super heated that it began melting. As soon as one began disintegrating, she moved on to the next. Sometimes, a black crystal warrior would only melt around the head and shoulders before beginning to cool. This left what appeared to be a row of melted statues standing in a field of broken shards.

Not wanting to be outdone, Jewel rode up to a duplicate of Flame and said, "Jump up and ride with me!"

Flame knew that Jewel was up to something and leapt onto the ruby-red woman's warhorse, sitting behind her. Since talking to one woman made of hot, burning coals was the same as talking to all of them, everyone got the message at once. Some of the Flames hadn't taken partners to become fire throwers, and so several paired up with several Jewels. The results were startling!

As each Flame wrapped her arms around the Jewel in front of her and pressed her body up against the ruby-red woman, laser beams shot out of Jewel's eyes. Each pair of women targeted a different black crystal warrior, and the beams began burning through them. The Jewels aimed for the legs of the black crystal warriors cutting them off at the knees.

However, a number of black crystal warriors had shaken off their surprise at having been thrown over Eldwyn's wall and began mounting horses that were uninjured. They were ordinary horses not made of black crystal, but the fire-breathing warriors riding them were now mounted once more and dangerous.

Chen and Andrina's women had done a remarkable job of destroying Lord Daegal's black crystal warriors who'd survived Eldwyn's surprise, but at first count, it looked like at least 25 were remounted and ready for battle. Extremely angry over having been duped, the black crystal warriors licked their wounded pride and charged at Flame, Jewel, Corson, Andrina, Gwendylln and Chen.

Chen dug her heels into her black stallion and tried to leap forward to meet the challenge but her horse didn't move. In a moment, the black leather panther found that she couldn't move either.

"Crystal what is going on?" Chen shouted.

"Oh, I'm saving you for a little surprise of my own," the dark sword said laughing, her tone of voice brimming with evil mischief.

Chen looked over at her uncle who'd been immobilized by Crystal earlier. Lord Daegal looked at his niece and the force of the hate pouring out of him shocked her. They had never gotten along, but this whole battle in Crystal Valley was his fault not hers. He came to her. She hadn't gone to him. But that's the way it had always been. This battle was just one more assault the warlord was making upon her. And the others in her bedchamber had been equally abusive, if not more so.

The black leather panther remembered back to when her father, Ritalso, had first turned up missing. Chen didn't know Lord Daegal had imprisoned him. As a young girl, Chen had felt frightened and alone, and thought he'd abandoned her.

Back then, Andrina hadn't as yet suggested to Lord Daegal that he form a cadre of 100 young women Chen's own age to serve as a personal guard for her. Thus the young girl had no one to whom she could turn, except for her loving uncle who sought to comfort her.

Lord Daegal had lied convincingly about his brother. He cast Ritalso's motives in as dark a light as possible. Chen had been both stunned and confused.

Many a night she'd fallen to sleep only after Lord Daegal sat on the edge of her bed providing almost constant reassurance that he would not abandon her as well. He had been gentle with her lightly stroking her hair until she fell asleep.

The gentleness ended when Crystal, in a particularly evil mood, suggested that he take his reassurance a step further. At the dark sword's insistence, and wanting to turn Chen into the type of scarred, shattered, angry young woman that Crystal would find appealing, Lord Daegal began visiting Chen's bedchamber with more than kindness in mind. He proceeded to terrify the teenage girl. This went on night after night for what seemed like an eternity. At first, fear had shocked her into passivity. But eventually fear turned to hatred. Then she rebelled.

In secret, Chen had enlisted the aid of her uncle's warriors to teach her to fight. One night she'd raked a knife across her uncle's ribs as a warning. He returned with less frequency after that, but when he got drunk nothing short of killing Lord Daegal would have stopped him. She wasn't willing to murder him, though she'd done it many times in her imagination. If he were dead, she'd be totally alone. At least this way, she was the niece of the ruler of the castle. If she killed him, she'd be defenseless. So on some nights, when nothing would dissuade him, not even a few wicked thrusts with a knife, she would give in to his needs.

With a great effort, Chen pulled herself back to the present. As the black leather panther continued watching her uncle, the hate filling his eyes was not unexpected, but the depth and intensity of it was shocking.

"I want Crystal Castle, and I want the dark sword. They're mine! Not yours, mine!" Lord Daegal shouted, his rage exploding.

Having a more immediate concern, Chen forced herself to tear her eyes away from Lord Daegal. Her warrior women and 25 of her uncle's fire-breathing, black crystal warriors were closing in on each other, the men being mounted on horses that Crystal had turned back to normal.

Many warhorses had suffered serious injuries when crashing into Eldwyn's invisible wall, but these animals had fared better than the others having no broken bones. These warhorses were shaken up and badly bruised but could still be ridden.

Being held firmly in the grip of Crystal's force field, Chen could do little more but watch as the two opposing sides sped towards each other. When the combatants were thirty yards apart, the Flames who'd doubled up began unleashing hell on the approaching black crystal warriors shooting streams of fire with incredible intensity. Also, pairs of Jewels and Flames began shooting laser beams at the enemy with feminine ferocity. That the men even thought they had a chance against an equal number of angry women showed how naïve they were.

The female flame-throwers were leaving behind a mangled collection of black crystal statues as partially melted warriors fell from their horses. The women who hadn't doubled up were swinging their maces with a vengeance. Body parts of shattered, black crystal warriors were flying everywhere. Broken limbs and chunks of crystal were falling to the ground piling on top of shards already covering the valley floor. Whether the black crystal warriors were melted or shattered, dead was dead.

To avoid being burned to a cinder, Andrina, Gwendylln and Corson had been riding behind the Jewels and Flames. A few black crystal warriors had broken through the maelstrom of fire, laser beams and maces only to find three female humans eager for battle. Even without special powers, these women were dangerous, and they made quick work of the fire-breathing warriors. The women snuffed them out.

Soon, the fighting was over, and the black crystal warriors were destroyed. Vanquished. Slaughtered. Undone. Beaten by a small group of proud, determined women.

All that was left of Lord Daegal's attacking forces were a few humans that Zenkak's wolfhounds had not, as of yet, finished off. As the ranks of human warriors had diminished, Zenkak's wolfhounds became increasingly playful. They were now chasing the few warriors who were left, knocking them down, pawing at them playfully and in general terrifying the men to death.

Looking back towards Jewel, Flame and the others, Zenkak noticed that Chen wasn't moving. Everyone else around her was, but not his master. The hairs went up on the back of his neck, and he raced to her aid.

Andrina, the first to notice Zenkak, said, "Chen, your lead wolfhound is heading this way, and he looks pretty upset."

"I'd be surprised if he wasn't," Chen said watching the shaggy beast charging towards her. "Crystal, if you hurt him, you and I are going to have a problem."

"Me, injure a faithful animal like Zenkak? How could you even think I'd do something that despicable?" Crystal said laughing.

"I'm serious."

"Okay, fine, have it your way. Sometimes, you're no fun at all."

"You're sick."

"No kidding? Wait till you see what I've dreamed up for you. Maybe you ought to think of yourself more and your faithful pet a little less."

When Zenkak reached Chen, he sprang up and bounced off the force field surrounding his master. Charging at it again, Crystal allowed the wolfhound to penetrate the invisible shield, and then the dark sword held him in place with it. Now Lord Daegal, Chen and Zenkak were all imprisoned and immobile.

"Flame, please remove the Crystal Medallion from Lord Daegal's neck," the dark sword said.

As one of the Flames dismounted, Crystal freed the warlord's head, neck and upper chest from the force field, though Lord Daegal's arms were still pinned to his sides. He was so furious that the 15-foot tall, black crystal warlord's face became red hot, and he spit smoke and fire with an alarming show of temper.

Flame had never known a man before who could do that, and it sort of turned her on. Walking over to Lord Daegal, she put her own pyrotechnic hand behind his head, placing her flame-engulfed lips in front of the warlord's mouth and opened hers to receive the pleasure of his heat.

At first, Flame was mostly yellow and orange, but the fire shooting out of Lord Daegal's mouth was red hot! As their lips touched, the warlord's burning intensity poured into her face and neck turning them a mixture of red, yellow and orange, but predominantly red! Gradually the red flames made their way down her back.

"If you stay a fire-breathing, black crystal hunk, we are definitely going to have to get better acquainted," Flame said when she pulled away.

Smiling, she looked over to Jewel and said, "Why am I always drawn to men who aren't good for me?"

"Have you ever met a man who was any good?" Jewel laughed.

"Not really," Flame lamented.

"Well, there is Pensgraft," Jewel said thoughtfully. "He's strong, handsome, caring, bold, sensitive, philosophical and intelligent."

"He's too smart to get involved with girls like us," Flame pointed out.

"There's one woman who might be able to entice him. I've noticed him glancing more than once at a certain dangerous woman clad totally in skin-tight black leather," Jewel said.

All the Jewels and Flames nodded in agreement.

Gwendylln and Corson stayed out of it. The black leather panther didn't like it when anyone teased her. Andrina, for her part, nodded approvingly and kept this bit of information for future reference. Always the strategist, she wasn't beyond playing matchmaker.

Chen just remained silent, but she brooded over the invasion of her privacy.

"Hello?" Crystal said. "Does anyone want to stick to the business at hand?"

"One last thing. How old do you figure Pensgraft is?" Flame asked.

"Well, I heard Pensgraft say he was 18 when his daughter was born. That could put him in his mid 30s, and Chen's in her early 20s," Jewel said.

"Hmm, sounds like a fit to me," Flame said teasing the black leather panther a little, but being more serious than not.

Chen held her peace but controlling her temper took an effort. Had she not been bound by a force field, her hand would definitely have been on the hilt of her sword as a warning for everyone to back off. Chen was well aware that Flame and Jewel were taking advantage of her being immobile in order to bring up the subject.

It wouldn't have been so bad if Chen hadn't been thinking the same thing. Pensgraft was the only man who ever made her feel safe and wanted. It was frightening for Chen to find herself wanting someone. Gwendylln and Corson she was used to having as friends but allowing herself to be open even to

Pensgraft was unnerving. It made her feel vulnerable. It gave her a panic attack just thinking about it.

Andrina watched the emotions moving across Chen's face and came to a conclusion. "That young woman's in love!" The matchmaker decided she would begin laying the groundwork for her "daughter" to conquer Pensgraft.

"People! People! Your attention please!" Crystal said loudly. "Before we go any further, Flame do you think you could get around to doing what I sent you over there for?"

"More kissing?" Flame teased knowing full well what Crystal wanted.

"No, the Crystal Medallion!"

"Oh, excuse me," Flame smiled as she slipped the thin chain with the circular medallion over Lord Daegal's head.

Flame held up the prize, not quite knowing what she held in her hand. No one really knew, except for Crystal, who now released Chen from the force field. Crystal was hanging from a belt around the black leather panther's waist and had been inside the force field with her. But Chen was free once more as Flame brought over the Crystal Medallion.

"Chen, this is my gift to you," Crystal said.

"I've always admired the medallion's beauty," Chen admitted. "But I never thought I'd be the one wearing it."

"Well, it's yours now."

Having no way of knowing what was coming next, Chen slightly bent her neck forward, and Flame slid the chain over her head. The medallion was made of black crystal and had a band of white gold encircling it.

"Yes!" Crystal almost screamed as the dark sword, Chen and the Crystal Medallion were finally together.

Crystal had yearned for this day since the black leather panther was barely in her teens. The dark sword had seen the outrageous displays of violent temper that leapt from Chen with almost no provocation. And after knowing her just a few days, Crystal had fallen in love, a warped, twisted love.

The dark sword had encouraged Glenitant and, through her, Lord Daegal to intercede in Chen's upbringing. But Crystal was careful to keep hidden in her heart the depth of her love for the young girl. Had Glenitant known that Crystal was plotting to overthrow her, the old crone would have killed Chen.

But now Crystal had what she wanted, and unbeknownst to Chen, the dark sword had just taken her prisoner. Or so Crystal thought.

"Everyone stand back. I'm releasing Lord Daegal," Crystal said, and the warlord immediately felt the force field letting go of him. Lord Daegal was so angry that he drew his sword as fire, smoke and ash spewed out of every pore of his body.

"You used me!" the warlord shouted at the dark sword. "You were after the Crystal Medallion all along!"

"Really, you figured that out for yourself, did you? Anyway, why should you have the medallion and not Chen? She's the rightful heir."

"If she's dead, there will be no heir!" Lord Daegal bellowed.

"Okay, if you can kill her, you can have both me and the medallion."

When Chen heard that, it sounded all too familiar. "Didn't you pull the same thing with Aunt Glenitant? You made me fight her to get you."

"Yes, and now, I'm letting you fight to keep me. Plus, this gives you a chance to get back at Lord Daegal for kidnapping your father and for the way he comforted you over your loss. When he came to your bedchamber, Lord Daegal went too far, too often, don't you think?"

Chen looked at her uncle and hate welled up inside her.

"Do you expect Chen to fight this black crystal, fire-breathing monster all by herself and with just a mace?" Andrina asked the dark sword.

"No, I'll level the playing field," Crystal said excitement filling her voice.

A "dark light" began radiating from Crystal. Suddenly it seemed as if a shroud was being pulled over all of them. Stars disappeared from the sky, and the light from the 14 Flames began to dim. Chen could sense the presence of something, or someone, invading the area around her. Within the nighttime darkness, there now seemed to be a deeper darkness illuminating pathways within everyone's consciousness creating an increased awareness of harsh thoughts and feelings. Negative possibilities and consequences seemed so much more real and inevitable, almost like the existence of a diabolical evil was a certainty.

"Crystal, what's going on here?" Andrina shouted as the stench of rot and decay filled the air around her. Suddenly, the older warrior woman felt the warmth of another body up against her back. Glancing around, she saw a decrepit, elderly woman looking at her. The ancient hag put her bony arms around the warrior woman's waist, and Andrina felt the heat of the evil, old crone's face as their cheeks touched. Stunned, Andrina realized that this was what it must feel like to be possessed by something dark and evil.

"Get away from me!" Andrina shouted putting all of her will power into the command. "Get away from me, now!"

Fortunately, the demon vanished. The warrior women were staring at Andrina, but Jewel and Flame already knew what had happened. They'd seen the decrepit, old hag before, and she was the presence of evil itself. The old crone had come out of Crystal, out of the deepest recesses of the dark sword's inner being.

Only Baelfire can deal with this, Andrina told herself. And she was right. The old crone would have to be confronted by an old wizard, a magic horse, a teenage girl and her sword.

Chapter 35

Back at Crystal Castle, the good sword looked out into the night sensing something had changed. A new danger, something very alarming, was hidden within the darkness. Baelfire had felt this evil presence before, and its reappearance sickened her. Looking around at the battle in the courtyard, she saw that the reinforcements, the dozens of Flames and Jewels, had turned the tide in their favor. But another fight was brewing. One even worse.

Will it never end? Baelfire asked herself while fighting feelings of despair and desperation.

Aerylln, Zorya, Eldwyn and the good sword were still lying exhausted by the castle entrance. They no longer had the energy to maintain a protective force field over themselves, but they weren't entirely defenseless. With the appearance of reinforcements, and with the methods Jewel and Flame had improvised for shooting fire and laser beams, the defenders had taken back much of the courtyard. Now, they were in the process of driving General Gornic's troops back over the castle walls.

The general was agitated and displeased with this reversal of fortune. Losing his sons, and now losing the battle, was proving to be too much for even this ferocious warrior. He'd attempted to rally his troops by staking himself out, so to speak, and refusing to retreat. Gornic had stood his ground and was determined to defend it or to die trying. It was a foolhardy display of courage that was meaningless, given that his troops had no hope of winning the battle. His behavior was more of a death wish, a simple desire to die before his time was over, before life as he knew it had ended.

The warrior women defending the castle showed him no mercy. However, Jewel and Flame realized the general wanted to go out in a blaze of glory, and in this they accommodated him. Flame paired up with a duplicate of herself, once more generating enough heat to become a humanoid flamethrower and hurled a stream of fire at a very dangerous, destructive warrior who, nonetheless, was seeking death with honor.

Even after being set ablaze, General Gornic gripped his sword with all his strength and rushed at a group of Chen's archers, the warrior women unleashing a torrent of arrows as a tribute to his bravery. When General Gornic dropped to his knees and fell face forward onto the courtyard floor, his body was riddled with over 20 arrows. With his last breath, he cursed the women who'd defeated him feeling humiliated by losing to Chen's warriors. Women should know their place, General Gornic thought as he died, refusing to give up his prejudice.

But for as much as he despised powerful women, his deep-seated insecurities preventing him from being open to change, the general was dead, and Chen's warriors were alive. His death had a demoralizing effect on his troops, who shared his prejudice about warrior women being inferior. Their general's death was a rude awakening. It seemed that women could defend themselves, and no amount of male denial could bring their general back to life. He'd died at the hands of women, which was a frightening thought, now that Gornic's men were on the defensive with women raining hell and damnation down upon them.

Chen's warrior women, and the Jewels and Flames, gradually took back more and more of the courtyard, and they reclaimed it for Chen, all the women recognizing the black leather panther's undisputed sovereignty.

However, somehow, a few of General Gornic's warriors had gotten past Chen's archers, the Jewels and the Flames and foolishly tried to attack Aerylln, Baelfire, Zorya, and Eldwyn. But the men were instantly incinerated by a tired and irritable Baelfire.

Now, the good sword realized General Gornic's remaining warriors were the least of her worries. A far more dangerous opponent had materialized. Looking out into the darkness, Baelfire could smell it, rot and decay.

"Aerylln get ready. You might need to take me out of my scabbard," Baelfire said, and the young woman got to her feet and picked up the good sword. However, sensing the sword's state of exhaustion, Aerylln protested saying, "Baelfire, you can't do more. You're worn out. We all are."

"Zorya, get on your feet," the good sword commanded, too tired to argue with Aerylln or explain their predicament.

"What's wrong now?" Zorya asked. "Jewel and Flame are making progress containing General Gornic's men, and they're also guarding the entrance. The tide has turned in our favor."

"At the moment, I'm not worried about the castle. Darker deeds are afoot this night, I'm afraid," Baelfire said.

"What do you mean?"

"Balzekior!"

"Oh not now, not today!" Zorya wailed.

"Crystal must have taken the Crystal Medallion from Lord Daegal," Baelfire said.

"It seems like only yesterday that we took the medallion from Glenitant and gave it to Lord Glenhaven for safe keeping," Zorya said.

"Lord Daegal was never the man his father was," Baelfire said displeased that a young Daegal had inherited the medallion.

"We should have taken the Crystal Medallion from Lord Daegal and given it to someone else," Zorya said.

"But who?" Baelfire asked. "Lord Daegal and Glenitant were always at each other's throats. Lord Daegal may not have had his father's sense of honor, but he was always determined to keep the Crystal Medallion away from his sister."

"And now he's lost the medallion! If Chen puts it around her neck, then Balzekior will try to get the warrior woman under her power," Zorya said.

"Only the Creative Light can save us now," Eldwyn said while lying on the courtyard floor, his face ashen and his eyes puffy and bloodshot. "It's unpredictable, and I have no idea when it will next show up, but without it, there's nothing more we can do."

"Eldwyn, I don't understand," Aerylln said. "If the creative energy's so powerful, why doesn't it take some kind of action? It must know the problems we're facing."

Having reached her breaking point, Baelfire almost gave up. The good sword didn't have the strength to explain their relationship with the Creative Light, and she wasn't really sure how it worked. It just did, usually.

Looking over at the teenage girl, Zorya wished she had more faith in the power of good over evil like Aerylln did.

"I've lost my way," Zorya lamented. "I used to see so clearly, but now I just don't know what to believe."

"It's your fatigue talking," Eldwyn said, his voice weak, barely a whisper.

"No, it's not. What if we've been wrong all along?"

"We're not wrong."

And with that said, the old wizard drew one last, ragged breath, let it out slowly and died.

Baelfire, Zorya and Aerylln were stunned.

"You can't leave us now, not now!" Baelfire shouted.

*

Marcheto was in the courtyard with his brothers and father battling General Gornic's men when he heard a voice calling to him, Eldwyn's voice. The young man looked around but didn't see the old wizard.

"Go to Aerylln, Marcheto. She needs you, and she needs you now!"

The young warrior looked around once more but couldn't see Eldwyn anywhere. However, the voice had the desired effect, and fear for Aerylln's well-being gripped Marcheto.

Running to his oldest brother, Kirnochak, Marcheto shouted, "Aerylln needs me!" That was all the young man said, and it was all he needed to say.

Kirnochak quickly ran to Xandaric, Adexsus and their father, Tark. The eldest son told them what Marcheto had said, and they watched as the young man began fighting his way through General Gornic's remaining warriors. Banding together as a family, as they always did in times of adversity, a father and his sons ran after the most intuitive member of their clan.

Fighting past General Gornic's warriors, Marcheto's family made their way behind the safety of the hundreds of Jewels and Flames who were now dominating the courtyard, and they reached Aerylln, Baelfire, Zorya and Eldwyn almost the same time as Marcheto. All stood around the dead wizard who lay crumpled on the courtyard floor.

"Without him, it's going to be hard to create a Trinity," Zorya said, weeping over the loss of her friend.

"Crystal has unleashed a devilish enemy, and we need the Trinity," Baelfire explained. "Without Eldwyn, there's little hope of defending ourselves against a demon as powerful as Balzekior."

"Who's Balzekior?" Tark asked.

"She's the complete opposite of what we call the Creative Light," Baelfire explained. "Up until now, a dark trinity has never successfully materialized, but now, all that may change. Chen's a protégé, and she could be dangerous, very dangerous."

Kneeling down next to the dead wizard, Marcheto put a hand on Eldwyn's chest and said, "I heard him calling to me, and he told me that Aerylln was in trouble. It sounded like the old wizard was right behind me."

"That's not possible," Zorya said.

Suddenly, Marcheto began feeling very heavy, like his body was made of iron. Then, losing his balance, the young man fell facedown onto the dead wizard. Immediately, prism light shot out of Eldwyn's body, and the purple, blue, green, yellow, orange and red colors enveloped Marcheto. Xandaric tried pulling Marcheto away from the dead wizard, but Tark stopped him.

"Let him go, Marcheto must discover his destiny," Tark said.

But the prism light intervened becoming blindingly bright and exploding with radiant intensity knocking everyone away from the old wizard and the young man. And before anyone knew what was happening, Eldwyn and Marcheto vanished. The wizard's wooden staff and his threadbare robe were all that was left behind.

However, after just a few moments, a human form filled with prism light materialized. There wasn't an actual physical body, just a crystal-clear shape filled with all the colors of a rainbow. At first, the human form was lying on the floor next to Eldwyn's robe, but soon it sat up, and then stood up.

With a blinding flash, prism light shot out in all directions filling the courtyard with vibrant colors, instantly followed by a tremendous clap of thunder reverberating throughout the castle. Next, a powerful force field blasted out of the humanoid form knocking down almost every warrior within the castle walls.

After the blinding intensity of the prism light subsided, the human form had transformed and taken on a familiar appearance. It was Marcheto, a rather naked Marcheto. In the next instant, Eldwyn's old robe began radiating multi-colored light and lifted itself off the courtyard floor. Marcheto raised his arms and slid them into the sleeves as the robe lowered itself onto him.

The wizard's robe looked good as new. Well, not quite new, but it wasn't more than 100 or 200 years old. However, to the humans standing around the young man, the robe looked sparkling and fresh.

Glancing around with vacant eyes, Marcheto seemed to be in a daze. But as his eyes cleared, the young man reached out for the wizard's staff lying on the courtyard floor, and it leapt into his hand.

"We will take back the night!" Marcheto declared. Yet after looking around, he asked, "But who am I? Where am I?"

"You're my man, that's who you are," Aerylln said going up on her toes and kissing him full on the mouth. And, wow, that woke him up!

"Why am I dressed like this?" Marcheto asked feeling rather confused.

Before anyone could even attempt an answer, another humanoid form materialized next to the young man followed by another blinding flash of prism light. When it subsided, a faint image of Eldwyn was standing next to Marcheto.

"That's a very nice robe," Eldwyn said feeling one of the sleeves. "When it was mine, I really should have taken better care of it, but I won't be needing it now."

"Eldwyn, what's going on?" Marcheto asked.

"Well, I was literally exhausted to the point of death, and given that there wasn't time for me to recuperate, I realized my only option was to pick a replacement, and to do so quickly," Eldwyn said. "And with you being close by, the choice was easy."

"What do you mean?"

"Since you first exhibited a natural ability to meditate, I've been keeping an eye on you. Meditation is vitally important to the development of any new wizard."

"New wizard?"

"Yes, we're facing another challenge, an extremely daunting one, and I fear I'm not up to it. I'm sorry to be saddling you with so much responsibility so quickly, but it can't be avoided."

"What sort of responsibility?"

"You'll know soon enough, I'm afraid. It will come to you. Just wait here."

"What's coming?"

"You'll see, very soon. And it's important that you trust your heart. Let it guide you. I'll direct your steps, too, at least I'll try," Eldwyn said as he began fading from view.

"But I don't know anything about being a wizard," Marcheto protested.

"Just don't panic."

"Why would I panic?" Marcheto shouted at the disappearing figure.

"Just don't. And don't go into that field of black crystal shards either. Let this trouble come to you," Eldwyn said as the last of his faint image disappeared from view.

"What's happening? I don't understand," Marcheto shouted, but Eldwyn was gone, at least it seemed so. Taking a deep breath, the apprentice wizard looked out of the castle entrance into the darkness. In the distance, Marcheto saw a black crystal Lord Daegal breathing fire. And there was something else.

In the shape of a decrepit, old hag, Balzekior was walking towards the castle. Sensing the old crone's malignant evil, Marcheto shivered.

"Yes, I'm coming for you, young man. And for your pretty girlfriend," a voice in Marcheto's mind said to him, though the ancient hag was still hundreds of yards away.

However, making such a threat was a mistake on Balzekior's part.

Had the old crone only threatened the new apprentice wizard, Marcheto could have handled it and stayed calm. But the evil, old hag had just threatened Aerylln. Now, the young man was prepared to fight.

Hovering invisibly nearby, Eldwyn smiled.

Chapter 36

Out in the darkness, amidst broken shards, shattered warriors, torn human flesh and dashed hopes, Lord Daegal had discovered he was no longer bound by Crystal's force field, but that did little to calm his anger. If inner rage, if inner fire, could consume one's body, then the warlord would have melted into nothingness.

Lord Daegal looked around at the wreckage of his black crystal army. He'd thought it was an invincible armada but saw it fall prey to Crystal's treachery.

Looking back at Crystal Castle, Lord Daegal was surprised to see the outside walls being consumed by fire. But after a moment, he realized that wasn't the case. Instead, hundreds of Jewels and Flames were on the walkways spewing fire everywhere and forcing his warriors to retreat. Almost in a panic, his men were climbing back over the outside walls and scrambling down the siege ladders.

Back out in the field of black crystal shards, Lord Daegal realized the 14 Jewels and 14 Flames near Chen were only a small part of the overall fire consuming his reign. Looking at his niece, the warlord was both resentful and amazed that she'd pulled off this dramatic coup.

But very soon, Lord Daegal would envy her a whole lot less.

Drawing upon the evil that Balzekior had brought forth, Crystal harnessed its power and poured it into Chen causing the black leather panther to retch from the vile, suffocating darkness.

The warrior woman began to age dramatically looking more and more like the decrepit, old hag that had crept up on Andrina. In a few seconds, there was nothing left of Chen's former beauty. The only remaining remnant was her black leather outfit, and it was no longer skintight. In fact, Chen appeared anorexic.

"You really should take better care of yourself," Crystal said laughing at the gaunt, haggard face of the emaciated woman. "Well, some of us age better than others, I suppose."

Finding this anything but amusing, Andrina asked, "Do you expect Chen to fight her uncle looking like this? Why, she couldn't lift a sword, let alone wield one."

What does it matter? the dark sword thought. I'll do anything I please with her.

But saving this torment for another time and getting back to business, Crystal said, "Okay, try this on for size. Here's Black Scarlet!"

Chen began changing, rapidly filling her outfit once again. Then, as her muscles and overall body continued growing, the outfit became so tight the leather started ripping across her back, shoulders and thighs. Next, appearing out of nowhere, the warrior woman found herself covered by a huge, scarlet tunic hanging down below her knees. Attached to it was a scarlet cape so long and massive that the material flowed across her shoulders, down her back and piled up in folds on the ground.

That is until Chen began to grow, and grow, and grow.

Taking a good, hard look at her master, Gwendylln watched as the black leather panther turned into a female version of Lord Daegal while firelight from the Flames reflected off powerful black crystal biceps and thighs.

Gwendylln was deeply concerned but kept her distance. Chen in human form was dangerous enough, but her master as a black crystal monster was even more terrifying.

Chen's features were recognizable, but her face had turned to black crystal like the rest of her, and she towered over everyone except Lord Daegal. The scarlet tunic once hanging below her knees was now a sleeveless blouse. The scarlet cape was also properly proportioned to her size and stretched out its full length rippling in the wind.

Scarlet fire sprang into Chen's eyes, and she began breathing out scarlet and yellow flames. When Crystal first surrounded the warrior woman with a force field, Chen's stallion had disappeared into the darkness. But it galloped back to her having transformed into a giant, black crystal warhorse with a long, scarlet saddle blanket, which provided a striking contrast.

Bending down, Chen, as Black Scarlet, picked up a huge mace that was lying on the ground. Her weapon's handle was now the size of a small tree trunk, the metal links of the chain the size of horseshoes with a spiked metal ball at the end of the chain the size of a large boulder.

Black Scarlet leapt into the saddle, swung the mace 'round and 'round above her head and let out a monstrous, billowing roar! She took a shield that was hanging from the pommel of her saddle and hoisted it up in front of her.

Taking one look at Black Scarlet, Lord Daegal did something no one had ever seen him do before, he backed down. At least that's what everyone thought he was doing, even

Andrina. But that wasn't it. Instead, Lord Daegal had finally wised up and was tired of being used and manipulated by Crystal.

The warlord had started adding things up. First, it was Glenitant, with Crystal's backing, who'd encouraged him to imprison their older brother, Ritalso. Their brother had always seemed incompetent, but the warlord had seen worse fools. Second, it was Glenitant who'd encouraged him to physically assault Chen, but the warlord realized this was Crystal's doing as well. Three, the dark sword had encouraged Lord Daegal to attack Crystal Castle before he was properly prepared. Four, Crystal had obviously double-crossed him by backing Chen and providing her with ruby-red warriors and the women made of fire.

Looking back to when he was a young man, Lord Daegal wondered if Crystal had been responsible for the death of his father, Lord Glenhaven. If so, the dark sword might also be responsible for the realm falling into civil war upon his father's death.

With a shock, the warlord realized he'd seen the decrepit, old hag once before, and he even remembered her name, Balzekior. Lord Daegal struggled to recall where he'd seen her, and then it hit him. When Lord Glenhaven had been pronounced dead, the ancient hag had been standing next to the court physician wearing the slightest hint of a smile, something a young Daegal found inappropriate given the circumstances, but now he understood.

Feeling sick to his stomach, Lord Daegal realized both Balzekior and the dark sword had been his father's enemies, and, way too late, he realized they were his enemies as well.

The warlord thought, The old crone's the one behind it all. Crystal's just her puppet, and Glenitant was the dark sword's puppet. And to some degree, I did Glenitant's bidding, at least when it came to Chen.

Furious with himself and feeling an overwhelming sense of frustration, Lord Daegal realized he'd been used and used badly.

Looking off in the distance, the warlord saw the decrepit, old hag heading for Crystal Castle, and he shifted his anger from Chen to Balzekior. Deciding to go after the old crone, Lord Daegal urged his warhorse forward but pulled back on the reins upon seeing a black crystal warrior woman riding at him wielding a giant mace and spitting fire.

As the monstrous apparition got closer, he realized it was Chen and tried veering around her, but the warrior woman cut him off. Backing up, he made another sweep hoping to slip past her flank, but Black Scarlet altered course blocking this attempt as well. Wanting Balzekior even more, Lord Daegal had counted on saving the destruction of his niece for later when he could enjoy it. But now, he prepared to fight to the death. Forgetting the attack on Crystal Castle was his doing, Lord Daegal thought, This confrontation is Chen's fault not mine.

Staring hard at his niece, Lord Daegal drew his sword, and Black Scarlet responded by whirling her mace around over her head. Mounted on fire-breathing, black crystal warhorses, uncle and niece glared at each other, then nudged their animals' sides and charged.

Black Scarlet's mace slammed against Lord Daegal's shield with such force it almost knocked him from his saddle. Quickly recovering, Lord Daegal spun his horse around and lashed out at Black Scarlet with all his might. However, pulling hard on her reins, the warrior woman sidestepped the blow.

The black crystal warriors separated, rode a short distance apart, turned and charged once more. When almost upon each other, Lord Daegal made his warhorse rear up but acted completely surprised and pretended to lose control. Black Scarlet swung her mace again, but Lord Daegal immediately regained control of his horse and ducked under the flailing chain and iron ball that barely missed his head. Before Black Scarlet could swing the mace again, Lord Daegal leapt off his horse, lunged at the warrior woman, grabbed onto her left leg and dragged her from the saddle.

Tumbling to the ground, Black Scarlet rolled over and over finally ending up on her stomach. To her surprise and chagrin, Lord Daegal landed on top of her and began grinding his pelvis against her and said, "Seems like old times."

"Stop it! I'm fed up with old times!" the warrior woman shouted.

Lord Daegal's drunken visits to her bedchamber held no fond memories, only pain and desperation. Reaching out and grabbing the chain part of her mace, Chen dragged the weapon towards her. Then, as Lord Daegal was kissing her neck, she took the iron ball with the sharp, pointed spikes and slammed it against her uncle's face. Lord Daegal yelled out as a spike jabbed into his right eye.

Rolling off Black Scarlet, the warlord staggered to his feet and put a hand over his wounded eye. Wracked with pain, he stumbled and appeared disoriented. Taking advantage of this, Black Scarlet swung her mace over her head, brought it down where the spikes brushed the ground before arcing upward and catching her uncle between his legs. Black crystal shards flew everywhere, and Lord Daegal screamed while bending over in pain.

The warrior woman paused and savored the moment. Next, she swung her mace 'round and 'round above her head building momentum and smashed the iron ball into her uncle's face. The warlord's head exploded into dozens of shards, and Lord Daegal fell to his knees looking at his niece with his one good eye that had somehow avoided destruction. Red flames were still flickering within it.

The warlord drew a few ragged breaths, collapsed onto the ground and rolled onto his back. Black Scarlet watched the red flames flicker and go out. Her uncle was dead.

Leaping back onto her massive warhorse, Black Scarlet raced towards the castle. As she passed Andrina, she shouted, "The old hag is our worst enemy!"

All the warrior women spurred their horses and followed their leader, a black crystal giant wearing a scarlet blouse and cape.

But ever the realist, Andrina thought, What can we possibly do against the hag?

Chapter 37

Back at the castle, Marcheto watched Balzekior getting closer and gripped his wizard's staff trying to draw courage from it. Earlier, peering into the night with the eyes of a mystic, he'd seen the dark sword turn Chen into Black Scarlet. Then, after the black crystal woman had crushed Lord Daegal and began chasing Balzekior, the apprentice wizard realized a major confrontation was inevitable.

By the time Black Scarlet caught up with the hag, Balzekior had reached the entrance to Crystal Castle. Turning around, the decrepit hag smiled at the black crystal warrior and said, "How nice of you to pay your grandmother a visit."

"You're not my grandmother," Black Scarlet said disgusted by the idea.

"I'm not? I could have sworn your granny was around here somewhere."

"Why would she be?"

"Many of your relatives live with me."

"I don't believe you."

"Would you like to join them?" the hag asked in a caustic tone of voice.

Hovering nearby, Eldwyn saw that things were rapidly coming to a head. Floating closer to his young apprentice, the old wizard said, "You must challenge Balzekior."

"That's easy for you to say, you're invisible," Marcheto mumbled. But then, to the apprentice wizard's surprise, he opened up spontaneously to an infusion of creative energy and with it came a new understanding. Calling out to Black Scarlet, Marcheto shouted, "Chen, if you take off the Crystal Medallion, the hag will disappear. She can't maintain physical form unless you're wearing it."

Swinging around and staring at Marcheto, Balzekior realized the young man was wearing Eldwyn's wizard robe and was also in possession of the crystal-clear staff filled with prism light.

"You're new to all this, aren't you?" Balzekior shouted to the apprentice wizard who was standing on a walkway above the main entrance.

Stretching out her right arm, the old hag pointed a finger at Marcheto, and the castle wall in front of him exploded hurling huge blocks of black crystal high into the air.

Quickly creating a force field to protect himself from the blast, Marcheto was nonetheless shaken by the sheer intensity of the attack. Eldwyn tried calming his apprentice's nerves by once again reminding him not to panic. This time, Marcheto understood the reason for his master's advice.

Pulling himself together, Marcheto shouted to Black Scarlet, "You've got to take that medallion off!"

The black crystal warrior began struggling with the Crystal Medallion trying to pull it over her head, but she couldn't remove it.

"Are you trying to defy me?" Balzekior screeched. "Maybe it's time you learned more about where you come from, more about your roots!"

With that, a huge pit opened up under Black Scarlet with smoke and ash billowing upward and flames leaping far into the nighttime sky. The black crystal warrior looked over her shoulder at a shocked Gwendylln before falling into the inferno and disappearing from view.

The raging pit of fire continued spewing out its blistering heat, but, undaunted, Gwendylln headed directly towards the flames. Although in the form of Black Scarlet, Chen was still her friend, and Gwendylln was going in after her. That Gwendylln would be instantly incinerated hardly seemed to matter, she was going in!

Racing to block the distraught Gwendylln, Andrina knocked her to the ground with one solid blow of her fist, hopefully bringing Chen's best friend to her senses. Then, Andrina spun her warhorse around and galloped through the castle entrance. It was not a retreat.

The older warrior woman rode her horse up the stairs to the walkway where Marcheto, Aerylln, Baelfire and Zorya were now standing by the battlements. After dismounting, she approached the young mystic.

"What can your wizard's staff do exactly?" Andrina shouted over the roar of the inferno.

"I don't know," Marcheto shouted back trying to be heard over what sounded like a volcanic eruption.

Before any more could be said, a huge explosion rocked Crystal Castle, and Balzekior appeared in the form of a 30-foot tall creature made of red-hot lava. The flaming demon scooped up a handful of molten magma flinging it over castle's outer wall onto the courtyard below.

Then the demonic, lava woman lashed out at Marcheto covering him with a flood of liquid fire. Balzekior smiled expecting the human to disintegrate, but instead she heard a fearsome incantation, words the evil demon hadn't heard since before Baelfire and Crystal were forged over 500 years ago. The lava woman began writhing in agony.

"Internu maduchez incarnum extrapitor!" Marcheto shouted. *"Illuminnor embrachtus kartum equasitatious!"*

The young wizard's prism staff began shining brightly, and as Eldwyn had done before, Marcheto stretched his arms straight out in front of him holding the staff in a horizontal position and braced himself. A thin, multicolored beam of light shot out from the entire length of the long, crystal cylinder. Rays of purple, blue, green, yellow, orange and red light cut through Balzekior slashing her across the chest. Screaming in pain and frustration, the demon fell back into the volcanic pit.

Quickly materializing next to Marcheto, Eldwyn shouted, "Seal the pit, and the monster will disintegrate!"

"How do I seal it?"

"Dive into the center!"

Without a moment's hesitation, Marcheto stepped onto the battlement and leapt into the volcanic mass of flame, smoke and ash.

"I was about to say I'd go with him," Eldwyn said surprised at his apprentice's bravery.

"Well, I'm going after him," Aerylln declared stepping onto the edge of the castle wall.

"Please, don't!" Eldwyn yelled. "We can't afford to lose both you and Marcheto!"

"I'm not remaining behind!" Aerylln shouted ready to leap into the pit.

"At least take your father with you," Eldwyn pleaded. "He has considerable experience with Baelfire."

Pensgraft stepped forward with a no-nonsense look on his face, but everyone could see the gleam of pride in his eyes over Aerylln facing danger so bravely.

"My father?" Aerylln asked glancing up at the tall warrior.

"No time to explain," the old wizard said.

"I'm coming, too," Zorya stated firmly. "Pensgraft, climb onto my saddle. I'll protect you from the fire."

Eldwyn's physical appearance began to dim and falter, but his friends became even more alarmed when the elderly wizard almost faded completely from view.

"Don't worry, I'm not as dead as I look," he reassured them. "I still have some tricks up my sleeve."

Greatly relieved, Baelfire turned to Aerylln and said, "Take me out of my scabbard."

Pensgraft braced for the explosion of power that always leapt from the good sword whenever she was unleashed, but he needn't have been concerned. Having used up much of her energy, and unable to renew herself without a reappearance of the Creative Light, Baelfire's strength was greatly diminished.

"My energy's badly depleted, but we still have to try," the good sword insisted. And so, steeling themselves for whatever lay ahead, Aerylln, Baelfire, Zorya and Pensgraft leaped into the pit.

Shielding his face from the flames with one arm, Pensgraft looked around for Chen, but she was nowhere in sight. Instead, Black Scarlet was far below in the very depths of the inferno. The warrior woman was alone, and there was no one to help her, no one to count on.

Well, almost no one.

*

Black Scarlet felt an arm sliding around her waist and gripping her tightly. The warrior woman stopped falling, but her warhorse fell from between her legs plunging deeper into the flaming abyss. Black Scarlet watched the animal disappearing into the fire below, but she found herself being whisked away from the main chasm into a narrow passage.

Red-hot lava was streaming down its walls while a river of molten magma flowed beneath her feet. Black Scarlet and her protector flew into a large cavern where the flames weren't so intense and all consuming. At this point, the river of lava turned into a waterfall dropping several hundred feet to the cavern floor below.

As Black Scarlet's eyes began to adjust, she noticed the waterfall was pouring down into a lake of molten fire serving as the source of several rivers flowing along the cavern floor. Between the rivers were sections of land made from cooling lava that had turned to solid rock.

After reaching the cavern floor, Black Scarlet was relieved to have her feet back on solid ground. Turning to see her rescuer, she found herself facing a woman made of molten lava engulfed in flames. This was either her guardian angel or guardian demon, but Black Scarlet wasn't sure which.

Quickly evaluating her own condition, Black Scarlet realized her cape and blouse had been burned away, and firelight was flickering all along her polished, black crystal body.

"Though you're very pretty, black crystal won't last long down here. It's not durable enough for these temperatures. I'm afraid we'll need to alter your physical form once more," the flaming, lava woman said.

"We? You mean there's more than one of you?"

In answer to her question, it seemed, a dozen red-hot lava women climbed out of the closest river of molten magma. And they all watched as the woman who'd rescued Chen gave her a big hug. Black Scarlet wanted to pull away, but she made herself accept the affection. The black crystal warrior didn't want to alienate these women, at least not until she found out what they were after.

"So what do you want?" Chen asked bluntly.

"As soon as possible, we must get you back to the surface."

"Why help me?"

"Balzekior tricked my friends and me into voluntarily entering this volcanic pit. There's no hope for us, but you deserve a better life."

"Why should you care?"

"Chen, I'm your grandmother," the lava woman said. "My name is Risella. Grandma Risella."

Chen was shocked but quickly recovered.

"Okay, Grandma Risella, how do you plan on getting me back home to Crystal Castle?"

"To start with, your friends are attempting to rescue you," Grandma said. "In fact, a young man is just about to join us."

Grandma Risella pointed up at the passageway, and Chen watched as another flame-covered, lava woman carried Marcheto into the cavern.

"Step one is to transform both of you into lava. Then, you'll find it much more comfortable here," Grandma said.

"What if I don't want to be more comfortable?"

"Are you always this argumentative?"

"Yes."

"I'm sorry, but we don't have time for tantrums," Grandma Risella said shoving the black crystal warrior into a river of molten magma. At the same time, another lava woman tossed Marcheto into the river.

Bobbing to the surface, Chen was burning hot in more ways than one. As she climbed out of the river, she was furious with her grandmother. The warrior woman, now made of lava, shouted, "Don't ever do anything like that again!"

"Sweetheart, you can yell later. Our window of opportunity is narrow. The longer you stay down here, the harder it will be to get you out."

"I won't accept your excuses," Chen fumed.

"Honey, a grandmother doesn't need excuses."

Looking over at Marcheto, who was also made of lava, Chen saw he was still wearing his wizard's robe and held the crystal-clear prism staff, both of which were indestructible.

"So, when do I leave?" Chen asked impatiently.

"As soon as everyone arrives."

"Who's everyone?"

Looking up at the passageway once more, Grandma Risella pointed at the flaming lava women escorting Aerylln, Baelfire, Zorya and Pensgraft, but Eldwyn was nowhere to be seen. Without preamble, Grandma Risella had the lava women toss all but Baelfire into the river of fire.

"I'm surprised they let you do that to them," Chen said disdainfully.

"Before we brought them here, they were told what to expect."

"I'd never have done it voluntarily."

"They didn't feel like doing it either," Grandma said. "But from what my friend just told me, Pensgraft gave them an ultimatum. To cooperate fully, or they'd have to answer to him. And did you see the look on Pensgraft's face when he arrived? Why, I've never seen a man so distraught. If I weren't already made of lava, I'd have jumped into the river myself. He was really worried about you."

When Pensgraft climbed out of the river, he was a roaring bonfire of lava and flames. Heading directly for Chen, the warrior woman pressed herself up against him, turned to Grandma Risella and asked, "Do you think this big guy and I could have some time alone?"

"First things first," Grandma said smiling. "The Crystal Medallion and the dark sword need to be neutralized."

Putting her hand to her chest, Chen was surprised to find the medallion was still there.

"It'll never come off, at least while you're this far down inside the pit," Grandma Risella said. "We have to get you closer to the surface. However, even then, we're going to need help."

Walking over to Marcheto, Grandma stood in front of his prism staff and said, "Eldwyn, I need your assistance, and it's urgent."

When the elderly wizard stepped out of the staff, he was already made of lava. And directly behind him were a dozen more wizards also made of lava and engulfed in flames. Each of these fiery mystics had once worn the robe Marcheto was now wearing, and they had all wielded the prism staff. These were but a few of the young wizard's predecessors, all belonging to the College of Wizards, a band of warrior mystics stretching back for thousands of years. The College was comprised of over 100 wizards inhabiting a parallel universe, and the prism staff was the gateway between the two worlds.

For the wizards, succession wasn't based on bloodline but on a unique, intuitive ability enabling them to sense the presence of the Creative Light. In a way, like bats flying in darkness, all the wizards were gifted with inner radar. But where bats could detect physical objects, wizards could sense the energy of everything and everyone around them. And an invisible thread of energy emanating from the Creative Light served to unite them, guide them and coordinate their actions.

However, even for the wizards, the Creative Light was a mystery, and its workings difficult to discern. At times, the Creative Light's power seemed undeniable. Yet, at other times, it seemed nonexistent. At best, wizardry was an imperfect science. It was risky and sometimes outright dangerous.

And now, the College of Wizards knew it was facing another unpredictable and perilous situation. Opening the prism staff gateway wasn't something they took lightly. In order to allow the good from their parallel universe to enter this world, they also ran the risk of giving evil the opportunity to enter theirs. But the College was not unfamiliar with Balzekior's volcanic pit of fire. They'd been here before, and all the wizards knew Risella, having worked with her previously as part of a resistance movement.

"Grandma, you have a dozen lava women with you, and Eldwyn just showed up with a dozen of his fellow wizards. What's going on?" Chen asked.

"We're going to have to fight our way out of here."

Chen smiled.

"I knew you'd like that," Grandma Risella said. "But first, we have to pack both the dark sword and the medallion in cooled, solidified magma. That will help neutralize them."

Several of Grandma's friends began scooping lava out of a river and poured it onto the cavern floor. After packing Crystal in flaming magma, the lava cooled and solidified becoming hard as rock. Then, kneeling down, Chen dangled the medallion into more molten magma and waited till it cooled as well.

"All right, let's go," Grandma said leaping into the air and flying towards the cavern entrance. Discovering that her own lava body enabled her to fly, Chen launched herself at the passageway speeding after Risella. Everyone followed close behind.

Upon reaching the entrance, Grandma stopped and gave a quick warning. "The higher up we go, the more resistance we'll have. And it's likely, as we near the surface, that Balzekior herself will show up and try to stop us."

"If we're fighting our way out, what's your plan?" Chen asked.

"After entering the main volcanic pit, let Marcheto be in front with his prism staff. The other wizards will be directly behind him, and then I want you, Pensgraft, Aerylln, Zorya and Baelfire in the middle. My lava women will guard your back. Shoot to the surface as quickly as possible. Don't stop for any reason. If there's trouble, and there will be, let my lava women and the other wizards handle it."

Chen started to object, but Grandma cut her off saying, "I'm serious, don't get involved. The evil forces inhabiting this underworld are way bigger than you are." However, Grandma Risella realized trying to reason with Chen was like talking to a stone wall. Shaking her head in resignation, Grandma realized she'd once been the same way.

After leading the group back through the narrow passageway, they arrived at the edge of the main pit of flames, and Grandma gathered Marcheto, Eldwyn and the other wizards together.

"Marcheto, I'll be flying next to you most of the way. But once we get closer to the surface, you'll be on your own."

"Where will you be?"

For a moment, Grandma Risella said nothing, but the young wizard saw the fear and foreboding in her eyes. "Just don't stop, no matter what!" she shouted grabbing his right arm and flying into the volcanic pit.

Quickly positioning themselves into a "V" formation, Grandma Risella, Marcheto, Eldwyn and the other wizards hurtled towards the surface. Risella was on the young wizard's right while Eldwyn flew on his left, that is until Aerylln leapt from behind bumping her boyfriend's mentor back a space. The young woman unsheathed Baelfire stretching out her arm and holding the sword high above her head. Marcheto followed suit gripping the prism staff and thrusting it over his head into the roaring inferno. Immediately, purple, blue, green, yellow, orange and red light shot out from the end with vibrant intensity.

Wide bands of individual colors split into dozens of thin, straight lines looking like strokes of a brush with spaces between the bristles. Some bands of a single color splintered yet stayed together in clusters, while other bands of light split into rays that began intermingling with different colors.

"What are they for? Why's this happening?" Eldwyn asked having never seen anything like it.

"They're not just lines of light. They're thin shafts, like arrows," Grandma Risella said guessing their purpose.

As Marcheto and everyone behind him propelled themselves up through the volcanic pit, the inferno became blisteringly intense with thick smoke and flames everywhere and red-hot lava streaming down the walls on all sides.

Then the battle for freedom began in earnest.

Dozens of humanoid creatures made of black, volcanic rocks with thin seams of molten magma descended upon them.

Grandma Risella's lava women quickly moved to the front taking thicker shafts of light and making them into bows, while using the thinnest rays of light for bowstrings. Soon, a dozen angry, lava women were shooting light arrows at their attackers.

At the same time, the jewels in Baelfire's hilt began shining brightly, and the good sword called to Zorya who flew over with Pensgraft on her back. The jewel-encrusted necklace hanging around the warhorse's neck, made with gemstones like the ones in Baelfire's handle, was also shining brightly.

"Zorya, I need you to ride out in front of us," the good sword said without explanation.

Taking a bow and quiver of light arrows offered to him by one of the lava women, Pensgraft began firing at any volcanic-rock creatures foolish enough to get near him. Zorya, for her part, obeyed Baelfire without hesitation shooting upward through the blazing inferno.

"Ready?" Baelfire shouted.

"Ready!" Zorya shouted having no idea what the good sword had in mind.

Immediately, Baelfire shot a blast of white-hot, plasma energy directly at the warhorse striking her in the backside. And although this must have hurt, it also had another major effect transforming Zorya into a clear-crystal warhorse with flames of prism light shooting from the back half of her body. That included part of her saddle, so Pensgraft had to lean forward to avoid being consumed by the multicolored fire. Purple, blue, green, yellow, orange and red flames propelled the warhorse upward with incredible velocity punching a hole in the raging inferno and creating a path for the others to follow. Pensgraft shot the remaining black-rock creatures with his light arrows and the group of freedom fighters soared up through the opening.

Grandma Risella had predicted that Balzekior would appear once they got nearer the surface, and she was right. Hovering in the center of the pit, the 30-foot tall demon was blocking their way. Undaunted, Eldwyn flew up to Marcheto shouting, “Here’s where you earn that robe you’re wearing!”

Dropping back to the other wizards, Eldwyn explained what he wanted, and the mystics became very determined, their eyes glittering like diamonds. Bright, yet hard.

The College of Wizards changed from the “V” formation into a new one. They flew in pairs, one pair behind the other in a straight line following Marcheto, the newest member of their elite squad of fighting mystics. And with the prism staff propelling them upward, they were regrouped into a living battering ram.

Suddenly, Chen flew ahead, and Grandma Risella wondered what kind of mischief she was up to now. Grandma hoped it was something really bad. She thought, After all, what’s the point of putting up with a violent, temperamental, young woman if you can’t count on her to be highly destructive when it really matters?

Chen didn’t let her down.

The unpredictable, hostile, young woman looked at Balzekior and found a target for her rage. A big one.

Baelfire gave Chen an assist bumping her forward with a jolt of pure, white, plasma energy catapulting the warrior woman towards Zorya and Pensgraft. Landing on the saddle behind the huge warrior, Chen grabbed Pensgraft around the waist, reached up with her mouth to his ear and bit into it.

“Ouch, that hurts!” Pensgraft said looking around at the only woman he knew who had the brass to voluntarily take a front-row seat while charging a 30-foot tall monster.

“Cut right through her!” Chen yelled trying to be heard over the roaring inferno. “Plow right into the center of her chest!”

As they shot upward, Pensgraft glanced at Chen and saw she was smiling. Taken completely by surprise at her audacity, he yelled back, "I'm glad someone's having a good time."

"Do you consider this a date? You know, us being out together for a ride?" she teased.

"Only you could joke at a time like this."

"The trick is putting your mind on something even more frightening than what you're facing," Chen yelled into his ear.

"What could possibly be more frightening than this?"

"I want to have a baby! Yours!"

Pensgraft was stunned. He thought about the problems involved in bringing a child into a violent, troubled world. He thought about the sleepless nights caring for a helpless, newborn infant. Finally, he thought about being married to Chen.

Suddenly, facing Balzekior didn't seem so bad.

Gritting his teeth, Pensgraft braced himself for the impact while Chen shouted encouragement to Zorya and began screaming a battle cry. The demonic monster tried knocking Zorya and her riders away with a huge hand, but they ducked under it and slammed into the flaming, lava creature. Following close on their heels, the wizards' battering ram, with Aerylln and Marcheto at its point, plowed into the monster's chest with such velocity they penetrated the beast coming out the other side. Grabbing hold of Marcheto's arm as they raced by, Pensgraft, Chen and Zorya flew along with the others.

After passing through the evil demon, Pensgraft looked back and saw Grandma Risella's lava women either standing on Balzekior or flying around the creature and attacking from every direction. They used their bows to shoot a barrage of light arrows into the beast.

Pensgraft watched Grandma Risella standing on the demon's shoulder and firing arrows into the creature's neck.

Grandma was doing an incredible job of keeping Balzekior busy so Chen and the others could try to escape.

Looking up at her granddaughter, Risella saw the Crystal Medallion packed in lava rock and still hanging from Chen's neck. "If we're going to defeat Balzekior, that medallion has got to come off," she shouted to the lava women around her.

Hoping to use Balzekior's own energy against her, Grandma grasped a light arrow and rammed it into the lava monster's right eye shoving it in deeply. Keeping hold of the arrow, Grandma Risella felt the monster's energy flowing into her. Then, gripping another light arrow with her other hand, she aimed its tip at the Crystal Medallion's thin chain, and a red laser beam burst from the arrow.

The beam struck so hard that Chen almost fell off Zorya, but the white-gold chain broke, and the medallion slipped from her neck. With incredible reflexes, Pensgraft caught the medallion preventing it from falling deeper into the pit and into Balzekior's grasp. As for Chen, now that she was free of the medallion, a cloak of darkness that had been clouding her mind and emotions seemed to be lifted from her. However, the effect on Balzekior was even more dramatic.

Looking back over his shoulder, Pensgraft saw the giant, lava monster beginning to crumble. Then Balzekior, Grandma Risella and her lava women disappeared from view as they dropped deeper into the blazing inferno.

But breaking the connection between Balzekior and Chen had an unforeseen consequence. The width of the volcanic pit began narrowing, and the opening on the surface was shrinking. The pit was closing.

Eldwyn and his fellow wizards realized what was happening. So, one by one, they approached Marcheto and reentered the prism staff gateway to their parallel universe. The last to leave, Eldwyn flew up to his apprentice and began disappearing into the staff.

"It's up to you now! It's all up to you!" the old wizard shouted before vanishing completely.

Proud that Eldwyn trusted Marcheto so fully, Aerylln put an arm around the young mystic and shouted, "We can do this!"

Chen and Pensgraft held on tightly gripping Zorya's sides with their legs while Marcheto took hold of the pommel of the warhorse's saddle. Aerylln wrapped both of her arms around her boyfriend but also kept a firm grip on Baelfire. And Crystal, packed in solidified lava, was being pulled along behind them. Attached to the base of Marcheto's wizard's staff was a chain made of prism light, and the other end was attached to the dark sword. Crystal, already feeling humiliated at being imprisoned in lava rock, was being dragged through the flames in a most undignified manner.

At the same time, the entire College of Wizards met inside the prism-staff gateway standing in a large circle, linking arms and projecting their force of will through the staff and into the volcanic pit of flames.

A powerful cloud of purple, blue, green, yellow, orange and red light flooded the raging inferno extinguishing the flames nearest the surface. Then, the prism light began radiating enormous energy and pressed hard against the walls of the pit forcing it to remain open as Chen, Pensgraft, Marcheto, Aerylln, Zorya, Baelfire and Crystal shot up towards the early-morning sunrise.

Reaching the surface, they catapulted out of the volcano, and it closed behind them with a thunderous crash of the earth's crust slamming together.

The energy from the College of Wizards continued pouring from Marcheto's prism staff. It swept through Crystal

Valley flowing over the black crystal shards that were blanketing the land. In a matter of moments, the vast acreage surrounding the castle was transformed back into rolling fields of fresh, green grass.

Chen, Pensgraft, Marcheto, Aerylln, Zorya, Baelfire and Crystal had all been thrown clear of the crushing force of the collapsing pit, and they landed with a thud by the entrance to Crystal Castle. No longer made of flaming lava or crystal, the prism light had turned their bodies back to normal.

Wanting to survey her domain, Chen leapt to her feet and watched as the remnants of Lord Daegal's army made its way over the mountain and headed back to The Rock, Lord Daegal's castle. Well, not his anymore, he was dead. Chen had shattered him along with his dream of dominating her.

Marcheto's father and brothers came running to him, and Chen's warrior women sprinted towards their leader. Reaching Pensgraft, Gwendylln said, "It's a good thing you brought her back, or you'd really be in trouble."

Chen hugged Gwendylln and Corson while Pensgraft stepped through the castle's entrance and glanced around the courtyard. Dead bodies were everywhere. Freedom had come at a high price but, thankfully, most of the price had been paid by the enemy.

Pensgraft saw Balder and the remainder of his men on the walkway along the western wall. Dartuke, Thordig and the other nobles who'd survived were above on the front wall's walkway.

Striding over to Pensgraft and Chen, Andrina said, "You're lucky she got back safely." Then, wearing a big smile, she hugged Chen so tightly the younger woman thought her ribs would break.

"That's what I told him," Gwendylln laughed.

Standing behind Andrina were Jewel and Flame who looked on smiling. No longer having dozens of duplicates of themselves, there was just one of each.

Aerylln and Marcheto were standing together holding hands. Walking over to the young man, Pensgraft gripped Marcheto's shoulder, gave it a hard squeeze as a warning and said, "It's okay with me if you date my daughter. Just watch yourself."

"Yes, sir."

"Your daughter?" Aerylln asked.

"We need to have a talk, young lady, a long one," Pensgraft said. Then turning back to Chen, the giant warrior realized again how beautiful she was and, in his eyes, always would be.

Both of them looked down upon Crystal, the dark sword, who was lying on the ground imprisoned in solidified lava, as was the Crystal Medallion. And that's how they would stay. The College of Wizards was determined not to allow either to go free.

Chen, back in skin-tight, black leather, pressed her body up against Pensgraft.

"Okay, big guy, Balzekior's defeated, at least for now, but what about the other challenge I mentioned?"

"Yes, let's have a baby," Pensgraft said hugging her.

"Are you sure?"

Leaning down, he kissed her and asked, "Will you marry me?"

"I'm going to be quite busy, so we'll have to see," Chen teased. "After all, I'll be running Crystal Castle, and you'll be taking over The Rock."

"The Rock? And just how do you plan on accomplishing that?"

"Anyone object to this man becoming Lord Pensgraft?" Chen asked as she glared around daring someone to challenge her authority.

Tark approached Pensgraft and said, "General Gornic's dead. That makes me senior officer of whatever's left of Lord Daegal's army. Many warriors at The Rock will rally to my banner. Plus, who'd have the stomach for fighting dozens of Jewels and Flames a second time?"

"But Crystal's a prisoner, so Jewel and Flame can't multiply."

"Who knows that but us? Believe me, after today, there won't be much resistance."

"We're talking about two castles, three-days ride apart. Chen, can we manage the distance between them?" Pensgraft asked.

"If you're man enough for it, then I'm woman enough for it," Chen said firmly.

"Well, I guess that settles it."

"I want them both for our child," she explained.

Having grandchildren will be nice, Andrina thought almost forgetting that Chen wasn't actually her daughter.

"So, you'll marry me?" Pensgraft asked again.

Chen remained silent.

"I love you," Pensgraft said.

"Then I accept."

They embraced and kissed for a long time while everyone applauded.

Caught up in the joy and excitement of the moment, no one gave the entombed dark sword a second thought. But Crystal was seething in anger and already plotting her escape.

They closed the pit of flames, the dark sword grumbled to herself, but I can sense new cracks in the earth's crust allowing demonic lava to flow north, and that could prove interesting.

I'll wait till your baby's born, and then I'll kidnap the child putting it in such grave danger Chen will have to set me free if she wants to save her family, Crystal thought filled with malicious evil.

Pensgraft kissed Chen again, unaware of the dark sword's plans.

"I'm really looking forward to this wedding," Crystal said exuding good will.

But a positive sentiment from such an unlikely source immediately made Andrina suspicious. She thought, *This sword needs to be watched and watched carefully.*

Glancing over at Aerylln, Crystal saw Baelfire sheathed in a scabbard hanging from the young woman's hip, and Zorya was next to her appearing more powerful than ever. A shudder of fear swept through the dark sword as she realized Aerylln's powers were just beginning to develop.

Crystal now looked at the future with a mixture of both excitement and foreboding. Baelfire had always been an enemy, but now Crystal wondered how much of a threat Aerylln would be in coming years.

Only time would tell. And evil would be waiting to challenge her.

CPSIA information can be obtained at www.ICGtesting.com
Printed in the USA
BVOW041304290612

294009BV00004B/1/P

9 780615 620886